PRETTY POISON

SINISTER IN SAVANNAH BOOK 3

AIMEE NICOLE WALKER

Pretty Poison (Sinister in Savannah Book Three)
Copyright © 2021 Aimee Nicole Walker

aimeenicolewalker@blogspot.com

ISBN: 978-1-948273-20-6

Photographer © Wander Aguiar—www.wanderaguiar.com
Cover art © Jay Aheer of Simply Defined Art
www.simplydefinedart.com

Editing provided by Miranda Vescio of V8 Editing and Proofreading
www.facebook.com/V8Editing

Proofreading provided by Judy Zweifel of Judy's Proofreading
www.judysproofreading.com
and Susie Selva—www.susieselva.com

Interior Design and Formatting provided by Stacey Ryan Blake of
Champagne Book Design—www.champagnebookdesign.com

I am dedicating this book to Breonna Taylor, a beautiful woman who was taken from this life too soon. I wish I could right the wrongs in real life as I do in my fictional stories. Maybe I can't make justice happen for you, but I can make sure people don't forget your name. #SayHerName

PRETTY POISON

SINISTER IN SAVANNAH BOOK 3

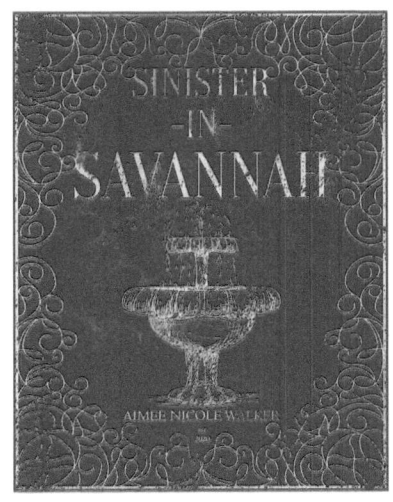

CHAPTER 1

Vegas, then…

"**C**ome on, Raphael," Rocky urged while staring through the lens of his camera. "Make your move already. My ass is going numb."

Rocky's phone vibrated in his pocket. His first instinct was to ignore the incoming text message, but Asher was due home any minute. He blindly removed the phone from his pocket and held it in front of his face, glancing at it long enough to confirm it was from his husband.

Where are you?

Rocky looked back through the lens and saw that Raphael Warner hadn't moved any closer to his mistress. He was starting to doubt these two were even having an affair. So far, Rocky had only presented photos to Mrs. Warner that depicted her husband dining out with this woman on three occasions—all seemingly innocent public outings.

Mrs. Warner insisted that something more devious was going on, and since she was paying handsomely for his time, Rocky had agreed to keep following Raphael's pursuits. After weeks of tailing the CEO of Warner Global Technologies, Rocky finally struck gold during a deep dive into the man's financials. WGT had acquired many companies over the years, and one of them had recently closed on a house in a neighborhood just outside Vegas. It was the only residential property any of his companies owned.

Rocky had dressed up in a power company uniform and let himself inside the residence the previous day to scope it out. The utilities were on, and someone had fully furnished the home, but he found no signs of anyone living there. The house was beautifully decorated but felt cold, lifeless, and sterile. It reminded Rocky of the dozens of model homes he and Asher had toured while trying to decide where they wanted to live. A big fenced-in backyard for a future pooch was the only thing the two men had agreed upon since they'd started house hunting. This property combined all the things Asher and Rocky were looking for, but the neighborhood was way out of their price range. They couldn't afford to buy the detached pool shack.

Rocky hadn't found food in the refrigerator or cabinets, even though there were plenty of dishes. Was it possible Warner's company had bought the place for visiting executives to stay? Rocky had almost convinced himself that his assumptions were wrong until he opened the closet in the master bedroom. It was full of sex toys, lubes, lingerie, and costumes, which told him everything he needed to know about the house.

He'd uncovered Raphael Warner's fuck pad, although it gave him no joy. He'd really come to like his client, Julia, and knew how much it would hurt her to learn the truth. She wasn't paying him to spare her feelings, which was why he was staking out the property at ten o'clock at night when he could be home with his husband. When Mrs. Warner received conflicting information from her husband's assistant regarding Raphael's return to Vegas, she called Rocky.

"Something is about to happen," she'd told him a few hours earlier. "Raphael's assistant told me he's flying home this afternoon, but my husband told me he wouldn't be back until tomorrow."

"I'm on it," Rocky had replied.

Watching Raphael charm this woman through the photo lens made him sick to his stomach. Four innocent kids were about to have their lives turned upside down, and he hated the role he was playing in the destruction. He loathed himself for wondering if Julia might give him a deal on this house when she sold off every single one of Raphael's assets. It had been a fleeting thought but lingered long enough to make his face heat in shame.

Ford? Asher texted.

He set the camera down and typed out a quick response. *On surveillance duty.* He glanced at the couple on the couch again and noticed they'd moved much closer. Warner was stroking his hand through the woman's long dark hair. Rocky picked up his camera and snapped a picture before tapping out another message. *Doesn't look like I'll be much longer. Where are you?*

The response came a few seconds later. *Home.*

The message included a photo of Asher sprawled in their bed, wearing a pair of tight briefs that hugged his bulge alluringly. Asher's hand rested on his lower abdomen, his long fingers splayed so the tip of his pinky grazed the waistband of his underwear. God, Rocky loved those hands so much, and he couldn't wait to feel them on his skin. Would they be possessive or tender? Both. Asher had been gone for almost a week, so he would start out one way and end with the other.

Fuck me. I'm one lucky son of a bitch.

Rocky had come to Vegas on a whim to attend a conference for private detectives. He expected to learn about the latest investigative technology available and ended up falling hard for the flashing lights and desert nights. When he won big at a craps table on his last night of the convention, Rocky had taken it as a sign he should stay. Little did he know he would meet the love of his life, US Deputy Marshal Asher Dunleavy, soon after.

Instead of responding to Asher's text, Rocky called him instead.

"Hiya," Asher said huskily.

"Don't distract me, or I'll miss the money shot," Rocky replied.

"Like the one I sent you last night?" Asher asked.

Rocky closed his eyes and recalled the image of Asher's cum-splattered stomach. Since his husband traveled a lot, phone sex and video chats kept them connected while apart.

"Stop," Rocky pleaded. "I can't afford to get a boner right now."

"Yeah, I don't want anyone to see you jacking off in your car."

"I'm not in my car," Rocky said. "I'm tucked inside a treehouse in the yard behind my subject's property. That's just gross, not to mention I'm concerned about the integrity of the structure."

Asher chuckled. "Then get out of there before it collapses and you break something vital."

Rocky checked on the lovebirds again and noticed the female was straddling Raphael Warner's lap, and the two were engaged in a deep kiss. He switched the phone to his left ear, picked up the camera with his right hand, and started taking shots.

"Here we go," he told Asher. "Won't be much long—" His words died in his throat when a third person stepped inside the room with a gun in her hand.

Bang!

Rocky fumbled the phone when the first gunshot blasted through the quiet night. "Oh no. God, no!"

Raphael Warner's head slumped forward. His mistress let out a bloodcurdling scream as she scrambled off his lap.

"No, no, no," Rocky tried to shout, but it came out as a hoarse whisper. Unable to tear his eyes away from the scene unfolding in front of him, Rocky searched blindly for his dropped phone, his hand scrabbling over rough wooden planks until he found it. "Help!" His voice sounded shrill, similar to the shriek of a wounded animal and like the woman screaming and crawling away from Julia Warner as fast as her hands and knees could carry her.

Bang!

The woman collapsed onto the tile floor, but that wasn't enough for Julia, who stood over her and fired the gun two more times into the woman's prone body.

"Ford!" Asher yelled. "What the fuck is going on?"

His husband's urgent voice broke Rocky out of his trance and spurred him into action. He hurried down the crooked ladder as fast as his shaking legs permitted, only to collapse as soon as his feet touched the ground. Rocky gripped the treehouse ladder and hauled himself to his feet while managing to stagger toward the house where Julia Warner stood sobbing.

She hugged herself and fell to her knees. "Why?" she screamed at the motionless woman. "Why did you do this to me?"

Rocky's legs got stronger with each step, and he was eventually able to run. Julia seemed lost in her own world until Rocky walked through the sliding glass door. Fear for his own safety hadn't even registered until Julia Warner lifted her head and stared into his eyes. All traces of warmth and humanity were gone.

Rocky shifted his attention to the hand holding the firearm. He assumed it was fully loaded when she came in, which meant there were plenty of bullets left if Julia decided not to leave behind any witnesses. Rocky's mind immediately began to lament all the things he'd miss and the dreams he'd yet to realize with the man he loved. No more lazy Sunday mornings where they fought over the crossword puzzle answers. No house with a backyard. No dog. No kids.

Rocky held up his hands in front of him, showing Julia he wasn't armed. He risked meeting her gaze, hoping against all odds that he'd somehow survive and get home to Asher. One look into her vacant eyes and Rocky knew all hope was lost.

Calm washed over him as soon as he accepted his fate. "I love you, Asher."

"Ford!" Asher's panicked voice came through the phone. "Where the fuck are you?"

Rocky had the presence of mind to disconnect the call so Asher wouldn't have to hear him dying.

Don't you dare give up so easily, a voice inside his brain whispered. It sounded a lot like Asher.

"No, Julia. Please." He had to try.

Julia lifted the gun and aimed it at Rocky. His body tensed as if bracing itself for impact. When staring into her vacuous expression became too much, Rocky closed his eyes and pictured Asher on their wedding day.

If this was it, he wanted to go out with Asher on his mind and love, not fear, filling his heart.

CHAPTER 2

Savannah, fifteen months later...

"**Y**ou're listening to Mornings with Mad Dog Mulroney on Kiss FM, and boy, do I have a treat for you. If you're a fan of my radio show, you know my latest obsession is the *Sinister in Savannah* podcast. What you didn't know is that my producer has been working hard behind the scenes to arrange a sit-down interview with the three hosts."

Rocky glanced over at Felix and Jonah, who both shrugged. The producer had sent one email asking if they'd be interested in an interview, and they'd agreed. They'd exchanged a few more emails to set a time that would work for everyone involved. How hard was that?

Rocky chalked it up to showbiz propaganda and urged his thoughts toward something more substantial, like how Mad Dog's deep raspy voice didn't match his physical appearance. He'd expected Joe Manganiello and got Pee-wee Herman. He'd had to tense his jaw to keep his chin from hitting the floor when the man introduced himself. The adage "you have a face made for radio" now made perfect sense to Rocky.

Had the producer implied they'd been hard to work with or had she exaggerated just to score points with her boss? Christ. *Move on, Rocky.* But he couldn't. It seemed like such a little detail, but their reputation was everything—collectively and individually. Rocky couldn't afford for bad press to negatively impact the PI agency he was building with Peter, and the podcast would falter if their listeners lost faith in them.

He opened his mouth to speak, but Felix clamped his hand on Rocky's knee. The gesture was both calming and unnerving. It scared him how well Felix could read him sometimes. Rocky nudged him with an elbow, and silent laughter vibrated through Felix.

"I want to welcome Jonah St. John, Felix Franklin, and Rocky Jacobs to the show. Guys, I can't tell you how excited I am to have you all here today."

"It's our pleasure," Felix replied.

"Thanks for having us," Jonah added.

"No problem," Rocky said. *No problem?* Could he broadcast any louder just how uncomfortable these appearances made him?

"I know you guys are super busy, so I'll jump right into the questions," Mad Dog said. "I know you must get asked this all the time, but why don't we start out with a little background. Can you tell my listeners how you met?"

It was the most common question they received, but Rocky appreciated starting off with something he could answer in his sleep. "We have mutual friends in the Savannah Police Department who introduced us." He left out the part about them joining forces for an off-the-books investigation.

"We didn't like each other very much," Felix added, which was something they'd never shared publicly.

"No," Jonah corrected. "Leave me out of that equation. You two couldn't stand each other on sight."

Mad Dog laughed. "Why not?"

The question was a natural sequitur, but one Rocky didn't have a ready answer for. Since Felix was the one who'd opened this can of worms, it was only fair for him to field the question. Rocky turned and met Felix's roguish gaze. "Tell the nice man why you didn't like me, Fee."

Felix narrowed his eyes. "You know why, Major."

"Yes, *I* do, but I'm not the one who brought it up," Rocky

countered. Then he sighed dramatically and faced Mad Dog, who stared at them with wide-eyed interest. "He thinks I'm prettier than him, and he's jealous."

Felix chuckled and shook his head. "Puh-lease." He hooked his thumb in Rocky's direction and leaned toward Mad Dog. "Major here is hung up on size. He's worried that he doesn't *measure* up."

Rocky snorted and looked over at Felix. "As if. I have nothing to be ashamed of." Facing Mad Dog once more, he said, "I'm a grower. He's a shower."

"Um, guys," Mad Dog said slowly. "You're making me really happy this isn't a live interview right now."

"What?" Felix asked.

"Why?" Rocky added.

"I can't afford to have my show yanked because you guys are talking about penis sizes."

"Penis sizes?" Rocky and Felix both asked, then looked at each other.

"Wait, were you talking about your dick?" Rocky asked.

"No, and you can't say dick on the radio," Felix replied.

"What were you talking about, then?" Mad Dog asked.

"Brains," Rocky replied. "Felix likes to show off by using big fancy words."

Felix shook his head. "And I was talking about muscles." Then he flexed his biceps for everyone to see.

Mad Dog's grin stretched from ear to ear. "I've been had."

"Lucky you," Felix and Rocky said at once.

"Jesus," Jonah groaned.

"Does this happen often?" Mad Dog asked him.

"Uh-huh, but you get used to it." Jonah laughed. "The reason these two jackasses didn't get along was because they're so much alike."

"Can he say jackass on the radio?" Rocky asked Felix.

"It means donkey," Felix said. "So, yeah. Just don't mention the donkey's dick, and you'll be fine."

Ignoring them, Jonah continued. "They're either hissing and spitting at one another or completing each other's sentences like they've been married for sixty-five years. You never know which interaction you'll get and will often witness both in a short span."

"Sounds like Jonah is getting sick of us," Rocky said to Felix, who nodded.

"Sure does."

Mad Dog chuckled. "This is the most fun I've had during an interview in ages. As a fan of your show, I've picked up on the chemistry between the three of you, but seeing your dynamic in action is a wonderful thing."

"Everyone should have friends like these two," Felix said.

"Aww," Rocky and Jonah chimed in together.

Felix narrowed his eyes. "Neither of you are going to reciprocate?"

Jonah and Rocky both leaned forward to make eye contact, then shook their heads. "Nah," they said.

Mad Dog laughed while Felix silently fumed. His expression promised retribution.

"So, what made you decide to start a podcast?" Mad Dog asked, getting them back on topic.

"We're passionate about true crime," Jonah replied.

"And we can't stand injustice," Rocky said.

"And even though we're all investigators, our individual experiences allow us to each bring a unique perspective to our show," Felix added.

Mad Dog tipped his head to the side. "Interesting. Are these personal or professional experiences?"

Felix gasped and placed a hand on his chest. Marla would be so proud of his theatrics. "Come now, Mad Dog. You can't expect us to divulge all our secrets on a first date."

"You should at least buy us a steak dinner first," Rocky added.

"Or seafood," Jonah suggested.

"Fine," Mad Dog said, waving his hand, "keep your secrets. Let's talk about the case that's garnered national attention for your podcast."

For the next several minutes, they discussed their involvement in the Cahill family's fight for justice. Jonah started the conversation since he was the one who'd introduced them to the case. He talked about Marla and her conviction that the wrong person had gone to prison for killing her friend, Earl. From there, they took turns telling the story and answering questions.

"It's in the governor's hands now," Jonah said.

"Do you think Governor Stanton will grant the posthumous pardon?" Mad Dog asked.

Rocky wasn't willing to hold his breath. "We hope so."

"Absolutely he will," Felix said.

Mad Dog chuckled. "This is where the differences in your personalities shine through."

"It's the showing-versus-growing thing I mentioned," Rocky said.

Felix opened his mouth to speak, but Jonah cut him off. "We're optimistic the governor will do the right thing."

"Uh-huh," Mad Dog said, slowly nodding as he studied each of them. His lips twitched at the corners as if he were fighting off a smile or wanted to say something but thought better of it at the last minute. "What's next for the trio of trouble? Have you decided which sinister Savannah crime you'll feature on your show next?"

"We have," Rocky replied.

Mad Dog quirked a brow. "Would you care to give us a hint?"

"Nope," all three of them answered.

"Ah, keeping things tight-lipped," the DJ said.

"It's the only way to earn people's trust," Rocky explained.

Mad Dog nodded. "Fair enough. Whatever it is, I'm sure your fans will be riveted each week when the episodes drop."

"We sure hope so," Felix said.

Rocky thought the DJ would wrap up the interview, but instead, he pivoted to other topics. Rocky checked his watch to ensure he was still good on time, then relaxed into the interview and went with the flow.

"I can't thank you guys enough for coming on my show today," Mad Dog said after they answered his last question. "It won't be long before your podcast outgrows small audiences like mine."

"There's no such thing as an audience too small," Felix replied.

"What he means to say is that we're humble people," Jonah said. "Fame isn't something we aspire to."

Rocky nodded. "We're in it for the justice."

"Speak for yourselves," Felix said. "I'm a Gemini, so I want it all."

Mad Dog chuckled. "I'd love to have you back on the show again, if you're interested. Maybe we could take questions from listeners?"

"That sounds like a lot of fun," Felix said. "What do you guys say?"

It sounded fucking scary to Rocky. They'd have no control over the questions posed to them. Instead of voicing his concerns, he smiled and said, "I'm in."

"Me too," Jonah added.

"Great. I'll have my producer contact you and set up arrangements."

They shook hands with Mad Dog and exited the studio room. Rocky rechecked his watch once they were in the elevator. They stopped a few stories down, and the other passengers disembarked.

"Have someplace you need to be, Major?" Felix asked him as soon as they were alone. "You've checked your watch twice in the last fifteen minutes."

"I have an appointment I need to keep. I'm still good on time."

"Does it involve a tall, dark, and handsome man?" Felix asked.

"You mean his secret husband?" Jonah asked.

Rocky groaned. "Come on, guys. I told you Asher and I are getting a divorce." Saying the words out loud made his chest ache. It felt like an invisible hand was trying to squeeze every last drop of blood from his heart.

Felix snorted.

"What's that mean?" Rocky asked.

"I've seen the two of you together. The man called you baby and kissed you in front of everyone. Is *he* aware you're getting a divorce?"

"I wish I would've been there," Jonah said wistfully. "Well, I don't mind missing out on the fake abduction part, but I wish I could've met Rocky's husband."

Felix fanned his face. "So freaking hot."

Rocky smirked at his friend. "I'm telling Jude."

"I wasn't lusting after your husband," Felix said. "I was talking about the chemistry arcing between you."

The elevator stopped, and two young ladies and an older man got on board. Rocky hoped Felix would let it drop, but he should've known better.

"And when he used that growly voice to demand you stop visiting sex clubs… Oh my."

Rocky looked over and glared at Felix, but it was hard to stay mad when Jonah's shoulders shook with repressed laughter. When the elevator stopped two floors down, the other passengers couldn't get away from them fast enough. Jonah gave up trying to hold back his laughter, and it bounced around the small space.

"He's going to kill you," Jonah managed to say in between guffaws.

"I am," Rocky agreed.

Ignoring him, Felix continued regurgitating that same damn scene for the millionth time since it had occurred three weeks ago. "What was it that Mr. Marshal McHotty Pants said during your private little chat?" What happened to Deputy Douchebag? Rocky liked that much better.

"Like I'm telling you," Rocky groused. And how fucking slow was this elevator? It felt like they'd been descending for ten minutes, but a quick glance at his watch said it had been less than two.

His annoyance only made Felix smile wider and Jonah laugh harder. Rocky wanted to be pissed at them, but he was usually the one causing the trouble. He deserved every second of the shit Felix gave back to him.

"He's transferred to Savannah," Felix told Jonah. "Does that sound like someone who wants a divorce to you?"

"Not at all," Jonah piped in as if they'd rehearsed this attack.

"Have you seen him again since then?" Felix asked.

"Nope. And that's enough chitchat about Asher," Rocky said when they reached the first floor. "I want to talk about Tess Hamilton."

They exited the elevator and stepped off to the side.

"What's up?" Jonah asked.

"I received an email from Jennifer Blossom, and she's decided not to participate in our show about Tess."

Felix's brow furrowed. "She's the claims adjuster who uncovered the forged life insurance beneficiary change form for hubby number three, right?"

"Yeah," Rocky said. Jennifer's assertion became the catalyst for the insurance fraud charges filed against Tess. Afterward, the conversation changed from whether Tess forged documents on a dying husband's life policy to whether she killed all three of her husbands.

The prosecutor had only found enough evidence to charge her with insurance fraud for her third husband. The first trial had ended in a hung jury and the second with an acquittal. The case had hinged mostly on circumstantial evidence, but that hadn't stopped the press from trying and convicting her, not only for the insurance fraud but for the deaths of all three husbands.

"Did Jennifer say why she was withdrawing?" Jonah asked.

"She's worried about losing her job," Rocky said. "She didn't mind speaking to me off the record when I'd first started putting the idea together for the podcast, but that was early days before *Sinister in Savannah* had taken off."

"I can understand her position," Jonah said.

"Me too," Felix agreed.

"Feels like we've hit one brick wall after another when it comes to Tess," Rocky admitted. "I've sent dozens of letters to her friends, families, and former coworkers and followed them up with phone calls. No one wants to speak to me. Tess Hamilton must've surrounded herself with the most loyal people on the planet."

"Or they're afraid of her," Felix countered.

Felix had been convinced from the very start that Tess Hamilton was a cold-blooded killer. Jonah had leaned more toward the mercy killer angle, since all her husbands had been seriously ill at the time of their deaths. Rocky thought she'd just been very unlucky in love. Since the three friends couldn't agree on the level of Tess's guilt and innocence, they'd decided to take a different approach.

They'd planned to interview all the participants together, then present the evidence to support their angle. The other two hosts would try to disprove it using the evidence they'd uncovered to support their theory. In the end, they'd let their listeners decide for themselves if Tess was guilty or innocent of killing her husbands. Without interviews, it would be next to impossible for them to proceed.

"There will be cases that just won't work out for us," Jonah said. "I think Tess might be one of them. There's no concrete evidence to prove or disprove her guilt or innocence. Her husbands were cremated without autopsies, so we can't even say for sure that foul play occurred. All we have is speculation, and that goes for Jennifer and her handwriting expert. It's junk science."

"It's too soon to wave the white flag," Felix said. "I say we take some road trips and knock on doors. It will be much harder for people to turn us down in person."

"I could easily shut the door in your face," Jonah countered, making Rocky laugh.

"I have a last-ditch plan," Rocky said. "Tess's youngest son also lives here in Savannah. I'm hoping I can reason with him."

"Do it in person," Felix suggested.

"Not my first rodeo, Fee," Rocky replied dryly. He glanced at his watch again. "I really do need to get going."

"To meet Asher?" Felix asked.

"Nope."

"A client?" Jonah inquired.

Instead of answering, Rocky said, "Are you jackasses available for breakfast tomorrow?"

"Sure. Meet you at Daisy's at eight?" Felix asked.

Jonah grimaced. "How about seven? I have a department meeting at nine."

"I'll be there," Rocky said, hugging his friends goodbye.

Rocky didn't want to be awake at seven, let alone dressed and eating, but their partnership required sacrifice and compromise. The two men were worth it. Then why wasn't he willing to talk to them about Asher, and why had he deflected questions about his destination? Why couldn't he just tell them he was working with a therapist?

The interior of his car had to be at least a thousand degrees. Rocky turned up his air-conditioning to full blast, hoping it would prevent his hair wax from melting. He had a reputation to uphold after all, and pretty hair was part of it.

At a red light, Rocky glanced over and saw two little girls skipping down the sidewalk while holding hands. He didn't know if they were best friends or sisters, but the two were so happy to be in one another's company. They seemed completely unaware of the world around them. Had he ever been that innocent and carefree? The woman walking behind them must've called out because the two girls stopped and turned to face her. They immediately linked hands again while they waited for her to catch up. The woman said something to make them jump up and down with glee before the trio turned the corner and headed west on Henry Street.

Henry. He'd seen that street name recently, but where? Then it hit him. Tess Hamilton's file. Her son, Grant Duncan, lived there. Rocky glanced at the clock on the dash and decided he had enough time for a quick recon mission before his therapy session.

"Just a quick detour for the good of the podcast." A home said a lot about a person. This had nothing to do with procrastination or avoidance. "I won't get out of the car. Hell, I won't even park."

Rocky flipped on his turn signal. When the light changed to green, he headed east on Henry.

What could go wrong?

CHAPTER 3

His first mistake of the detour occurred when he saw the SPD barricade a few blocks down but didn't view it as an omen. Reasonable people would've used the first available cross street to get away from trouble, but Rocky used it to cut over to the avenue that ran parallel to Grant's street. His second lapse in judgment came when he chose to park his car and walk the rest of the way around the block. He'd had no way of knowing how far the barricade extended, but he for sure wouldn't be able to drive past Grant's house without having to turn around in someone's driveway. The police activity would lure the residents out onto their porches and sidewalks to see what was going on. It was another reason Rocky should've just driven on to his appointment and circled back another day.

But Felix had hit on something with his off-the-cuff remark about investigation techniques. It had irked him at the time, and he felt like Felix was trying to micromanage Tess's investigation, not because he was a dick, but because it was his control-freak nature. Felix needed to be in charge to feel secure, and Rocky both respected and understood it. But he'd felt more like a sidekick than an equal partner in the first two investigations. Tess Hamilton's story had been his idea. Rocky had pushed for it when the other two had exhibited only mild interest or shown hesitation. That meant he couldn't give up at the first setback.

Decision made—poorly or otherwise—Rocky grabbed a ball cap from the glove box. This one read ACME Home Inspections and had been a birthday gift from his grandmother, Queen Bea. It was both a practical disguise and a tribute to his favorite cartoon characters. The Roadrunner had never fallen for the traps Wile E. Coyote set, but luckily the citizens of Savannah weren't as observant as him. Rocky grabbed the aluminum clipboard he'd purchased to complete his disguise. If stopped and questioned, he'd open it and produce a phony business card and standard home inspection forms. That scenario hadn't happened yet, but it paid to be prepared.

He set off down the street, then hung a left at the next intersection and another one at the next corner to get back on Grant's road. Luckily, the police barricade began and ended at the opposite end of the block. All the curious residents were focused in that direction, freeing Rocky to check out Grant's house.

"Jeepers," Rocky whispered as he stared up at a house that belonged in a *Scooby-Doo* episode.

It was a massive gothic revival but wasn't quite as ornate as the ones closer to Forsythe Park, or at least not in its current state of utter disrepair. There was scaffolding on one side and construction material stacked neatly on the ground next to it. A few of the second-story windows were boarded up and a tarp covered a portion of the steep roof. Even though the structure appeared to be in the middle of major renovations, its potential was still evident. It would cost six arms and eight legs to restore the mini mansion to her former glory, but she'd be a knockout in the end.

The ornamental wrought iron fence surrounding the property had been neglected for far too long, and its run-down condition lent an air of spookiness to the tall edifice. When Rocky reached the gate, he noticed the reddish-brown rust had only eroded the surface. Duncan would be able to salvage the metal with a good sandblaster and a protective coat of paint. It would be a time-consuming job but much less expensive than replacing the fence.

The gate creaked loud enough to wake any spirits who might still call the spooky place their home. No car was in the driveway or parked directly in front of the house, so it didn't appear anyone was home. Christ. Did Duncan actually live there? Even if he weren't afraid of things that went bump in the night, he'd have to exist in a constant state of chaos and filth from home renovations. Then again, maybe the interior was finished already.

He kept an eye out for shifting shadows in the windows as he approached the house. A breeze picked up, making the hairs on the back of his neck stand up.

"Pretty sure this slasher movie has been made a dozen times already," he whispered. The urge to make the sign of the cross over his chest grew stronger with each step, as did his self-flagellation. Was this really where he needed to be right this minute? Then again, would coming back tomorrow be any less creepy? No. So Rocky kept moving forward.

The breeze got stronger as he stepped onto the porch and carefully approached the door, which was solid and new and stood out in contrast to the dilapidation all around it. Rocky kept his eye out for any rotten spots in the porch boards. He didn't want to fall through holes, and he really wanted to avoid skeletal hands that might rise up and grab his—

Screech.

Rocky's feet and heart slammed to a stop at the same time. *Oh God. What was that?* This time, Rocky made the sign of the cross as his brain cycled through all the possibilities—none of them good. He shook his head, thinking he'd imagined the whole thing, then continued toward the front door. Rocky raised his hand to knock but froze when he heard the eerie sound again.

It was more of a scraping sound than a screech, and that one had been louder than the first. Metal grating against something, but what? Concrete? He paused and waited to hear it again so he could determine what it was.

Why? Run, dumbass!

Once again, Rocky ignored his instincts and hoped for the best. When he heard the noise again, Rocky realized it was coming from the side of the house, so he retraced his steps. Instead of continuing down the sidewalk and away from the noise, as any sane person would, Rocky rounded the corner and crept along the side of the house.

The structure's condition wasn't quite as bad there, but he could see where the contractor had set up the scaffolding to replace the bricks on the chimney. There were no curtains on the first-floor windows, at least not on that side, so Rocky confirmed the disrepair and renovations did indeed extend to the home's interior. He was momentarily awestruck by the woodwork that had been restored in parts of the living room. A dog barking in the neighbor's house shook him from his trance. It sounded big and ferocious, so Rocky decided to get the hell out of there in case the dog's owner was home.

But the wind kicked up again, whistling through the narrow gap between Duncan's house and his neighbor's. *Screech.* Rocky lifted his head to follow the sound and saw that the scaffolding was scraping against the newly replaced bricks, leaving white marks where the metal was cutting into the clay.

"Hey!" a man shouted angrily, making Rocky jolt. "What the fuck are you doing?"

Typically, Rocky would've plastered a smile on his face and showed the neighbor his false credentials. But the man threw open his front door and yelled, "Sic 'em, boy!" The dog growled in response, and a brown blur streaked out the door.

Rocky wasn't about to stick around to see if the dog's teeth were as aggressive as his bark. So he ran for his life. Rather than go back in the direction he came from, he sprinted toward the rear of the property hoping to find a gate or break in the fence. Luck was on his side, because most of the ornate iron was missing along the back. The shouting behind him intensified, and Rocky knew his pursuer was closing in on him fast. The urge to look over his shoulder was strong, but he'd lose precious seconds if he did. So, Rocky channeled his junior high track coach and gave himself a pep talk.

Pump those puny arms and legs, Jacobs, and haul your skinny ass across that finish line.

Ahhh. Coach Nivens had never been one to mince words. The

students had joked that their shop teacher must have lost a bet and got stuck coaching track instead of a sport more befitting a man of his size. Christ. The coach's thighs had looked like they'd been carved from oak tree trunks, and his ass was made for those shorty shorts. It was no mystery why those two years in junior high saw a record number of kids trying out for track.

Coach Nivens was crass, rude, and dominant. The school board hadn't bestowed the esteemed coach-of-the-year award on him, but Rocky credited the man with awakening his sexuality and obsession with thick thighs. That had to count for something. Rocky had pumped his puny arms all right, especially when alone in his room and—

Sharp teeth chomped down on the ass of his jeans, interrupting his meandering thoughts.

"Attaboy, Snickerdoodle," a man yelled.

Fuck me. He was about to lose his life to a dog named after a cinnamon cookie. On the bright side, Snickerdoodle's owner sounded winded. Rocky's escape looked promising if only he could get away from the dog.

Rocky pumped his not-so-puny arms and legs harder and nearly shouted with relief when the fabric gave way with a loud rip, tearing a long strip of denim all the way down his leg. The air against his bare skin was an incentive for Rocky to run as he'd never run before. Snickerdoodle gave an indignant growl when Rocky pulled free from his grasp. He risked a glance over his shoulder and saw that the dog had stopped his pursuit to shake his head victoriously, flinging the strip of denim from side to side like a dead animal.

"Get him, Snickerdoodle," his owner shouted. "He's getting away."

Rocky didn't look back to see if the dog had obeyed the command. He assumed he had and used it as motivation to churn his legs faster. Rocky cut sharply to the right and sprinted between two houses toward the street running parallel to the one he was on. He'd headed in the opposite direction of his car, but he could circle back later. If he survived, that is. Rocky hurdled over an abandoned tricycle and dodged and weaved through a group of kids riding their bikes down the sidewalk.

"Watch it, mister," a little girl retorted.

"Stranger danger," another cried. "Blow your whistles."

Oh God. That was the last fucking thing he needed. Before he could react, a little boy hollered, "Look! A doggie!"

A chorus of *awws* rang out, and the kids forgot all about Rocky as they threw their bikes down and ran toward Snickerdoodle. Rocky risked another glance over his shoulder and saw the dog had dropped his strip of denim and rolled onto his back for belly rubs. How fucking cute was he? Just as Rocky decided he could let up, Snickerdoodle's daddy caught up to his dog.

The man pointed at Rocky and said, "Get him, boy."

Rocky faced forward and prayed he still had gas left in his tank. Unfortunately, his distraction meant he'd miscalculated the distance to the street and darted out in front of a big, black SUV. Screeching brakes and burnt rubber assaulted his senses, but luckily the vehicle managed to stop before plowing into him.

Rocky leaned on the hood to catch his breath and stared through the windshield at the car's inhabitants. It took a second for his oxygen-deprived brain to register the identity of the man with the pirate's smile sitting in the passenger seat.

"Oh fuck" seemed hardly adequate, but it was all he could come up with under the circumstances. Asher unbuckled his seat belt, pushed open his door, and stepped down from the hulking SUV.

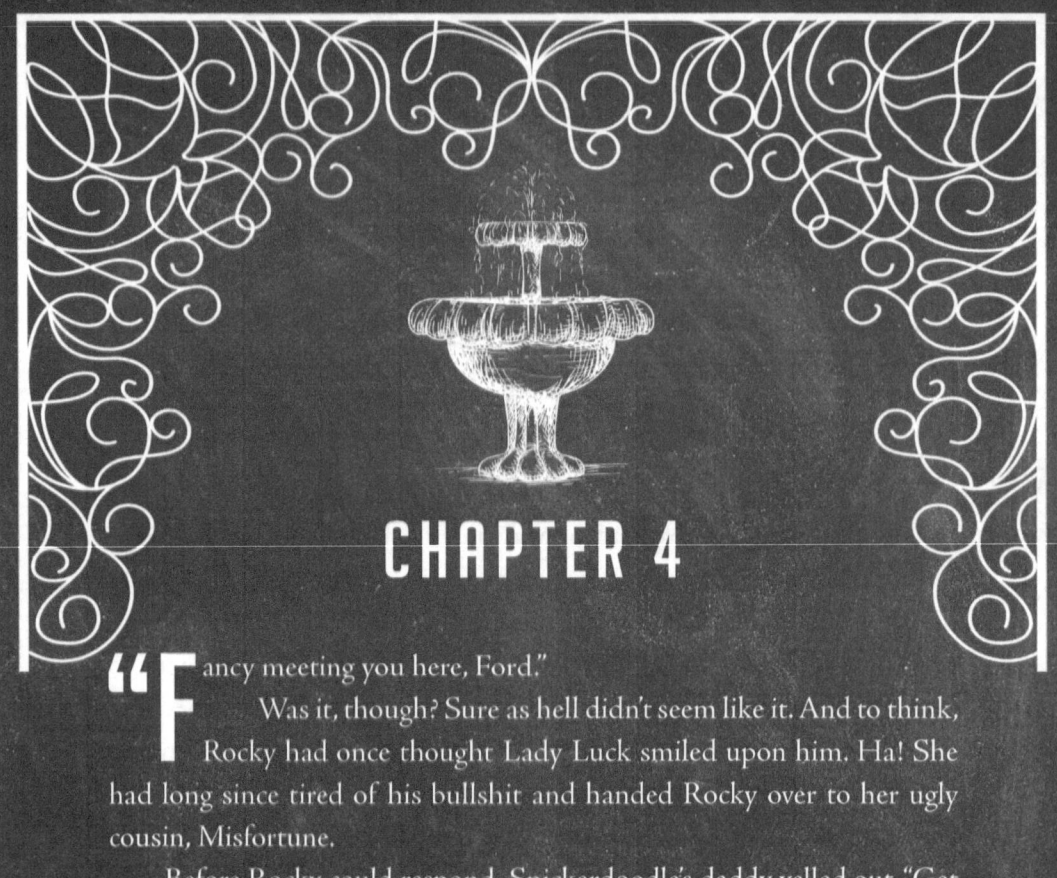

CHAPTER 4

"**F**ancy meeting you here, Ford."

Was it, though? Sure as hell didn't seem like it. And to think, Rocky had once thought Lady Luck smiled upon him. Ha! She had long since tired of his bullshit and handed Rocky over to her ugly cousin, Misfortune.

Before Rocky could respond, Snickerdoodle's daddy yelled out, "Get him! He's a Peeping Tom!"

When the man started in their direction, Rocky had to act fast. He lowered his head so the brim of his hat shielded most of his face. "Get out your handcuffs."

"Oh, that's new," Asher said, his voice deep and rumbly and so fucking delicious. Rocky's toes curled inside his sneakers tight enough to snap. "Don't think we tried that—"

"I'm on a case," Rocky said urgently. "I don't want to blow my cover. Please help me."

From the corner of his eye, he saw Asher turn to face the fast-approaching man. "I'll take it from here, sir."

The man didn't even slow down. "But you haven't let me tell you what he did. I want to file an official report."

Asher held up his hand, and the man jerked to an abrupt stop. "My partner will take care of that," he said. Then he ducked his head inside the SUV to speak to the deputy Felix had dubbed Gingersnap after their run-in with the marshals on the Spencers' property.

After a brief exchange, Asher's partner got out of the vehicle and walked over to the man. They shook hands, and Gingersnap gestured for them to step even farther away, freeing Asher to approach him. Rocky wanted to insist on dealing with Deputy Gingersnap instead, but his bargaining position was fragile at the moment.

Asher's stride was powerful, confident, and assertive, epitomizing three of the characteristics Rocky had been drawn to from the onset of their relationship. The closer Asher came, the harder Rocky's pulse pounded.

"Place your hands on the hood, spread your legs to shoulder width, and don't move," Asher commanded.

A surge of longing gripped Rocky by the balls and squeezed hard, rendering him immobile. Too bad he couldn't say the same for his lips. "Whose shoulder width? Mine or—"

Rocky's words died when Asher grabbed his wrists and placed Rocky's hands on the SUV's hood. The warmth of the engine seeped into his palms, but it couldn't compete with the heat rolling off the man behind him. Christ. Did Asher always stand so close when he arrested people? Rocky wisely kept his mouth shut this time and kept his eyes trained on the ground. Asher's black combat boot came into view when he slipped it between Rocky's feet. He tapped his boot against Rocky's right instep, encouraging him to move it. Rocky inched it over a bit, and Asher tapped him again. They repeated this until Asher was satisfied with the width of his spread.

Asher hummed his approval. "Yeah, that looks good."

"Why do I get the feeling you're not talking about the space between my feet?"

Asher chuckled, then leaned in so close that his lips nearly touched Rocky's ear. "Stop talking."

Longing tightened the vise on his nuts a little more. But before he could acknowledge Asher's demands, his husband stepped back. Rocky's relief was short-lived because Asher squatted down behind him and started feeling around his ankles.

"W-what are you d-doing?" he stammered.

"Checking you for weapons."

Rocky sighed and shook his head. "I asked you to *pretend* to arrest me."

"You did, and I am. Everyone knows a suspect gets patted down before they get placed in the vehicle." Asher slid both hands up the inside of Rocky's legs. He had to tense his body to keep from reacting when Asher's fingers brushed over his bare flesh. God, how he'd missed those incredible hands. Rocky fought the urge to spread his legs wider or to push his ass out. "New undies?"

Rocky racked his brain to remember the pair he'd chosen that morning. All he could think about was how close the tips of Asher's fingers were to his balls.

"I've never seen this shade of orange before," Asher said when he dropped his hands and stood up.

Rocky breathed a sigh of relief, but it got caught in his throat when Asher began patting down his chest.

"What would you call it? Burnt orange?" Asher asked, coasting his hands over Rocky's pecs and abs. His nipples hardened, and he bit his bottom lip to hold back the moan until the urge passed.

"Sienna sunrise," he rasped. Why did his voice sound like he'd been smoking three packs a day since birth?

Asher checked Rocky's waistband for hidden weapons before examining his front pockets. His fingertips nearly grazed the head of Rocky's dick before he pulled his hands free. "Well, they look surprisingly good with your complexion."

"Are you a federal marshal or the fashion police?" he asked.

Asher chuckled as he dropped his arms and stepped back. "I was just making conversation. I didn't realize it was such a sensitive topic."

"You're just being an ass."

"Is that how you treat everyone you ask for a favor?" Though Asher had put some space between them, it wasn't enough. Rocky could still feel the heat rolling off his much bigger body. "Turn around," Asher instructed before Rocky could respond.

Rocky pivoted around but didn't lift his head to meet his husband's gaze.

"Look at me," Asher said firmly.

Rocky took a deep breath and raised his head on the exhale. Asher's dark brown eyes glittered with conflicting emotions.

"It's good to see you, Ford."

Rocky could only manage a nod before Asher slapped a handcuff on his right wrist, then the left. The metal clicks felt ominous, but he didn't have time to dissect it because Asher led him around to the rear passenger door behind the driver's seat. He risked a glance toward Gingersnap and nearly laughed when he saw the man squatting down next to Snickerdoodle, giving the dog belly rubs.

Asher got in the front passenger seat and turned so he could make eye contact with Rocky. "You want to tell me what's going on?"

"Why are you here?" Rocky asked.

"Dandridge and I were assisting SPD with an outstanding warrant."

Rocky shook his head. "I wasn't asking what you were doing on this street. I want to know why you're in Savannah."

"I think we already talked about this on the dock behind the Spencers' house."

"We did no such thing," Rocky replied. "You insulted my friends and me, then avoided answering my questions. So, I will ask you thrice. What are you doing here?"

Asher snorted. "Thrice?"

Rocky rolled his eyes. "It's a *Schitt's Creek* reference."

"A what?"

Rocky growled his frustration. "Answer the damn question."

"You're so fucking cute, Ford."

"Shut up."

"And I didn't insult you or your friends," Asher countered.

"You called us meddlesome idiots."

Asher nodded. "I only spoke the truth."

Rocky balled his hands into fists on his lap. "Maybe you should've handcuffed my hands behind my back. I can still reach you."

Asher's lips curved into a dangerous smile. "You're welcome to try, baby."

"Still evading my question, I see."

"I'm not trying to be coy. You want answers I can't give."

Rocky narrowed his eyes. "I specifically asked you if the transfer Spencer mentioned was permanent or temporary. You responded with 'time will tell' before the goon squad called you away. If that's not coy, I don't know what is."

"Goon squad?" Asher's big shoulders shook with laughter. "Wait until they hear your nickname for them." He checked on Dandridge's progress with Snickerdoodle's dad, then returned his gaze to Rocky. "I think us running into one another is fortuitous."

"Speak for yourself," Rocky grumbled.

Asher ignored him and kept talking. "I helped you out, and now you can return the favor."

"I'm fresh out of them."

"Fine," Asher said, reaching for Rocky's bound wrists. "Let me just release the cuffs so you can step out of the vehicle and explain to Snickerdoodle's owner why you were peering into people's windows." Asher grinned because he knew he had Rocky exactly where he wanted him.

"Fine, but I'm not sucking your dick."

Asher held Rocky's gaze in a silent standoff like two gunslingers waiting for the clock to strike twelve. They both knew it wouldn't take much for Rocky to eat his words.

"What do you want?" Rocky asked, breaking the silence.

He checked his partner's status once more, then shook his head. "Dandridge is coming back. We can talk about it later."

"How much later?"

"You have someplace you need to be?" Asher asked.

Fuck. During the excitement, Rocky had forgotten all about his therapy appointment. He checked his watch and was relieved when he saw that he would only be a few minutes late if he could get on the road soon. "Um, yeah."

"Dressed like that?"

"Well, I hadn't planned on Snickerdoodle ripping my jeans off."

"What time do you think you'll be home?"

"Six."

Rocky started to push Asher for more details, but Dandridge opened the door and climbed into the SUV.

After quick introductions, Dandridge asked Asher what they were doing with Rocky.

"We'll drop him off at his car," Asher said.

Rocky told Gingersnap where he'd parked. The marshal shifted the SUV into drive and said, "Mr. Sexton has made some serious accusations against you."

"Like what?"

"He claimed you were prowling around his neighbor's house and peeping into windows," Dandridge said.

"Bullshit. I was following up on a letter I'd sent to Mr. Sexton's neighbor regarding an investigation."

"Fair enough," Dandridge said, "but it doesn't explain why this man caught you peering into the neighbor's first-floor window. Are you going to deny it happened?"

"Nope," Rocky said, shaking his head. "I heard a weird noise and decided to investigate."

"Define this weird noise," Asher said.

"It sounded like metal scraping against concrete. It's like nails on a chalkboard." Rocky shivered dramatically. "At first, I didn't think anything of it because the house is clearly undergoing a major overhaul. But there were no construction vehicles or workers on site."

"Mr. Sexton said they didn't show up today," Dandridge added. "He said it was the first day in weeks where there wasn't constant noise coming from his neighbor's house. When Snickerdoodle started barking, he assumed you were part of the crew until he saw you creeping along the side of the house and peeking through windows. That's when he opened the door and unleashed the dog."

"Hellhound," Rocky countered.

"What kind of case are you pursuing?" Asher asked.

"I'm not obligated to divulge that information to you."

Asher smirked. "Fine. You can have your secrets for now."

"My car is just up ahead on the right."

Dandridge pulled to a stop next to it. Asher got out of the passenger seat and opened Rocky's door, then released the cuffs around his wrists once he stepped out.

"I'll be over around six," Asher said as he started to get back in the SUV.

"Wait. What?" Rocky asked.

Asher furrowed his brows. "You said you'd be home at six."

"Yeah, I did. Why can't you just call me?"

"This is a request that should be made in person."

Rocky just blinked.

"It's not sexual," Asher said.

From inside the car, Dandridge started laughing. "Never a dull moment with you, Dunleavy."

Asher's lips twitched but didn't curve into a smile. "I'll call you if something comes up and I'm running late."

Rocky should've told him not to bother, then insisted he didn't want to see Asher again. Instead, he said, "You remember where I live?"

Asher's gaze darkened, and Rocky had no trouble interpreting his emotion. Longing—absolute and undiluted after all their time apart. Rocky had fled to Savannah fifteen months ago and Asher had followed. They'd spent a weekend locked together in the tiny house but hadn't resolved anything by the time Asher boarded his plane a few days later.

"Oh yeah," Asher said huskily before climbing into the SUV.

Dandridge drove off as soon as Asher shut the door, leaving Rocky with a heart more tattered than his jeans.

Karen Hollingsworth looked up from the newspaper in her hands. "You're late."

"Would you like to see my manager, Karen?" Rocky asked.

"Ha, ha, ha," she said dryly. "Like I've never heard that one before." She set the paper on her desk, then folded her hands on top of it. Karen wore the same navy blue nail polish each week. It was calm and cool like the woman who'd chosen it. Was it her signature color or was she just on a kick? Time would tell. Fuck. There were those three words again. "Close the door and sit your smart ass down."

Rocky flopped down onto the couch. "You're not what I imagined a psychologist would be like." He'd pictured soft voices and empathetic gestures, and he'd received them when the situation warranted it, but more often than not, she'd demonstrated what Rocky would call tough love.

She smiled at him. "Thank you."

"I'm not sure I meant it as a compliment, Karen."

"I'll take it as one anyway," she replied. "I guess we're even because you're not what I imagined a private detective would be either." She picked up a remote from her desk. "What are you in the mood for today?"

"Blues rock," he replied. Rocky closed his eyes and focused on his breathing like she'd instructed him during his first visit. "Always blues rock."

The familiar music of BB King filled the room, soothing the tension in his body. Rocky opened his eyes and slowly brought her office into focus. He liked the pale blue walls and the various watercolor paintings of wooded landscapes and lighthouses on rocky shores. If he stared at them long enough, he could almost hear the wind whipping through the tall blades of grass or the waves crashing against the rocks.

"Would you like something to drink?" Karen asked. "You seem a little frazzled and disheveled." There was the empathy and kindness he'd expected.

"Some water would be nice."

"You know where the refrigerator is," she reminded him. There was the tough love he admired.

Rocky smiled as he rose from the couch and crossed the room to retrieve a bottle of water.

"Whoa," Karen said. "Somebody is having a rough day."

"Just don't psychoanalyze my underwear choices," Rocky said when he returned to the couch.

A wry smile briefly tugged at her lips. "I wouldn't dream of it."

Rocky sipped the water, then set the bottle down on the table. "So, where do we begin our session today?"

"We're on your dime, so you tell me," Karen said.

Scrunching up his face, Rocky said, "Shouldn't you have some kind of master plan to guide me along this journey of healing and self-discovery?"

Karen quirked a brow. "Who says I don't have a plan?"

"You're letting me steer the ship."

"And that can't be part of my strategy?"

Rocky considered it for a second, then shrugged.

"There are two things at work here," Karen said. "First, I haven't earned your trust yet. We haven't known each other for very long. Once you believe I can help you, I will adjust my approach."

Rocky nodded. "What's the second issue?"

"Forcing you to talk about traumatic events before you're ready will only cause you more harm, and that's the last thing I want."

He'd completed the necessary intake forms, which had asked the reasons he sought therapy. Rocky had included a summary of the incident in Vegas, so she wasn't merely making an educated guess that he'd lived through something dark and devastating.

"I'm here to help you, Rocky, which cycles back to the first issue," she said. "Once you have faith in the process, you'll be ready to open up to me. Until then, I want to help you in any way I can."

Rocky repositioned himself to lie on the couch so he could stare up at the ceiling. It was the same pale blue as the walls, but someone had painted puffy white clouds on it to mimic the sky. It reminded Rocky of his lazy summer days when he was a little boy. He'd lie on his back and look for clues hidden in the clouds that proved his mother was really watching over him. On most days, Rocky felt like three centuries separated him from the boy he used to be instead of three decades.

Karen was right. Rocky didn't fully trust her yet, but he needed to start somewhere if he ever wanted to find some semblance of peace. He had told the therapist he was tired of running during their initial consultation. Karen had asked follow-up questions to clarify if he'd meant literally or figuratively. Rocky had answered "both." He had fled from Vegas a few months after the incident, and he'd been running in one form or another since. Today, he literally ran from Snickerdoodle, but most of his fleeing occurred in his sleep. The terrors differed from night to night, but they were all variations of him trying to get away from the awful event and the blood that still coated his soul.

He'd never be able to outrun the tragedy, wash it away, and he'd sure as hell never forget it. Rocky just needed to learn how to coexist better with the trauma. Karen assured him she could help, and he had to trust that much at least.

"I'm still not sleeping very well," he said after a brief pause.

"Is it because of insomnia or nightmares?"

"Both," Rocky admitted. "Mostly I just feel like a giant elephant is sitting on my chest."

"Are the breathing exercises helping?"

He nodded, then reminded himself to use his words. "Yeah. The relief just doesn't last. The pressure comes back when I least expect it sometimes."

"That's very normal. The breathing helps you deal with the symptoms, but it's not a cure for anxiety."

Rocky crossed his arms over his chest. "I'm just not sure how talking about my problems will make anything better."

"Bottling up your emotions isn't working for you very well."

"Touché."

"So, why not try something different," Karen asked.

"You mean like acupuncture?" Rocky knew it wasn't what she meant, but he preferred the prospect of someone sticking dozens of needles into his skin over talking through his problems.

"I know a practitioner if it's something you're interested in trying. I've never done it myself, but I have clients who swear by the practice. Would you like a referral?"

Rocky shook his head. "Not yet. It feels so extreme."

"What have you tried before?"

"Herbal teas." Prior to therapy, Rocky had done his own research and tried melatonin supplements, but they'd left him feeling hungover the next morning. "Oh, and essential oils," he added, turning his head to smile at her. "I took a lot of shit for the last one. I showed up at a recording session smelling like a field of lavender two nights ago. I'll never live it down with my podcast partners."

"You don't sound upset," Karen remarked.

Rocky chuckled. "I'm not. My smart mouth is always getting me in trouble with my friends."

"I can't imagine," Karen said drolly.

"I may not trust you yet, but I do like you, Karen."

She smiled. "High praise, indeed. Thank you."

"Isn't this the point where you admit that you like me too?" Rocky asked.

She shrugged. "It's not relevant to my ability to help you."

"Fair enough."

Karen tilted her head to the side. "Your entire demeanor changes when you mention your friends. You seem calmer and more at peace."

"They just get me," Rocky said. "Jonah knows what it's like to survive a traumatic event, Felix has a chip on his shoulder the size of Texas, and I'm like a hybrid of the two. We just mesh. We don't question it. There's no need for pretenses. When I'm with them, I feel at peace." Rocky took a deep breath. "If I could just fix this sleeping thing, I'd be on my way to recovering."

Karen smiled. "Have you tried CBD oil?"

"Not yet, but it's something to consider."

"Let's circle back to the reasons why you're not sleeping well," Karen said. "Is it triggered by recent events?"

"Yeah."

"Anything you'd like to talk about?"

"We're not there yet, Karen." He couldn't just casually discuss Asher's reappearance in his life. Rocky was afraid to consider what kind of impact today's interaction would have.

"Okay, Rocky." She smiled warmly, and he was glad to see she wasn't upset by his reticence. Then again, she'd probably dealt with more complicated patients than him. They probably weren't as cute as him, but they couldn't help it. "Do you mind telling me why you decided to become a private detective?"

The topic felt safe enough. "I come from a long line of avid mystery readers. My father's favorite character is Sherlock Holmes, and my grandmother favors Agatha Christie's Miss Marple. I cut my teeth on Encyclopedia Brown, Nancy Drew, and the Hardy Boys as a kid, but my obsession didn't truly kick in until I bought a copy of *The Maltese Falcon* at a yard sale. I'd had my heart set on spending my allowance on baseball cards until my dad picked up the battered paperback and said, 'Oh my goodness. This was your mom's favorite book. I think she might've loved Sam Spade more than she loved me.'" Rocky smiled up at the ceiling, reliving the twenty-year-old memory. "Dad had smiled fondly at the book in his hands, and I needed to know why my mother had loved it so much."

"Did you?"

Rocky turned and met Karen's serene gaze. "Did I what?"

"Figure out what drew her to Sam Spade?"

"I think so," Rocky replied. "It's impossible to know unless you have a direct line to heaven."

Karen shook her head. "I'd charge a whole lot more."

Rocky chuckled. "I felt connected to my mom when I read the story and even convinced myself that the book I found had belonged to her. Then I started imitating Sam Spade. I thought if I could be like him, it would make my mom proud."

"How did that manifest itself?"

Rocky chuckled. "I solved my first mystery when I was twelve. My grandmother had erroneously put my beloved book in her yard sale. When I realized what happened, I scoured the neighborhood, interviewing people who were there that day to find out what they bought and who they saw. I drew charts and graphs for crying out loud."

Karen smiled. "I can picture you doing that. I bet you solved the case?"

"Sure did. I tracked the book to a lady who lived a few streets over. I explained to her why *The Maltese Falcon* meant so much to me. I offered to buy the book back for double what she paid for it."

"I bet she was touched."

Rocky nodded. "She gave me back the book, told me to keep my money, and even handed me a pie she'd just baked. From there, my investigations moved on to stolen skateboards and bikes and ended with me figuring out who slashed the prom queen's tires. Making a career out of investigating seemed like the next step, but it didn't happen right away."

"Why not?"

"I went to college first because my maternal grandmother convinced me it was what my mother would've wanted. I decided to follow in my grandfather's footsteps and got a degree in finance and accounting. After graduation, I landed a lucrative job at my grandfather's firm, but I was miserable."

"You were living the life they expected and not the one you wanted."

"Yep," Rocky agreed. "One day, I was feeling low, so I decided to read my favorite book. That's when I knew I needed to make big changes. How could I make anyone proud if I was living a lie?"

"Do you think your mother would be proud that you pursued your own dreams?"

The question hit him with the same velocity as a bullet from a gun, knocking the air from his lungs.

"Take a deep breath in through your nose while counting to four," Karen coached, her voice calm but firm. "Hold it for seven seconds, then exhale through your mouth over eight."

He could only hold his breath for four seconds on the first attempt but hit the four-seven-eight ratio on the second try. Rocky kept repeating the process until his ears quit ringing and the pressure in his chest eased.

"I'm sorry, Rocky," Karen said.

He shook his head. "Don't be. We talked about my mom's death last visit. She's not off-limits."

"Until I connected her to your career," Karen said, jotting down notes.

Rocky considered the question Karen had asked before he freaked out. "I want to think my mother would be proud of me, even though I've made mistakes." *Mistakes.* It seemed like such an insignificant word to describe the error in judgment he'd made that had ruined so many lives. Rocky rubbed a hand over his sternum, focusing on the up-and-down motion of his rib cage as he breathed. "I'm trying to atone for them," he whispered. "On most days, I think it's the most any of us can do."

"And on other days?" Karen asked.

Rocky focused on her direct gaze once more. "I realize it will never be enough." He sighed. "I blame that on my Catholic upbringing. Where most people need food and water to live, we can sustain ourselves on guilt alone."

Karen chuckled. "Are you still a practicing Catholic?"

Rocky shook his head. "It doesn't prevent me from feeling like I'm permanently stuck in purgatory." He picked at a hangnail on his thumb. "Do you really think you can help me?"

"I know I can," Karen replied.

They continued talking until his time was up. Rocky walked to the door and paused with his hand on the knob. "See you next week, Karen."

"Try to be on time."

Rocky nodded, then opened the door.

"Hey, Rocky," Karen called out.

He stopped and faced her. "Yeah."

"You'll do in a pinch."

Rocky laughed as he rubbed a hand over his heart. "Ouch."

He'd heard therapy was supposed to make you feel better, but he felt as drained as a battery from an overused dildo when he left Karen's office.

CHAPTER 5

Rocky drove home on autopilot but got a little burst of energy when he turned on to his street and his house came into view. He absolutely adored the white bungalow he'd purchased from his grandmother when she moved into her retirement community. The exterior was quaint and cute with its bold, red front door, navy blue shutters, and a trellis archway over the porch. His nana had planted colorful flowers in the window boxes and the blossoming vines that climbed up the intricate latticework on both sides of the entrance. Rocky had no idea what any of them were called, but he watered them faithfully to keep them looking nice.

The home had been his safe place when he was a lonely kid, then a confused teenager, and especially when he was a brokenhearted mess of a man seeking refuge after leaving Vegas. The bungalow represented so much more than four walls and a roof over his head; it was love.

Which was why Rocky was kicking himself in the ass for saying yes to Asher coming over. He would disrupt the harmony inside the home, and his husband's presence would linger long after he left. Rocky wasn't interested in starring in a Dickens novel. He didn't need the ghosts of Asher past and present to disturb his nonexistent sleep any more than they already had, dragging him to memories he didn't want to relive. He didn't want to think about Asher's future without him, and he sure as hell didn't want to see Asher fall in love with someone who wasn't him. Fuck no. Just the idea of it had him pacing the floor. And how fucking stupid was that? He was the one who'd left Asher and filed for a divorce. What right did he have to deny Asher the happiness he deserved?

None. Fucking none at all. But it hurt so damn much. Rocky would be furious if he didn't deserve the punishment. He jerked to a stop in the middle of his living room.

Was that why Asher was here? To torment Rocky and get even? And what was this favor that couldn't be asked via text or phone? He shoved his hands into his hair, gripping his skull and willing his brain to settle down. Each thought made it harder to breathe until he felt like his chest was caving beneath the pressure. His heart galloped like a race-horse at the Kentucky Derby until he felt lightheaded. Rocky closed his eyes and cycled through the meditation exercise Karen had taught him. After a few minutes, the weight on his chest eased, and his heart set-tled to a leisurely trot. He'd almost returned to Calmville when a knock sounded at the front door.

Shit! Rocky looked around the living room to assess its condition, then laughed at his ridiculousness. He'd been the meticulous one in their relationship while Asher had been the slob. Rocky hadn't changed and was willing to gamble Asher hadn't either. With nothing to tidy up to delay the inevitable, Rocky crossed the room and opened the door. A beautiful queen stood on his front porch. Miss Marla had her beloved Betty, a black-and-white French bulldog, tucked beneath her right arm and carried an aluminum tray in her left hand. The sight of her never failed to boost his mood.

"Well, hello there. You look stunning," Rocky said.

"I know." Marla set Betty down and handed the pan to Rocky. Betty darted past Rocky's legs on her way to the rear of the house. The little dog loved his backyard, and he knew she'd be waiting patiently for Rocky to let her out to enjoy it. Marla slowly turned in a circle, giving him the three-sixty view. The skirt of her white and black polka dot '50s style hal-ter dress twirled around her knees. "Hello, Pretty Boy," she said, angling her head and offering her cheek.

Rocky kissed her warm skin, then lowered his head to breathe in the delicious aroma escaping the foil covering. "Smells like butter and cinnamon."

"There's the private dick we all know and love. Can't fool you for a second. Cinnamon rolls for my cinnamon roll."

Rocky snorted. He wasn't sure that kind and sweet were terms many people would ascribe to him, but he was happy Marla thought so. Rocky fought the urge to pull the foil back and shove his face into the pan. He stepped aside and gestured for her to enter. "To what do I owe this pleasure?"

"Do I need a reason to do something nice for my boo?" Marla batted her eyelashes and attempted an innocent smile. Attempted was the keyword.

Rocky wasn't fooled for a second. Marla was the one who'd referred him to Karen. If she made a habit of turning up after his appointments to soothe him with baked goods, he'd gain thirty pounds before he even worked up the courage to delve deeper into the source of his pain.

"You have an ulterior motive for everything you do," Rocky teased.

"Taking care of my boys gives me a purpose. And you're very welcome."

"Thank you," he said, kissing her cheek once more. "It has nothing to do with you hoping to learn what was discussed at therapy?"

Marla gasped and literally clutched her pearls. "Are you implying I'm nosy?"

"Does the douche nozzle fit?" Rocky quipped.

Marla's mouth hung open for so long Rocky worried he'd actually offended her. Then her head fell back, and she laughed so hard she needed to lean against the doorframe for support. After a moment, Marla composed herself and said, "I may resemble that."

Rocky quirked a brow. "A nosy queen or a douche nozzle?"

Marla swatted his arm. "You can tell Mama about your troubles," she said silkily.

Rocky nodded. "I could."

"You could also offer a lady a drink and someplace to sit." Marla craned her neck to look down the hallway. "Unless you're trying to hide something…or someone."

"Nope."

He suspected Marla knew about Asher, even though she'd never mentioned it directly. Jonah wouldn't divulge his secret, but Felix sure as fuck would and most likely had. Fucking Felix. Betty came to the rescue by running back into the living room and letting out a series of short barks. Marla turned to look at her beloved dog. "What is it, Miss Thing?"

Betty responded with two more barks.

"Outside?" Rocky asked. Energy radiated through Betty's wiggling body as she spun around in a circle. "Why don't we go out back so Betty can play in the yard while we drink lemonade and get caught up."

"Sounds simply divine, baby."

Rocky set the cinnamon rolls on the counter and filled two glasses before heading outside with Marla.

"Thank you, darling," Marla said before taking a big drink. "That hits the spot."

Rocky took a sip, then set his glass down on the table. "Sure does."

"I absolutely love your home, and Miss Thing won't want to leave this big ole yard."

Rocky watched as Betty sniffed her way across the grass until she found the perfect spot to squat and pee.

"Did everything go okay with Karen?" Marla asked, yanking Rocky's attention back to her.

"She's nice."

"Nice?" Marla asked with a grimace.

"Okay, Karen is a bit of a smartass, which is why I like her a lot. I have a tough time opening up to anyone, let alone a perfect stranger."

Marla placed her hand over his. "It takes time to build a bond. I happen to be a great listener."

"I wouldn't even know where to start."

She gave Rocky an encouraging smile. "The beginning is usually a good place."

"It all started thirty-five years ago on a rainy day in September. I think it was a Tuesday."

Marla snorted. "Maybe not back to the beginning of your existence, dear. I was thinking more along the lines of the origin of your current problem."

Rocky released a deep sigh. "When I was thirteen, I realized I had a crush on my track coach."

Marla patted his hand. "Fast-forward a little, my pet." Rocky had to bite the inside of his cheek to keep from laughing at her eager expression. "I'm thinking maybe a few weeks ago."

"Okay. It all started when Felix called me fat."

Marla growled, and Rocky couldn't keep up the pretense any longer. He burst into laughter, earning a scowl.

"I'm going to smack the sass right out of you," she warned.

Rocky sobered and straightened in his chair. "Oh, the day is starting to look up now."

"Maybe you can start with an explanation about your pants. Is this the new trend? Kids these days."

Somehow, Rocky had forgotten all about his jeans. "I finally met a dog I didn't like." Well, he'd met a dog who hadn't liked him. Snickerdoodle—God, what a ridiculous name—was the kind of dog he and Asher had hoped to adopt. Rocky was surprised Asher hadn't left him in the SUV and joined everyone else in the neighborhood to rub the dog's belly.

Activity at Rocky's neighbor's house caught his attention. He groaned when the man wheeled his ancient lawnmower out of the garden shed.

"What is that relic?" Marla asked.

"Are you talking about the man or the machine?"

Marla laughed. "Both."

"That's my neighbor, Cal. I don't know if his lawnmower has a name, but it would be something old, like Alfred."

"Surely it doesn't still work."

"I think work is a subjective term."

Cal gave the pull-chain a good yank. The beast sputtered a few times, then roared to life.

"I don't think I've ever heard a mower so loud," Marla yelled over the noise.

"I'm used to it," Rocky replied. The noise grew louder as Cal pushed the rusted hunk of metal along the fence separating their properties. Fortunately, the neighbor kept walking to his front yard to tackle it first, making the noise more tolerable.

"At least you're not trying to sleep late on a Saturday morning," Marla said.

The mower cut off suddenly, and Rocky cringed as he anticipated what would happen next. Before he could warn Marla, a loud boom echoed through the neighborhood. Even though he'd braced himself, the noise reminded him of gunshots blasting through a quiet desert night.

Marla flinched and clutched her chest. "What the fuck was that?" Her shrill tone kept Rocky grounded in the present and prevented him from traveling back fifteen months to when his world had imploded.

"The damn lawnmower backfires every time he cuts off the engine," Rocky said.

"Dude needs a new one."

"Or at least new sparkplugs," a new voice added.

Son of a bitch.

Asher had let himself in through the gate, but they'd been too deafened and distracted by Cal to notice. Rocky's mouth went dry at the sight of him. He was dressed in the same clothes he'd worn earlier—black cargo pants, black T-shirt with US Marshals emblazoned on the front, and the same wicked-looking gun holstered at his hip. Something was different, though. Then Rocky's gaze fell to the oversized black duffel bag in Asher's hand.

The monstrosity went everywhere with his husband. How many times had Rocky tripped over that damn bag when Asher dropped it by the front door after returning home from an assignment? Rocky would often find a trail of clothes from the front door to the bedroom because it was all Asher could muster in his exhausted state. His heart stuttered to a stop when he realized the significance of Asher standing in his yard with the duffel bag. He knew precisely what Asher's favor was. *Oh hell no.*

Rocky's pulse impersonated a race car competing in the Oh Fuck 500.

Beside him, Marla gasped, signaling she hadn't missed the mountain of muscle standing ten feet away. "Oh my," she husked.

"Shall I get the smelling salts?" Rocky asked drolly.

"Oh, shush. Hello, Marshal," Marla purred. Rocky turned to face her, not that she noticed. She was too busy batting her eyelashes at Asher and fanning her pink cheeks.

Marla leaned toward Rocky and whispered, "Do you still want to stick with the dog-tore-off-my-pants story?"

Before Rocky could respond, Asher said, "You didn't tell me you were expecting company tonight, Ford."

"Ford?" Marla asked.

"It's short for Rockford."

"Oh, that's cute," Marla said. Still not meeting Rocky's gaze.

"Thanks," Asher said.

Betty realized someone new had joined the mix and barked ferociously, charging toward the threat to her mom. Rocky pivoted in his seat in time to see Asher squat down and extend his open arms to the charging beast. Betty, the little slut, launched herself at Asher, who caught the dog midair. His husband cradled the dog securely against his chest as he stood up and carried her onto the deck.

"And who do we have here?" Asher asked when he reached the table.

Marla's chair scraped across the wood as she vacated it in a hurry. She sashayed to Asher and extended her hand. "This is Betty, and I'm Betty's mama, but you can call me Marla. Miss Marla, if you're nasty."

"I'm Asher or Mr. Asher Dunleavy, if *you're* nasty."

Marla tipped her head back and laughed throatily. "I've heard of you."

Asher quirked a brow. "You have?"

"Mmmmhmmmm," Marla purred as she wrapped a hand around Asher's bicep. "Seems to me that some of the details were left out of the telling, though. Child, you're one big motherfucker. Look at these guns."

Asher flexed his arm, making Marla squeal in delight. "Ford, why didn't you tell your beautiful friend about my big *guns*."

"I didn't tell her anything about you," Rocky said. *Fucking Felix.*

Asher's smile faltered. "Of course you didn't."

Marla held out her arms for Betty, and Asher carefully transferred the wiggling dog to her mama. "I don't think you're entirely blameless here, Big Guns. I've known Pretty Boy for nearly a year, and we're just now meeting. Do better by my boy."

"Yes, ma'am."

Marla's loyalty soothed the panic rising inside Rocky but didn't squelch it.

She smiled at Rocky. "Walk a lady out, won't you?"

"You're leaving so soon? I didn't get a chance to tell you about my shitty day." Marla's presence was a much-needed buffer. Without it, he'd... Rocky wasn't sure what the hell he was going to say or do.

"I have people to see and places to go, and I need to get Amos's Cadillac back before he wakes up from his nap and sees it missing." She faced Asher once again. "It was lovely meeting you. I hope to see you again real soon."

"The pleasure is all mine, ma'am," Asher said.

Marla looped her arm through Rocky's, and together, they walked back inside the house. As soon as he shut the sliding glass door, she leaned into him and said, "I think the pleasure is about to be all yours. Lord, I bet he's going to pound you like a cube steak. You'll be just as tender afterward too."

"Marla!"

"Listen to you, sounding like a virgin on their wedding day."

Rocky laughed. "No one saves themselves for marriage anymore. Are you on a regency romance kick again?"

"Perhaps." Marla batted her fake eyelashes at him. "At least tell Mama one thing."

"Maybe," Rocky replied noncommittally, earning a *tsk* and a playful slap on the arm.

"How'd the two of you meet?"

"Felix didn't tell you that?"

"Only because his smart ass didn't know," she quipped.

Rocky grinned, despite his annoyance and frustration. No matter what happened, he'd never regret the night his eyes had landed on Asher Dunleavy for the first time. "A nineteen-year-old woman met a guy online and ran off with him. Her parents had been able to trace her as far as Vegas before her trail went cold. They hired me, and I found her within twenty-four hours."

"Alive?" Marla asked nervously.

"Yes, but her new boyfriend was the worst kind of human being. I'm pretty sure he peddled everything from stolen laptops to humans. I had no doubt my client's daughter would disappear for good once he grew tired of her."

"Oh, that's awful, baby. What did you do?"

"I knew I had to build a case to show the authorities, but unbeknownst to me, this loser was already on their radar. I ended up being near the scene when the FBI and the marshals executed their arrest warrants and liberated the girl in the process. I got so caught up in watching the scene play out through my binoculars that I'd somehow missed the mountain of a man approaching my car."

"Mountain is right. Get to the good part."

"Saving the girl was the good part."

Marla rolled her eyes. "Get to the dirty part. Did you invite him into your back seat?"

Rocky chuckled. "All I saw at first was his torso. Then he leaned down to make eye contact, and I nearly swallowed my tongue. The red and blue flashing lights from the emergency vehicles accentuated his high cheekbones and square jaw."

"Nearly came in your pants, didn't you?"

"I was rendered speechless. All I could do was think about how badly I wanted the deputy marshal to take me home and pin me to the bed." Rocky smiled at Marla. "You've seen those thighs, right?"

"Hard to miss."

"Anyway, I recovered my ability to think and speak enough for Asher to interview me. I went home alone afterward."

"Without getting his phone number?"

"Asher was very rigid and borderline hostile. I just assumed he was straight."

"Until…"

"He showed up at my door a few hours later." The memory had Rocky's heart knocking against his rib cage.

Marla laughed. "He wasn't there to ask you follow-up questions, was he?"

"Nope." Rocky grinned. "Apparently, I'd spoken my initial thoughts out loud. Asher showed up to pin me to the bed." *Boy, had he ever.*

"I'm dying to know more, but a deal is a deal." She leaned forward and kissed Rocky's cheek. "Come on, Miss Thing. We're going to stop at the grocery store because I have a sudden craving for Swiss steak." She blew Rocky an air kiss, then headed out the door. "I love you, Pretty Boy."

"Love you too."

He waved as she drove away and cringed when she nearly side-swiped a parked car. Once back inside his house, he leaned against the closed door for a moment to pull himself together. As beautiful as Marla looked and as vivacious as she seemed, there was a frailness about her, reminding Rocky that their time together was limited.

Tears welled behind his closed eyelids, and he willed them away. He promised not to mourn her while she was still living, and it was a vow he planned to keep.

Vow. The sobering thought reminded Rocky of the gorgeous hulk of a man on his deck. He could get in his car and drive away, but Rocky wasn't the type to live off the grid. Asher would easily track him down. And besides, he loved the life he was rebuilding in Savannah. Running wasn't an option, and he couldn't hide in the house forever, so Rocky squared his shoulders and headed outside.

Maybe the therapy stuff was starting to kick in.

CHAPTER 6

Asher wasn't where Rocky had left him, but his giant duffel bag marked the spot where he should've been. He saw Asher standing at the fence, chatting with Cal, who'd decided to take a break from mowing. Rocky softly groaned when Cal looked over at him and waved excitedly.

"I never knew you had a husband," the elderly man yelled out. "Why didn't you say so? You've known me all your life. Did you think I'm one of those bigots?" Before Rocky could answer, Cal looked back at Asher. "Where the hell have you been all this time?"

"We're getting divorced," Rocky announced as he joined the two men at the fence.

"Ah, that explains all the men parading in and out of his house lately." Cal might not be a bigot, but he sure as hell was a blabbermouth.

Asher looked over at him with a quirked brow, and Rocky rolled his eyes.

"Those are just my friends, Cal, and there haven't been a ton."

Cal's wife poked her head out the back door. "Dinner's ready, Cal." She spotted Asher, then said, "Oh, hello."

"Hi, I'm Asher."

"It's nice to meet you. I'm Elaine."

"Did you know Rocky was married?" Cal asked his wife.

"No, but *I* mind my own business, dear. Come on in and eat while the food is still hot." She popped back inside the house and shut the door.

"Well, I best get going. It's meatloaf night."

Asher chuckled. "It was nice meeting you, Cal."

"Same to you," the older man said over his shoulder as he shuffled toward his house.

Asher grinned from ear to ear as he made his way up the deck steps. Someone needed to knock him down a peg.

"Will you tell me what you're doing in Savannah now?"

"I told you I would as soon as I got Spencer settled."

He'd said "time will tell," which sounded way more ominous than this paraphrased version. Instead of pointing it out, Rocky said, "That was three weeks ago."

Asher tilted his head. "You're going to tell me how to do my job now? Do you know how much work goes into establishing new identities for one person, let alone an entire family?"

"No."

"It's extensive and exhausting when things go according to plan, so imagine the ensuing chaos after three knuckleheads crash my investigation."

"You called us meddlesome idiots," Rocky reminded him. Asher replied with a shrug and an easy smile that did nothing to ease Rocky's nerves. "I'm not disputing that your job is complicated, but I have a tough time believing you couldn't find a spare moment to call or text me."

"And allow you to throw up roadblocks?" *Or run away.* Asher hadn't said the words out loud, but Rocky could see the accusation in his husband's gaze. Asher shook his head, and the incrimination disappeared. "A stealth approach works best."

Rocky's eyes fell to the monstrous bag at Asher's feet. "You can't stay here."

"It'd just be for a few days."

Rocky shook his head. "Absolutely not." The house was too small and only had one bathroom. He didn't want to hear Asher in the shower or smell his bodywash lingering in the air. He didn't want to imagine water sluicing down his husband's incredible body. *Yet here you are doing just that.*

"I don't see why there'd be a problem. You've done a great job of erasing me from your life."

"I have not," Rocky scoffed.

Asher quirked a raven brow. "Really? You've either told people we were divorced or pretended I didn't exist. I'm not sure which hurts the most."

Asher's verbal arrow would've struck center mass if not for the shields Rocky had worked hard to erect against such attacks. "I'm going to ask you one more time."

"What comes after thrice?" Asher asked.

Rocky took a calming breath. He'd passed the road sign welcoming him to exhaustion several miles ago and was coasting on fumes. "Why are you here, Asher?"

His husband matched Rocky's deep breath with one of his own. Great. They'd huff and puff and blow the house down without Rocky being any closer to understanding what the hell was going on.

"You're not going to like it," Asher finally said.

"That goes without saying."

"I'd requested a transfer to Savannah soon after you left me. The logical step in my mind had been to follow and fight for you—us."

Rocky leaned against the deck railing for support, gripping the wood so hard the edges cut into his skin like his husband's words shredded his soul. Of course Asher hadn't given up easily.

"There were no openings at the time," Asher continued. "We grew further apart each day, and you seemed to be blossoming in a life that didn't include me. Then came the divorce papers."

Rocky choked down the guilt and heartbreak. "Which you contested."

Asher nodded. "It gave me time to win you back."

Time that was quickly running out. Was that the real reason Asher was in Savannah? Rocky could ask him, but did he want to know the answer?

"Does that mean a position here in Savannah recently became available?"

"Yes, and it came with a promotion to inspector." The one he'd been passed over for because of the embarrassing media attention Rocky had garnered after the fallout from the Warner shootings. "Things hadn't been right in Vegas for a long time. I'd fallen out of love with the city before we met. All of my family still lives in Brooklyn, so I had no reason to stay in Vegas."

"Congratulations."

Asher's pride shone in his smile. "Thank you. I figured I'd get to know the city you loved more than me."

"I don't love Savannah more than I love you."

The sweet curve of Asher's mouth morphed into dark, dangerous pirate territory, knocking Rocky off-kilter. Then he closed the distance between them, his gait every bit as cocksure as his grin. "Good to know."

"Know what?" Rocky asked, sounding as breathless as one of Marla's romance novel heroines. He had butterflies in his stomach to match.

"That you don't love Savannah more than me."

Rocky shook his head. "I said I *didn't* love Savannah more than you."

Asher chuckled. "Oh, I must've misheard you."

"Yeah, that's it."

Asher stopped mere inches away, and Rocky had to tilt his head back to look into his glistening, dark eyes. Reaching for the man felt as natural as breathing, so Rocky gripped the wooden railing harder to stave off the urge. It didn't stop Asher from crowding his personal space even more by lowering his head. Asher was close enough that his breath ghosted over Rocky's lips. The longing he felt was echoed in Asher's expression, and with it, Rocky saw a silent challenge. Asher was going to kiss him, and Rocky was going to let him.

The intensity was too much. Rocky closed his eyes at the last minute. But he didn't turn his head away. Instead, he braced himself for an onslaught of feelings and sensations that never occurred because Cal fired up his obnoxious lawnmower again.

Rocky and Asher jerked apart and stared at each other, both of them breathing heavier than usual. He was both happy and dismayed that Asher reacted to his proximity in the same way.

"Wow, Cal eats fast," Asher shouted, breaking the standoff.

"You can't stay here," Rocky shouted back.

"Why not?"

Luckily, Cal wheeled the beast back to the front yard, making it easier for Rocky to shut Asher down. Maybe everything he'd said was true, but none of it explained why the hell Asher was there with his duffel bag in tow.

"Let's start with something easy. Why do you even want to stay here in the first place?" Rocky asked.

"The house I rented isn't ready for me to move into yet."

"Why?"

"The landlord insisted on giving the place a fresh coat of paint and shampooing the carpets before giving me the keys."

Rocky narrowed his eyes. "How long is that supposed to take?"

"A few days at most."

"Where have you been all this time, and why can't you continue to stay there? Better yet, why can't the marshals put you up in a hotel or sock you away in a safe house or something?"

"I just returned to Savannah a few days ago, and I've been crashing at Dandridge's place. He's been really cool, but I don't think his fiancé is happy about it. You'd really rather I stay at a hotel or a safe house than crash here with you?"

"Yes."

"Ouch." Asher rubbed a spot over his heart. "I understand if you don't trust yourself around me."

"What?" Rocky said. "You're the one who almost kissed me."

"It was closure. Nothing more," Asher said.

"Mmmhmmm."

"I'll be on my best behavior." Asher crossed his heart for good measure. "If you don't have any feelings for me, then I don't see why it would be a problem. You still have a guest bed, right?"

"Your feet will hang off the end."

"I've slept in much worse conditions, baby." Rocky scowled at him for using the endearment and Asher grimaced. "It's just a habit."

"I only have one bathroom."

"So? Are you implying we should conserve water and—"

"No." He'd aimed for a firm voice, but it came out shaky with a hint of a whimper.

"Then, I don't see a problem."

Guilt and misery made Rocky feel like a cornered rat. From the moment they'd met, he had brought nothing but chaos into Asher's life, turning his orderly world upside down. Offering him his spare bedroom for a few days was the least he could do.

"Fine, but no more trying to kiss me."

Asher lifted his right hand to show his index, middle, and ring fingers extended in salute. "You have my word."

"Put that away," Rocky said. "You were never a Boy Scout."

"It's never too late to start," Asher said, a smile tugging at his lips.

Rocky rolled his eyes. "And don't flirt with me either."

"I wouldn't dream of it, but can you behave? What was it you once told me? You're from the South, so flirting is in your DNA?"

"I was quoting Blanche Devereaux."

"Who?"

Rocky snorted. "You really need to work on your pop culture knowledge."

"I don't have time for that. I'm always chasing someone." His pointed gaze said present company included.

"Well, I'll do my best to fix some of your inadequacies while you're here."

"Can it start with some of the Southern cooking you've bragged about for as long as I've known you? Dandridge is a vegetarian and a health food nut. It didn't feel right ordering barbecue while staying there."

Rocky chuckled. Now they were getting to the real reason he was vacating his partner's place. "Come on. Let's get you something to eat." When Asher didn't budge, Rocky narrowed his eyes. "What?"

"You weren't planning on cooking food, were you?"

Rocky rolled his eyes and headed inside. "There's nothing wrong with my cooking. I only faked my ineptitude because I'm lazy."

"Uh-huh," Asher said as he followed. "So, what drawer do you keep your takeout menus in?"

"What takeout menus?"

Asher walked straight to the drawer beneath the microwave. He laughed when he saw the vast array of menus tucked inside. "Glad to see some things are still the same."

It was true that not much had changed for Rocky during the year they'd been apart. It both irked and delighted him that his husband still found his habits endearing. The ornery gleam in Asher's eyes and the responding tightening in Rocky's core made him second-guess his decision to let Asher stay.

It's only for a few days, a voice inside him whispered. *What could go wrong?*

Unfortunately, it was the same voice that always led Rocky astray. Even knowing he should change his mind, Rocky casually shrugged as if an epic battle between want and need weren't raging inside his brain. He wanted Asher there more than his next breath, but he needed him to go away.

As if Asher picked up on his inner turmoil, he narrowed his eyes and studied him. "Ford?" What was he asking? If Rocky had changed his mind about the divorce? Or if he regretted leaving Asher? Maybe he wanted to know if Rocky still loved him. The questions fired one after another until Rocky's brain hurt. Asher tapped the stack of menus in his hand. "What do you feel like eating?"

Asher's tense posture, knitted brow, and borderline grimace said his husband was worried about more than just Rocky's food preference. He looked like he was prepared to battle. Or was he braced for rejection? This was the moment to speak up. He could tell Asher to go, and he would. Then what? They'd pretend to be strangers whenever they ran into one another? Would his soul continue to bleed out every time Rocky thought about everything they'd lost? Or could he use these few days to find some closure? His heart said hell yes, but his brain called him a fool.

"It sounds like you're jonesing for barbecue. Trish's Diner is the best. If you don't mind, I'll let you call in the order while I shower and throw these jeans out."

"Are you sure?" Asher pressed.

"Positive." Thanks to Miss Marla, Rocky suddenly craved cube steak in its best form—pounded, double breaded, and fried. "Can you order a chicken-fried-steak dinner for me?"

The tension melted from Asher's broad shoulders right in front of Rocky's eyes. "Of course. Mashed potatoes and cream gravy, green beans, and a roll for your sides, right?"

Rocky smiled. "You don't have to specify cream gravy with Trish. No self-respecting Southerner puts cream gravy on their meat and brown gravy on their mashed potatoes. Mixing types of gravies is illegal in these parts."

Asher nodded. "Good to know. Is there some kind of handbook to give a Yankee like me? Sounds like I could use some pointers on how to navigate my new landscape and negotiate with the natives."

"Not that I'm aware of, but it's probably because we wouldn't want to encourage hordes of Northerners to flood our beautiful city. All those harsh tones and clipped syllables." Rocky shuddered in mock horror.

"Yeah, it's much better to turn a two-syllable word into ten," Asher replied. "We wouldn't want to get directly to the point, would we? It would be best to meander down three generations of history before we tell a person to turn right at the next light."

Rocky laughed. "I feel so seen, and yet I find it so cute that you think we'd ever give such simple directions, even after extolling three generations of history. We use landmarks here. God help us all if anyone changes the paint colors on their homes or businesses or if lightning takes out the weirdly shaped tree that signifies you should be turning left."

"Jesus," Asher muttered.

"Having regrets yet?" Rocky asked. "Maybe it's not too late for Director Bradshaw to take you back."

Like earlier outside the SUV, a myriad of emotions washed over Asher's face before settling on one that made Rocky far more nervous than the lust he'd witnessed. Determination furrowed his husband's brow.

And it spelled big trouble.

It's only for a few days.

CHAPTER 7

Ashower was as good of an excuse as any to avoid Asher long enough to regain his equilibrium. Standing beneath the spray, Rocky felt like he'd been punched in the face by a prizefighter. He was seconds away from being ruled down for the count. He took his time washing his hair and body, then sat in the bathtub while the hot water rained down on him. Rocky pulled his legs to his chest, wrapped his arms around his calves, and rested his chin on his knee. Steam filled the bathroom, creating a private fog that matched the landscape of his overtaxed and fatigued brain.

He couldn't hide here forever, but he could hold out until the water turned cold. Lucky for him, he'd replaced the hot water tank not long after he'd moved in. The new model was larger than the original, but all good things must come to an end. At the first sign of a temperature drop, Rocky rose to his feet and shut the water off. He ran the towel over his hair and body before wrapping it around his waist and stepping out of the shower.

Not willing to leave the serenity of the steamy bathroom, Rocky wiped a circle in the condensation on the mirror to study his reflection. He looked as tired as he felt, and he couldn't believe no one had remarked on the circles beneath his eyes. The baby blue irises people described as mischievous or seductive looked dull and flat to him. Looking at who he'd become reminded Rocky of where he'd been and what he'd lost. Those trains of thought would lead to others equally as morose and depressing, and he was tired of existing in the quagmire of his own making.

Rocky hoped therapy would help because he didn't feel any closer to the man who'd fearlessly tossed those dice onto the craps table. He wasn't any closer to being the kind of man Asher deserved. Maybe he'd never been that guy and had just fooled himself.

Rocky slammed on the mental brakes before he caused himself more harm. He busied himself by turning on the shaving gel warmer his parents had given him for his birthday. Michelle might technically be his stepmother, but she was the only mother he knew. His father, Roger, had remarried when Rocky was five. Michelle had never tried to take his birth mother's place. She'd preserved Amelia's things such as the journals she'd written in, her favorite vinyl albums, the photographs his mom had taken, and the artwork she'd painted. Michelle had given them to Rocky when he was old enough to appreciate the keepsakes. He loved her with every fiber in his being, even when she'd presented him with a little sister when he was eight. CeCe was still giving him hell all these years later.

Rocky worked the warm cream over his face, then shaved with the straight razor from the kit. He'd been nervous as hell about attempting a barbershop-style shave on his own, but after several YouTube videos, he'd worked up the courage to try it for himself. He'd never go back to disposable razors or electric models now.

He had to wipe the mirror a few more times while shaving because it kept fogging back up. Opening the door would let the steam out, but it could also let his unwanted company in. Rocky set the razor on the countertop and leaned closer to his reflection to study his handiwork. He tilted his head to the left and right and lifted his chin to inspect his neck. Rocky ran his fingers over his skin, feeling for any stragglers, before applying aftershave to his face.

With no more legitimate excuses, he picked up his dirty clothes from the floor—sans the jeans he'd tossed into the trash—and stepped into the hallway. The unimpeded trip he'd hoped for didn't happen because Asher stood a few feet away.

He waved his hand in the air, dispersing the fog rolling out of the bathroom. "Christ. It looks like a scene from a Cheech and Chong movie."

"You know how I love my long showers," Rocky said glibly.

"I do." Asher's gaze roamed over Rocky's bare skin, lingering on the towel wrapped around his waist. He felt the gaze just as strongly as if Asher had reached out and trailed a finger down his torso. Goose bumps popped up all over Rocky's body, and something warm and not entirely unwanted unfurled in his core. He wanted to make sure he'd tightly tucked the end of the towel at his waist but didn't want to draw Asher's attention to his discomfort.

"Were you looking for me?" Rocky asked before he noticed the bulky bag in Asher's hand.

"Uh," Asher said, then cleared his throat. "I was going to drop my bag in your guest room. Dinner should be here any minute."

"That's quick."

Asher smirked. "Not really. You were in there for at least twenty-five minutes."

They lapsed into an awkward silence as they stared at one another. The narrow hallway walls seemed to close in on them like one of those fun houses at a carnival. Rocky hadn't liked them as a kid, and he liked them even less as an adult.

Rocky said, "Well, I—" at the same time Asher tilted his head toward the guest bedroom door and said, "I should—"

Their stumbling words only made Rocky's discomfort grow. This was so unlike them. They'd been in tune from the very start, but now... Rocky smiled, hoping to reduce Asher's apprehension. The doorbell rang before Asher could respond.

"I'll get the door so you can drop your stuff in the guest room," Rocky offered.

"Dressed like that?" Asher growled.

Rocky looked down at the towel riding low on his hips. He'd been so caught up in this weird conversation he had forgotten about his state of undress. "Yeah, maybe not. Give me your bag, and I'll drop it in the room."

Asher accepted Rocky's offer and held it out to him. Rocky took the duffel bag and laughed when the weight of it jerked him slightly off-balance. Christ. It felt even heavier than it used to.

"What do you have in here? A dead body?"

Asher scoffed and waved him off before pivoting and walking away. "Get dressed and let's eat," he tossed over his shoulder.

Rocky quickly dumped the duffel in the spare bedroom and retreated to his own. He found a pair of ratty gym shorts and an old Braves T-shirt that was a decade past its prime. They were a perfect way to prove he wasn't trying to impress anyone.

By the time he joined Asher in the living room, he'd separated the meals and had plopped his ass into Rocky's recliner and dug into his food. The Braves game was playing quietly in the background. His husband narrowed his eyes and studied Rocky intently as he made his way across the room.

"Did you run out of clean clothes?" Asher asked.

"No, why?"

Asher continued to study every inch of him, and Rocky's skin tingled anywhere Asher's gaze landed until it felt like an army of ants marched under his flesh.

"Hmmm," Asher said after a moment. What the hell kind of answer was that? He tucked into his meal, and Rocky's clothes were all but forgotten. "This is damn good."

"I know," Rocky said smugly as he dropped into the club chair on the opposite side of the couch from where Asher lounged in his recliner.

"You don't find food like this in Vegas," Asher said after a few bites of ribs, macaroni and cheese, and green beans. "I could definitely get used to this."

"Your waistline will too."

Asher lowered his fork and glared at Rocky. "Are you calling me fat?"

"Not yet."

"I'll add extra reps with the weights and longer bouts of cardio to keep me in proper form."

"For fighting?" Rocky asked, then nearly kicked his own ass for opening this can of worms.

Asher quirked a brow. "Yeah, for fighting, although the stamina sure comes in handy at other times."

Rocky's face flushed as image after image of Asher dominating him in bed flashed in his brain. His husband had a sex drive and endurance like he'd never witnessed before. Whenever Rocky erroneously allowed his mind to go there, he'd transition to wondering who was satisfying Asher's needs in his absence. The mere thought of Asher touching anyone else sparked a fire deep in his belly.

"Ford."

Asher's firm voice yanked him back from the brink. Rocky blinked a few times to refocus his eyes and realized he'd been staring at his husband's crotch.

"Ask me," Asher said.

Rocky swallowed hard. "About what?" He'd perfected the dumb blond act for when it suited him. This was one of those times.

Asher shook his head. "I'm not playing your games." Then he continued shoveling food into his mouth while staring at the baseball game on TV like it was the most enthralling thing he'd ever seen. "Why are these green beans so good?" Asher asked a few bites later.

"They're swimming in a pool of bacon grease and onions."

Asher grunted. "What about this macaroni? What's this crunchy stuff on top?"

"Breadcrumbs and butter," Rocky replied. "Trish makes the cheese sauce from scratch. I can't imagine how many batches of macaroni and cheese they bake in one day."

"I'm guessing the cheese sauce isn't made with Velveeta." The processed cheese product was one of Asher's favorite things in the world.

"Hell no."

"I won't hold it against her when she can make something this good."

Rocky chuckled. "I'll be sure to pass along your praise next time I see her."

Asher's phone rang, and Rocky muted the volume on the television.

"Duggy Bear," Asher said into his phone instead of his typical greeting. Of course, Duggins would interrupt their dinner. Tim Duggins had made no attempt to hide his attraction to Asher in front of Rocky, but his husband had seemed blissfully ignorant of the other man's feelings. He'd taken advantage of every bad thing that happened in Vegas to drive a wedge between Rocky and Asher.

And you let him win, dumbass.

"Yeah, I made it to Savannah okay," Asher said.

The remark caught Rocky off guard. Asher had been here for a few days and hadn't told Duggins? He glanced over at his husband, but Asher's face was an impassive mask. Also odd. Where was the smile that usually tugged at his lips when talking to his best friend? Why weren't his eyes dancing with laughter? Had something happened to drive a rift between them? Rocky's mind spun with all the things that might've happened to cause friction between the longtime partners. He didn't like a single one of them.

"It's not been without hiccups, though," Asher said.

Rocky faced the television and tried to appear as if he were caught up in the game. He couldn't have told anyone what inning they were in or what the score was, even though the information was right there on the screen.

"My rental house wasn't ready, so I crashed with Dandridge for a few days." Asher stopped and listened to Duggins's reply. "Yeah, I kind of wore out my welcome with his fiancé. The guy seems nice enough, but he didn't seem keen on juggling his routine. Huh?" Asher asked. From his periphery, Rocky saw his husband glance over at him. Was he figuring out how much to divulge to Duggins? "Luckily, I ran into Ford this afternoon, and he's letting me stay with him."

Rocky turned his head and met Asher's gaze. Rocky fell into them, tumbling ass over head just like Alice down the rabbit hole.

"Yeah, he's here now," Asher said.

"I live here," Rocky snarled.

"What's that?" Asher asked. Rocky wasn't sure who his husband was talking to until Asher grinned and added, "Duggins says hello." Rocky held up both middle fingers. His husband smirked at the immature reaction. "Ford sends his best wishes." Asher chuckled at Duggy Bear's response. "Nope. Both of them."

Rocky could hear Duggins's laughter coming through the phone, and his appetite disappeared. He took his leftovers to the refrigerator, then headed into the home office he'd set up in the smallest of the three bedrooms. The space was barely big enough to turn around in once he'd installed a desk and some bookshelves, but Rocky liked the cozy vibe he'd created by hanging some of his mother's photos and vibrant watercolor paintings on the wall.

Asher's laughter taunted him from the living room, but Rocky was determined to drown it out and ignore both the man and the feelings he inspired. The only way to accomplish his goal was to throw himself into his work. Rocky powered up his computer and clicked on the icon for the software Avery created for the podcasters. It allowed the partners to upload documents, photos, and case-file notes so that everything was in one tidy place. The setup also linked the guys to all the search engines and databases they used to run background checks and investigate people. Since they were a team, each of them could access any of the uploaded files.

His favorite features were the chat boxes and link for teleconferences. Whenever one of them was using the program, their avatar showed up in the upper left corner. Rocky glanced up and saw that Felix was online. He clicked on the cartoon version of his favorite reporter and selected "chat" from the menu. Avery had made it possible to chat one-on-one or in a group.

Rocky typed, *What the hell are you doing on here?* He hit enter and the chat box changed from blue to green when Felix clicked it open. A reaction message let him know Felix was responding.

What the hell are you doing on here? Asher already pounded that cube steak?

Rocky buried his head in his hands. Damn Marla. He shook his head and typed a response. *I bet she called you as soon as she got home.*

Ha! You're so cute. Marla called me before she left your street.

Rocky chuckled as he typed, *I hate you.* Bantering with Felix was exactly what he needed to decompress.

You love me, Felix fired back. *Everything okay?*

Rocky assured Felix he was fine and gave him a quick explanation of why Asher had shown up with a duffel bag in hand. There's no way Marla missed that detail or left it out of her story, although she might have embellished it a bit.

We still on for breakfast? Felix asked.

Absolutely.

See you then. Gotta run. Dinner's ready.

Rocky started to tell Felix to pass his greetings on to Jude, but his avatar disappeared before he got a chance. *Fucking Felix.*

He pulled up the file notes for Tess and scanned over the detailed timeline he'd created, which dated back to the late sixties when Tess, an army nurse, met Bob Duncan, an army pilot. The couple married within a year of returning to the States and started a family soon after. Since none of Tess's or Bob's friends, families, or coworkers were willing to speak to them, Rocky had been forced to rely on public records, employment history, property searches, and printed articles about the couple. The latter mostly came after the third husband passed away, and rumors circulated that Tess had killed all three husbands.

Bob's obituary didn't state the exact reason he'd died, but the family had requested donations be made to the American Heart Society. Since anyone could request a death certificate, Rocky had ordered Bob's, which listed congestive heart failure as the cause of his death.

Very little was known about her marriage to Donald Trout, aka husband number two. The only thing Rocky found was his obituary notice in the paper. It didn't say much about the couple and had only identified Tess as his surviving spouse. Rocky had uncovered their marriage certificate. The couple married fifteen years after Bob Duncan died and were still married when Donald Trout died nearly two years later. Rocky had obtained a copy of Mr. Trout's death certificate too, which stated his cause of death was advanced stage COPD.

Tess married Arnold Hamilton four years later. She stayed off everyone's radar until Jennifer Blossom, the claims adjuster, declared the beneficiary change form was a forgery. Previously, his policy was to be paid out to his four adult children. The alleged fraudulent form included a payout for Tess. Arnold Hamilton wasn't just an average citizen. He owned one of the largest trucking companies in the Southeast, with assets totaling in the billions, not millions.

The couple had only been married for a year before Arnold's death, and he hadn't changed his will to include Tess. Jennifer had explained to Rocky that all large life insurance payouts are closely scrutinized before the company releases the funds. During their interview, she acknowledged a person's handwriting changes over the years, especially when age or illnesses contribute to shakiness. She even went as far as to say she would've paid out the claim had her company not received an anonymous tip alleging that the witness on the form was a fictional person.

When Jennifer dug further, she uncovered it was true. No one by that name resided at the address provided and never had. The phone number listed on the form was also a dead end. Jennifer then delayed releasing the funds and hired a handwriting expert, who compared recent known samples of Arnold Hamilton's signature to the one on the beneficiary change form. It was close, but even Rocky suspected it was forged. That didn't mean Tess was the one who'd done it, but both the insurance company and a federal prosecutor hadn't felt the same way. They'd determined Tess was the only one to gain from the fraudulent act and pursued a conviction.

A case is only as strong as the evidence presented to the jury, and the prosecutor's case had been as shaky as Bambi's legs during his first time on the ice. Rocky hadn't been surprised by the hung jury or the subsequent *not guilty* verdict. Rocky had no way of knowing whether Tess was innocent or guilty, but no one should be sent to prison on such flimsy evidence.

Rocky sat back in his chair and thought about what he knew, which wasn't a lot, and what he didn't, which was a fuck ton. Then he pulled out a legal pad and a pen from his middle desk drawer. He wanted to form a backup plan if he couldn't convince Grant Duncan to help him, so he started by making a list. His top strategy was to contact lawyers from both sides of the aisle. The prosecutor and the defense attorney were rising stars and probably had big ambitions. Saying no to publicity wasn't likely. The second option was a road trip to Augusta, where Tess had lived with Bob, and to Albany, where she'd lived with Donald. He'd knock on the doors of anyone who knew the couples. Coworkers. Neighbors. Friends. Family. He'd find out who was the nosiest person in their circles and hit them up.

Rocky paused to think of another alternative to speaking to Tess herself but lost his train of thought when he heard Asher moving around in the bathroom, which abutted his office. When the shower turned on, Rocky pushed his chair back from his desk so hard he crashed it into the wall behind him, rattling the bookcase. He heard a soft thump and looked down to see his battered old copy of *The Maltese Falcon* had fallen off the shelf and onto the floor.

Rocky saw it as a sign and logged out of his program before exiting his office. He'd get nothing accomplished with Asher showering. Rocky wouldn't be able to stop himself from thinking about how Asher looked wet. He grabbed his battered paperback off the floor and headed outside to enjoy the evening. Children's laughter carried on the breeze, joining the birds serenading him. He dropped down in the chaise and closed his eyes, willing serenity and peace to find him.

Control what you can. Let the rest go.

Isn't that what Karen was teaching him? After several rounds of mindful meditation, the heaviness in his chest eased up, and his body felt more relaxed.

I got this.

It was his last conscious thought until a noise jarred him awake sometime later. He blinked in the dark, trying to figure out what had woken him and why his body was so stiff. The second question was easy to answer when he remembered lounging on the chaise after dinner. The chair was comfortable for short reprieves but couldn't replace a bed.

What the hell had woken him?

The clouds shifted, allowing a sliver of moonlight to wash over his yard and deck. That was when Rocky saw the shadowy silhouette of a huge man standing over him.

CHAPTER 8

"**F**uck!" Rocky shouted as he jackknifed into a sitting position. His outburst triggered barking from a few dogs in the neighborhood.

"It's just me, Ford," Asher whispered. "I didn't mean to startle you."

"Why were you hovering over me while I slept?" Rocky grumbled as he rose to his feet. "And you didn't startle me. I recognized your shadow right away."

"Why'd you let out the girlie scream, then?" Asher asked.

Once Rocky's eyes adjusted to the dark, he noticed Asher held a familiar aluminum foil container in his hands. It provided him with the perfect explanation for his outburst. "I smelled butter and cinnamon. *My* cinnamon rolls, to be more precise."

"Oh," Asher said. "Since we're married, half of these rolls are mine."

"Are you fucking kidding me right now?" Rocky asked, marching toward his husband. "First, you turn my whole world upside down by moving to my city, and now you've helped yourself to the baked goods my friend made for me."

Asher retreated a few steps but not out of fear. Rocky saw the brilliance of his white teeth flashing in the dark. The smug son of a bitch was smiling over Rocky's irritation. "Your friend liked me, and I don't think she'd mind you sharing your cinnamon rolls." Asher took another bite and moaned. "That's not really the issue here, though, is it?"

"It isn't?"

"Nope," Asher replied smugly. "You're projecting."

"Am not," Rocky said, reaching for the tin.

Asher cut to the right, deftly evading Rocky's hands. "Are too."

Rocky lunged for Asher, but the big man was surprisingly graceful. He darted away again, leaving Rocky empty-handed and fuming. "Give me the fucking cinnamon rolls."

Asher's laughter echoed in the dark. The deep rumble sounded strained as if the man were teetering on the edge of madness. It was a warning for Rocky to proceed cautiously, but it only made him want to push his husband even harder. "You're transferring your anger to something you're willing to vocalize," Asher said.

"Yeah, Dr. Dunleavy? What is it I really want?"

Asher stopped dodging Rocky, and that's when he realized his husband had maneuvered him up against the deck rail. *Damn him.* "If you aren't willing to be truthful with yourself, then you won't be honest with me."

Asher lifted a forkful of ooey-gooey cinnamon roll to Rocky's lips. He wanted to resist the peace offering, but the tantalizing aroma was Rocky's undoing. It was totally the pastry and not the man's words or the heat rolling off Asher's body that made Rocky part his lips.

The cinnamony decadence exploded on his tongue, making Rocky sway.

"Was that so hard?" Asher asked.

Rocky ignored him and swallowed before opening his mouth for another bite. Asher's laughter was much lighter as he obliged him. The two men kept their eyes locked on one another as they shared the dessert in alternating bites. It was deliciously intimate and dangerous. By the time Rocky swallowed the last forkful of a second roll, he had nearly forgotten his resolve.

Asher set the pan on top of the deck rail and reached for him. Rocky froze because his brain couldn't choose between his fight-or-flight instincts. Then it was too late because Asher rested his hand on Rocky's jaw and tilted his chin upward. His husband slowly lowered his head, giving Rocky many chances to jerk away or say no. Before Asher's mouth reached his, his husband swiped his thumb over Rocky's lips. "You had a little something on the corner of your mouth. It reminded me of other things and made it hard for me to concentrate."

Asher pulled his thumb away and revealed the icing he'd swiped from Rocky's mouth. He should've been embarrassed he hadn't even felt it, but that was the last thing on his mind. Rocky wanted Asher to push the digit between his lips and demand he lick it clean. How many times had his husband done just that when a blow job had gotten extra messy?

"You wanna do the honors, or shall I?" Asher asked.

The urge to suck Asher's thumb into his mouth was so strong it nearly scared Rocky. If he acted on his impulse, there'd be no going to separate rooms. They both knew it. Asher was leaving the decision up to Rocky. He took a breath and gave a slight shake of his head. If Asher was disappointed, he didn't show it.

"More for me," his husband said, then lifted his thumb to his own mouth. Asher licked the icing in the most indecent way possible from base to tip, leaving no doubt about what he wanted to do to, and with, Rocky.

His mouth watered, but Rocky didn't take the bait. A moment on his knees would undo a year's worth of carefully distancing himself from Asher.

"There's no need to sleep in a recliner or chaise lounge just to avoid me."

"It wasn't intentional. I'd decided to read for a bit before bed and fell asleep."

"Come to bed now," Asher said.

It sounded more like an invitation than a command. Rocky quirked his brow.

"Go to bed is what I meant," Asher said, rebounding quickly.

Refusing his request was on the tip of Rocky's tongue, but he stopped himself. Asher would see through his stalling tactics and subterfuge.

"Let me grab my book." Rocky sidestepped around Asher and retrieved the ancient paperback.

When they stepped inside the kitchen, Asher recovered the foil pan and placed the fork in the sink. He went to the refrigerator and pulled out a carton of milk. Rocky took advantage of Asher's distraction to ogle the way the red shorts clung to his husband's muscular ass. It was a thing of beauty, and Rocky nearly sighed out loud.

Asher poured them each a small glass of milk, which they drank before heading down the hallway.

"I hope you sleep well," Rocky said, pausing outside his bedroom door.

"Sweet dreams, Ford," Asher replied.

Not likely. Rocky nodded and opened the door to his room as Asher continued past him. Fuck, it felt so wrong. His heavy heart thudded miserably as he made his way to his bed. Rocky set the book on his nightstand, then stripped down to his underwear before climbing between the sheets.

After staring at the ceiling for what seemed like hours, he was no closer to falling asleep. Who could blame him with so much on his mind? But he required sleep to remain sharp, so he reached for his earbuds and opened up the meditation app Karen had suggested. He listened to a few recordings, and even though Rocky felt more relaxed afterward, they hadn't eased him into sleep.

Rocky flipped on his reading lamp and picked up another of Karen's recommendations. This one was a book on not only surviving trauma but thriving afterward. It was valuable guidance, if not a little dry, so it didn't take long for his eyelids to get heavy and his brain to feel hazy as sleep moved in like a dense fog.

Rocky waited for the final deafening gun blast. Would he die quickly, or would he slowly bleed to death on the tile floor in this strange house? The potent aromas of sulfur from the gunpowder and copper from the blood burned his nostrils and made Rocky's eyes water, even behind his closed lids.

He'd long since abandoned the Catholic faith over their pushback against homosexuality, but he prayed to the father, the son, and the holy ghost. Not to save him but to ensure Asher never saw what became of Rocky. He prayed Duggins had the wherewithal to keep Asher away from the crime scene and photos.

It wasn't a sign from above or the sound of a gunshot that made Rocky open his eyes again; it was soft weeping. The kind that was bottomless, rising from one's soul.

Rocky locked eyes with Julia Warner and saw she'd returned from the desolate place in her brain that had allowed her to gun down her husband and the woman in cold blood. Her eyes were no longer vacant; they were filled with so much dread and despair, and it pained Rocky to hold her gaze. Yet, he did because he wanted to survive and go home to Asher.

"Julia," he said softly, taking a small step toward her. Rocky didn't dare look at Raphael or the petite woman sprawled on the floor. There wasn't anything he could do for either of them. If Rocky hoped to survive this night, he needed to make sure he held on to this Julia, not the one who'd so easily pulled the trigger. She still had the gun in her hand, but her arm now hung by her side. Rocky could think a little more clearly when the weapon wasn't aimed at him. "Drop the gun and let's talk."

Sobs racked Julia's small frame, and her chest heaved as she struggled to catch her breath. She shook her head once, then a second time. Rocky took a few more steps, closing the distance between them.

"You won't put the gun down, or you don't want to talk?" he asked. If he could just get Julia to talk, he stood a chance. Gunshots wouldn't be an everyday occurrence in this swanky neighborhood. The cops had to be en route.

"I'm not sorry," Julia said. "I hate them."

Rocky didn't ask her any stupid questions; he just kept inching closer.

"Do you know who this dead whore is?" Julia asked.

"I don't," Rocky replied, realizing he'd made a big mistake. He'd have been wise to identify the woman in the pictures before showing them to Julia. If Rocky had, this could've all been prevented. Raphael might've been a shitty husband, but had he deserved to die like that? Did his children deserve to lose their father?

"Her name is Melissa, and she's married to my brother, Carlos. He has terminal cancer, and instead of taking care of him like a good wife does, she's out seducing my husband and looking for a soft place to land once Carlos dies. I knew this bitch was nothing but pretty poison the moment Carlos introduced her to my family. My brother is a good man—the best. Melissa destroyed my entire family. She's the one who should die, not Carlos."

Rocky thought it wasn't fair to blame this affair solely on her, but he kept his mouth shut. Besides, Raphael had paid the ultimate price for his faithlessness. While Rocky could understand Julia's desire to kill Raphael and Melissa, he couldn't condone her acting on the urge.

"I thought it would be easy," she said as tears streamed down her face. "I hate Raphael for not being strong enough to say no, but I can't imagine a life without him."

By this time, Rocky was almost within grabbing distance. He saw the moment Julia decided her life was no longer worth living.

"Julia, no," Rocky said, lunging forward just as she swung the gun up toward her face.

He gripped her arm at the same time the gun went off. The blast from the weapon reverberated through him, making his ears ring and slowing his response. Then he was on his knees trying to stop the blood flowing from the gaping hole where her chin had been.

"Oh my God. Oh my God," Rocky said as the blood kept coming.

They needed help. Rocky didn't hear police sirens, so maybe the neighbors hadn't called the cops. He'd had his cell phone at one point, but where was it? Keeping both hands pressed against Julia's face, Rocky scanned the room. He spotted it near Melissa's fallen body, but it was out of his reach. Rocky would have to leave Julia to get it but worried she'd bleed out. There was so much blood. If he didn't go for the phone, though, she'd surely die.

"Please don't die," he said as he pulled his hands away from her face and crawled to his phone. "Please don't die." The blood made his hands slick, and it took several attempts before he could hold on to the phone without dropping it. "Please don't die. Please don't die."

"Please don't—"

"Ford, wake up." Strong hands gripped Rocky's shoulders and shook him hard. "Wake up, Ford."

Rocky's eye popped open. Asher hovered over him with a concerned expression etched on his face. He released a deep sigh as he sat on the bed. Unfortunately, his big shoulders no longer blocked the bright bulb in the ceiling fixture. Asher must have switched it on when he came into the room. It felt like the light was burning his retinas, so Rocky lifted his hand to shield his eyes.

"Can you turn that off?" he asked hoarsely.

"Sure," Asher said, easing off the bed. "Sorry."

"S'okay." Rocky scrubbed his hands over his face, then dropped them when Asher flipped the switch. "Sorry for waking you."

"Don't apologize." Asher's voice sounded close, which meant he'd returned to the bed instead of staying by the door.

Once Rocky's eyes adjusted to the darkness, he saw that Asher stood next to his bed. His husband reached out and caressed his cheek. "Scoot over. You know this is my side of the bed."

Instead of arguing, Rocky moved over to make room. He should send Asher away, but he wouldn't. Not tonight.

Asher lifted the top sheet and slid in beside him. "Still having those awful dreams?"

"Sometimes."

"Ford," Asher said gruffly.

"Yeah. It's not always the same one, though. It depends on the trigger."

"Am I the trigger tonight?" Asher whispered into the darkness.

"God no," Rocky said, scooting closer to his heat. "Never you." Asher released a shaky breath, and Rocky moved closer still. "I think it was Cal's lawnmower. The damn thing sounds like a gunshot."

"Someone should fix it for him."

"Or maybe I need to fix the parts of me that are broken," Rocky said, stopping when he was a few inches away from Asher's strong body.

"You're not broken, Ford. The fucking world is."

"I'm trying to get better, you know."

Rocky heard Asher's pillow rustle and felt his husband's intensity aimed in his direction. He turned his head and met Asher's stare in the darkness. "I started seeing a therapist."

He waited for an "I told you so" because Asher had recommended Rocky seek help when the nightmares first started. "That's good," Asher said, sounding relieved instead of smug. "That's real good, Ford."

"I'm tired of running from that night. I'm tired of feeling broken. I'm tired of the nightmares. I'm just so fucking tired."

Asher rolled to his side and placed his hand on Rocky's chest. "Go to sleep, baby."

The endearment should've annoyed Rocky, but he held it close to his battered heart. "I can't."

"Why?" Asher's warm breath ghosted over Rocky's cheek. He was so close, yet so far away.

"You know why, Asher."

"Do you want me to do it?"

Rocky sighed. "Yes."

Asher chuckled, then lifted his leg and draped his big thigh over Rocky's pelvis. The weight was enough to bring tears to Rocky's eyes. He rested his hand on Asher's outer thigh, the springy hairs tickling his palms. Fuck, he'd missed any part of Asher pinning him to the bed.

"Thank you," he said, his voice sounding thick and raw from the emotions battering his heart.

"Go to sleep, baby."

And he did.

CHAPTER 9

Rocky was on fire. It was the only explanation for the insufferable heat radiating throughout his body. Was it a fever? Had he died and gone to hell in his sleep? Would the devil rise from the fiery pits and taunt Rocky with reminders of all the lives he'd help destroy? Those poor kids.

"Ford."

Oh fuck. Satan hadn't shown himself yet, but he sounded an awful lot like his husband. Was that part of his punishment? Would Lucifer look like Asher too?

"Ford, your cell phone is ringing."

"They allow them in hell?" Rocky asked.

Satan chuckled. "Wake up, baby."

Wake up? Baby? Who the fuck—

Asher!

Rocky jerked awake and became aware of two things simultaneously: during the night, he'd draped his body over Asher's, and the raging inferno he'd dreamt was actually his husband's body heat. Then his other senses stirred, such as his cell phone ringing in the living room, the musky scent of sweaty men stuck together, and Asher's morning wood pressed against him.

"I can only take so much, Ford," Asher said, his voice rough with sleep and raw with need.

"Sorry," Rocky said, not bothering to lift his head off Asher's chest. "I'm going."

Asher wrapped both arms around Rocky and held him tighter. "You don't really want to go." Asher kissed his temple and stroked his hand down Rocky's spine. "I don't want you to go either."

Panic should've flooded through Rocky's nervous system, restricting his lungs and making it hard for him to breathe. Alarm wasn't one of the many emotions surging through him, though. The fatigue weighing down his limbs didn't require an exploratory committee. Lust coiled in his belly, responding to Asher's arousal. What worried him the most was the contentment he felt deep down in his soul. Rocky broke free of Asher's hold and rolled off him to lie on his back. He stared at the ceiling as his phone finally sent the caller to his voice mail.

"Do you want to talk about it?" Asher asked.

It could mean so many things, none of which he wanted to discuss with Asher. Not before coffee, not during coffee, and not even afterward. So he shook his head and kept his gaze locked on the ceiling as he said, "No." He wanted to quantify his response by adding that he hadn't changed his mind about the divorce, but his lips remained immobile.

They lay there—inches away but miles apart—until the awkwardness became too much for either of them to bear. Asher threw back the covers and climbed out of bed. Rocky closed his eyes because he knew what would come next. The familiar sounds of Asher stretching out his stiffness taunted Rocky, making it nearly impossible to ignore the masculine beauty on display. If he turned his head, he'd be able to watch the play of muscles under Asher's skin. His husband worked out a lot to keep his body in top shape, but the job's physical demands still took their toll.

Rocky rolled onto his side, facing away from Asher, and burrowed deeper into the sheets. The activity stirred up the intoxicating mixture of scents that made up his husband's shampoo and bodywash. Vanilla, patchouli, and leather. The combination sounded pretentious, but it was incredible. If heaven were real, Rocky was confident it would smell just like Asher.

His husband cleared his throat, and Rocky cracked one eye open.

Big mistake because it put him almost eye level with the erection straining against Asher's briefs. Christ, how he missed the days he could ride that beautiful cock until he didn't have a care left in the world.

"Eyes up here before I get the wrong idea, Ford."

It was on the tip of Rocky's tongue to tease Asher, but he squelched his instincts to peer up at his husband. "Yes?"

The corners of Asher's lips twitched like he wanted to smile, but he fought it off. "Are you going to be okay?"

The question was like taking a sucker punch to the gut, knocking the breath out of him. Of course, Asher wanted to know if he was okay. He'd heard Rocky crying out in his sleep and was forced to coddle him back to dreamland.

And what would he do if Rocky said no? Call off sick to work, then get back into bed? Would he hold Rocky until the pain went away? Fuck, he was tempted to say no just to see what Asher would do.

"Ford?" Asher asked, pressing him for an answer.

He could give a flippant answer to appease the concern in Asher's eyes, or he could be honest. "I'm getting there." And he was, just not as quickly as he would have liked.

Asher held his gaze for a few seconds, searching for God only knew what. He must've been pleased with whatever he saw, or didn't see, because Asher nodded. "Do you mind if I shower first? Dandridge will swing by to pick me up in a bit, and I want a chance to eat before he arrives. I can't survive on twigs and berries like he does."

"Of course," Rocky replied. "I can start breakfast for you."

"Please don't," Asher said.

"Fine." Rocky closed his eyes once more, pulling the covers up to his chin and preparing to linger a little longer in a bed that smelled like Asher. His husband chuckled when he left Rocky's room. He'd just started to doze off when his phone rang again.

"Damn it," he grumbled as he slid from beneath the covers.

Rocky zombie shuffled into the living room and answered his cell without checking the caller ID.

"You owe me twenty bucks," his nana said into the phone.

"What for?" Rocky adored Beatrice Jacobs with every fiber of his being, but it was too early in the morning to deal with Queen Bea's shenanigans.

He didn't doubt a bet had occurred because the two of them frequently wagered on the silliest things. Nana usually won, and Rocky loved the gleeful look in her eyes whenever he settled their score. Just because he didn't remember the conversation didn't mean it hadn't happened. His nana's mind was a steel trap while Rocky's acted more like a traveling circus lately, bouncing from town to town and never lingering in one place too long. He'd read it was one of the brain's coping mechanisms, but knowing it was common didn't make him feel any better.

"Could you give me a hint?" he asked.

"Nurse Ratchet is gone. I said she wouldn't last a month, but you gave her six."

Rocky bit back a groan. "Which one was she again?" The residents had a bad habit of attaching the nickname to any nurse they didn't like, and it was hard for him to keep them straight.

Queen Bea huffed out a sigh. "The new one."

Still nothing. "When exactly did this bet occur?"

She released another sigh, this one much more chagrined than the first. "Rockford, you're working my last nerve. Are you senile, or are you just playing me? If it's the former, I can see if they have another room for you here at the home."

The pipes rattled in the wall a bit when Asher turned on the shower. Rocky knew he was looking at a significant expense to replace the worn plumbing and hoped it would hold off a while longer. His mind started to drift to images of his husband soaping himself in the shower.

"Rockford, are you still there?" Nana asked.

He chuckled. "Go easy on a guy, Nana. You woke me up, and I haven't had coffee yet." *And I have a naked, hot-as-fuck husband in my bathroom.*

"Oh, did you stay out late working on a case?" As if someone flipped a switch, her voice shifted from irritated to excited. "Tell me all about it."

"You know I can't, Nana."

"You always say that," she countered.

"Because it's true. I can't blab about my clients. My reputation is everything in this business."

"Not even a tiny hint?" she asked.

"Nope. About this bet…" he said, shifting her back on topic.

"It occurred during my birthday dinner. You do remember the occasion, don't you?"

Rocky snorted. "Of course."

"Well, I introduced you to a new nurse and told you she wouldn't make it a month. You gave her six. Since she left after two, I win. I'm going to need my money before Friday so I can enter the poker game with Eunice."

"Okay, Nana."

"That's my good boy. Are you watering my flowers and feeding my birds?"

"Yes, ma'am."

"Are you being respectful to the neighbors?"

"Yes, ma'am."

"Has Cal fixed his awful lawnmower yet?"

"No, ma'am."

"I love you with my whole heart, Rockford. You're my favorite grandson."

"I'm your only grandson," Rocky reminded Queen Bea.

"One with a smart mouth. Learn when to take a compliment."

"Yes, ma'am."

His nana snorted. "I'm going to box your ears next time I see you."

"You'll have to catch me first."

"You're a pain in my ass," she grumbled. "Twenty dollars by Friday. Don't make me send people after you." Queen Bea hung up the phone before he could respond.

Rocky stared at his phone for a second before returning it to the table. Five fucking thirty? Jesus. Why was she up so early? A thump against the front door made him jump until he realized it was just the newspaper hitting it. His delivery guy launched the rolled-up paper like a hand grenade before driving off to the next target. Rocky headed to the door to retrieve the newspaper from the front porch. Opening his door triggered the motion sensor in his porch light. The damn thing was bright enough to illuminate his entire front yard. It had seemed like a great idea when his nana was living there alone, but he could've done without the temporary loss of eyesight.

Rocky heard a sharp intake of breath. He blinked until the black dots cleared his vision. Mrs. Baylor and her standard poodle, Clark, stood on the sidewalk in front of his house, both staring at him. Mrs. Baylor's mouth hung open in shock, but Clark appeared to be grinning.

"Morning," Rocky said, waving at her.

She made a harrumphing sound and resumed her walk without so much as a wave or a middle finger.

"What's her problem?" Rocky shrugged and shut the door. Maybe she was just surprised to see someone else awake at the awful hour.

He headed to the kitchen to start the coffee. Once the pot was brewing, he checked the refrigerator's contents to make sure he had something Asher could whip up for himself. He couldn't remember the last time he'd stopped at the grocery store, but Rocky usually had breakfast food on hand since it was one of the few things he made well. Asher had insisted he not cook, so Rocky grabbed a fork and dug into the cinnamon rolls.

He was still leaning against the counter, stuffing his face, when Asher walked in sometime later. He was dressed in black from head to toe again. His shirt looked even tighter than the one he'd worn yesterday. Rocky briefly debated making jokes about the effects of eating Southern food already kicking in, but he was the one shoving thousands of calories into his face before sunrise.

Asher raked his eyes over Rocky, a half smile flirting with the right corner of his mouth. "Is that what you plan to eat for breakfast?"

Rocky swallowed his bite and said, "Cinnamon rolls are breakfast food."

"Okay, let me rephrase my question. Is that all you're going to eat?"

"I plan to have a cup of coffee in a minute. Caffeine and carbs. The breakfast of champions."

Asher pursed his lips and nodded. "After a night of little sleep, you're setting yourself up for a hard crash. How about we offset the coffee and the carbs with some protein?"

"Two cinnamon rolls," he corrected. Either Asher had taken his sweet time in the shower, or Rocky was greedy. Both of those things were a possibility. The latter would explain why he couldn't prevent his mind from imagining what would keep Asher in the shower for such a long time. Gluttony was definitely to blame for Rocky quirking a brow and asking, "What did you have in mind?"

Asher's lips slowly spread and curved upward into a smile that would make any villain proud. "What do *you* have in mind?"

Rocky swallowed again and nearly choked on air. "I was thinking of scrambled eggs."

"Uh-huh," Asher said, turning to the refrigerator.

Setting the aluminum pan on the counter, Rocky pulled the mixing bowl from the cabinet and a whisk from the drawer while Asher pulled out ingredients from the refrigerator.

"How old is this ham?" Asher asked.

"Honestly, I'm not sure. Sniff it."

"*You* sniff it."

Rocky crossed the room. Asher lifted the deli bag up, and Rocky took a deep whiff to see if the contents were still fresh. "It's good."

"Forgive me if I doubt your food freshness test."

Rocky shrugged. "It's never let me down before."

"They say there's a first time for everything, but I'll happily go the rest of my life without experiencing food poisoning."

They locked eyes and started to laugh because it was a conversation they'd had many times during their short marriage. Rocky reached inside the deli bag and tore off a hunk of meat and popped it into his mouth. Asher's eyes dropped to Rocky's lips and he seemed mesmerized by their movement. And maybe Rocky chewed the tiny piece longer than necessary before swallowing and declaring it safe enough for Asher to eat.

"Where do you keep your skillets?" Asher asked.

Rocky crossed his arms over his chest. "And you claim to know me so well." He muscled Asher out of the way and opened the oven door, then gestured to the pots and pans stacked neatly inside. "Tah-dah."

Asher chuckled and shook his head. "I'd hoped this habit had changed in my absence, especially considering this kitchen is twice the size of the one we shared in Vegas."

Rocky would never forget the playful bantering that followed when Asher discovered he kept his pots and pans in the oven. He'd had very little storage in the tiny kitchen, and Rocky rarely used the oven part of the appliance. The storage solution made perfect sense to him. Asher hadn't agreed. Their bantering back then had turned into teasing touches and kisses, which led them to abandon food altogether.

It would be easy for them to fall into the same routine, but Rocky wouldn't allow it. So he said, "It's not about size, you queen. It's about practicality. I don't need an oven, so why not use it for storage?"

Asher placed his hands on his lean hips, squaring off against Rocky like an outlaw. "I might accept that as reasonable logic if your other kitchen storage decisions followed the same path. Your kitchen layout is a mess."

It absolutely was. Rocky had never cared about where things went in a kitchen, only that they were put away. He hated clutter more than he loathed cooking. There were exceptions to his ridiculousness, and he had every intention of pointing them out until Asher held up his index finger.

"I'm going to need coffee for this."

"Fine. Allow me to demonstrate my first point," Rocky said as he crossed the room. He opened the cupboard door above the coffee pot and pulled down two travel mugs. "Coffee mugs near the coffee pot." Then he pulled open the drawer directly below his magic bean machine. "Spoons below it."

Asher chuckled. "Show me your next trick."

"You're in no way prepared for it," Rocky teased.

"True," Asher agreed. "I'd be more impressed if the cupboard that held your cups and plates and your silverware drawer weren't on the opposite side of the room from the dishwasher."

Rocky scoffed. "As if I use that thing to wash dishes. I wouldn't waste the electricity or water on the few cups and plates I use a week."

Asher scrubbed his hand over his mouth like he was trying to erase his smile, but it still lingered on his husband's lips. "I'm afraid to ask what you wash in the dishwasher if not dishes."

Rocky let loose an evil laugh as he applied the right amount of cream and sugar to both mugs. For someone who bitched about Rocky consuming too much sugar at breakfast, his husband sure swallowed his fair share in the form of coffee.

Asher looked at the dishwasher, then back at Rocky. He took a few steps and opened the appliance, revealing a stack of random Tupperware pieces and their lids. His husband closed the door and howled with laughter. Rocky flipped him off, even though he couldn't be mad. He'd had as much use for the containers as he did the appliance Rocky stored them in.

"I expected dildos," Asher said once he caught his breath.

"Dildos?" Rocky asked.

Asher shrugged. "I recently saw it in a rerun of *CSI*."

"And you somehow equated that with me?" Rocky wasn't sure if he found the thought horrifying or humorous.

"You were the one who asked me to get out the handcuffs within seconds of running into one another," Asher pointed out. "Not to mention your new underwear choices."

"Orange underwear isn't a kink." Not that Rocky knew of, anyway.

"The shade of blue you're wearing today is pretty," Asher said, saluting Rocky's crotch with his coffee mug before taking a sip. Rocky had forgotten all about his state of undress until Asher had literally pointed it out. Not that his husband seemed to mind since he just continued talking. "Then there are all the guys Cal mentioned."

"Oh my God. There have been no guys here other than my friends."

Rocky could see the question in his husband's gaze. He was willing to accept Rocky hadn't brought men into his home, but had Rocky parked his boots under someone else's bed? It wasn't like Asher not to ask, which meant the answer scared him. A part of Rocky said this was his moment to drive home the point that they'd been living apart for over a year and remind Asher of their impending divorce. With just a few words or even a silent gesture, he could nail the coffin closed on their time together.

Rocky couldn't force himself to lie. "There's been no one. Not here or anywhere." He'd flirted and danced with the idea of trying to find someone to chase Asher from his mind, but no one would do. He only wanted Asher.

"For me either."

Asher's confession sucked the air out of the room. Rocky hadn't asked because he hadn't wanted to know and now didn't want to think why he suddenly felt dizzy with relief. The subsequent reaction occurred much lower, reminding Rocky that he'd been parading around in his underwear this entire time. No wonder Mrs. Baylor was miffed.

Gesturing to his bare torso, he said, "The kitchen probably isn't the best place to be wandering around in your underwear."

Rocky could tell Asher had much more to say, but he bit his bottom lip and nodded instead. Rocky slipped off to his bedroom and pulled on the same T-shirt and shorts he'd worn the previous night. When he returned to the kitchen, Asher had lined up the onions, peppers, and mushrooms in a neat row. Rocky pulled the cutting board and a knife from a drawer and set them on the countertop. While Asher started chopping vegetables, Rocky retrieved the olive oil, spatula, and skillet. They moved like they always had, a well-choreographed dance of give and take. The only difference was that Rocky had to suppress the urge to slip his arms around Asher's waist and place kisses between his husband's shoulder blades.

Rocky suspected Asher would accept the gestures, even welcome them, but it would be a big mistake. He couldn't let Asher's proximity lull him into a false sense of security or normalcy. This arrangement was temporary, but the repercussions for lowering his shields would be everlasting. So he shook off his melancholy and focused on making small talk about the weather while assisting Asher with breakfast.

"Who the hell bought you food storage containers? Don't they know the takeout ones you get from restaurants will suffice?"

"Most of it belonged to Queen Bea, and the rest was given to me as housewarming gifts."

Asher's face softened. "How is your nana?"

"Ornery as ever. That's who called this morning and woke us up."

"I'd been awake for a while."

"Oh my God. Why didn't you shove me off you?"

Asher briefly averted his gaze to stare down at his feet. When their eyes met again, the earnest expression in his husband's eyes made Rocky regret he'd asked. Asher took a deep breath. "You were sleeping so peacefully, and I didn't want to disturb you."

The response sounded right, but it didn't match the intense emotion in Asher's gaze. It seemed as if they were both dancing around the elephant in the room instead of acknowledging its presence. Instead of pressing the issue further, Rocky nodded and repeated his conversation with Queen Bea, which entertained Asher.

"Do you like your new team?" he asked while setting the table.

"A lot," Asher replied. "They've all worked together for a long time, and it shows. I worried they wouldn't welcome an outsider, but other than some Yankee jokes, the guys have made me feel right at home."

"I'm glad to hear it," Rocky said.

Once the food was ready, they sat together at the small table. Asher unfolded the newspaper and checked out the headlines. "You can tell a lot about a city by looking at their newspaper."

"What does ours tell you?"

Asher smiled. "You people are eclectic."

"Understatement of the century," Rocky replied.

Asher glanced at his watch, then began shoveling fluffy eggs into his mouth while he continued perusing the paper. "Ouch," he said a moment later. "Your friend Felix hits hard."

Rocky wasn't sure what Felix's recent story was about since they hadn't had much time to talk lately. Even though he'd just seen his best friends the previous day, the interview had taken up most of their time together. Rocky suddenly remembered their parting words and the plans to meet for breakfast at seven. Fuck. He might've forgotten all about it if

Asher hadn't mentioned the article. His lack of sleep was catching up to him. Right now, he was forgetting little things, but if he didn't get a handle on his problem, those small blunders would multiply and could turn into life-altering mistakes.

Unaware of Rocky's inner turmoil, Asher continued talking. "I'm not sure it's a great idea to antagonize the governor when you're hoping for a posthumous pardon."

That got Rocky's attention. "What?"

Asher pushed the paper across the table to him. There in bold, black print was proof of Felix throwing down a verbal gauntlet. The headline read: "Questions Remain about Governor Stanton's Mob Connections."

"What kind of vetting process does Felix go through before he publishes articles like this?" Asher asked.

Rocky stared at the newspaper until his vision blurred. He'd only read the first few sentences, but it was enough to make him feel like his lungs had turned to lead. Or was it stone? Something brittle and dry and on the verge of crumbling to dust.

"Ford?"

Asher's voice brought him back from the brink of panic. He blinked, bringing the room back into focus. "Huh?"

"I asked if you trust Felix's decisions to go public with these types of allegations."

It sounded like such a simple question, but everything about Felix Franklin was complicated. He was both the most honorable and the most infuriating man Rocky had ever known. Even so, there was only one person Rocky trusted more than Felix and Jonah, and that man was waiting for an answer.

"I may disapprove of his methods, but I trust his motives. If Felix says there's a connection between the governor and Jack Mercy, then you can believe it exists." Rocky smiled wryly. "Felix was the one who figured out Spencer was about to shed his identity and disappear, after all."

Reminding Asher that the three of them messed up his mission might not have been the wisest choice, but it illustrated how smart Felix was. "Point made," Asher said wryly.

He shoveled the rest of his food into his mouth while Rocky abandoned his plate to read Felix's article. Each sentence evoked both pride and fear. Felix was brilliant, but this kind of hit piece could bring a lot of unwanted attention to Felix and everyone close to him. Rocky had survived one media shitstorm; he wasn't sure he could last through another.

"Gotta go," Asher said, rising to his feet. "Dandridge will be here any minute." He walked his plate to the sink, then glanced over at Rocky. "I'd put my plate in the dishwasher, but it's full."

Rocky rolled his eyes. "Why is Dandridge picking you up? Doesn't the branch here provide their deputies with vehicles?" Rocky knew for a fact that the deputies got to choose their rides from the vehicles the USMS confiscated.

Asher grimaced. "Slim pickings. My car will arrive from Vegas in a few weeks."

"You hired someone to drive it here?" The car was his pride and joy. Rocky shuddered to think about the vetting process Asher would put them through.

"Enclosed hauler," Asher said as he rinsed his plate.

"What about the rest of your stuff?"

"The movers should be here in a few days."

"What are you going to do with your things if your rental house isn't ready?"

Asher shrugged. "Store them in the garage."

"No way," Rocky said. "Your vinyl record collection will be ruined. You can store them here if you need to."

"Thank you." Asher nodded at his plate. "Eat your breakfast."

Rocky gave him a playful salute with his fork before tucking into his eggs. "Be safe."

"Always."

Rocky heard the front door closing a few moments later. He finished his breakfast, tidied the kitchen, then headed into the bathroom to get ready for the day. The small space was still humid from Asher's recent shower, and the scent of his husband's shampoo and bodywash lingered in the air, wreaking havoc on Rocky's heart. Asher's razor, comb, toothbrush, and aftershave were scattered all around the sink. He touched each one as a reminder that he wasn't dreaming. Asher was in Savannah, presumably to stay.

If Rocky had viewed his random luck at the craps table as a sign, why couldn't he also see Asher's promotion in the same light? Had fate granted them a second chance?

If so, was he brave enough to seize it?

CHAPTER 10

Daisy's Place had become the trio of trouble's favorite hangout. They'd met the drag queen while probing Earl Ison's murder at Marla's behest. Through the investigation, Rocky, Jonah, and Felix had uncovered Bo Cahill's coerced confession, which had garnered national attention for their podcast. Everyone working at the diner dressed in full drag and served up snarky banter with the delicious, homemade food. Asher would eat his weight in Daisy's homemade pies if he ever found out about the diner.

Rocky caught the tail end of the queens dancing to "Raise You Up" from *Kinky Boots* as he walked in. The patrons clapped and cheered while dropping tips into a hat being passed around by a barrel-chested leather daddy.

Edgar, Daisy's husband, stopped in front of him and quirked a brow. Even though Rocky had only caught the last few seconds of the performance, he dropped a five-dollar bill in the hat.

The older man narrowed his eyes and studied Rocky. "Something is different about you this morning."

"New aftershave," Rocky said.

"Nah, that's not it." Edgar tilted his bald head to the side. "You look… less pretty."

Unsure if it was a backhanded compliment or an insult, Rocky just smiled and said, "Thank you. It's good to see you, Edgar."

"Likewise. You should come around more often," Edgar replied before moving on.

Rocky searched the crowded diner and located Jonah and Felix in a corner booth at the rear. Jonah glanced up and smiled at him, and Felix pivoted in his seat to watch him approach. Felix's cocky grin spelled trouble, so Rocky walked to Jonah's side of the table and dropped onto the bench beside him.

"You don't want to sit next to me?" Felix asked.

Rocky shook his head. "It's easier for me to kick you from over here."

"Ouch," Felix said. "Why bother with physical abuse when your words are as sharp as razors?"

"Says the man who eviscerated the governor on the front page of the paper this morning," Jonah said, saluting Felix with his coffee cup before taking a sip.

Felix shrugged. "It's only going to get worse for the asshole the longer he drags out the posthumous pardon for Bo Cahill. I will leave no stone unturned."

"Don't you worry that your approach will have an adverse reaction?" Rocky asked as he poured a cup of coffee from the carafe on the table. "People might view it as you bullying the man into pardoning Bo."

Felix slid the sugar and creamer to him. "I'm all out of fucks. Are you worried my exposé on the governor's questionable business dealings will backfire on us?"

"I believe wholeheartedly in our mission to obtain a pardon for Bo," Rocky replied.

"But?" Jonah prodded.

Rocky suddenly felt like he was walking a tightrope. One false move wouldn't send him careening to his death, at least not a physical one. The ramifications on his professional and personal life, though, were enormous. Not just his, either. What about Jonah and Felix? What about Asher? Resting his hand on his sternum had become automatic, and he wasn't even aware of it until Felix's gaze followed the motion.

Dropping his hand to his lap, Rocky said, "Not a but. More like an asterisk. I'm just saying we should put what the Cahill family wants first and foremost and not use them to grind an ax against a politician you can't stand."

"Direct hit," Felix said, slumping back against the bench. "Maybe you shouldn't project your media bias onto me and my motives."

"What's happening here?" Jonah asked.

"I believe they're having an argument," Daisy said as she strode up to their table. "And Marla told me you're brilliant."

Jonah chuckled. "I recognize an argument when I see one, but these two are usually thick as thieves. I haven't seen them argue like this since the first night they met."

"Unresolved sexual tension?" Daisy asked.

"No," Felix and Rocky said at the same time, both smiling at one another.

"Oh," Daisy said, sounding disappointed. "Renee will be over to take your order in just a second. I want to talk to you guys about something before you leave, okay?" After they all agreed, she said, "There's no squabbling in Daisy's Place unless you're prepared to snag a bitch's wig. You hear me?" she asked.

"Yes, ma'am," all three of them said as she sashayed away.

"Hey," Rocky said, reaching across the table to squeeze Felix's hand. "I'm sorry. I am letting my past history with rabid reporters cloud my objectivity. I know you're not like them, and I never meant to imply otherwise."

Felix rotated his hand and linked their fingers. "I'm sorry too. Your words struck too close to the truth, and I lashed out at you."

"I'm sorry too," Jonah said.

Rocky looked over at him. "For what?"

Jonah shrugged. "I just felt left out. Give me a second, and I can probably think of something to apologize for."

Rocky bumped his shoulder against Jonah, but the bigger man didn't even budge. "I can't imagine what it's like dealing with the two of us."

"I wouldn't trade the experience for the world," Jonah said.

"Do you think my article was a mistake?" Felix asked Jonah.

"While I personally loved every scathing word you wrote, I think we do need to give the process a fair shake." Jonah was always the voice of reason that counterbalanced Felix's and Rocky's high energy. "The Cahills have a brilliant legal team working on their behalf, but they have something even more powerful going for them."

Rocky nodded. "The court of public opinion."

"That's right," Jonah said. "If this fool doesn't issue the pardon, then we can mobilize Bo's supporters to flood the governor's office with phone calls, emails, and letters. If that doesn't work, we use our platform to vote the fucker out of office."

Felix nodded. "As always, you make an excellent point. The outcry of many has a greater impact than a singular voice of dissent."

"It's one hell of a strong voice," Rocky said. "I'm proud to call you my friend."

Felix tilted his head down to sip his coffee but not before Rocky saw the flush creep across his friend's cheeks.

Jonah leaned closer to Rocky and mock whispered, "Is he blushing?"

"I think so," Rocky replied.

"Is there a reset button we can push?" Felix asked. "I feel like we've veered off track."

Rocky leaned forward and tapped the tip of Felix's nose. "Boop."

Felix looked as stunned as Rocky felt. What the hell had possessed him to do such a silly thing? Jonah was the first to recover and chuckled. Felix scowled at their stormy friend, which must've tickled Jonah's funny bone even more because his amusement turned into a full-on belly laugh. Jonah had a wicked sense of humor, but a reaction like this was rare, making Rocky glad he'd done it.

"Did you just boop my nose?" Felix asked.

Rocky shrugged. Jonah wiped the moisture from his eyes. He looked back and forth between Rocky and Felix, then started laughing harder. He got choked up at one point, so Felix slid his glass of water closer to him.

"Easy there, big guy," Felix said. "You can't let decades of suppressed joy out all at once. You might strain something."

"And Avery had plans for it," Rocky added.

Jonah's broad shoulders continued to shake for a few more minutes before he reined himself in. "I love you two assholes."

Felix and Rocky made cooing noises and reciprocated their affection when Renee stopped by to take their orders.

"Should I come back?" she asked.

"Nah, we know what we want to eat," Felix said. He rattled off what he wanted, then Jonah placed his order.

Renee smiled at Rocky. "And for you?" she asked.

"I'm just having coffee this morning."

"Okay," she said. "Your food will be out shortly."

Once they were alone again, Felix quirked a brow. "No appetite?"

"Skipping meals isn't like you," Jonah added.

"I had breakfast already," Rocky said.

"Mighty early for you to be so bright-eyed and bushy-tailed," Felix said. "Perhaps it has something to do with your houseguest."

"Shut up, Fee."

"So, when do I get to meet your deputy marshal?" Jonah asked.

"He's not *my* deputy marshal."

"Fine," Jonah said. "When do I get to meet your husband?"

"I'm not sure there'd be a point in introducing the two of you," Rocky said. "We're getting a divorce."

Jonah shrugged. "I still want to meet him."

"As a professional courtesy, if nothing else," Felix added. "They're both in law enforcement, and Jonah could be of benefit to Asher someday."

Asher would be fascinated by Stella, the supercomputer sleuth Jonah created. Still, introducing the two men would be another thread tying Rocky and Asher together. "Maybe." It was all he was willing to give them right now.

"Fair enough," Jonah replied.

Tired of talking about himself, Rocky decided to steer the conversation in a more palatable direction. "Speaking of beneficial, I absolutely love the software Avery developed for us to beta test."

Jonah laughed and Felix smirked, telling him that his transition wasn't as smooth as he'd planned. Neither of them tried to veer back to discussing Asher, though, so Rocky viewed it as a win.

"I'll be sure to tell him," Jonah said. "His internship is coming to an end soon, and he's decided not to pursue a career with the GBI."

"Really?" Felix and Rocky asked at the same time.

"Avery seems to enjoy working there," Rocky added.

"He does, and I love working with him too. We just worry it's not healthy for our relationship in the long run, not to mention unethical since I plan to make him my husband someday."

Rocky couldn't wait to share that day with them. "What would Avery like to do?" he asked. "I'd think his skill set would be in high demand."

Jonah nodded. "Neither of us is worried about him finding a job, but I'd hate to see him use his talent to make someone else a fortune instead of himself."

"Maybe he can find some freelance work to cover expenses while he creates his own magic," Felix suggested.

"That's the goal," Jonah said.

Rocky smiled as the solution came to him. "I know a guy."

Felix snorted, and Jonah turned his obsidian gaze to Rocky. "Who?"

"Me," he replied. "Our cyber caseload continues to rise, and I prefer fieldwork to feeling like I'm chained to my desk. I never thought I'd see the day when cyber cases exceed cheating spouses, but nowadays, a lot of the cheating is occurring over the internet."

"Is emotional cheating grounds for divorce?" Felix asked.

Rocky quirked a brow. "How would you feel if you caught Jude jerking off in a video chat with some dude he met online? Would you feel like he was being unfaithful to you?"

Felix's nostrils flared and he bared his teeth a little. "Yes."

"I don't know about the legal ramifications of virtual affairs because I'm not a lawyer. Maybe it won't justify alimony payments or trigger a clause in their prenup, but it sure speaks to a person's character."

Felix whipped out his phone and began typing.

"What are you doing?" Rocky asked.

"I'm making sure Jude knows I will not tolerate him jacking off with some stranger online." Unfortunately for Felix, Renee arrived with their food.

"You tell him, honey." She waited for the guys to inspect their plates to make sure everything was okay before leaving them alone to eat.

"Those peacocks finally came around to liking him," Felix said, typing even faster. "I'll sic them on Jude's nuts so fast he won't even know what hit him."

Rocky reached across the table and snagged Felix's phone from his hand.

"Hey," Felix said. "I wasn't finished typing my message."

"There's no message to send," Rocky said as he deleted every stupid letter. "I'm very sorry I used your relationship to illustrate my point. My intention wasn't to start a fight over something Jude hasn't even done." Rocky returned the phone to Felix but jerked it back just as his friend reached for it. "Promise me you won't send a stupid text when I'm not around to save you from yourself. That man is crazy about you."

Felix smirked. "This reaction is a far cry from the one in the nightclub. Remember when you punched him in the mouth for breaking my heart?"

"That was before I knew how much Jude loves you," Rocky replied. "Don't fuck this up."

Felix took a deep breath, then nodded. "Thanks, Major."

"You're welcome, Fee."

His two best friends dug into their food. Rocky snagged a piece of this and a chunk of that off their plates every few minutes because it looked scrumptious, and he wasn't sure what to do with his hands. Karen had explained to him that keeping his hands busy would help to distract his brain. He was pretty sure she hadn't meant stuffing his face.

Daisy returned to their table once Renee had cleared their empty plates. She shooed Felix over and sat beside him. "I've been thinking about our Marla a lot lately, and I want to do something for her. She's touched so many lives, and I want her to know it before—" Daisy shook her head, unable to finish. She didn't need to. They all felt time slipping away from them.

Rocky, Jonah, and Felix all reached for her hands at the same time.

"We all took a solemn vow not to mourn her while she was still alive, right?" Daisy asked them.

"Yes," the guys agreed.

"We didn't say anything about not celebrating her life and all the fabulous ways she's made us better people," Daisy said.

Rocky smiled. "I like the way you think."

"Me too," Felix agreed.

"Yeah," Jonah added, his voice thick with emotion.

"Let's show her how much we love her," Daisy said. "I want Marla to know the community she loves so much will honor her every single day. I can't think of a better gift."

Neither could Rocky. "What did you have in mind?"

"A drag show at The Dive Bar, of course," Daisy replied. "A night of endless tributes fit for the queen of all queens."

"Sounds amazing," Felix said.

Jonah laughed. "This reminds me of one of her favorite episodes of *The Golden Girls*. Do you remember the one where Sophia decides she wants her memorial while she's still alive so she can hear the nice things people have to say about her?"

"But Rose sent out the invitations without including the tidbit that Sophia was still alive," Felix replied.

"And they all arrived thinking Sophia had passed away and got pissed off when they found out she was there," Rocky added.

The four of them shared a laugh before the reality of their situation sobered them.

"We'll do better than Rose," Daisy assured them.

"Do we make it a surprise party?" Felix asked.

"Nah," Jonah said. "She'd want her family there. Amos goes to Atlanta and picks her folks up every other weekend so Marla can spend time with them. I suspect he'll start picking them up every weekend before much longer."

"Marla would be really pissed if we sprung a party on her and she wasn't dressed appropriately," Felix added.

"When isn't she dressed appropriately?" Rocky countered.

"True," Felix agreed, "but I think Marla would love the buildup to her party."

"That we can all agree on," Daisy said. "Let me start throwing some ideas together with the girls, and I'll be in touch." She kissed Felix since he was close and blew air kisses to Jonah and Rocky before sliding out of the booth. She snatched the bill from the table. "This one's on me. Just take good care of Renee."

"Of course," Rocky said, reaching for his wallet. He dropped his last twenty-dollar bill on the table, which meant he'd have to stop at an ATM to get money to pay off his debt to Queen Bea.

Jonah and Felix each contributed to the tip, then they slid from the booth and exited the diner. On the sidewalk, the three men hugged before setting off for their vehicles. Rocky felt lighter for having spent time with them, even if part of it was spent bickering and another chunk was dedicated to planning a life celebration for someone they didn't want to lose.

His friends had given him a purpose to live when he needed it the most and kept him grounded when he felt as if he were drifting away. Rocky's overactive brain spewed out an endless spiral of thoughts about how delicate and precarious life was. He was so tired of constantly being afraid of fucking up or losing the people he loved or even living.

It was no way to exist.

What happened if Rocky confronted the fear head-on and laughed in its face? What if he mentally slammed on the brakes every time his mind pointed out all the bad things he'd witnessed and replaced it with something beautiful? How much better off would Rocky be if he swapped out what might've been with what could be? It sounded simple enough, but he knew damn well it required a herculean effort to shift those negative thoughts on some days.

Rocky's cell phone rang, startling him from his daydream in the diner parking lot. He glanced at the caller ID and saw it was Peter calling. "Hey, partner," Rocky said. "What's up?"

"Shelly's water broke, and I'm driving her to the hospital," Peter said calmly, even though Rocky knew how excited he was to meet their first child.

"Already?" Rocky asked. He didn't know the mortality rate for expectant mothers, but after losing his own at birth, he knew that losing one was too many.

"Already?" Shelly asked. Peter had either called him on speakerphone or Rocky had yelled really loud. "It's been thirty-eight weeks."

"But who's counting, right?" Rocky teased.

"I am," Shelly growled.

"We knew this was a possibility, so I've updated the notes on all my current cases," Peter said.

"Wait, you're not just dropping her off and coming to the office for a few hours?" Rocky asked.

Shelly laughed. "I'd kick his ass from here to Seattle."

"Okay, fine," Rocky said. "I'll head to the office now and look through your notes and juggle my schedule around. You'll be back to work tomorrow, right?"

"Why did I ever think he was adorable?" Shelly asked Peter.

"Beats me," Peter replied. "Seriously, Rocky, I know this leaves you in a bind with your cases and your podcast commitments."

"Don't you worry about it. You need to focus on taking care of the little mama and fussing over your bundle of joy." Staying busy would keep Rocky out of trouble and prevent him from getting into trouble with Asher. "What do you think about hiring Avery as a freelancer for our cyber investigations? We both love the software he developed, and he's a whiz at ferreting out information on the web."

"I was just about to suggest the same thing since most of my workload is the cyber stuff you can't stand. Why don't you talk to Avery and see if he's interested and find out how much he'd charge us? I'm okay with paying per billable hour or by the job. Bring him on board now to work these cases since we're short, and we can always renegotiate if the arrangement isn't working for either party."

"Sounds good."

"One last thing," Peter said. "I'm supposed to have a meeting with a new client this afternoon. If you're busy, Trudy can meet with her to gather information and go over our pricing schedule. This relationship has the potential to be lucrative for our firm, so I want to avoid rescheduling it."

"I'm free, so don't worry. Keep me posted on the baby, okay?"

"Will do."

After they disconnected, Rocky did something that felt both foreign and familiar to him. He prayed.

CHAPTER 11

"**O**h my God," Trudy said when Rocky walked through the door of Baxter and Jacobs. It was one of those frosted glass numbers with the severe black lettering, which Rocky thought looked retro and sleek at the same time. "Did Peter call you?"

"He did," Rocky replied, hoping he sounded as excited as their gal.

"Isn't it the best news?"

"It is," Rocky agreed.

He felt slightly better after praying, but it wasn't the relief he'd hoped for. He still felt powerless and afraid. There wasn't a single thing he could do to ensure Shelly and the baby would be okay, but he could step up and make sure the agency caseload was appropriately managed. That would give Peter peace of mind so he could be a good husband and dad.

He and Peter were as different as night and day in both their personalities and professional approach. Peter had the financial resources, intelligence, and people skills to run a successful business, but being a private investigator required additional tools. It wasn't enough to be smart; you had to stay two steps ahead of the person you were investigating. The job required gut instincts, dogged determination, and the type of resourcefulness they don't teach you at pricey universities. Luckily, Rocky had both of those things.

He would never forget the night Peter had found him drinking away his sorrows on a barstool soon after returning from Vegas. Rocky worked on his dad's construction crew from dawn to dusk to keep his body and brain busy. Every inch of him ached but nothing more than his heart or the gaping hole in his chest where it had once been. He'd thought Peter was hitting on him when he'd first introduced himself. Rocky had looked him up and down, noting the polo shirt, khaki pants, and expensive leather loafers. Peter's wedding band glinted in the dimly lit tavern. Was he trolling for a dirty lay before he went home to his missus?

"Go home to your wife," Rocky had sneered.

Peter smirked. "Planned on it, but I wanted to talk to you first."

"Talk?" Rocky asked. "That's new."

Realization slowly dawned on Peter's face, and his surprise turned into laughter. "I'm not hitting on you," he said a few moments later.

"This is a gay bar," Rocky pointed out. "You can understand my confusion."

"Is it?" Peter asked, then pivoted to look at the patrons. Same-sex couples moved together on the dance floor, and others were playing pool. The rest either chatted and laughed with friends or were drowning their sorrows in ice-cold beer like Rocky had been attempting to do before the interruption. "Huh," Peter said. "I guess it is."

"Why are you here if not to fuck me?"

Peter tipped his head. "Is that all you think people want from you?"

"Pretty much."

"Not tonight. I'm here to talk business," Peter said. "Why don't you let me buy you dinner?"

Narrowing his eyes, Rocky had said, "This still feels an awful lot like a proposition, pal."

"It is, but I have a business proposal for you. Peter Baxter," he'd said, extending his hand.

Rocky had studied it, then looked down at his own. Dirt and dust covered the scrapes and cuts in various stages of healing. "You don't want to shake my hand."

"But I do," Peter insisted.

Rocky reluctantly shook his hand and gestured for Peter to take the empty stool beside him. Peter parked his ass on the stool and gestured the bartender over.

"Dazzle me with your proposal, Peter," Rocky said once the man had his drink.

"I've started a private investigation firm, and I'm looking for a seasoned investigator to teach me the ropes."

"So you're trolling all the bars looking for a poor schmuck who might happen to have a PI license?"

Peter threw his head back and laughed. "I asked around town and your name kept coming up. They even told me I might find you here." He looked around again. "They didn't tell me everything, though." Rocky was charmed by how little the kissing men on the dance floor affected the man. That was big points in his favor.

"I'm flattered, but I'm not interested," Rocky said. Except he was. He fucking missed the thrill of investigating, but his confidence was shaken. "I'm sorry you wasted your time on me. Let me buy you dinner for your trouble. I know this place doesn't look like much, but the food is delicious."

"What do you recommend?"

"They make the best burger and fries in town, if you like that kind of thing."

Rocky sized Peter up again and figured he was a salad guy, but Peter surprised him and ordered wings and fries. The surprises kept coming when he talked about his dreams for his agency over dinner.

Fuck, it had sounded so good. "You don't need someone with my baggage dragging you down."

"I know about the trouble you ran into in Vegas. I still want you to come work with me."

Rocky had wanted to hang his head in shame, but Peter's piercing gaze hadn't allowed it. "Just give me a chance."

Rocky took a deep breath and something other than pain and sorrow unfurled in his chest. He hadn't recognized it then, but he understood now. Hope. "Tell me more," he'd said.

By the end of the night, Peter had convinced Rocky to give him a shot, which he'd found hilarious since it should've been the other way around. They clicked together so effortlessly that Peter proposed a full partnership within a few months. This was Rocky's chance to thank Peter for believing in him.

Trudy let out a soft squeal, snagging Rocky's attention. "We're having a baby!" she said, clapping between each word and making her blonde halo of curls bounce.

Rocky chuckled. "Pretty sure Shelly is doing all the hard work."

Trudy waved him off. "You know what I meant. I can't wait to hold him or her."

Unlike most parents, Peter and Shelly had no idea the sex of their baby. Rocky thought he'd want to do the same thing if he were ever brave enough to go the surrogate route. He and Asher had discussed a future that included children, but they hadn't decided how to go about it.

Rocky gave himself a mental shake. No good would come from him pining. "We need to order flowers and balloons. Should we do it now or wait?"

Trudy tilted her head. "With it being her first child, she could be in labor for quite some time. Maybe we should wait."

"Okay," Rocky said. A mother of three would know much more about this than he would. "What about one of those edible arrangements instead of flowers that will die?"

"Perfect," Trudy said. "I'll order it as soon as our little angel arrives. Oh!" She moved a cardboard box in front of her. "Speaking of deliveries..." Trudy grabbed a pair of scissors from her desk caddy and sliced through the packing tape. "I've been waiting for you to arrive before I tore into it."

Rocky suddenly felt as giddy as a kid at Christmas. "You didn't have to wait."

Trudy removed several sheets of bubble wrap, then looked up at him. "You pouted the last time I dove in without you."

"Did not," he scoffed.

"There," she said, pointing at his face. "That's the look. You have sad puppy eyes, a puffed-out bottom lip, and the corners of your mouth are turned down. I've seen the look a million times when one of my kids or my husband tried to make me feel guilty or manipulate me into doing something for them."

"I'm wounded," Rocky said.

"Save it and come see what we got."

He never argued with Trudy. The woman's instincts were the best he ever witnessed, and her bullshit meter was never wrong, even when Rocky was the one tripping it.

They fussed and fawned over their new high-tech gadgets. To be the best agency, they had to stay up with the current trends. Their recent haul of listening devices and cameras disguised to look like everyday objects made Rocky particularly gleeful.

Holding up a key fob for closer inspection, he said, "This might be my favorite one. Not everyone owns a smartwatch or other high-tech gadgets, but nearly all of us have a key fob."

"Check this out," Trudy said, lifting a lightbulb from the box. "Designed to look like an LED bulb used in those smart homes where you can control everything from a phone app."

Rocky took it from Trudy's outstretched hand and marveled at the flawless design. He knew without screwing it into a lamp that it would also function as an ordinary lightbulb and would sync with a smart home's technology. The bulb would only act as a listening device when triggered remotely on an app. "Okay, this is my new favorite."

They also ordered hollow coins which would store microchips, a recorder disguised to look like a desk calculator, and a digital picture frame that snapped pictures and videos and recorded conversations while displaying the images the owner uploaded. They purchased new GPS trackers in various sizes and a pair of sunglasses to match the eyeglasses Rocky and Felix had successfully used at Jack Mercy's nightclub.

"That's not all," Trudy said, sounding like a game show host.

"What else have I won, Johnny? A new car? A yacht? A year's supply of soup?"

"Smartass," Trudy grumbled as she pivoted her chair to reach inside another box and pulled out a dozen legal pads shrink-wrapped together. "Christmas came early."

As much as Rocky loved technology, he still did his best thinking when he put pen to paper. There wasn't a problem he couldn't solve with a legal pad and a good pen. Then why had Rocky resisted the suggestion to write in a journal? It was like he self-sabotaged his efforts to get better.

"Rocky," Trudy said, interrupting his musings before he could drift too far away.

"Yeah?"

"I've given your advice a lot of thought."

"I say a lot of things, so maybe you help me out here a little."

Trudy chuckled but averted her gaze. When she began chipping away at her nail polish, Rocky knew she was nervous. He also understood what she was working up her courage to say.

"Remember how you told me I blended into every room like drapes?"

Rocky snorted. "I said no such thing, Trudy. I called you a chameleon."

"Only after you hemmed and hawed and stumbled over your words because you were trying not to offend me."

That part was true. Rocky had tried to extol the way she adapted to every situation. Trudy's smile was a universal language, and she had a trustworthy face and a peaceful demeanor. He'd simply wanted to say that Trudy would make an excellent investigator if she'd ever wanted to branch out a little. He'd botched it miserably with his stammering about, allowing her to make suggestions. All of them were awful.

"I'm not the one who claimed you blended in like drapes, sofas, and throw pillows. You were. I think a blooming cactus describes you well. Pretty, low maintenance, and nice to have around."

"Let's not forget prickly when provoked," Trudy said, waggling her brows.

"What conclusion have you drawn?"

Trudy shook her head. "No conclusions. I'm still in the thinking phase. Well, I did discuss it with Darren."

"And?"

"As much as I love taking care of you and Peter around here, I do need something more challenging. Do you think Peter would go for it, though? I don't want to hamstring the office with this career move. On the other hand, I don't want to try to do both jobs or get stuck filling in for the new receptionist when she calls in sick."

"Hold up," Rocky said, sensing she was about to get worked up. There was only room for one nervous Nelly in this firm, and he'd claimed the role first. "Peter would never discourage you from pursuing a path that made you happy. You wouldn't become a licensed investigator overnight or even in a few weeks or months. We'd have time to train you properly and hire someone to take over your office management duties. You could even help us interview prospects and train your replacement."

"You make it sound so easy."

"It can be that simple if you want it badly enough. What does Darren think?"

"He's worried I'll become cynical and suspicious."

"Tell him to toe the line, and he'll have nothing to worry about."

Trudy laughed. "Good one. I'll want to use it later." She picked up her phone and began typing a note.

"We'll probably have other changes happening sooner," Rocky said. He told her about his conversation with Peter regarding Avery doing freelance work for them.

"Oh, good," Trudy said. "You hate cyber stuff."

"I don't hate it, but I much prefer to be in the field. Peter is much better at handling face-to-face meetings with clients and tackling cyber work."

"That's why our agency rocks and why I'm hesitant to throw a wrench in the cogs."

"Change is inevitable," Rocky said. "Sure, we can insist on doing things one certain way, but our agency won't prosper because we won't be able to meet demands."

"You're so smart."

Rocky smiled. "So my nana says."

"And speaking of face-to-face meetings, are you working with the new client this afternoon, or am I?"

"I told Peter I was free for the appointment, although I didn't get any information about who I was meeting or what we'd be discussing. Peter just mentioned it could be a lucrative development. What do you know about it?"

"Her name is Lillian Travers, but I don't know anything more than that," Trudy said.

"Lillian Travers," Rocky repeated. "Why does that name sound familiar?"

"Beats me."

"I'm going to get in touch with Avery to see if he's available to discuss freelancing opportunities, and I'd like the two of us to look over Peter's caseload to make sure we have all the bases covered."

"We got this," Trudy said, holding up her fist for Rocky to bump.

Rocky called Avery once he reached his office. "How'd you like to do some freelancing for my agency?" he asked once they got the initial greetings out of the way.

"Seriously?" Judging by the surprise in Avery's voice, Jonah hadn't mentioned their conversation at the diner to his boyfriend. Maybe he hadn't wanted to get Avery's hopes up in case it didn't pan out. "When?"

"As soon as you're available," Rocky said, then told Avery what was going on. "A whiz like you could probably resolve these cases in a few hours tops."

"No pressure," Avery mumbled. "I have no idea how much to charge."

"Why don't you do some research and see what kind of numbers you can come up with. We don't care if you want to charge per hour or job. Whatever we agree to now doesn't have to be our arrangement forever."

"This sounds like a great opportunity. Can I call you back later this afternoon or early evening?"

"Of course."

They chatted a few more minutes before disconnecting. Trudy stopped in a few minutes later with a tablet in one hand and a coffee cup in the other.

"Thank you," Rocky said. Even though he'd gotten more sleep than usual last night, it hadn't been enough to shake the fatigue that always seemed to cling to him. He'd take all the help he could get to clear the mental fog, especially now that he had more responsibilities on his shoulders.

"Let's see how the next few weeks look," Trudy said as she accessed their caseload.

Rocky and Trudy went over the open investigations, shifting the workload between them based on skill set and priority. He kept the cyber bullshit under his tasks but hoped he'd be handing them over to Avery in the next day or so. Once they finished, Rocky shifted his attention to the top priority cases. The morning flew by, and before he knew it, Trudy was knocking on his doorframe.

"How about I get you a sandwich from the deli across the street before the mystery client arrives?"

His breakfast had worn off long ago. "That sounds perfect."

"Reuben on rye?" she asked.

"I'd probably lapse into a carb coma before the client arrived."

"Tuna salad?" Trudy asked.

"Would you like to sit across from someone who'd just eaten tuna?"

Trudy laughed, then said, "Chicken salad it is."

After she left, Rocky decided to google the name Lillian Travers to see why she sounded familiar. He was glad he was sitting down when the results popped up on the screen. Lillian's daughter, Halianna, had been abducted, sexually assaulted, and strangled during her freshman year of college.

Rocky clicked through several articles. The images were a kaleidoscope of heartbreak, starting with the initial missing person report where Lillian pleaded for her daughter's safe return. After a few months passed with no word from Halianna, the outlook grew dimmer, and Rocky could see the hope vanishing from Lillian's expression. She tried to put on a brave face for those around her, but Rocky could see the toll it was taking on the woman.

Rocky sucked in a sharp breath when he came across the pictures taken at the press conference where the sheriff announced Halianna's remains had been discovered by hunters in the woods. Lillian stood to the right of the podium while he spoke and fielded questions from the press. Farther down in the article, Rocky read that Lillian had given a statement too. She'd thanked those who'd worked hard to bring her Halianna back home. Though the outcome wasn't what she'd prayed for, Lillian was grateful for the kindness that law enforcement and total strangers showed her family during the most challenging time in their lives.

Rocky recognized the look of utter devastation on Lillian's face because he'd seen it in Julia's eyes before she turned the gun on herself. Due to the salacious nature of the shooting, the local media outlets kept the Warners' story in the forefront. They were constantly flashing images of Julia's face as they described the most sordid details about the woman's life. Facts he hadn't been privy to before taking the case; things which made him look like a pathetic patsy or maybe even partially culpable for the murders.

The images the media used depicted Julia as a loving mother, wife, sister, and daughter. Rocky hadn't doubted those things were true, but they only told half the story. Were there no pictures capturing the darkness and brokenness he'd witnessed? Had she been that good of an actress that she never let on about the hurt she felt? Or were the signs ignored? Wasn't it easier to pretend life was as perfect as the depictions on social media? Those were questions that haunted him.

Rocky clicked on the next articles, which detailed the search and eventual arrest of Halianna's killer. Lillian's face was once again plastered on every news piece as they worked their way through pretrial, trial, and the sentencing hearing. Rocky noticed a shift in Lillian's expression in each one. The sadness still lingered, but something else was brewing in the woman's hazel eyes. Determination.

It might've started out as a quest for justice, but it morphed into so much more. The most recent article Rocky found talked about Halianna's Hope, a nonprofit organization that Lillian formed to honor her daughter's memory and to help other victims and their families. Rocky scanned the article and saw that they were creating a committee to lobby for stricter laws against sex offenders. Halianna's killer had been convicted and sent to prison twice for violent sex crimes before killing her. The fucker never should've been free to roam the streets. Rocky wasn't sure why Lillian Travers needed Baxter and Jacobs, but he was honored to assist her in any way he could. And maybe assisting Lillian would help him make peace with himself at long last.

A moment later, Trudy breezed through the door with his lunch. "Here you g—" She set the paper bag and bottle of soda on his desk and rushed around to his side. "What's wrong?"

"What do you mean?" he asked. That's when he became aware of the tears streaking down his face. Fuck. He truly was losing it. How helpful would someone like him be to Lillian when he couldn't take care of himself? Blowing out a frustrated breath, he said, "I googled Lillian Travers's name and realized why it sounded familiar." He gestured to the screen and Trudy read the article over his shoulder.

"Oh," Trudy said. "Is there anything I can do to help you, Rocky?"

He smiled up at her, then shook his head. "You've already done enough. Thank you."

"For walking across the street to get your lunch?" she asked.

"It's more than that, and you know it. You're always looking out for us, and we're lucky to have you."

Trudy leaned forward and hugged Rocky tight. "I love working with you guys." She dropped her arms from around his shoulders and stood up. "Now eat your damn lunch. Mrs. Travers is due in thirty minutes." Then Trudy narrowed her eyes and tapped her finger against her lips as she appraised Rocky's appearance. "You said this meeting is super important to Pete, right?"

"Yes," Rocky said. After reading the articles, it was also important to him.

"You need to change your clothes."

Rocky looked down at his gray T-shirt, jeans, and boots, then back up at Trudy. She was right. He'd dressed to work in the field or at his home office. "I'd already left my house for a breakfast meeting with Jonah and Felix when Peter called me."

"It's a good thing you keep spare clothes here at the office."

"Do you think business casual would work, or should I go all out and wear dress pants, a pressed shirt, and a tie?"

"Either would work." Pointing to his lunch, she said, "Eat. You're getting too skinny."

Was he? Rocky glanced down again but didn't notice anything different. His clothes still fit him properly. Well, except for the jeans he'd thrown away after his run-in with Snickerdoodle the previous evening.

"Just eat," Trudy said firmly on her way out the door. "You're probably down to twenty-five minutes now."

That spurred Rocky into action. Trudy hadn't just purchased the sandwich and chips; she'd also included a juicy dill pickle and three chocolate chip cookies. Rocky's stomach was still tied up in knots over the articles he'd read about Lillian and her daughter, Halianna, so he only ate a fraction of the food Trudy had bought for him. He stored the leftover sandwich in the refrigerator in the breakroom but tucked the cookies and chips in his desk drawer so he could grab them quickly later.

Afterward, he checked the spare clothes he had in his office closet. He decided to go with the proper slacks, dress shirt, and tie combo. The pants he chose were charcoal gray, and the shirt was a lighter hue of the same color. Rocky stared at the different ties hanging in his closet. He'd narrowed it down to lavender stripes and mint-green paisley but couldn't decide which he liked best. Rocky quickly changed clothes and headed out to the reception area to get Trudy's opinion.

"Which tie do you like best?" Rocky asked.

Trudy smiled when she glanced up. "You look really handsome."

"Thanks," he replied.

Trudy was one of the few people who didn't call him pretty. The compliment didn't offend Rocky's sensibilities or threaten his masculinity, but it reminded him of the numerous headlines in Vegas that had started referring to the crime as Pretty Poison after someone leaked the contents of Julia's goodbye letter to the press. If that wasn't bad enough, Duggins had started calling him Pretty Poison when Asher wasn't in the room. If Rocky ignored the jabs, Duggins would hit harder.

"You might be pretty, but you poison everything you touch," Duggins had said one night after learning Asher wasn't home. His husband had run to the store to pick up Rocky's favorite ice cream to cheer him up. Duggins saw it as the perfect time to let him have it with both barrels. Rocky had told him to fuck off, but his bite had lacked venom after a terrible stretch of sleepless nights and botched attempts at intimacy. Stress, anxiety, and depression had taken a horrific toll on his libido.

Duggins had sensed Rocky was down, so he went for the knockout punch. "Asher got passed over for a promotion because of you, asshole," Duggins had shouted at him. "You've turned him into a laughingstock at the office. If that's not bad enough, you can't even muster the energy to jerk him off." Duggins had laughed dryly. "The man is getting screwed at work while getting blue balls at home." Rocky had been horrified to realize Asher discussed their sex life, or lack thereof, with Duggins. Then he saw the wicked gleam in the man's eyes and knew Asher hadn't betrayed his confidence. "You should be more careful about leaving your laptop open and unattended."

Rocky had bristled. "You had no right to look at my browsing history."

"Asher was my best friend long before you came along. I had every right." Duggins blew out a deep breath. "You're like a drug he can't stay away from. If you love Asher as much as you claim to, then do him a favor and take your pretty face out of Vegas before he overdoses on you."

Duggins had confirmed every fear Rocky had, so leaving made the most sense.

"Hmmm," Trudy said, startling Rocky from his memory. She rose from her chair and studied the ties. "Hold them up to your neck one at a time."

Rocky did as she asked. "Have you heard from Peter or Shelly?"

"No, but I didn't expect to either. First baby, remember."

"How much longer do you think it will be?"

"Could be a few more hours," Trudy said.

"Or a few days," a soft feminine voice said.

Rocky turned around and locked eyes with Lillian Travers, who'd just stepped out of their restroom. He hadn't been aware she'd arrived yet. "A few days?"

109

Lillian smiled and nodded. "I was in labor for thirty-six hours with my daughter. It was worth every second. I'm sure your friends will feel the same way once they're holding that tiny gift from heaven in their arms." She stepped forward and extended her hand. "I'm Lillian Travers."

Rocky shook her hand. "I'm Peter's partner, Rocky Jacobs," he said. "As you've heard, Peter and his wife are having a baby today"—Rocky grimaced—"or sometime this week." Indeed, there had to be an easier way to bring children into the world than torturing their mother for days on end. Ouch. "I hope you don't mind meeting with me instead."

"Not at all," she said. Lillian shifted her focus to the ties Rocky still held in his hand. "I'd go with the lavender stripes. The color will pop with your blue eyes."

"Thanks," he said, looping the purple tie around his neck and shoving the mint-green one in his pocket.

"If the tie is for my benefit, please don't bother. I couldn't care less about formal clothes."

Rocky took in the classy navy blue sheath dress and nude heels she wore for their meeting. She'd pulled her hair into a low ponytail and applied her makeup with a light hand, choosing to highlight her features rather than create an entirely different face. This was a woman who cared very much about her own appearance at least.

"You did tell me the tie would complement my eyes, so I'm going to wear it. I'll just be a moment. Can we get you anything to drink, Mrs. Travers?"

"No, thank you. And it's Lillian. Please don't rush on my account. I'm early as usual."

"And I don't want to keep you waiting." He just needed to take a few deep breaths to get himself under control. Dredging up all that shit with Duggy Bear had put him in a strange headspace.

He left Lillian in Trudy's capable hands and returned to his office to finish getting ready. Once there, the tie felt more like a noose around his neck than a piece of men's clothing. He cycled through meditative breathing, and it still didn't work. Rocky felt like he was choking, so he removed the tie and shoved them both in the closet. He took a few more deep breaths, then returned to reception to get Lillian. If she noticed the lack of tie, she didn't say anything. Rocky saw numerous questions in Trudy's eyes, though.

"Are you sure I can't get you something to drink?" Rocky asked her. There was an unwritten Southern rule that said you had to ask your guests at least twice if they wanted refreshments.

"I'm positive," she replied.

Satisfied that he'd made both his grandmothers proud, he smiled at the older woman. "What can our agency do for you?"

"Are you familiar with my story, Mr. Jacobs?"

"Rocky," he corrected. "Yes, ma'am. I'm so very sorry for what happened to your family."

"Thank you," she said, then launched into a conversation about what she'd like to do to honor her daughter's memory.

Her plans extended well beyond lobbying the legislature. She wanted to open shelters for abused women. Lillian planned to call it Halianna's House. Another one of her passion projects was raising money to help fund search and rescue teams to assist law enforcement when someone vanished. She explained that the sheriff's department had been hamstrung by tight budgets and other issues when Halianna disappeared.

"I'd like to call this service Halianna's Heroes," Lillian said. "Because these people worked tirelessly for her. And it's not just about helping the people who have been victimized. We need to do more to prevent these crimes from happening."

The more she talked, the harder Rocky found it to breathe. Here was this woman who'd lost so much, and she was trying to make the world a better place while Rocky ran, hid, and made the trauma about himself. Shame washed over Rocky, making it hard for him to maintain eye contact.

Lillian stopped midsentence and reached across his desk to grip his hand. "I know that look."

"Excuse me?" Rocky asked, trying to pull himself together.

"I know trauma when I see it," she said softly. "Judging by your reactions, it must've been pretty recent."

Rocky ran a hand through his hair. "It was long enough that I should be doing better."

"Bullshit," Lillian said. The crass word sounded weird coming from someone so elegant. Maybe her wardrobe was a façade, her shield against the world. "Everyone heals differently. I don't just mean the methods either. Are you talking to someone about it?"

Rocky nodded. "Well, kinda. I'm still warming up to the idea of therapy."

"It's an adjustment. I sometimes think it's harder on men. Boys are taught to be stoic and emotionless from a young age. Feelings are a sign of weakness and all that other nonsense. Do you like the person counseling you?"

"I do."

"Stick with it, Rocky. You'll be better off in the long run."

Rocky studied her open expression and kind eyes. "How'd you do it?"

"Do what? Get out of bed? Stop crying? Start living again?"

He nodded. "All of it. I feel like I'm still there. That night plays on an endless loop in my brain. I get little breaks now and then, but they're like commercials. The relief fades, and the horror show resumes. I want to run, but my feet are stuck in something thicker and stickier than mud. I want to break free."

Lillian tilted her head to the side. "Do you really?"

"Want to break free?"

Nodding, Lillian said, "It's easy to say those words, but sometimes hard to mean them. Survivor's guilt is an insidious enemy. Do you think you deserve to be free of the pain?"

Rocky stared at her without speaking for so long that Lillian started to look worried. She probably thought she'd overstepped, but in reality, she flipped on the "aha" switch in his brain. As much as Rocky wanted to heal from witnessing the double murder, a huge part of him didn't believe he deserved it. That's where he needed to start his recovery.

Lillian tightened her grip on Rocky's hand instead of letting go. "Are you okay, Rocky?"

"Not yet, but I'm getting closer." Rocky shook his head and pulled free from her grip, then scrub his face with his hands. "I'm so sorry."

"For what?"

"For breaking down this way. It's highly unprofess—"

"Knock it off," Lillian said, cutting him off. "Helping other victims is how I honor my daughter's life. I think it was destiny that we met today. I believe God puts people in our lives when we need them most."

Rocky had once believed that too, so he nodded.

"My first task is putting together the absolute best board of directors and officers to ensure all the money we raise is being put to its best use. That's where you come in. I have a list of candidates for each position. I'd like you to run full background checks on each of them. Every person attached to Halianna's Hope must meet certain criteria."

"I'd be honored," Rocky said.

"Later, we'll look at political candidates our organization can support to ensure we have friends in the state capitol and in Congress."

From there, they discussed the timelines for the various phases of staffing the organization. Lillian wanted to focus on the board of directors first, who could then help her choose the rest of the staff.

"I think I've taken up enough of your time," Lillian said once they'd gone over the agency's pricing and invoicing processes. "I'll have my assistant email the dossiers for each of the candidates once we've made our final selections. It will probably be sometime next week."

Rocky rose to his feet and walked her back to reception. "Perfect. I'm looking forward to working with you, Lillian."

"As am I," she said.

Unlike waiting rooms at doctor's offices, their reception area was on the small side. It looked even smaller with a mountain of muscle sitting in one of the chairs. Rocky's steps faltered when he spotted Asher. His husband glanced up from the magazine he'd started reading and smiled.

"Hey," Rocky said, internally rolling his eyes at how breathy he sounded.

Glancing over at Trudy, he saw her eyebrows creeping up toward her hairline. Yeah, she'd noticed his reaction too. He read the curiosity in her gaze, which meant Asher probably hadn't introduced himself as Rocky's husband.

He said goodbye to Lillian at the door and thanked her for entrusting their agency with such an important mission.

Lillian patted his arm. "We'll be in touch soon."

After she left, Rocky turned and caught Asher staring at his ass. Something dark, delicious, and dangerous sparked inside him.

"To what do I owe this pleasure, Inspector?"

Asher closed the magazine and set it on the small coffee table before he rose to his feet and crossed the short distance. "I have a problem that only a smart-mouthed private eye can help me with."

"You've come to the right place," Trudy announced.

Rocky looked over, and she'd propped her elbow on her desk and rested her chin in the palm of her upturned hand. Her eyes shimmered with pure, unadulterated glee. "Don't you have something to do?"

"Don't you?" she fired back.

"I really like her," Asher said, then crossed the room and extended his hand. "I'm Asher Dunleavy." Rocky waited for him to drop the bomb, but he didn't.

"Trudy Robinson," she said, shaking Asher's hand. "I don't recall seeing your name on the schedule."

"It was a spur-of-the-moment thing," Asher said to Trudy before facing Rocky again. "I won't take much of your time."

"Pity," Trudy said as she turned back to her computer.

Rocky chuckled and gestured for Asher to follow him back to his office. He felt his husband's eyes on his ass during the short walk, so Rocky was a mess of jumbled nerves by the time he shut the door to give them privacy.

Rocky turned away from the door and smacked into a concrete wall of muscle. Asher placed his strong hands on his hips, and Rocky slowly lifted his head to meet his husband's gaze. Asher took a few steps forward, which meant Rocky had to back up a little if he didn't want to be plowed.

Oh, but I do. I really, really do.

Asher didn't stop moving until Rocky was sandwiched between the unyielding door and his husband's substantial body. He liked it a lot and suddenly found himself at a loss for words.

"Hi," Rocky managed to say.

Cupping his face, Asher brushed his thumb over Rocky's cheek, then he lowered his head until his mouth was an eyelash away from Rocky's. He didn't mean one of those two-inch-long fake lashes like his drag queen friends wore. He was talking about the short and stumpy kind most people were burdened with.

Rocky's brain and heart launched into a battle of "kiss me" and "don't kiss me." Rocky was quickly falling into the kiss-me camp.

The mixture of scents that had intoxicated Rocky in the bathroom was even more potent now, taunting him. He could so easily press his nose against Asher's throat and breathe him in. His husband was right there for the sniffing and... taking? Is that what Rocky wanted?

"Hi," Asher said. How could one little word awaken so many emotions and stimulate hundreds of nerve endings inside him? It wasn't the word; it was the husky voice and the man with the hungry eyes who spoke it.

For the love of all things holy and unholy, please kiss me.

CHAPTER 12

Asher didn't budge from his position. If Rocky wanted a kiss, he'd have to take the initiative. The heat radiating from his husband's body and the smoldering look in his eyes said he was also in the kiss-me camp. Asher's ardor slowly downshifted the longer they stared at one another, but that thumb never stopped moving. Rocky guessed where Asher's thoughts were going, and he wanted to throw up a stop sign.

"Are you okay?" Asher asked softly.

Too late. Pity had replaced lust in Asher's dark gaze.

Biting back a groan, Rocky stepped out of Asher's quasi embrace and walked toward his desk. Rocky could tell him about Shelly going into labor or his conversation with Lillian, but it would only make Asher worry more. "I'm fine. Why do you ask?"

"I'm not allowed to express concern?"

Rocky dropped down in his chair and forced himself to meet Asher's eyes. How many fucking times had Asher asked Rocky the same question? Too many to count. No matter how Rocky answered him, it led to an argument. Rocky had no interest in rehashing old fights, so he ignored him instead. "What brings you by?" he asked.

Rocky caught a spark of anger in Asher's eyes before he erected a mask of indifference. He hated that expression as much, if not more, than pity.

"I left this morning without grabbing a spare key out of the menu drawer." Technically, it was a catch-all or junk drawer. Rocky kept batteries, spare keys, and small hand tools such as screwdrivers in the same drawer with the menus. Obviously, Asher knew that but wanted to get in another dig at his nonexistent kitchen skills. "Can I borrow yours? I'm going to finish up early today, and I'd like to do something nice to thank you for letting me stay."

"Bet it won't involve cleaning," Rocky replied, getting in his own jab.

Asher snorted. "Hell no. I thought I'd cook a nice dinner for you. When was the last time you ate a homecooked meal?"

"My friends are great cooks, and we get together a lot."

Asher's shoulders slumped. He wanted to do something for Rocky that no one else could. And, boy, could he ever. It just didn't involve food.

"But none of them cook amazing Irish dishes like you can," Rocky said as he opened the middle drawer and removed his keyring. He worked the house key loose, then extended it to Asher. "So, if you're in the mood to show off your skills, I'm in the mood to reap the benefits."

Asher accepted the peace offering with a crooked grin. "I'm definitely in the mood." Something dark, dangerous, and oh-so-alluring danced in his gaze, and his pirate smile made a reappearance, promising Rocky that he'd reap the benefits. "Dinner will be at six," Asher said on his way to the door. "Don't be late."

Several snappy responses came to mind, but none of them formed on his lips. Rocky stared off into space for a few minutes after Asher left, trying to get his mind back on his caseload. Until Avery officially signed on, the brunt of the investigating was on his shoulders. Feeling needed was much preferred to being pitied, so he dove back into his work and pushed every other thought to the back burner.

A loud commotion outside Rocky's second-story office window caught his attention sometime later. He pushed back from his desk and wandered closer to check out the newest dispute between the pair of blue jays who had taken up residence in the beech tree outside his office. Mrs. Blue Jay stood on the edge of her nest while Mr. Blue Jay perched two branches higher.

"Out of pecking range. Smart move, buddy," Rocky said.

The missus tore into her mister with a litany of loud jeers and short whistles while he stared off into the distance as if he didn't hear her. Everyone in a two-block radius could hear her shrieking. What had he done to deserve such a beatdown? Was he home late with supper? Had she caught him cuddling up to a different female? One who was outside their species, perhaps?

"I bet it was the slutty cardinal I saw hanging around here," Rocky whispered. "I thought he chased her out of the tree, but maybe he just followed the tramp back to her nest."

The more Mr. Blue Jay ignored his little lady, the more agitated she became. Rocky slowly rose to his feet and eased closer to the window, approaching at an angle so he didn't frighten them away. Mrs. Blue Jay jumped down off the nest and began hopping along the branch. Mr. Blue Jay was probably many things, but stupid wasn't one of them. He flew higher up in the tree and returned her jeers and chirps.

"Whoa ho," Rocky said. "Someone's feeling plucky this afternoon, although that's the equivalent to a passive-aggressive remark, buddy."

Whatever Mr. Blue Jay had chirped didn't sit well with the missus because she began flapping her wings. Her mister continued running his beak but kept moving toward the end of the branch, making a quick getaway a possibility. Rocky once again acknowledged the bird's cunning display of survival instincts. The missus wasn't one bit impressed, however.

"Men are such assholes," Rocky said. Christ, he was losing his freaking mind. Talking to birds? Thank fuck he hadn't really expected an answer. *Right?*

Mrs. Blue Jay flew up to his branch, and Rocky expected Mr. Blue Jay to make a break for it, but he surprisingly held his position as she hopped toward him, flapping her wings. Then they were beak to beak for a few seconds, and their shrill yelling at one another turned to a softer cooing. The knot of tension in his core tightened in recognition of their antics.

"I don't believe it," Rocky said. "Fighting is part of their foreplay."

Sure enough, after a few more seconds of cooing and rubbing their beaks together, the female turned around. She lifted her tail feathers and exposed her cloaca; a term he'd learned from watching hours of Animal Planet when he couldn't sleep.

"Hussy," Rocky said. "Make his sorry ass work harder for it."

Someone cleared their throat from the doorway. Rocky turned and found Trudy standing on the threshold. Her loony grin matched his behavior. What a pair they made.

"It's time to go home," Trudy said.

"Can't be." Rocky checked his watch and was stunned to see it was five o'clock already.

"*Your husband* told me he was making you a special dinner tonight." Trudy's voice was a mixture of curiosity and incrimination.

Rocky sighed. "It's complicated."

"Things are always convoluted when a man is involved," she said while tipping her head toward the activity outside his window.

"Yeah, pretty much."

"It's best not to keep your man waiting," she said. "He plans to have dinner ready at six."

"Do you always do what your husband tells you, Trudy?"

"Of course not. Sometimes defiance is the spice of life," she replied, waggling her brows. "Other times, I trick him into thinking my rebellion was his idea all along."

Laughing, Rocky said, "We're really not that hard to trick."

"Nope," she agreed. "Have a good night. I'll see you in the morning."

"Goodnight."

Rocky considered working a little longer because his commute was short. It wouldn't take an hour to get home, and Rocky didn't want to look too eager. He could work on his investigations a bit longer or even stop by Grant Duncan's house to see if he was home. Then he remembered the Snickerdoodle fiasco and nixed the idea. It was too soon.

Home it was. Rocky powered down his computer and packed some things into his messenger bag to work on later. He couldn't see himself hanging out with Asher in the living room all night. Work would be the best kind of distraction.

During his commute, his favorite Mazzy Star song came on the radio. Damn, the feelings "Fade into You" evoked were dangerous. It was the song he'd been listening to when Asher knocked on his door hours after the bust that had brought them together. The bluesy, sexy melody was the perfect soundtrack for touching, kissing, and melding bodies together. It became their anthem of sorts because they just faded into one another, sharing breaths, kisses, and eventually their lives. One minute, Rocky was a single man who thought he was living his best life in Vegas, and the next, he learned how wrong he'd been. Loving Asher was the best part of his life.

A car horn blared, interrupting his travel down memory lane. Rocky realized the red light had turned green, and the people behind him didn't care that he was drowning in his feels. He accelerated through the intersection and changed the radio station. The song was the last thing he needed to hear.

"What the fuck?" Rocky asked when his house came into view a few minutes later, and he saw a beat-up, rusted car in his driveway.

Rocky parked beside it and went inside. Blues rock was a passion they both shared, so Rocky wasn't surprised Asher had chosen to play one of his Stevie Ray Vaughan albums while he cooked. The sultry beat seduced Rocky's senses just as much as the smells emanating from the kitchen.

He'd never had corned beef and cabbage together before meeting Asher, and he hadn't eaten the combo since returning to Savannah.

"Is that you, Ford?"

"No, it's the ghost of husbands past."

Asher poked his head out of the kitchen. "Really? I don't have an ex-husband, nor do I have a future husband. Just the present one." When Rocky didn't reply, Asher narrowed his eyes. "No witty comeback?"

"I'm trying, but all I can think about is food."

Asher smiled wolfishly. "Dinner will be ready in a few minutes. I'm just waiting for the skillet to get hot enough to fry the boxty."

He ducked back into the kitchen, leaving Rocky to hang out in the living room by himself or follow Asher. How many more opportunities would he get to watch his husband in action? He went into the kitchen where Asher was plopping scoops of boxty into a greased cast-iron skillet. Rocky had never heard of the Irish potato pancakes until Asher had prepared them for him. Talk about fantastic hangover food.

"Remind me to take a picture when everything is ready. My seanmháthair loves when I make her recipes."

Rocky loved the brogue that crept into Asher's voice whenever he spoke Celtic words. He pulled a bottle of beer from the refrigerator. He wanted to hold the cold glass against his heated skin but twisted off the cap and tossed it in the trash instead. After a long drink, Rocky asked, "Do you want to eat inside or out?"

"Will Cal fire up that obnoxious mower again?" Asher asked.

"Not until tomorrow."

Asher nodded as he transferred the boxty to a plate. "Out on the deck." He plopped four more dollops of batter into the skillet to make another round of potato pancakes.

"Speaking of outside, why is that monstrosity parked in front of my house?"

Asher laughed. "Lady Luck isn't a monstrosity. She's a Lincoln Continental and would've been a real showstopper back in her day."

Rocky snorted. "About what era would that have been? Pretty sure her luck ran out a long time ago."

"Mideighties. Lady might look rough, but she runs really well." Asher flipped the boxty over to cook to the other side.

"What are you doing with Lady Luck?"

Asher smirked. "She was the only car available in the asset forfeiture lot."

"So, you're the one whose luck ran out."

Asher backed Rocky up against the cabinet, not stopping until their bodies were flush. Then he placed his hands on the counter, bracketing Rocky in place. Asher looked at him with the hungry determination of an apex predator. Rocky was the prey, but it wasn't fear pumping through his body. Lust was the devil riding him hard and whispering dirty things in his ears.

"I won't be relying on luck to get what I want, Ford."

The kiss-me-don't-kiss-me battle began waging inside Rocky again. As if he sensed it, Asher chuckled as he opened the cupboard door to the right of Rocky's head and pulled down two plates. Stepping back, he handed them to Rocky. "Mind setting the table?"

Thankful for something to do with his hands besides dragging Asher to the floor, Rocky said, "Sure."

He retrieved the silverware and another beer from the fridge for Asher, then carried everything out to the table on the deck. The weather was mild for a summer evening, and Rocky was grateful for the respite. Too bad he couldn't get a break from the emotional storm brewing.

Rocky returned to the kitchen where Asher had just finished transferring the final batch of potato pancakes from the skillet. His husband snapped a picture and sent it off to someone who would show it to his grandmother, who didn't own a cell phone. Rocky had only met the matriarch of the family once. He'd marveled that someone so tiny had brought four mountainous men into the world. Maeve had laughed, kissed his cheek, and assured him that her sons had started out as wee babies. Well, she'd used an Irish word he couldn't pronounce.

Asher's father, Ian, and his three brothers all had sons too. Asher's generation had all introduced little girls so far, a fact that Maeve adored. Rocky would never forget the gentle way Asher had cradled his niece against his chest. She'd only been a week old when they'd visited Brooklyn, and his husband had been smitten at first sight. That moment felt like a million years ago.

"Hey," Asher said, forcing him back to the present. "You okay?"

"Yeah, my mind just wanders sometimes. This looks delicious."

Asher gestured to the platters of food lining the counter and said, "After you."

Rocky took a plate and began assembling his boxty. He laid a potato pancake down first, then smeared horseradish-mustard on it before adding the corned beef and cabbage mixture on top. He didn't even wait for Asher to make his plate before folding the pancake in half and eating it like a taco.

Rocky grunted when the flavors burst on his tongue. Damn, it was better than he remembered.

"My seanmháthair would get all fired up about your methods."

Rocky laughed. Asher ate his boxty the traditional way, meaning he dipped it in the mustard instead of smearing it on the pancake as a layer. "Why does it matter how I eat the mustard? It all goes to the same place."

"She's big on tradition."

"Yet, she doesn't have a problem with you being married to a man," Rocky pointed out.

"She's just happy someone was willing to put up with my slovenly ways."

Rocky looked over at the stove and cringed at the mess splattered all over the glass surface. It looked as if Asher had dropped the batter from the top of a building or a giant bird had shat all over his kitchen.

"I'll clean it up," Asher said as he assembled his boxty. Once finished, they headed outside.

Rocky attacked his dinner as soon as his ass hit the chair. He closed his eyes and barely refrained from doing a happy dance.

"I had a hard time deciding between making boxty and Irish stew, but it looks like I made the right choice."

"This is so delicious."

"I'm glad you like it. I really do appreciate you letting me stay a few days." Asher took a bite of his dinner and looked over the backyard while he chewed. After taking a sip of beer, he said, "It's so peaceful out here. I can see why this property means so much to your family." After a quiet pause, he asked, "So, which one is the magic magnolia tree?"

Rocky was glad the question came when he was between bites, but then he got choked up on emotion instead of food. He bought himself some time by taking a drink of his beer. It wasn't so much that Asher had asked about the tree but that he'd remembered its significance. Asher had seen the framed photographs of Rocky's parents beneath the majestic magnolia, but they'd only talked about the stories behind them once. The first image captured his father on bended knee asking his mother to marry him, and the second was taken just a week before Rocky was born and his mother had died. Amelia Jacobs had looked so serene and happy as she lay on a blanket, using his dad's thigh as a pillow. She rested her hands on top of her swollen belly as she stared up at the sky. Rocky's dad held a book in his hands and was reading it out loud to her, a playful smile tugging at the corners of his mouth.

It took him decades to work up the courage to ask his dad what he'd been reading that day. He'd chuckled and said it was a book about parenting. "Your mom just laughed at some of the suggestions and told me to throw it away. She said we'd do things our way."

Rocky had lain under the same tree more times than he could count. Sometimes he read, and other times he just stared up at the clouds floating by. Rocky had always found so much peace there, and it made perfect sense why Savannah was the place he'd run to.

"It's that one," Rocky said, pointing the tree out for Asher.

"I bet she's a beauty when she blooms."

Rocky nodded. "And smells incredible."

"You know what this backyard is missing?" Asher asked. Rocky looked over at him and shook his head. "A dog."

"Huh-uh."

"Why not? You love dogs."

"I did until I met Snickerdoodle."

Asher scoffed. "He was just doing his job like a good boy. You can't take it personally."

Snickerdoodle was a beautiful dog, and under different circumstances, Rocky would've loved to rub his belly like all the others had. Even though the dog destroyed his favorite pair of jeans, Rocky couldn't hold a grudge. That didn't mean he was ready to be responsible for a dog of his own. "I work so much it wouldn't be fair."

"You could hire someone to walk him during the day when you're at work or use a doggy daycare."

"Sounds simple enough, but I work a lot of evenings too."

"So put him through personal protection training and take him with you," Asher said.

That was one option Rocky hadn't thought of, but it made sense. Rather than admit it, he said, "You assume I'd want a male dog, huh?"

"Nope. I just refuse to use the word 'it' to refer to a living thing. From now on, I'll use *she* and *her* when referring to our—*your*—future dog."

Rocky nearly choked on his next bite. Christ, Asher never relented.

"A German shepherd would make a great personal protection dog. They're smart, fierce, and very loyal. I think you should name her something super girlie like Fifi."

"Fifi?" Rocky asked. "No fucking way. She'd hate us—*me*." Great, now he was doing it too.

"No one would expect a badass dog to answer to such a harmless name."

"No way," Rocky said again.

"Fine. We'll pick something a little edgier."

Rocky was about to remind him that there was no "we," and they wouldn't be owning a dog together, but his phone rang. He checked the caller ID and saw it was Peter. His breath caught in his throat as dozens of possibilities raced through his mind.

"Ford?" Asher asked as the phone rang for the third time.

Rocky shook himself free of the fear clawing at him and answered the phone. "Hey, Peter," he said. "How's everything going?"

"We have a baby girl!" Pete said proudly. "Seven pounds eight ounces of amazingness. We named her Skylar Rose."

"That's wonderful news. Congratulations, Peter. How's Shelly?"

"Exhausted but otherwise doing great. She's a badass, my wife."

"She is," Rocky agreed. "Give her my love and send me some pictures of Skylar Rose. I can't wait to meet her."

"Will do. How'd it go with Lillian Travers?"

"No business talk," Rocky said. "Everything is handled at the agency, including a successful meeting with Lillian. I really like her."

"Good. Okay, I'll relax."

"You'll try," Rocky corrected. In the background, Rocky heard the soft cries of a newborn baby. "Sounds like your little miss needs her daddy's attention right now."

"Holy shit, I'm a father."

Rocky laughed. "Yes, you are, and you'll be a great one."

"Thanks, Rocky."

"Talk to you soon."

"You didn't tell me Peter and Shelly were expecting," Asher said once Rocky hung up the phone.

"We haven't really talked much this past year," Rocky replied. The last thing Rocky wanted to do, then or now, was discuss their unrealized dreams, yet there they were. First, they'd talked about backyards and puppy dogs, and now they'd progressed to babies and children.

The food he'd eaten suddenly felt like a brick in his stomach. Rocky drained the last of his beer and stood up with his empty plate and bottle. "Thanks for dinner. I'll take care of the dishes in a bit."

"Where are you going?"

"With Peter on paternity leave, I have some urgent work I need to take care of tonight," Rocky said.

Asher held his gaze for several heartbeats. "Don't work too late."

"I'll try not to. Thanks again for dinner," Rocky said before ducking inside the house. He rinsed his plate and set it in the sink. He stopped by his bedroom to change into a T-shirt and a pair of shorts before heading to his office.

Once there, Rocky unpacked his messenger bag and dove into his work. They had a little bit of everything going on, but nothing that required surveillance. He tackled the highest priority items left on his list, even if they were dull. He blamed his boredom for the reason he kept nodding off in his chair, not exhaustion. Rocky jerked awake when his cell phone rang. He felt like he'd been asleep for a long time, but there was still daylight coming through the cracks between the blinds.

He cleared his throat, then answered his phone. "Hey, Avery."

"Hi." Avery's voice shook a little. Was he nervous? "Do you have a few minutes to talk?"

"Of course."

"I feel like I've come up with a plan that's profitable for both of us."

"I'm listening."

126

Avery summarized what his research had turned up. "The problem is, neither arrangement is fair a hundred percent of the time. I think the solution is a hybrid of the two." Rocky listened as Avery went into great detail about what he should charge under certain circumstances and why. It was utterly adorable. "I'm not out to rip anyone off. I—"

"I'm sold," Rocky said before he could finish making his pitch.

"Really?"

"Yeah," Rocky said. "I know Peter will appreciate the amount of time you put into your research. Like I said earlier, we can modify our agreement later down the road if it's warranted."

"Oh, that's great," Avery said, sounding relieved. "What's next?"

"Can you meet me at the office tomorrow morning around nine? Trudy will go over the paperwork and get you set up with computer access. Afterward, I'll go over the cases I need immediate help with."

"Absolutely. Thank you so much for this opportunity. It means so much to me."

"You're going to be worth every penny we pay you and then some. See you in the morning, Avery."

After they hung up, Rocky heard voices outside one of his office windows. He recognized Asher's low rumble but wasn't sure what the hell he was doing creeping around the perimeter of the house. Rocky walked to the window and cracked open the blinds to peer outside. Asher was crouched down next to Cal's lawnmower with his hands in the belly of the beast. After a moment, Asher stood up and dusted off his hands.

"That ought to do it." Gesturing to the machine, he said, "Give it a tug."

Cal leaned down and gave the pull cord a hard yank. Instead of sputtering, the lawnmower fired right up, sounding probably like it had when it left the factory. Cal gave it a little push before letting go of the handle. Rocky braced himself for the blast of the backfire, but nothing happened when the machine cut off other than Cal whooping and giving Asher a high five. His husband bent over to collect a spray can and a lawnmower part from the ground before he turned and headed back toward the house.

Rocky dropped the blinds and stepped back before Asher caught him peeking. If he'd wanted Rocky to know he'd bought sparkplugs for Cal's lawnmower, then he would've told him. Which brought Rocky to his next thought. Why the secrecy? It wasn't abnormal for Asher to do nice things, especially for an elderly man. He was willing to bet his next paycheck Asher had even offered to mow the grass for the guy. But Cal's yard was his pride and joy. He wouldn't trust it to just anyone. Rocky knew because he'd made the offer at least once a month since he moved in.

So, Asher had ulterior motives, and Rocky knew precisely what they were. He'd told Asher the backfiring lawnmower reminded him of Julia's gunshots. Asher couldn't heal the trauma in Rocky's brain, but this was something he could fix. So Asher had.

Hiding in his office suddenly felt ridiculous and cowardly, so Rocky logged off his computer and went to find Asher. He stood at the sink, washing mower grease off his hands. Rocky noticed the muscles in his back working beneath his shirt and the way his sweatpants clung to his ass. Sensing he wasn't alone, Asher glanced over his shoulder.

"All finished?"

"Yep. Now I'm reporting for kitchen du—" Rocky's words died when he finally noticed how spotless the room was.

"Too late," Asher said as he dried his hands.

"What else have you been up to?" Rocky asked. This was Asher's chance to tell him he'd helped Cal.

His husband shrugged. "A little bit of this and a little bit of that. I was thinking about eating another cinnamon roll. I shouldn't, though."

"You should," Rocky said. "Let me elevate the experience for you." He warmed up two rolls, topped them with a scoop of ice cream, and drizzled caramel sauce over them.

"My teeth hurt just looking at this concoction," Asher said, but he accepted the bowl when Rocky handed it to him.

They went back outside to enjoy the lovely evening, swapping stories about things that had happened since the last time they'd talked to one another. Asher was mostly curious about his work with the podcast, while Rocky kept his inquiries to Asher's family and his new team. He didn't want to hear Duggy Bear's name mentioned one single time.

By the time the lightning bugs came out, Rocky was ready to turn in for the night.

"I've got an early morning too," Asher said. "I have to be at the command center at four."

"Gross," Rocky said.

"Yep."

Asher locked up the front while Rocky secured the rear, and they met in the middle, which was the hallway to the bedrooms.

"Goodnight, Ford," Asher said when they reached Rocky's bedroom door. "I hope you sleep better tonight."

Rocky reached out and placed his hand on Asher's forearm before his husband could disappear farther down the hall.

"What's wrong?"

Rocky took a deep breath while digging deep for courage. The few hours he'd slept in Asher's arms had been the deepest sleep he'd had since before the shooting. He craved the peaceful abyss as much as the body that had comforted him. "I have no right to ask this, but will you..." Rocky's voice trailed off as his bravery waned.

Asher said nothing. He just nodded, then pushed open the bedroom door and followed Rocky inside.

CHAPTER 13

Rocky woke up alone and on the wrong side of the bed when his alarm went off the next morning. He must've rolled over to Asher's side when his husband left for work, or like the previous morning, Rocky had pinned Asher to the mattress at some point in the night. If that were the case, how had Rocky slept through him leaving?

Stretching like a cat, Rocky marveled at how good it felt to sleep without interruption for the first night in…he didn't know how long. Asher's scent was even stronger on his bedding now. Rolling onto his stomach, he buried his face in the pillow and breathed the fragrance in. Rocky let himself pretend it was a lazy Sunday where the only thing he and his husband cared about was making love and eating a ridiculously overpriced brunch someplace. He pictured warm sunbeams on naked skin. Asher would kiss a trail from the nape of his neck to the crack of his ass. He wouldn't stop there either. Rocky squirmed as memories flooded his brain, and that's when he became aware of his erection.

Flopping onto his back, Rocky shoved the sheet and his underwear down to his thighs. He wasn't a narcissist who loved looking at his nude body, but erections had been a rare occurrence since the shooting. So, yeah, he was beyond happy to see his dick standing at attention and reporting for duty.

He traced his fingertips over his hard-on, noting the way his cock jerked beneath his touch. Heat pooled in Rocky's core, spreading throughout his body and making his toes curl. The ceiling fan overhead stirred the air, making it feel like a caress against his skin. His flesh pebbled and his nipples hardened in response. One part of his brain spurred Rocky to hurry up and jerk himself off, but the other urged him to take his time and savor the feelings. There was no telling when this would happen again. So, instead of spitting in his hand and rubbing one out quickly, he took his time reacquainting himself with his body just as Asher would if given the choice.

Rocky ghosted his fingers over his skin, pretending they were his husband's mouth until his entire body trembled. Only then did he retrieve the lube from his nightstand and slick the length of his cock. He massaged the sensitive spot under his crown until a bead of precum glistened at the slit. Closing his eyes, Rocky relaxed his head into the pillow and allowed his mind to wander to Asher. He pretended it was his husband's hands fondling his sac and stroking his cock. Rocky spread his thighs and dipped his hand between them to tease his puckered entrance, wishing it was Asher's wicked tongue taunting him.

Christ, this felt too damn good to slow down. He increased the tempo of his strokes and lifted his other hand up to pinch a nipple, rolling it between his thumb and forefinger. Pleasure arced through his body, and he lifted his hips off the bed to fuck his fist. The lube had dried out a little, but he was too far gone to stop and reach for more.

Rocky's ass puckered, aching to be filled. His thoughts drifted to the last time he'd had sex with Asher. They'd gone to New Orleans to celebrate their one-year wedding anniversary and to check out the blues-rock scene there. They'd spent most of their time in bed, alternating between hard fucking and tender lovemaking. Rocky had fallen asleep with Asher's dick still inside him. Rather than pull free, Rocky had pushed his ass tighter against Asher's pelvis, hoping to hold on to him even longer. It had been the sexiest thing ever, and he hadn't felt that same level of contentment since.

He couldn't remember one of the happiest weekends in their marriage without his mind veering to what happened after they got home.

Asher had left for a task force mission as soon as they returned, then Julia... *Fuck, don't go there.* Rocky worked his cock faster, willing the pleasure to triumph over the pain for once. The friction was almost painful, but he didn't let up. Rocky's balls drew up tight seconds before he came with a euphoric shout.

Rocky had never been so glad to see cum coating his stomach as he was then. He really needed to roll out of bed, take a shower, and get ready for work, but his body felt too heavy. Or maybe there was a disconnection between his brain and his limbs. Rolling over onto his stomach and burying his face in Asher's pillow was the dumbest thing he could do, but it's exactly what he did.

He woke sometime later when his cell phone rang. He lazily rolled across the bed until he could reach it. "Hello?"

"Um, hi," Trudy said. "You doing okay?"

"Yeah. Why?"

"Well, Avery is here because you asked him to meet you at nine, but you're not here."

Rocky jackknifed into a sitting position. "I'll be there in twenty minutes. I got caught up in something unexpected."

"I just bet you did. Is the unexpected thing about six and a half feet tall with dark eyes, black hair, and a chin dimple to rival all action heroes?"

"Christ," Rocky grumbled as he ran a hand over his face. "I'll be there in thirty minutes."

"A moment ago, you said you'd only take twenty. Why do you suddenly need ten more minutes?"

He hung up without a response and texted an apology to Avery before dropping the phone on his bed and running to the bathroom to shower.

Rocky made it to the office in fifteen. Trudy and Avery assessed him with varying degrees of curiosity when he breezed through the door.

"I'm so sorry, Avery. I, um..."

"Got caught up in something unexpected," Trudy finished for Rocky. The mischievousness sparkling in her blue eyes spelled big trouble for him. She cleared her throat and tried to wipe the smartass smile from her lips, but it still lingered. "So, I've taken the liberty of getting Avery all set up with access to our systems. It didn't require a whole lot of training since he was the one who designed the system we use now." Trudy narrowed her eyes and continued her gentle rebuke. "That information might've come in handy and saved me from embarrassing myself."

"You have nothing to feel embarrassed about," Avery said to Trudy before turning his attention back to Rocky. "Put me to work, boss."

Rocky hooked his thumb in Trudy's direction and said, "She's the real boss, but I'm sure you've deduced that already."

Trudy scoffed. "Flattery gets you nowhere, but I do accept small tokens of appreciation."

"Good to know," Avery said, then whipped out his cell phone and started typing. "Flowers? Candy? Perfume?"

"Tea," Rocky said.

Avery lowered his phone and smiled. "Really? I happen to be a big fan myself."

"We're going to get along smashingly," Trudy declared. "Now, the two of you get out of my reception area so I can get to work. I have billables to work on so we can keep Rocky in the grand style he's accustomed to."

"You mean electricity and functioning toilets?" he teased.

"That too, but I was leaning more toward spy gadgets and notepads."

Rocky placed his hand on Avery's shoulder. "Come on before Trudy gives away all my secrets."

"Thanks for all your help," Avery said to Trudy as Rocky led him away.

"My pleasure," Trudy said. Rocky knew she genuinely meant it too. "Welcome aboard."

"I assume Trudy gave you the grand tour?" Rocky asked.

The office space wasn't massive, only boasting three offices, a reception area, a small conference room, an even smaller breakroom, and two closet-sized bathrooms. The commercial-grade carpet was charcoal, and the walls had been painted a dove gray. The color scheme was bland, but

Rocky liked it much better than beige. This space represented more to Rocky than a way to earn a living; it had restored a sense of purpose in his life.

He hadn't disliked working construction jobs for his dad. At the end of a long day, he'd been able to step back and see the fruits of his labor. There was something to be said about that. He'd even gotten to use critical-thinking skills to solve problems that popped up on the job-sites. It just wasn't his passion. Private investigating might've started out as a way to connect him to his deceased mother, but somewhere along the way, it had come to mean something much more. Right or wrong, investigating had become a part of who Rocky was, not just something he did.

"She did give me a tour," Avery confirmed. "It's a good space."

"We might outgrow it someday, but it works really well for now."

Rocky sat at his desk while Avery checked out the watercolor paintings of wildlife hanging on his wall.

"These are beautiful," Avery said as he moved from one piece to the next. "Are they a local artist?"

"My mother," Rocky said.

Avery turned widened eyes on him. "Wow. She's incredibly talented."

"She was," Rocky agreed. "She passed away a long time ago."

Avery's expression fell. "I'm so sorry."

"Thank you," Rocky said. "But I'm the one who is sorry."

Avery tilted his head to the side. "Why?"

"For bringing the mood down." Rocky gestured to one of the empty chairs in front of his desk. "Ready to get started?"

"Oh, of course," Avery said, then hastened to sit down. He removed a laptop from his messenger bag, reminding Rocky that he'd left home without his. "Put me to work."

Rocky logged on to his computer and accessed the entire agency's open cases. Avery's brand-new avatar had an empty task box just begging to be filled. Rocky clicked on the investigations he'd earmarked for Avery, then dragged and dropped them into Avery's task box. The action only took seconds but left him feeling almost lightheaded with giddiness.

They spent the next ninety minutes going over each case. Avery asked intuitive questions and made detailed notes, not hesitating to ask for clarification if he was unsure. Rocky was thoroughly impressed and grew smugger by the minute since hiring Avery had been his idea.

"I unintentionally skipped breakfast and left my messenger bag at home. I'm going to duck out for a minute to retrieve it and grab a bite to eat on the way. Care to join me? I'll treat."

Avery glanced at his watch and grimaced. "I wish I could," he said, sounding genuinely disappointed. He returned his laptop to his bag and stood up. "Jonah has an important meeting this afternoon, and I need to make sure he's prepped and ready to go."

Rocky quirked his brow at the double entendre.

Avery's face turned bright pink. "You have no room to talk right now."

Rocky laughed and shrugged. Maybe he should've been embarrassed that he'd fallen asleep after jacking off, but shame was the last thing on his mind. He walked with Avery back to reception where he hugged the younger guy before leaving him alone to chat with Trudy about tea. Rocky fell into Jonah's tea-hating camp, so the words they spoke might as well have been a foreign language.

"I need to run home and pick up my messenger bag," he told Trudy. "I'm going to grab a bite to eat. Would you like anything?"

"No, but thank you," she said. "Oh, I talked to Peter this morning. He said Shelly and Skylar should be going home today. I was thinking about having their edible arrangement sent to their house tomorrow. What do you think?"

"Skylar was just born less than twenty-four hours ago," Rocky said, even though it wasn't the opinion she'd asked him for. "How can they send her home already? What about Shelly? Couldn't there be complications?"

"That's just how it goes," Trudy said. "Both mom and baby will need to pass some medical milestones first. I know it sounds terrible."

"Try barbaric," Rocky said.

"Most women are all too happy to recover at home. There's no rest to be found in a hospital."

But that's where the life-saving equipment was. What if Shelly had internal bleeding they'd somehow missed? Rocky felt pressure building inside his chest. He worked hard to control his breathing and reminded himself that not all new moms ended up like his mother.

"So, are you okay with sending the arrangement to their house tomorrow?" Trudy asked. "I just don't want to miss them at the hospital today."

Rocky nodded. "Get them a really nice one."

"I'd like to contribute," Avery said.

Trudy patted his arm. "You're so sweet. I know they'll appreciate it."

"I'll leave you to it," Rocky said as he headed for the door. "Tell Jonah I said hello."

"Will do."

Rocky had to reroute his trip home to avoid a traffic jam due to an accident. "Damn tourists," he mumbled. The detour took him away from where he wanted to eat, which was Daisy's, and forced him through a fast-food drive-thru.

A teenage boy's voice came through the speaker, and he sounded as enthused about being there as Rocky was. "What can we make for you?" The kid's voice was without any kind of inflection or personality. Rocky wondered if it was one of those robotic recordings.

He rattled off a breakfast combo without looking at the menu. He liked what he liked and rarely tried anything new, which was why a particular taco joint was on his shit list for removing his favorite things and replacing them with new-age bullshit no one asked for or wanted.

"We're now serving lunch, sir," the kid said. "That's why you don't see any breakfast items on the menu right now." The punk had so much disdain dripping from his tongue that Rocky hoped he choked on it.

Fucking smartass. Rocky changed his order, then pulled up to the window. He was prepared to verbally blast the kid or at least glare menacingly. The bubbly girl who took his money wasn't the same person who'd taken the order, so he couldn't be pissy toward her. Rocky could see the little jerk punching orders into the computer behind her, but he wouldn't look in his direction. Glaring was off the table, and Rocky wasn't in the mood to scream like a lunatic or demand to see the manager like some fucking Karen.

What was the male equivalent of a Karen, anyway? Todd. He'd never met one that wasn't a total douche bag.

"Here you go, sir," the bubbly gal said. "Have a great day." The gesture was part of her job, but her bright smile said she meant it.

"You too," Rocky said.

The encounter with the young lady boosted his mood but wasn't enough to dampen his ire after he bit into the burger and encountered a pickle after he'd specifically ordered it without the slimy green things. At the next red light, Rocky removed the top bun to remove the rest of the pickles. Instead of one or two like you'd expect to see, there were six or seven. Their juices would've soaked into the bun, meaning there'd be no escaping the nasty dill flavor.

He glanced at his receipt and saw the words *extra pickles*. No wonder the little asshole who'd taken his order had refused to look in Rocky's direction. He'd said "no pickles" when he repeated Rocky's order but entered extra pickles into the computer. That's what Rocky got for not paying attention to the menu or the ordering screen. Sadistic little fucker. Rocky knew that pimply-faced pickle punk would be featured on a future podcast episode about sociopaths.

Rocky flung the pickles into the bottom of the bag and forced himself to eat the rest of the burger during his drive home. He parked his car and was halfway to the front door when he realized Asher hadn't returned his key to him last night, nor had Rocky grabbed the spare from the menu drawer. *Junk drawer*. Damn it. He jogged back to his car and opened the glovebox, expecting to find a set of bump keys there. Then he realized he'd left them in the messenger bag, which was inside the home he was locked out of.

Rocky cycled through his options. He could try to pry a window open and crawl through it or use a credit card to try to jiggle the lock loose. He was weighing the pros and cons of each when his cell rang.

"Rocky Jacobs," he said without looking at the caller ID.

"Where's my twenty bucks?" Queen Bea said. "Did you forget?"

"Oh, hi, Nana. No, I haven't forgotten." He had, but who could blame him with so much going on? "I'm sorry I haven't dropped by yet. Things are crazy at work with Peter out on paternity leave."

"Okay, but I need the money for my bingo tournament tonight."

"I thought you said it was for poker on Friday," Rocky said.

"Now he pays attention," Queen Bea groused. "Just bring my money to me. Okay, kid?"

"Or what? You'll send your debt collectors after me?" Rocky teased.

Queen Bea snorted. "You don't want to find out."

"I hear you loud and clear," Rocky said. "I'll be by soon. Love you, Nana," he said, then hung up before she could bust his chops even more. His phone rang almost immediately after, and Rocky figured his nana was going to give him hell about his phone etiquette. "I'll be there tomorrow with your money. Give a guy a break, okay? I locked myself out of the house like a dumbass."

"Oops," Asher said. "My bad."

Rocky had been expecting to hear his nana's voice, so Asher's voice caught him off guard. "Oh, hey. I thought you were Queen Bea calling back."

Asher laughed. "She's still hustling you for money, huh?"

"Yeah."

"She's a hoot." Then Asher asked Dandridge if he would swing by Rocky's house.

"That's not necessary," Rocky said quickly. "I have a backup plan."

"Shut up, Ford," Asher said before hanging up.

A few minutes later, the big black beast of an SUV rolled to a stop in front of Rocky's house. Asher climbed out of the front passenger door and strolled toward him. With the dark tinted windows, it was impossible to know how many federal agents were inside the vehicle. With his luck, probably all of them. Why wouldn't the entire Savannah branch of the USMS be on hand to witness yet another humiliating chapter in his life?

"How many deputy marshals are witnessing my embarrassment?" Rocky asked when Asher reached him.

"There's nothing to be ashamed of, Ford. I'm the one who fucked up," Asher said as he slid the key inside the lock. He rotated his wrist, then opened the door for Rocky. "After you."

"You don't have to come in too," Rocky said.

"Oh, I think I do," Asher replied, guiding Rocky inside like an errant toddler before closing the door behind them. "This might be a big mistake, but I'm doing it anyway." It was the only warning Rocky got before Asher tugged him into his arms and captured Rocky's mouth in a searing kiss.

Rocky gasped in surprise, and Asher slid his tongue between Rocky's parted lips. He grabbed on to Asher's broad shoulders to shove him away, or so he told himself, but really, he just used that big, beautiful body as an anchor to keep from falling at his husband's feet.

Asher tightened his grip on Rocky's hips at the same time he angled his head and deepened the kiss, rubbing and rolling their tongues together. Rocky released Asher's shoulders to slide his hands up into his husband's hair, the silky strands sliding through Rocky's fingers until he made double fists and yanked. Asher just grunted and upped his seductive attack, walking Rocky backward until he was flush against the door. This was the kiss he'd silently begged for the previous day.

Rocky pressed harder against Asher's chest, trying to get closer even though the only thing separating their bodies was their clothes. A quick remedy for sure. Rocky relaxed one hand from Asher's hair to reach between their bodies. He'd intended to unbuckle Asher's belt, but his husband suddenly jerked away and put a few steps between them.

Rocky kept his back pressed against the door and marveled that he was still standing upright. The two men stared at each other, chests heaving as they sucked precious air into their lungs. Uncertain of what to say, but knowing something was required, Rocky cleared his throat and said, "You're forgiven."

Asher blinked a few times before he found his voice. "Excuse me?"

"You were apologizing for not returning my key, right?"

Asher slid his hands over his head, taming the mess Rocky had made. "Yeah, that's it." Asher stepped forward but stopped just before he reached Rocky. "It had nothing to do with spending two nights in your bed. My motives were not at all influenced by the way you dry humped my thigh both nights or that I stared at the ceiling for hours while wishing I could roll you onto your back and bury my cock deep inside your sweet ass."

Rocky's face heated, but it wasn't from shame or remorse. "I'm not sure separated husbands talk to one another in such a dirty manner."

Asher narrowed his eyes. "Are you flirting with me, Ford?"

"I don't know," Rocky replied honestly. "I might be. I need to think about it." He nearly snorted. Thinking was all he'd done for the past fifteen months. Maybe he should act first, think later.

Asher's mouth twitched, and his eyes glittered with humor and heat. "Well, the guys and I are heading out of town to track down a fugitive. We might not be back for a few days. Why don't you think about it while I'm gone?" Asher pressed a quick kiss to his lips. "Try not to overthink it, though."

Rocky had gotten used to Asher's abrupt departures and reappearances when they lived together in Vegas, but that seemed like a different lifetime. He should be grateful to have his solitude restored, but he was anything but. "Be safe, okay?"

"Always." Asher brushed the back of his fingers over Rocky's cheek. "Take care of yourself, Ford."

Rocky nodded, his emotions making his words too heavy to speak.

"Try not to dry hump anyone else's thigh."

Rocky laughed and shoved off the door. "Get out of here." He brushed against Asher as he headed to his office. All traces of his husband and the SUV full of feds were gone by the time Rocky retrieved his messenger bag and the spare key from the menu drawer. Junk drawer, damn it.

The second half of Rocky's day was busy but uneventful in the way that he hadn't locked himself out of his house, the office, or his car, and no one snuck pickles by him again. He thought he'd be able to breathe a little easier with Avery taking point on the cyber investigations and Trudy managing the fiscal tasks and other clerical things that kept the agency going. He was wrong.

He'd met with and signed three new clients, each of them requiring different services. A corporation suspected one of their employees was leaking confidential information to a competitor. A gentleman hired him to prove his husband was hiding assets in a run-up to their divorce. The third new client was another small-business owner who suspected flaws in their bookkeeping and inventory. The company hired Rocky to determine if this was a software glitch, as their employees claimed, or an act of theft, as the owner suspected.

It wasn't often that Rocky got to put his finance and accounting degrees to investigative use, but he really liked it when his two worlds collided. He and Peter had talked about doing more forensic accounting investigations, but as of now, most of those jobs went to prominent accounting firms in Atlanta like the one his maternal grandfather owned.

Rocky chatted with Avery about checking out the company's software for flaws and manipulations while he focused on the accounting side of things. Between the two of them, they'd be able to ferret out any discrepancies.

"Go home," Trudy said from the doorway.

Rocky had been so deep in thought he hadn't heard her approach. He jerked his head up to meet her shrewd gaze. "I will if you do."

"I mean it, Rocky. You won't do us any good if you run yourself ragged during the first week of Peter's paternity leave."

"And what about you?"

She scoffed. "I'm a mother. We never rest."

Rocky shook his head but wisely logged off the system and pushed back from his desk. "Fine. You win this battle."

"And I'll win the next one and the one after that," Trudy said.

"What do you think about locking the office during lunch tomorrow so we can go meet Skylar?"

Trudy smiled. "I think that's the best idea you've come up with since hiring Avery."

"What you're saying is that I'm having a banner week."

"The week isn't over, so I wouldn't get cocky if I were you," Trudy cautioned.

When they reached the front of the office, Trudy logged off her computer, and they exited the building together.

"Have a good night. I'll see you in the morning, Trudy."

"Night," she said.

On his ride home, the local radio station played a promo for the interview he, Jonah, and Felix recorded with Mad Dog Mulroney. Rocky smiled as he recalled the bantering and bickering that had gone on in the little studio and then again when they met for breakfast the next day. Those thoughts inevitably led to Tess Hamilton, the case Rocky desperately wanted to investigate, and his botched attempt to speak to her son.

Rocky was only a few blocks over from Grant Duncan's street, so he decided to drive past the man's house to see if he was home. If this avenue didn't pan out, he'd switch tactics and call the attorneys involved in the case. Without Tess's consent, her lawyer would only discuss the public aspects of the trial and his approach to her defense. It would still give his investigation some insight and might help steer Rocky toward people he hadn't thought to interview.

He slowed down when Grant's house came into view, then parked at the curb when he saw a silver SUV in the driveway. Rocky got out of his car and waited for Snickerdoodle to attack, but all was quiet on that end. Nothing about the *Scooby-Doo* house looked different. The building materials, tools, and equipment were still in the same place, and the structure was in the same state of disrepair. The gate was still squeaky and obnoxious, but Rocky straightened his shoulders and lifted his chin, striding toward the spooky place like he had a right to be there. He wasn't afraid of ghouls reaching through the rotten boards on the porch to grab his ankles. Nope. Not him.

Rocky jogged up the porch steps and rang the doorbell. When no one immediately answered, he knocked on the door. Rocky heard footsteps approaching from inside the house and plastered a friendly smile on his face. *Here we go. This could be your last chance. Be nice. Be courteous. Be—*

The door swung open, and Rocky lost his train of thought. Holy fuck. Grant Duncan was naked except for the white towel wrapped around his waist. Pictures of the man accompanied almost every article about his mother, and even though the camera clearly loved him, those images didn't do him justice.

The dark-haired man was tall, broad-shouldered, and had the kind of thick thighs that could pin a guy down in bed. Had this been one of those noir PI films or classic novels, Rocky, the main character, would entertain the invisible audience with a witty, unforgettable inner monologue extolling all the ways this man represented trouble. Instead, the guy's physical appearance was so similar to his husband that it robbed him of the ability to speak.

Grant's eyes were a nice, warm brown, where Asher's were so dark they looked black. This man sported a nice tan, but Rocky wouldn't call him a swarthy pirate as he'd often said about his husband. Grant had excellent bone structure, but Asher's face looked like it had been chiseled from granite, which only made his full lips look even softer in contrast to his square jaw. Grant didn't have a superhero jaw and chin dimple like Asher. This guy wore what some people called designer scruff—enough to make him look edgy without going full-on caveman. Asher's position required him to stay clean-shaven, but he abandoned his razor during his time off. Just thinking about it made Rocky long to feel the coarse hair scraping against his sensitive skin.

Rocky wasn't the only one taken aback. Grant stared at his face long enough to coax a blush out of him, which was a rare reaction. Rocky was used to his blond-haired, blue-eyed looks attracting the attention of men and women alike, but this man's open-mouthed gape was a little over the top.

"Grant Duncan?" Rocky asked, breaking the awkward silence.

"Yeah, but I'm not interested in buying cookies."

Rocky watched a droplet of water glide over Grant's broad chest and washboard abs before disappearing into the terry cloth. "I can tell you don't eat them."

Grant chuckled. "Everyone eats cookies." Rocky forced his eyes back up to meet Grant's amused gaze. "I'm a vegetarian, so I'm not interested in buying steaks or seafood either."

"Do you have anything against vacuums?" Rocky teased. Flirting and disarming people with his charm was his superpower.

The corner of Grant's mouth tipped up into a smile. He studied Rocky's face before his gaze drifted down Rocky's body. "I will be in the market for one once these renovations are completed, but I'm running late for a date and don't have time for a demonstration."

"So, you don't have time for me to save your soul either," Rocky quipped.

Grant laughed, the sound husky and contagious. "I should've left already. Maybe you can leave your card in case this date is a bust and I have time for a demonstration later."

Rocky had no doubt about the kind of demonstration he was referring to. He retrieved a business card and handed it to Grant, whose entire demeanor changed when he read Rocky's name.

"Fuck off," Grant snarled and stepped back.

"Wait," Rocky yelled before Grant could slam the door in his face. "I only want five minutes of your time."

"I have nothing to say to you."

"Come on. How could you possibly know that?" Rocky asked.

"You're the guy who's calling my mom's former friends and coworkers."

Former friends and coworkers? Did he mean to imply they were no longer her friends, or was it an innocent slip under stress? It only made Rocky hungrier for the truth.

He nodded. "I am."

"You can't possibly think I'll participate in a smear campaign against my own mother."

Rocky had met many people who'd do much worse than that. "Of course not," he said, hoping not to alienate the man further. "I'm not here for nefarious reasons."

"She's seventy-four years old," Grant continued as if he didn't hear Rocky or just didn't care. "She's lost so much already, including her anonymity. You should be ashamed of yourself."

"I'm not trying to smear Tess's name," Rocky said again, this time in a louder voice. "I'm trying to tell her story. Just let me give you my elevator pitch."

Grant narrowed his eyes. "What's that?"

"It's where someone pitches their idea or makes their case in the amount of time it takes to ride an elevator."

"How'd you find me, anyway?"

"I'm a PI. I'm very good at finding people," Rocky replied.

"Sounds sketchy to me. You have two minutes."

"I only need one," Rocky quipped. "*Sinister in Savannah*."

Grant's brow shot up. "What's that?"

"A podcast I produce with my two best friends. Listen to our first season. It's called 'Ride the Lightning.' You'll see what we're all about. My contact information is on the card."

Grant looked at the rectangle of cardstock in his hand, then back up at Rocky. "Look, you seem like a nice enough guy, and I like your sense of humor."

"They call me Mr. Congeniality."

Grant chuckled, shook his head, and extended the card back to Rocky. "I'm sorry, but I can't accept it. I really have nothing more to say to you. I will ask you nicely to leave my mother alone. She's already been tried and acquitted for the alleged crimes. This will all die down eventually." His words were spoken without real conviction. It was wishful thinking on his part, and both he and Rocky knew it. "Anyway, if you'll excuse me, I really need to get dressed and get on the road." Grant's rejection wasn't reflected in his tone or body language. He was curious, and Rocky claimed it as a small victory.

Knowing it was time to retreat, Rocky took a few steps backward.

"Keep the card. Your curiosity will get the better of you, and you won't be able to resist checking out the podcast. When you do, you'll want to call me."

"You're awfully sure of yourself."

Rocky shrugged. "Your mom has something to prove, and we're the best chance she has."

He felt the weight of Grant's stare when he walked away. When he reached the squeaky gate, Rocky turned and glanced back at the porch. Sure enough, Grant hadn't budged from the doorway.

"Oh, and good luck on your date," Rocky said.

Grant replied by slamming the door shut. Rocky chuckled all the way back to his car. Once inside, he glanced over at Grant's house in time to see a first-story window curtain flutter back into place.

Yeah, Grant was totally going to call him, and Rocky needed to be ready when he did.

CHAPTER 14

Rocky wasn't ready to go home to a quiet house yet, so he swung by the ATM and withdrew some cash. He had a debt to pay after all, and besides that, he loved spending time with his grandmother.

Rocky found Queen Bea in the middle of a hotly contested game of canasta. She was too busy cursing out some guy named Harvey to notice Rocky had entered the room. Then again, her eyeglasses probably hadn't been updated since Nixon left office. Rocky had tried to tell her that the cat-eye frames she preferred were back in style, but she insisted she wouldn't be able to find pink ones with rhinestones.

His nana's face lit up like a Christmas tree when she saw him. "My best boy is here," she said, throwing open her arms for a hug. Queen Bea didn't do delicate embraces; she held you tight like it could be the last time.

"Hi, Nana. You still give the best hugs." She smelled like lavender, vanilla, and cedarwood. "You're wearing the perfume I bought you for your birthday." He'd seen it at a department store and bought it on a whim because the perfume's name matched the phenomenal woman he loved so much.

"I can't resist a perfume called Fucking Fabulous." Several scandalized gasps and a few masculine guffaws echoed around the card table, and Queen Bea soaked up the attention. "Are you here to pay up?"

"A deal is a deal." Even if he couldn't remember it. Rocky pulled a twenty-dollar bill out of his pocket and placed it on the table. "Are you having a good day?"

"Harvey felt me up," Nana said loud enough for people two counties over to hear.

"I did no such thing," Harvey said in a gravelly voice. He tossed his cards down onto the table and glared at Nana. "All I did was catch you when you started to fall."

"By grabbing my breasts?" Nana shrieked.

"Hey," Harvey said, "my reflexes aren't as quick as they used to be. What would you like me to do next time? Let you fall and break a hip?"

"Try wearing less cologne," Nana snapped. "The stench bowled me over and enabled you to grope my tits. Or was that your plan all along?"

"Listen here, you meddlesome old bitty," Harvey said, pointing a trembling finger at Nana. "I don't need to resort to such ridiculous tactics to pick up the ladies."

"Ha!" Nana shouted. "You can't keep your hands off me. Just admit it."

Harvey's face flushed bright red, and Rocky worried Nana had just caused the man to have a stroke. "Why...you...I oughta..."

"Now, Nana. That's no way to flirt with a man," Rocky said, hoping to de-escalate the brewing fight.

Nana picked up the twenty-dollar bill from the table. "How'd you like to win your money back, Rocky?"

Eager to divert a disaster, Rocky said, "Sure."

"I bet you twenty bucks Harvey shows up at my room to prove how wrong I was." She glanced at her watch. "I'm guessing around eight o'clock."

Rocky noted the twinkle in Harvey's eyes as he stared at Nana. "No way in hell I'm taking that bet."

"Double down?" she asked.

Rocky laughed. "If I don't want to gamble on twenty bucks, then I'm certainly not eager to lose forty."

Queen Bea shrugged. "It was worth a shot."

"I admire your effort," Rocky said.

"Want us to deal you in?" one of the ladies asked Rocky.

"I can't stay long, but thank you," Rocky told her.

"You working a case?" Queen Bea asked. Then she looked at her friends. "My grandson is a private detective." They all nodded because Queen Bea had most likely told them at least once a day. "I think I would've made a great lady detective." She looked up at Rocky. "Do you think it's too late for me to start a new career? Things go missing around here all the time."

Rocky frowned. "What kind of things?" His mind automatically went to jewelry, cash, and prescription drugs.

"Dentures, eyeglasses, and canes," Queen Bea said as she looked at her fresh hand.

Rocky bit back his laughter. Those items were most likely misplaced or forgotten rather than stolen. Queen Bea liked to keep her mind sharp, so he said, "I think it's a good idea to help your friends."

Queen Bea whooped, but it turned into a cough. The player beside her pushed Nana's glass of water closer to her. She patted the woman on the shoulder, then took a drink. "I'm going to need a hat. I want one like Humphrey Bogart."

"We can do that," Rocky said.

He glanced up and spotted a familiar woman crossing the room at a brisk pace. She was tall and still had an athletic build, even though she had to be in her seventies. Like Grant Duncan, photos of this woman often accompanied articles about Tess, though her name was never provided. Grant and this lady always sat directly behind the defendant's table, and the pair made an interesting contrast. The woman with her snowy white hair and cold blue eyes was the exact opposite of Grant's dark good looks. Light and dark. Cold and hot.

"Is she a resident here?" Rocky asked, tipping his head in the woman's direction.

"She's too old for you, son," one of the fellas playing cards said.

Queen Bea snorted. "She should be so lucky, Herb. Besides, he doesn't swing that way."

The man named Herb looked up from his cards and met Rocky's gaze. "Really?" There was no judgment in the man's scrutiny, only curiosity.

"Yep."

"Her name is Helen Girard," Harvey said. "She's a physical therapist and mostly works in the rehab unit."

"Is she part of your case?" Queen Bea asked.

"Nope," Rocky lied. He smiled down at his grandmother, who squinted up at him. She didn't believe him for a second.

"Full-time residents get to use her services too," Herb added.

"You ought to know," Queen Bea said. "You're in there every week to work on one body part or another."

"I'm eighty-nine years old," Herb said. "Shit hurts."

Rocky chuckled. "That would make a great T-shirt." Herb held up a thumb, then took his turn.

"Herb has a crush on Ms. Girard," the lady beside Nana said.

"I do not, Dottie. You're just jealous."

Dottie scoffed as she looked up at Rocky. "Herb likes his ladies a little on the naughty side."

"Counts you out," Herb countered.

Dottie leveled the man with a death glare before returning her attention to Rocky. "Rumor has it that the lovely Ms. Girard got fired from her previous nursing home."

"It's just a rumor," Herb said. "Kinda like the one I heard about you being easy."

Dottie took a deep breath. "Herb, I can't be both boring and slutty at the same time. Stick to one insult. Christ," she said, shaking her head.

"What did she steal?" Rocky asked.

"Yep, she's part of his case," Queen Bea said.

Dottie shrugged. "No one has said what she took."

"Allegedly took," Herb reminded Dottie.

"Interesting," Rocky said. He'd bet money it wasn't dentures, eyeglasses, or canes. It could've been money or jewelry, but drugs were the safe bet since they had the highest street value. "Do you guys remember which nursing home?"

The card players looked at one another, then shook their heads collectively.

"Ow, my neck," Herb said, lifting his hand up to massage it.

Queen Bea crooked her finger for Rocky to come closer, so he bent toward her. "I'll ask around for you."

Rocky kissed her cheek. "It's not necessary. I'm not on a case."

Queen Bea patted Rocky's cheek. "Don't bullshit a bullshitter."

Rocky grinned. "Yes, ma'am."

"Be careful, Rockford."

He hugged her tight. "Always."

He didn't need his nana to snoop around now that he knew her name and current employer. The rest should be child's play to uncover.

Rocky debated going through a different drive-thru but decided against it when he remembered he had leftovers from the Irish feast Asher had made. Rocky reheated and assembled the boxty, but this time he skipped smearing the mustard on the potato pancake. Since Asher wasn't there to get his feathers ruffled, Rocky decided to eat the meal the traditional way and dip the boxty in the mustard. He regretted his decision when the healthy dose of horseradish made his nose burn and his eyes water. It didn't stop him from wolfing down three potato pancakes loaded with corned beef and cabbage.

Afterward, he cleaned his dirty dishes and headed to his office to see what he could find out about Helen Girard. It didn't take him long to discover she'd worked at Whispering Willows, a retirement community similar to Queen Bea's but a whole lot swankier. They wanted more than a hundred thousand dollars upfront to secure a villa, and the monthly bill depended on the level of care a patient needed. Independent residents like Queen Bea would still pay a small fortune, but the ones who required more nursing care could spend upwards of ten thousand dollars a month.

An establishment like Whispering Willows had a reputation to uphold and couldn't afford a scandal. They would hire the best and fire the rest, so Rocky was more curious than ever about why they'd parted ways with Helen Girard. He didn't question how Queen Bea and her friends had even heard about this woman's employment history. Nurses and aids like to gossip like everyone else. The question was, how could he get someone from Whispering Willows to loosen their lips? The obvious solution was to call them up and pretend to be a potential employer looking for a work reference. Rocky could play it by ear based on the reaction he got from his request.

He didn't bother updating Felix or Jonah because he knew nothing more now than he had when the day started. Okay, he knew Grant Duncan had a rocking hot body and that Tess's friend worked at Queen Bea's retirement village after supposedly getting fired from another facility. That wasn't enough to tap out in a text message, let alone call an emergency meeting.

Rocky switched gears and logged in to his agency program. There were a host of little, low-priority tasks he could knock off his list. Those small items started to pile up after a while, so Rocky worked his way through them. Trudy would never know if he didn't give her a reason to check the activity log.

Fatigue started to seep into his bones, weighing him further down the longer he sat, so Rocky pushed back from his desk. He could scrub the bathroom, check the bird feeders, and water the flowers. After that, he could—

His eyes snagged on one of his mother's watercolor paintings as he crossed the room. Instead of her usual wildlife, this one looked more like a fairy tale complete with a blond-haired prince, a castle, and a white horse with a flowing silvery mane. She'd painted it for his nursery, and though he'd long outgrown fairy tales, Rocky favored this piece more than the others. He had been the little prince his mother dreamed about but never got to hold. On most days, he felt more like the fabled frog.

Rocky thought of the photos he kept hidden in a box inside the office closet. Opening the door felt similar to breaching Pandora's box, but he couldn't stop once the idea came to him. He wanted to see the photographs of his mother again. They deserved to be displayed and treasured, not hidden away because he was ashamed of himself.

He retrieved the box from the closet and carried it out to the living room. Rocky grabbed a beer from the refrigerator and sat down on the rug next to the coffee table. Pandora's box didn't just include his parents' framed photos; it held his mother's journals and sketchbooks and her favorite throw blanket. The collection wasn't only a tribute to his mother either; he'd find proof of the life he'd started to build with Asher too.

It was hard to say what hurt the most: losing a person he'd never met or letting go of someone that was the other half of his soul. Asher's reappearance felt like a second chance, but what had changed since he'd left Vegas?

Nothing.

Christ, if he was going to scratch open old wounds and rip his heart out, he'd need a proper soundtrack. His go-to back in the day was Mazzy Star, so that's what he played. Rocky pulled up the music downloaded to his phone, chose the album *So Tonight That I Might See*, and set it to repeat.

Then he unpacked the memories, one photograph and memento at a time, until all the ghosts he'd laid bare were stacked around him like some sort of fort. By the time the box was empty, Rocky's untouched beer had gone warm, his throat felt raw and dry, and his eyes felt gritty from lack of sleep.

He checked the time and was stunned to see it was two in the morning. His head snapped around when he heard a key in the front door. Seconds later, Asher walked through it just as "Fade into You" started playing. His husband looked both exhausted and relieved, reminding Rocky of the first time Asher had knocked on his door.

"This feels so familiar," Asher said, a smile tugging at his lips as he dropped his duffel bag to the floor. He briefly tilted his head, and Rocky knew why when he said, "The soundtrack is the same, and so are your night owl tendencies."

Rocky stood up in the middle of his fort of memories, his heart racing. "What else is the same?" he asked.

"I still want to pin you to a bed and do very wicked things to you," Asher confessed. "I'd settle for any surface, though."

Like he'd done in Vegas, Rocky crossed the room and took both of Asher's hands in his.

His husband smiled and played along. "I don't know how…" he said. Like the night they met, Asher let the sentence trail off so Rocky could fill in the gaps.

He'd instinctively known that Asher was confessing to not knowing how to be with a man. But now? Asher was more than a little familiar with Rocky's body. "What do you mean?" he asked, going off-script.

"I told you I didn't know how to be with a man, and you led me into your bedroom and showed me the things I'd been missing out on my entire adult life. You put a name to emotions, yearnings, and truths I'd denied myself for over two decades. And I'm still just as lost now as I was then."

"How?"

Asher's voice broke, and he cleared his throat. "I don't know how to let you go."

This was it. The moment Rocky either said goodbye to all that they were or embraced what they could be. He dropped Asher's hands so he could step into his arms. He buried his nose in his husband's neck and whispered, "Then don't."

CHAPTER 15

"I'm not sure I heard you correctly," Asher said. The shiver that worked its way through his husband's big body told Rocky otherwise, but he decided to play along.

Raising his head, Rocky met Asher's stare head-on. "Don't let go."

The war of emotions raging in his husband's eyes was a testament to the amount of pain Rocky had unintentionally put him through. If they hoped to make their marriage work, they'd have to lay it all out in the open. Rocky understood that now. Burying emotions would only get a person so far because they never truly went away. The pain and misery festered in the background, silently feeding off the brain like a zombie and poisoning the soul.

"Are you sure, Ford?"

There were still so many things Rocky couldn't be confident of, but that, he knew. "Yes."

Asher briefly closed his eyes and took a deep, shaky breath. When their gazes collided again, the battle was over, at least temporarily. Rocky only saw peace and contentment now. "Thank fuck," Asher said as he framed Rocky's face with his large hands.

They moved toward one another at the same time, their mouths meeting in the middle and lips parting invitingly. He sucked Asher's tongue into his mouth, letting his teeth softly graze over the flesh until it slid free from Rocky's lips. Asher dropped his mouth to Rocky's neck, licking a path upward until he reached Rocky's ear. Asher tugged the lobe between his teeth, then sucked the sensitive skin just beneath it.

Lust spiked through Rocky's blood, pooling in his groin. One part of his brain wanted to rejoice and shout to the heavens when his dick started to harden. A small, mean voice reminded him that getting an erection and maintaining it were two different things. He'd had his first orgasm in months less than twenty-four hours ago. What if he couldn't do it again for days, weeks, or even months? How long would Asher be satisfied with blowjobs and hand jobs? Suddenly, the shortness of breath he felt wasn't due to anticipation and excitement. A cold sweat broke out over Rocky's skin.

"Hey," Asher said, pulling back so he could look into Rocky's eyes. "Nothing needs to happen tonight. I just want to hold you again. We both need to sleep."

Asher had never made him feel bad about the side effects of his trauma. He'd been patient and understanding, which had only intensified Rocky's yearning to please him. Their sex life had been intense and physical before the incident, and Rocky couldn't believe that Asher could settle for anything less. So, Rocky tried harder, his dick got limper, which made him grow angrier. He would drink, then they'd fight. Asher would plead with him to seek professional help, and Rocky would lash out in any way he could. No make-up sex ever followed, only self-hating recriminations. It was an ugly, vicious cycle that Rocky refused to repeat.

He'd taken the first step by seeking Karen's help, but it would take more effort on his part. Rocky was finally at the place where he was willing to put in the work, no matter how painful it was or how long it took. He couldn't magically let go of the blame he'd been harboring for ruining Asher's career, but the desire to do so was there. That was a damn good start.

"I need to shower first before we turn in," Asher said, his voice breaching Rocky's thoughts.

Rocky stepped out of Asher's embrace and linked their fingers together. "I'll help."

With the soundtrack of their past still playing in the background, Rocky led Asher past his fort of memories and down the hallway toward a new beginning. He didn't stop until they reached the bathroom, where he only let go of Asher long enough to twist the shower faucet on. While the water heated, Rocky turned his attention to stripping his husband's clothes off before tackling his own.

Rocky's cock was only semi-erect, but for once, he wasn't embarrassed. In fact, he had something to brag about. Rocky placed his husband's hand on his dick. "This might be the best I can do for now, but I need to feel your touch."

Asher curled his fingers around Rocky's flesh. "There are other ways of being intimate that don't involve sex," Asher said. "I'll explore each and every one of them with you."

Keeping his eyes locked on Asher's, Rocky said, "I woke up on your side of the bed this morning—well, yesterday—with my face buried in your pillow. Smelling you on my sheets made me so fucking hard, and I came while thinking about you."

"God, getting out of bed had been the most difficult thing I'd ever done in my life."

Rocky scowled up at him as steam filled the small room. "You apprehend the scariest fugitives in the world."

"I do," he agreed. "You were draped over me again and sleeping hard enough to drool on my chest. You made the most pitiful noise when I tried to roll out from under you. You even whispered for me not to go." Asher cupped Rocky's face and pressed their foreheads together. "I'd much rather track down drug cartel members who've infiltrated our cities than disappoint you." After a quick kiss, Asher released Rocky's cock and shoved the shower curtain aside. He stepped over the edge of the tub and extended a hand toward Rocky. "Didn't you mention something about helping me?"

Rocky placed his hand in Asher's and stepped into the tub. "I did." Asher closed the shower curtain, then pulled Rocky into his arms for a languid kiss. Desire thrummed through Rocky's body, and that alone was a huge victory. Rather than trying to build on it or twist it into something he wasn't ready for, Rocky just let it wash over him.

When they separated to catch their breaths, Asher reached for his shower gel. "I'd love to stay in here all night with you, but we both need sleep."

Rocky took the bottle from him and poured a generous amount into his palm. "For once, I'm not afraid of falling asleep."

"You're not?" Asher said.

Rocky rubbed his hands together to form a lather. "Huh-uh." He placed his palms on Asher's chest, rubbed the soap over his skin in large circles. His husband sucked in a sharp breath when Rocky's thumbs grazed over his hard nipples. "I thought I was fighting sleep because of the nightmares, but that wasn't it, or at least not the entire reason."

"What was?"

His hands stilled on Asher's torso. While it was too late at night for the conversation they needed to have, Rocky wanted to show Asher that he was ready to bare his soul. "I woke up each morning regretting that I left you and not knowing how to fix it, or if I should even try."

"Christ, Ford," Asher groused. "And here I thought you were happily building a new life without me."

"I was building a life without you, but I wasn't happy about it. I stumbled along okay until my jackass best friends fell in love and re-minded me of everything I'd given up. Then you appeared out of the darkness like an apparition at Cameron Spencer's house, and I realized my life had become a fucking Dickens novel. The ghosts of my past, pres-ent, and future visited me each night in my sleep. I just wasn't as smart as Scrooge."

Asher grinned. "You didn't shove open your windows and yell at the kid on the street to go buy the biggest goose?"

Rocky chuckled. "No."

He slid his hands lower on Asher's belly, relishing the feel of his husband's muscles flexing and responding to his touch. Rocky continued the downward trek until his fingers slid through Asher's pubic hair and curled around the erection jutting from his pelvis. Rocky cupped Asher's balls with his other hand.

"You don't need—"

"I want to," Rocky said. And he did. After the shooting, Rocky had reached for Asher out of obligation or fear of losing him. Now, pleasuring his husband felt like the thing he wanted most in the world. No, not wanted. Needed.

Rocky dropped to his knees in the tub and took his time washing Asher's legs. Christ, he loved the strength in this man, but most especially his powerful thighs. He loved being under them, between them, or bouncing on them as he rode Asher's cock. Rocky wanted to sink his teeth into them, so he did. His husband grunted and flexed his muscles but made no move to get away. Rocky lifted his head and met Asher's hungry gaze as he slid his hands down to wash his husband's tight calves. Hell, even his feet were sexy, but Rocky ignored those for the time being. He stayed on his knees and tilted his head up to meet Asher's intense gaze. Placing his hands on Asher's hips, Rocky guided him back a step to rinse the soap off his husband's body. Rocky ducked his head under the spray and wrapped his lips around the tip of Asher's cock, circling his glans and rubbing his tongue against the sensitive spot beneath it.

Asher balled his hands into fists at his sides instead of sliding them into Rocky's hair as he usually would. Rocky wanted to feel those strong fingers digging into his scalp and yanking on the strands as Asher surrendered to the pleasure. He released Asher's cock and balls to guide his husband's hands to where he wanted them—needed them. Rocky dropped his hands to his lap and silently begged Asher to treat him as he would have before the shooting.

Asher's caress was gentle at first. He ran a hand over Rocky's hair without tangling his fingers in it. His husband ghosted the backs of his fingers over Rocky's cheek and traced his stretched lips as he slowly inched his cock deeper inside Rocky's mouth. Asher's long eyelashes fluttered, and his lids drooped but didn't close. Rocky pressed his tongue up to tease every inch of Asher's dick as he fed it to him. Those tentative fingers tightened ever so slightly against Rocky's head. He knew which buttons to push to drive his husband crazy, and he would press them over and over until all of Asher's hesitation washed down the drain.

Rocky tightened his lips around Asher's cock, applying more suction and earning a grunt from his husband as his reward. Still, Asher maintained rigid control over his forward thrusts, keeping them short and halting before hitting the back of Rocky's throat. Asher's body trembled with restraint, and Rocky tasted his husband's salty essence on his tongue. He knew it wouldn't be long before Asher gave in and fucked his face properly.

Asher cupped the back of Rocky's head and snapped his hips forward, this time going deeper and making Rocky gag a little. His husband's eyes widened in alarm, and Rocky feared he'd call the whole thing off. He gripped Asher's ass in both hands and shoved his face forward, swallowing Asher's cock all the way down until Rocky's nose was buried in Asher's pubic hair.

Rocky swallowed around Asher's cock, and his husband let out a roar loud enough to make any Celtic warrior proud. Asher eased back out of his throat, allowing Rocky to catch his breath before pushing back in deep. Rocky's eyes watered, and his throat burned, but it was the most alive he'd felt in a long time. The tears that slipped down his cheeks were tears of joy, not pain or sorrow.

"Guess what I was thinking about when I took a shower this morning?" Asher asked, snapping his hips hard enough to make his balls slap against Rocky's chin. "This right here. You on your knees and staring at me with those fuck-me eyes. Christ, it's even better than I remembered." Asher's hips jerked as he lost rhythm, and more of his essence landed on Rocky's tongue. He was getting closer.

Rocky teased the crack of Asher's ass, circling the puckered rim and tapping the pad of his finger against his entrance. Rocky relaxed his throat and breathed through his nose as Asher increased his tempo. His pucker flexed against Rocky's finger, so he pressed harder but not enough to penetrate him. He knew the frustration would drive Asher wilder, so he circled, tapped, pressed, and repeated until Asher's hips jerked one last time, and he spilled down Rocky's throat.

Asher continued to buck against his face until the last drop fell, then he helped Rocky to his feet. Asher wrapped his arms around Rocky and kissed him deeply, not minding the taste of his own cum. Asher continued devouring his mouth until the water temperature started to drop. Rocky was reluctant to leave their steamy oasis, but they could continue their exploration someplace where they weren't at the mercy of a water heater.

Rocky reached around Asher to switch off the water and snagged their towels from the rack outside the shower. They made quick work of drying off before heading to Rocky's bedroom. The air-conditioning's chill caused goose bumps to form all over Rocky's body during the short trip, but Asher rubbed them away when he pulled Rocky into his arms.

Asher kissed him with a renewed fervor that made Rocky tingle in all the right places, but he wasn't sure it would be strong enough, and he didn't want to disappoint his husband.

Asher broke the kiss and stared into Rocky's eyes. "Don't overthink it."

"Who, me?" Rocky teased, even though he knew Asher was right. Rocky had read about stress-induced erectile dysfunction enough to know that fretting about his performance would cancel any shuttle launch he'd hoped for. He took a deep breath and nodded.

Asher pressed his lips to Rocky's neck. "Focus on sensations instead of function," he whispered against his skin.

Asher sank his teeth into Rocky's flesh and tugged, and Rocky felt a similar reaction in his core. His husband licked the spot he'd just marked before sucking it between his lips. Asher resumed kissing Rocky's neck, working his way upward until he reached his jaw. Then he nibbled along the jawline to get to Rocky's ear.

"How did that feel?" he asked.

Rocky let out a little moan and swayed on his feet.

Asher chuckled. "That good, huh? I have more tricks."

That, Rocky knew well. He opened his eyes and fell into Asher's bottomless gaze. Rocky didn't fight the fall, or even fear it, because Asher would be there to catch him. He understood this now. Rocky's only regret was that he'd lost a year with the man he loved while he figured it out.

"I want to touch you," Rocky said. "I only explored a few key parts in the shower."

Asher opened his arms in invitation, so Rocky slid his hands beneath them and caressed Asher's broad back, loving the feel of his strong muscles. He felt Asher stiffen beneath his touch and didn't understand why until Rocky's fingers ghosted over a puckered scar on his husband's lower back that hadn't been there the last time he'd seen Asher naked.

He stepped out of Asher's embrace and walked around him to get a better look. He could tell by the angry red color that it was pretty new. Rocky dropped to his knees behind his husband, then ran his fingertip over the blemished skin. He hadn't seen it the other night in the kitchen because Asher's shorts had covered it up. Rocky pressed his lips to the puckered flesh. The scar tissue twitched beneath his ministrations, so he shifted to kissing the skin around it instead.

"Is this a knife wound?" he asked hoarsely.

"Yes."

A mixture of rage and shame washed over Rocky. He wasn't a medical professional, but there was no doubt in his mind the knife had come close to hitting one of Asher's vital organs. Fucking Duggins had promised Rocky he'd always have Asher's back. Where the fuck had he been when some asshole was shoving a knife in it? And what about Rocky? He had been thousands of miles away while Asher recovered from nearly losing an organ, and no one had even thought to call him. Asher was his husband for fuck's sake. He—

Fuck. Why would the marshals have called him? Rocky had left Asher, then filed for a divorce. Rocky must've made a sound of distress because Asher turned around and hoisted Rocky back to his feet.

"I'm fine," Asher said softly. Maybe he was now, but he'd bet big money Asher hadn't been fine immediately after taking a blade to his back.

"How bad was it?" Rocky asked.

"The knife missed my vital organs, but the blade was dirty. I developed a nasty bacterial infection that took longer to recover from than the knife wound itself."

Rocky closed his eyes and tried to swallow back the tears, but they still slid down his face. "I'm sorry I wasn't there to take care of you."

"Hey," Asher said, brushing away his tears. "Look at me." Rocky opened his eyes. "What I'm about to say is going to sound really bizarre, but I promise it makes sense."

"If not, I could talk to Karen about giving us some kind of discount for therapy."

Asher chuckled. "Buy one get one free?"

"At least half off," Rocky countered, then gripped Asher's strong shoulders. "Okay. I've braced myself. Let's hear this bizarre but perfectly sensible thing."

"You might want to sit down," Asher said.

"And you might want to rethink your approach." But just in case, Rocky stepped out of Asher's embrace and led him over to the bed. They settled between the sheets, facing one another.

"I think getting stabbed might've been the second-best thing to ever happen to me."

"What?" Rocky asked, rolling onto his back. "I am definitely calling my therapist first thing in the morning. I bet Karen will work you into her schedule."

Asher laughed and scooted closer, throwing his big thigh over Rocky so he couldn't escape. "Hear me out," he said.

"Like I have a choice," Rocky fired back. Asher started to lift his leg, but Rocky reached out to stop him. "You know damn well how much I love this. I'm ready for an explanation now. You were saying something about how getting stabbed and developing a nasty infection was the second-best thing that ever happened to you." Rocky turned his head and looked at Asher. "I'm afraid to ask about the best thing."

Asher pressed a kiss to his lips. "You know damn well that meeting you takes the top spot."

Rocky pursed his lips while he considered it. "I'm not sure how I like sitting next to a stab wound in the pecking order of priorities."

Asher laughed. "That stab wound put me on medical leave for six weeks, which meant I had a lot of time to think and think and think."

"Sounds familiar."

"I took stock of my life and didn't like what I found. I'm a miserable son of a bitch without you."

The admission stole Rocky's breath. "Same."

"When the position opened in the Savannah field office, I viewed it as fate sending me to you." Asher smiled wryly. "I also figured out where I'd gone wrong with you."

"You didn't do anything wrong, Asher. I couldn't have asked for a better husband. I'm so fucking sorry that you spent even a second wondering what you could've done differently."

Shaking his head, Asher said, "You're wrong, Ford. I was too busy trying to give you what you claimed to want when I should've been focused on what you needed. Me," he added in case Rocky was confused.

Rolling on to his side to face Asher again, Rocky shifted the weight of his husband's thigh to his hip. "I'm an analytical guy."

Asher quirked a brow. "You don't say."

Rocky chuckled as he tried to parse together the right words. "I could never figure out why the sums of my highs and lows never added up." He reached out and cupped Asher's face. "As much as I love the friendships I've made since returning to Savannah, you're the missing piece I need to make my equation complete."

His husband's smile was so sweet, he couldn't resist closing the short gap to taste it for himself.

"That's a fancy way of agreeing with me," Asher said. "I can tell you've been reading more than just Sam Spade books."

Rocky snorted. "Marla started a book club, and she's big into romance these days. I might've picked up a thing or two." He nuzzled his nose against Asher's. "I love you."

Asher swallowed loud enough for Rocky to hear it, so he pulled back to look at him. Too much, too soon? The pirate smile slashed through his panic like a rapier.

"I love you too," Asher said.

They kissed until Rocky barely had enough breath and energy left to yawn. He didn't care that an erection hadn't materialized, and for once, he wasn't worried about falling asleep. But there was something he needed to know first.

"Why me?"

"Hmm?" Asher asked in a drowsy voice. His eyelashes fluttered but his lids remained shut.

"Why was I your first guy?"

Asher slowly opened his eyes and stared at him. "My only," he corrected.

Rocky smiled. "Why am I your only?"

"We've talked about this before."

"We have," Rocky agreed. They had similar stories. Both were raised in Catholic homes and hadn't wanted to upset their families. Like Jonah, Asher had joined the military after school and wasn't free to be out. The longer he kept his secret, the harder it became to tell the truth. "But you never said what it was about me that coaxed you out of the closet."

Asher snorted. "You have such a way with words." Then he took a deep breath. "You might recall that I was part of the task force that took down that douchebag in Vegas."

"I have a hazy recollection."

"Well, we didn't just happen on to the scene. We staked out the place for days." Asher laughed, then said, "Well, more specifically, I was staking out you, who was staking out the place."

"And you thought I was cute?"

"Fishing for compliments, are we?" Asher asked.

Rocky shook his head. "Maybe a few."

Asher cupped his cheek and pressed a quick kiss to his lips. "You were and still are the sexiest person in the world. When the bust went down, I volunteered to take your statement. I just had to see if you were as hot up close."

Rocky laughed. "Then I propositioned you without realizing it."

"And I knew you weren't aware the words had come out of your mouth," Asher admitted.

"And still you came over."

"I'm not even sure I was consciously aware of it when I drove to your apartment. I remember telling the guys I was heading home instead of the bar to celebrate the big takedown. Next thing I knew, I was knocking on your door. I told you I didn't know how to be myself, and you showed me the way." Asher made a little growly noise and tightened his hold on Rocky. "I told myself we'd have sex once and that would be it."

Rocky slid his hands through Asher's hair. "Except you never left."

Asher laughed. "I couldn't. You were everything I never knew I needed. Your handsome face and sweet ass might've lured me to your door, but your wit, loyal heart, and exceptional taste in music is what hooked me. And three months later, I convinced you to marry me. The twelve months that followed our wedding were the happiest of my life."

"The past fifteen months have been the worst," Rocky whispered. "But our dreams weren't broken."

"Only delayed." Asher kissed him once more. "Go to sleep, baby. I'll be here to help you fight all the ghosts," Asher whispered in the dark just before Rocky drifted to sleep.

CHAPTER 16

"Christ, is this going to be an everyday occurrence?"

Asher's gruff morning voice stirred Rocky from a deep slumber, but he refused to open his eyes or lift his head from his husband's chest.

"You should be more concerned if you wake up and I'm not draped over your body like a cheap suit." Rocky yawned. "Fine. I'll go back to my side of the bed."

Asher chuckled and slid his hand down Rocky's back to grab a handful of his ass. "I like you right here," he said, then pressed a kiss to the top of Rocky's head. "Your sleeping position wasn't what I was talking about, though."

Rocky lifted his head and cracked his eyes open. He immediately regretted his decision because it felt like sand had gotten trapped under his lids during sleep. He blinked to clear the grittiness, but it only made Rocky's eyes water and blurred Asher's roguish face. Taking it as a sign, he closed his eyes and lowered his head back to his husband's chest. He started to clarify what Asher had meant, but his exhausted brain finally registered something other than his husband's hunky body. His cell phone was ringing in the living room again. When it finally quieted, faint strands of "Fade into You" teased Rocky's consciousness. He'd left it playing all night.

How apropos, considering their current position. Rocky hoisted his leg higher over Asher's thighs, doing his best to meld deeper into his husband. "Probably a wrong number," Rocky said. Reality snuffed his wishful thinking a second later when the phone started ringing again. "Fuck," he grumbled as he tore himself away from Asher. "Don't go anywhere. I'll be right back."

Asher rolled onto his side and burrowed his head into his pillow. "Hurry."

Indeed. Rocky moved swiftly into the living room and nearly tripped over his forgotten fort when he retrieved the phone from the coffee table. He wasn't at all surprised to see his nana was the one waking him up.

"Good morning, sunshine," he said into the phone.

"You sound like death warmed over," Queen Bea said. "Are you sick?"

"No."

"Hungover?"

"Definitely not. Just tired," Rocky said, rubbing the sleep from his eyes.

"I can't believe you're still in bed."

Her incredulous tone made Rocky panic for a second. Was he late for work again? Rocky squinted at the cable box and groaned when he saw the time.

"It's barely seven o'clock, Nana."

"Hey, it's better than five thirty."

"What in the world propels you out of bed so damn early?" Rocky asked.

"Maureen," Queen Bea answered.

Rocky ran his fingers through his hair, scratching his scalp while trying to conjure a face to go with the name. "Is she one of the ladies you played canasta with?"

Nana snorted. "Hell no. She's one of the night nurses who drags us out of bed at ungodly hours. The dayshift nurses get pissy if we're not up and dressed when they start their rounds at seven. Isn't that right, Deidre?"

This Deidre person responded but Rocky couldn't make out what she said. Queen Bea cackled like a lunatic, so it must've been something witty and not mean.

"They think getting up and sticking to a routine is good for us," Nana said. "I wasn't a believer at first, but now I see the merits. Besides, when you're at the short end of your lifespan, you need to make the best of each minute."

"You'll outlive us all," Rocky said.

"Probably," Nana agreed. Then she had a brief conversation with her nurse before she said, "Oh, good. Deidre is a sweet girl, but she hovers. The coast is clear now, so we can get to the reason for my call."

"What's going on?"

"I asked around and uncovered some answers for your investigation."

"What investigation?" Rocky asked.

"The one involving the rehab nurse," she whispered. "Helen Girard worked at Whispering Willows before coming here."

Rocky had already uncovered that tidbit, but Queen Bea sounded so proud of herself. "Did you find out why she left?"

"Nope. And that only makes me more suspicious. These nurses love to gossip and often forget we're in the room. They share some ridiculously personal things with one another. All of them complain about their former employers. Not Helen. She's been unusually tight-lipped about her former position."

"So, it could all be speculation."

"Wrong, Sherlock. Deidre has a cousin who works at Whispering Willows. She's the one who said Helen left on bad terms, but management shuts down any inquiries about her tenure there."

"Interesting," Rocky said. "Whispering Willows is a pretty swanky place. Maybe she signed a nondisclosure agreement." He'd find out how much information Helen's employer was willing to divulge when he requested a work reference.

"Could be," Nana said. "Do you want me to get the cousin's name so you can interview her?"

Rocky considered it, but how much could this person tell him? Then again, a pattern in speculation and rumors could help guide him toward where to look. Where there's smoke, there's fire. "Sure. You can leave a voice mail if I don't answer when you call back."

"Or I could just give you her name now."

Rocky shook his head. Of course she already had the name. He turned and picked up an envelope from the stack of yesterday's mail and a pen. A shaft of early morning light streamed through the part in the curtains, projecting his shadow onto the wall. It took him a second to realize the protrusion from his midsection wasn't a funhouse effect or kinky shadow puppet.

Glancing down the length of his body, Rocky confirmed that he was indeed sporting a glorious erection. He couldn't wait to get back to the bedroom and show Asher. He'd push his husband onto his back and—

"Rockford," Nana said firmly.

"What?" he asked, cringing because he was sporting wood while talking to his grandmother.

"I said her name is Bethany Fields."

Rocky scribbled the name down on the envelope. "Thank you so much. I gotta run."

"To where? You were sound asleep when I called."

"Asher is here," Rocky said.

"Hell's bells, Rockford. Why didn't you say so? Is he here to stay?"

"Yes."

"Good. Bring that hunk for a visit," Nana said before disconnecting the call.

Rocky plugged his cell phone into the charger, then ran back to the bedroom. He slid to a stop next to Asher's side of the bed. His husband cracked open an eye and stared at his face. Rocky gestured at his morning wood with both hands. "It's not going to ejaculate itself."

Asher snagged Rocky's right wrist and yanked him down onto the bed. As soon as their bodies collided, Asher rolled and pinned Rocky to the mattress. "Good morning."

"Sure is shaping up to be," Rocky quipped, hooking his legs over the back of Asher's thighs.

His husband snapped his hips forward, and Rocky knew it wouldn't take long for Asher to go from semi-interested to full-on let's fuck. Rocky wrapped his arms around Asher's shoulders, holding him even tighter as Asher nuzzled his nose against Rocky's neck.

"I love you," Asher whispered before capturing Rocky's mouth in a hungry kiss.

Rocky parted his lips and welcomed Asher's tongue, sucking it deeper inside his mouth. He wasn't about to break the kiss to tell Asher how he felt; Rocky would show him instead. Asher growled his approval as he increased the tempo of his thrusts, their combined precum acting as a lubricant to aid the glide. Rocky's pucker flexed, desperate to be filled.

Tearing his mouth free, Rocky said, "Get the lube. I want to feel you inside me."

Asher stilled his hips, then lowered his head to nibble Rocky's earlobe. "And you will. There's no need to rush."

Rocky choked back a frustrated groan as he canted his hips to get more of the delicious friction he craved. "I don't agree."

Asher raised his head and met his stare. "Do you have someplace to be?"

"Nooooo, but your dick does. Let's make it happen before things go sideways." Just voicing his worries out loud took some wind out of his sails. *Please no.*

Asher cupped Rocky's face. "Things won't go sideways." He looked and sounded so confident, and Rocky wanted to have that same faith.

"How can you be so sure?"

"It's the want-versus-need thing," Asher said, rubbing his thumb over Rocky's mouth. He pressed down, and Rocky parted his lips to suck the digit into his mouth. Asher's nostrils flared when Rocky rolled his tongue around the tip. "You need to turn off your big, beautiful brain and give control of your pleasure to me."

Like it would be so easy.

"It is that easy," Asher said, pulling his thumb free.

Rocky nuzzled his cheek against Asher's palm. "I sometimes hate that you know me so well."

Asher reached between their bodies and wrapped his fingers

around Rocky's cock. "Seems to me that you like the idea of surrendering everything to me." Asher slowly slid his hand up and down Rocky's shaft. "Put your hands up over your head and keep them there. I want your eyes on me the whole time so I know you're staying in the moment with me."

A dark, delicious shiver hummed through Rocky as he followed Asher's command. His husband inched lower down his body, licking and kissing a trail across Rocky's chest. Asher sucked one nipple between his lips and pinched the other. Rocky fisted his hands in his pillow to keep from tangling his fingers in Asher's thick black hair.

"Just feel," Asher whispered against his stomach as he continued his downward trek. "Just watch."

Rocky jerked when Asher dipped his tongue inside his navel. Asher chuckled, then gently tugged the ticklish flesh with his teeth.

Heat and need continued to build and spread from Rocky's core until every inch of him tingled from his curled toes to his scalp. He felt feverish and delirious with hope. Yesterday morning hadn't been a fluke. He—no, *they*—were going to break the curse.

Asher sank his teeth into the tender flesh at Rocky's hip, making him grunt. "Stop thinking."

Rocky canted his hips, shoving the tip of his dick closer to Asher's mouth.

Cupping Rocky's balls, Asher quirked a brow and said, "I'm in charge. Feel and watch. Remember?"

Rocky observed as Asher lazily licked his cock from root to tip, only breaking their connection when his eyes briefly rolled back in his head.

"I'll allow it once," Asher said before moving on to Rocky's balls. He spent a long time there, licking and sucking while massaging Rocky's taint. He unabashedly spread his legs wider to give Asher easier access.

Rocky was desperate to feel Asher's lips around his cock, but his husband traded off between licking his shaft and sucking his nuts.

"Look how you tremble," Asher said. "I know what you want, but I'm giving you what you need."

"I need to come," Rocky whispered hoarsely.

"Yes, you do. And you will," Asher said as he leaned over to open the bedside table. He retrieved the bottle of lube and returned to his position between Rocky's legs. "In due time."

Asher flipped open the bottle and drizzled a generous amount of lubricant over his fingers. Rocky's nerves kicked back in, threatening to ruin the party before it got started. It had been over a year since they'd had penetrative sex. He expected discomfort, but would it cause him to lose his erection? That had never been an issue before—

Asher sucked the head of Rocky's dick into his mouth, making Rocky forget about everything else but how good his husband made him feel.

"Ohhhh God," he groaned, bucking his hips as Asher swallowed him down inch by inch. Had his mouth always been this hot and wet? His tongue this wicked? "Don't stop, baby. Please don't stop."

With his dark eyes locked on Rocky's, Asher worked his mouth up and down Rocky's shaft. The growling sounds Asher made were indecent and only turned him on more. Rocky yanked his own hair, wishing it was Asher's instead. Then his husband pressed a lubed finger to his ass. Rocky tensed at first but relaxed when Asher just circled the rim without attempting penetration. It stimulated his nerve endings, triggering deeper cravings and allowing Rocky to relax his bunched muscles.

Asher sucked Rocky down to the root and swallowed. With his throat muscles milking Rocky's glans, Asher slipped a finger inside Rocky's ass. He tried not to buck deeper inside his husband's throat when Asher curled his finger up and pegged his prostate, but he'd forgotten how sensitive he was. Asher was supposed to be in control, but Rocky was a greedy bastard.

He bucked his hips, riding Asher's finger and fucking his mouth. "I'm going to come," he warned in case Asher wanted to pull back. He didn't.

Asher slipped a second finger inside his ass, pumping and priming the well as his saliva dripped down Rocky's cock from his efforts. The pleasure built and built until the tension became painful, making Rocky feel like an unstable pressure cooker. He wanted the release more than anything, but he fought against it because he wasn't sure when, or if, he'd be able to do it again.

Asher let Rocky's dick slide free from his mouth and pulled his fingers from his ass. "Stay with me," he said as he crawled up Rocky's body with the lube in his hands.

Rocky took the bottle and drizzled it over Asher's cock before stroking his fist up and down to slick his husband's erection.

Asher captured his mouth for a deep kiss as he positioned his body between Rocky's legs, lining up the head of his dick and slowly pushing inside. The penetration burned, and Rocky's worst fears started to manifest when his arousal started to wane.

"Relax, baby. Let me in," Asher said. "I'll make you feel so damn good."

Rocky breathed through the stretch and shifted his thoughts to how Asher felt in his arms. He raked his fingers through his husband's hair and explored the broad muscles of his back. Then he dropped his hands to grip his husband's ass with both hands, pulling him deeper inside. Asher's hips bucked forward, and the head of his cock nudged Rocky's prostate.

"Yes," Rocky cried out. "More."

Asher buried his nose in Rocky's neck and began making love to him. Rocky locked his legs around his husband's hips and his arms around Asher's shoulders. His husband growled and increased the tempo of his thrusts, pushing Rocky past the pain and into pleasure so acute it stole his breath.

Rocky's orgasm rippled through him with the strength of a tsunami, making his back bow up from the bed. His lips parted on a silent scream as wave after wave of pleasure rushed over him. Asher grunted like a caveman as his body bucked and jerked, spilling inside Rocky. His husband went completely lax, his massive body pushing Rocky deeper into the mattress and making it harder for Rocky to breathe. Unlike the panic attacks, Rocky welcomed this kind of breathlessness.

Asher started to shift away from him, but Rocky tightened his embrace. "God, you wreck me." His husband's voice was a mixture of anguish and awe, echoing the volcanic emotions building inside Rocky. "Don't you ever leave me again."

"I won't," Rocky promised.

Asher peeled himself free a moment later. He reached down to snag his discarded T-shirt off the floor and cleaned the messes off their stomachs and cocks before tossing the shirt back onto the hardwood. Rocky wanted to protest his slovenly ways, but his body was still in the limp-noodle stage.

"Roll over," Asher said.

"Are you always going to be this damn bossy, or just in bed?" Rocky asked, even as he turned onto his side, facing away from Asher. He knew what was coming next, and he loved it just as much as when his husband pinned him to the bed.

Asher curved his body around Rocky's and pressed a kiss under his ear. "We're still in bed, aren't we?"

Rocky wanted to come up with a smartass reply and probably would have if he weren't so exhausted. The orgasm was a much stronger sleep aid than melatonin or meditation, but Rocky tried to blink it away. If he gave in, he ran the risk of sleeping until noon. He was eager to dust off his accounting skills and—

"Stop thinking and go to sleep, Ford."

"I should get up and start caffeinating my brain." But he relaxed deeper into his pillow.

"When do you need to be in the office?" Asher asked.

If this were a typical week, he could work from home because Peter and Trudy would handle anything that walked through the agency door. This week was anything but ordinary, though it was hard to work up any regret when he was snuggled up next to his husband. Rocky pushed his ass harder against the spoon Asher had formed around him and yawned. "Not until nine thirty or ten. What about you?"

"I'm off today," Asher said. "Go back to sleep for a little bit. I'll make sure you're awake in time." His husband tightened his hold around Rocky's waist. "I'll even make you an omelet first."

"Fine."

Asher chuckled. "Like you ever stood a chance."

As promised, Asher kissed Rocky awake ninety minutes later. "Go hop in the shower. I'll start coffee and breakfast."

"Or you could get in the shower with me."

"I promised to make you breakfast." And Asher always kept his promises. Unlike him. Asher swatted Rocky's ass, then rolled away from him. "That wasn't a dig, Ford."

"Stop reading my mind," Rocky groused.

"Stop being so predictable."

Rocky rolled onto his back, prepared to argue with his husband some more, but ended up just watching Asher work through his stretches. Fuck, his husband was stunning. Beneath all the masculine beauty beat the heart of a romantic warrior. Someone bold and brave and loyal. Most importantly, Asher was all Rocky's. He swallowed down his disappointment when his dick didn't join the I-love-Asher fan club. Then his eyes fell to the scar on his husband's lower back. He could've died. Rocky took a few deep breaths, loosening the pressure in his chest before it could take hold.

"And if I want breakfast in bed?" Rocky asked, trying to command his thoughts instead of letting them control him.

Asher paused halfway through pulling on a pair of shorts. "Weren't you the one fretting about getting to work?"

"That was then."

His husband chuckled and resumed the awful task of covering his private parts. "Up and at 'em."

"Fine," Rocky said as he threw back the covers. "Rain check on breakfast in bed."

Instead of lingering in the shower, Rocky rushed through his routine. The smell of crisp bacon made his mouth water when he stepped into the hallway.

"I didn't know we had bacon," Rocky said.

"Because you didn't buy it. I did."

Unlike the first morning when they made breakfast together, Rocky didn't resist the urge to touch and kiss Asher. The sun streamed through the windows, bathing the table in cheerful light as they ate and worked on a Sudoku puzzle together. Something stronger than protein and caffeine fueled Rocky's brain, and something warmer than sunshine filled his soul.

Hello, hope, my old friend. It was so good to see her again.

Rocky tapped the newspaper. "The four can't go there. See?" he said, gesturing to where the number appeared in the same column a few rows down.

"Damn it," Asher grumbled as he scribbled out the four.

"That's why you use a pencil for these puzzles." They'd had the same debate over the *New York Times* crossword puzzles that had become their Sunday morning ritual. Asher's dogged determination and Rocky's broad vocabulary made for a potent combination. Still, neither of them were smart enough to avoid the need for an eraser.

Asher smirked up at him. "You don't need a pencil if you're good enough."

Rocky looked at the messy puzzle, then back at Asher. No words were needed.

Asher chuckled and set the pen down. "While you were in the shower, my landlord called and said my house will be ready for me to move in this weekend."

"A little early for him to call you, wasn't it?"

"Nah," Asher replied. "It's just how he operates. He inherited the early-bird trait from his mother."

Rocky narrowed his eyes as jealousy crept in like a storm cloud. "You sound like you know this guy pretty well." How many times had they discussed the rental contract or set a move-in date?

Asher laughed and leaned forward to kiss the pout from his lips. "I should know him well since I'm married to his son."

Rocky flopped back against his seat. "You called my dad to let him know you were moving before you told me?" And why had his father kept Asher's secret?

"Don't look so betrayed," Asher said. "We weren't conspiring against you."

Rocky ran a hand through his hair. "Since when does my dad have rental properties?" How had he not known this?

"Ford," Asher said calmly. "Before I accepted the position in Savannah, I phoned your parents and asked for both their forgiveness and their blessing."

"What? Why?" Rocky wasn't offended. It just seemed like such an antiquated practice—one Asher hadn't followed the first time around.

"I'd vowed to love you and put your needs above all others, including myself, and I didn't do that. I'm deeply sorry."

It felt like the invisible hand was wringing Rocky's heart again. The anguish in Asher's voice and the pain etched on his face rendered him speechless. Rocky's lips moved, but no words came out.

"I didn't just let you down. I let your parents down also," Asher continued. "So I wanted to apologize for my selfishness, state my intentions to win you back, and get their blessing."

Rocky shook his head. "I can't believe you think any of this is your fault."

"None of it was your fault either, Ford," Asher said. "You can't see that, though. You're still blaming yourself for Julia Warner's actions. You see her as another victim instead of the woman who set you up."

"She was really sick, Asher."

"You don't know that. She used you to ferret out the location of their hookups, then followed you. This wasn't a spur-of-the-moment decision, but it's easier for you to believe that she was sick. Either way, it doesn't excuse her actions. What her husband and sister-in-law did was fucking awful, but she's the monster here. Her nieces and nephews were already losing their father, and she killed their mother. And what about her own kids? They're parentless too." Asher's voice shook with anger, and he shoved back from the table and began pacing the length of the room. "Fuck, I didn't mean to start this conversation before you went to work." He took a calming breath and said, "You might be ready to forgive her for involving you, but I'm not. I don't know if I ever will be."

Rocky sat quietly and stared at the table. This was the same argument they'd had countless times, but it was the first instance where Rocky was willing to admit there was some truth in what Asher said. He now understood that his husband's anger hadn't been directed *at* him; Asher had been—and still very much was—furious on his behalf. He pushed back his chair too and went to him. Asher stopped pacing and opened his arms.

"You did nothing wrong," Asher whispered, folding Rocky into his embrace. "One day, you'll believe it too. Until then, I'm going to remind you."

Rocky rested his forehead against Asher's shoulder. "Tighter," he whispered.

Asher obeyed, squeezing Rocky harder. "I love you so fucking much. I promised your parents I wouldn't fuck it up this time."

Rocky lifted his head. "Did you use that salty language? My mom is a sophisticated lady."

Asher scoffed. "Michelle is indeed, but I believe her exact response was 'you better not fuck this up.'" Tilting his head, Asher pursed his lips together while he thought. "Or maybe she threatened to fuck me up."

Rocky laughed. "That sounds more like something my sister would say."

"Yeah, we did have some conversations over Zoom, so it could've been CeCe."

"Tell me how this rental thing came about again? Did my dad venture off into a new business? I knew he bought a fixer-upper to flip."

"It's the same house," Asher said. "I called at just the right time. All the major renovations were nearly done when our paths crossed at the Spencer home. By the time I returned from getting them settled, the house only needed the carpets shampooed and fresh paint."

Rocky narrowed his eyes. "Did you really plan to move into the house, or was this whole thing a setup between you and my folks?"

Asher shook his head. "I'm being a hundred percent honest. I had every intention of moving into the house until I could win you back."

"Had, huh?"

Asher took a deep breath. "I'll still accept your parents' kind offer if you need more time. I don't want to rush you into anything. Maybe you should hold out for romantic dinners and slow dances under the magnolia tree." Rocky's heart melted from the earnest and hopeful gleam in Asher's eyes. "What do you want me to tell my landlord?"

They still had so much to discuss and work out, but one thing was for sure. Rocky didn't want to live apart from Asher for one more second.

"Call the guy and let him know you've already found a place."

CHAPTER 17

"**F**ord."

"Hmmm?" he asked without looking up from the pot of chili. Rocky mentally reviewed the spices and the amounts of each he'd added as he continued to stir. Had he forgotten a seasoning or added too many? His backyard was brimming with people—some familiar faces and some new—and Rocky didn't want his dish to suck. God, how he longed for the days when he didn't care what people thought of him or his limited ability to cook.

Asher stepped up behind Rocky and slid his arms around his waist. "Oh, good, you're back."

Rocky chuckled. "I haven't gone anywhere."

"Maybe not physically. I said your name thrice before you heard me."

The *Schitt's Creek* reference made Rocky smile. It hadn't taken Asher long to get hooked on the show. They'd binged most of the seasons the past few evenings, usually while sharing Ben & Jerry's. Ice cream kisses had become Rocky's new favorite thing.

Asher rested his chin on Rocky's shoulder. "The chili looks done to me and smells incredible."

Rocky smiled at the *Schitt's Creek* reference.

"Was this barbecue a bad idea?" Asher asked. "Our friends seem to be getting along really well. My team might be a little suspicious of

Felix, but it comes with the territory. They'll warm up to him. They think Jonah and his supercomputer Stella are pretty badass. And everybody loves Marla and Betty."

Rocky glanced out the kitchen window and saw that the party was going strong. Their friends were mingling and having a good time, so why couldn't he relax? Rocky had nearly made himself sick, worrying what Asher's team would think about him. He'd wanted to make a better first impression than the one he'd made on Duggins, but things weren't looking too good.

Rocky had earned his first strike when the trio of trouble's snooping interfered with the Spencer family's relocation plans. The second strike came when Dandridge caught Rocky showing his ass after the Snickerdoodle fiasco. He'd prepared himself for cool indifference at best and outright hostility at worst, but the guys had been really nice when they introduced themselves.

But by that point, he'd put so much pressure on himself not to fuck things up he had unintentionally erected shields. Rocky knew he was coming off as stiff and aloof. They probably felt unwelcome, which couldn't be further from the truth. It was nice putting a different name with their faces besides the goon squad numbers Felix had assigned them. He learned Dandridge's first name was Kurt. Goon Three, with the tawny hair and cumin-colored freckles, introduced himself as Zack Beaumont. Goon Four, with the white-blond hair and vibrant green eyes, was really named Eddie Chandler. None of the guys brought dates, which was a bummer because Rocky was curious about the guy Dandridge was engaged to.

All of them seemed happy for the invite and had even brought potluck dishes of their own. Even though their contributions were little more than frat-boy fixings, Rocky appreciated the thought and used it as an excuse to retreat to the kitchen. Once there, he became fixated on the chili instead of pulling himself together. Asher recognized the ploy and followed Rocky, but he was already sinking into the cognitive quicksand before his husband arrived and pulled him to safety.

"Ford?" Asher prodded.

It took him a second to remember what they'd been discussing. "No, the barbecue wasn't a mistake." Rocky heaved a sigh. "I just hope I can say the same about making this chili. It's not too late for me to tuck it away in the refrigerator. No one has to know. There are plenty of other things to eat."

"Don't be silly," Asher said. "If it makes you feel better, I'll act as quality control." He maneuvered Rocky out of the way, then got a clean spoon out of the silverware drawer.

"How brave of you," Rocky said, snatching the utensil out of his hand and dipping it into the pot. He blew on the chili to cool it off before holding it up to Asher's lips.

"Your chili is delicious. Nice and thick and full of flavor without being too spicy. I want to eat this on top of my burger."

Rocky blew out a relieved breath.

Asher cupped his cheek and drew him in for a brief kiss. "I know it's easier said than done, but stop worrying and just enjoy yourself, okay?"

He nodded. "I'll try." Rocky turned the stove off and set the lid back on the pot. "Let's get back out there."

Asher's phone rang. Rocky glanced down and saw Duggins's name lit up on the screen. Asher declined the call and returned his cell to his pocket. "Let's take the fruit and veggie trays out to snack on until it's time to throw the meat on the grill."

Rocky had so many questions, but it wasn't the time to delve into them. He opened the refrigerator and pulled out the trays, handing one to Asher and taking the other himself.

"Oh, good," Dandridge said, "here they come. Maybe Rocky can settle this debate."

Rocky laughed. "Um, I can try."

"What identifiers did you give to the goon squad to give them away?"

Rocky set the fruit tray on the picnic table. Then he pivoted to his husband, who wore a sheepish grin on his face. "You really told them about the goon squad moniker?"

"I told Dandridge," Asher replied. "He must've told the others."

"Yeah, yeah, yeah," Zack said. "We need to know how you ranked us."

He looked to Felix and Jude for help, but those two assholes just shrugged. "You can't remember, Felix?" Rocky asked. "You're the one who numbered them."

Felix flipped Rocky off while Jude laughed and checked out Felix's back.

"The bus didn't leave tread marks when it ran over you, Ace," Jude said.

Felix flipped him off too.

"Oh, they assigned us numbers. How did you rate us?" Eddie asked, waggling his brows. "Was I number one? I have bigger muscles."

"Bigger mouth, maybe," Zack countered.

"Okay, here's how it went," Rocky said. "Asher was goon one, Dandridge was two, Zack was three, and Eddie was four."

"Why did Asher get the top spot?" Dandridge asked, an adorable pout playing at his lips.

"Who cares?" Eddie asked. "They clearly saved the best for last, right, Rocky?"

"Care to field this one?" Rocky asked Felix.

"Not when you're handling it so well," his friend replied drolly.

"Fine," Rocky said. "The Felix Franklin goon ranking system was based on the order in which you spoke. Asher was the first, then Dandridge, and so on."

Eddie cupped his mouth with both hands. "Boooo."

"Lame," Zack added.

"Speaking of lame," Felix said. "Please tell me you're serving us more than celery and strawberries."

"Of course," Rocky replied. "We have burgers, hot dogs, brats, and Impossible Burgers. Lots of sides to choose from like coleslaw, baked beans, mac and—"

"Go back," Jonah said. "A what burger?"

"Impossible Burger. It's a plant-based mixture that mimics hamburger," Avery said. "You've eaten it before."

Jonah screwed up his face in mock horror. "I have not."

Avery snorted. "I used it to make tacos last week."

"No, you didn't. That was beef," Jonah said adamantly.

Avery shook his head. "No, it wasn't."

"Huh," Jonah said. "I didn't notice the difference."

"Yeah, well, your heart and liver did," Avery said, tucking himself under Jonah's arm.

Jude narrowed his eyes at Felix. "Have you pulled that switcharoo on me?"

"Hell no," Felix said. "If this fake-meat tomfoolery is the result of Avery and Rocky working together, then I say we break them up. And who here today doesn't eat meat?" He scanned the gathering like the mere thought was an egregious act of sedition.

Dandridge raised his hand. "I'm a vegan."

Jude and Felix stared at him like they couldn't fathom such an awful thing.

"Really?" Jonah asked. "You seriously don't eat meat?"

"What kind of meat are we talking about?" Marla sassily asked as she sauntered over. She'd worn a shimmery western-style shirt, a flouncy skirt in the same ivory color, intricately designed leather boots, and a red glittery cowgirl hat atop her head. She'd plaited her wig into two long braids that nearly reached her waist. "All meat isn't created equal." They laughed at her obvious double entendre. She looped her arm through Dandridge's. "They pump so many additives, hormones, and other bad things into our food. Don't let them bust your balls for doing the healthy thing."

Dandridge smiled. "I'm getting used to the teasing. To be honest, it's a rather new lifestyle change since I met my boyfriend."

"Fiancé," Eddie corrected.

"Another recent development," Zack added.

"Congratulations, darling," Marla said, leaning forward to kiss his cheek. "That's a whole lot of change all at once."

Dandridge smiled. "I've struggled with it at times."

"With the man or meat?" she asked.

"The meat," Dandridge admitted. "I'm looking forward to trying the Impossible Burgers, though. I've heard great things."

"Don't you try to sneak one of those on my plate," Felix said, bouncing his menacing glare between Rocky and Avery.

"You wouldn't notice if they did," Jonah replied.

"Sounds like a challenge to me," Jude said. "You up for it, Ace?"

"Only if you do it with me," Felix replied.

Avery rubbed his hands together. "This should be good."

Jude narrowed his eyes. "Who's cooking? No offense, Rocky, but I hear it's not your best gig."

Rocky couldn't deny it but flipped Jude off anyway.

Asher raised his hand. "I'll be doing the grilling."

"I'll help you with the seasoning," Avery said. "There are a few tricks I've learned."

"Wait a minute," Jonah said. "This sounds like you've been substituting my meat with the plant stuff for a while."

Avery just smiled and shrugged.

"Fine," Jude said. "I'll join the challenge."

"I'll put Marla in charge to ensure neither of you cheat," Rocky told them.

She shimmied her shoulders. "Well, I am dressed for such an honor."

Eddie leaned toward her and said, "I could've loaned you my pearl-handled six-shooter to complete your outfit."

Marla threw her head back and laughed throatily, then kissed Eddie's cheek. "Oh, I like you." The marshal's fair skin flushed a bright pink, making his hair look even whiter and his eyes greener.

"Who forgot to invite Morty Fishbein?" Avery asked.

"This isn't a Texas-style barbecue," Felix replied.

Those who were familiar with *The Golden Girls* laughed. Those who weren't looked at each other in confusion.

"Another Blanche Devereaux reference," Rocky told Asher.

"Ah," he said. "I guess we'll start that series next."

Asher lit the charcoal in the massive grill they'd purchased that morning at the hardware store. They'd stood in the aisle debating gas versus charcoal when the owner, Sal, pointed out a model that offered both options. Of course, it happened to be the biggest one the store sold, which suited Asher. Rocky wasn't the only size queen in this relationship. The gigantic grill also happened to be on sale, which made Rocky happy. Win-win.

They'd both loved their joint purchase, but their approach to assembling it was as different as night and day. Even though they were both mechanically inclined, Asher preferred to build things without reading the instructions. Rocky liked to scan the directions from start to finish before taking the pieces out of the plastic. They'd compromised. Rocky read the step-by-step instructions out loud while Asher removed the plastic and laid things out where he thought they'd go. They made a great team.

"Want my help?" Rocky asked when Asher and Avery came out of the house carrying the platters of meat.

"No," everyone said.

Rocky took it for the good-natured jabbing they'd intended. He hoped to make them eat their words after they sampled his chili.

"How many more people are you expecting to show up?" Dandridge asked when he saw the volume of meat lining both parts of the grill. His voice sounded a little strained, so Rocky glanced over at him. The man's eyes looked glassy as he stared at the food.

Rocky bumped his shoulder against Dandridge's to nudge him out of his trance. "Want to help me set out the side dishes and condiments?"

"Uh, yeah, sure," he said after one last longing look at the meat sizzling on the grill.

Rocky and Dandridge arranged the food on the large, rectangular folding table, another new purchase, while the other attendees launched into an animated discussion about the best side dishes. Rocky never expected it to get so heated, but Asher threw down the gauntlet when he remarked that Trish's Diner made the best macaroni and cheese he'd ever had.

Marla placed her hands on her hips. "Honey, have you ever sampled my macaroni and cheese?"

Asher blinked, then looked at Rocky for help. Rocky held up his hands and backed away, signaling to Asher that he was on his own. "No," his husband slowly said, "but I do know your cinnamon rolls are amazing."

Marla cackled like a villain. "Nice try, darling."

"Your cinnamon rolls are the best I've ever had," Asher amended.

"That's more like it." She crooked her finger, and Asher lowered his head for a kiss on his cheek.

Asher glared at Rocky when Marla sauntered away and he answered with a shrug. His husband would have to learn how to become a proper Southern gentleman by trial and error. He'd survived the first battle with a Southern lady but just barely.

Once Asher finished grilling, Avery and Marla worked together to administer the taste test. Rocky couldn't tell by looking if the plant-based burger was option A or B. Marla made the guys write down their answers so they wouldn't influence one another. Jude guessed correctly, but Felix didn't.

"How'd you know?" Felix asked him.

"There was something slightly different about the texture," Jude said, then took another bite. "It's delicious, though." He looked at Avery. "This is really healthier?"

Avery launched into a spiel about lower saturated fats and other health benefits while everyone loaded their plates with food.

"Better watch out, Jude," Jonah cautioned. "Next thing you know, Avery will have you drinking sweat-sock stew as part of a weekly cleanse."

"Gross. What's that?" Jude asked.

Avery rolled his eyes and elbowed Jonah. "Thundercloud is adamantly opposed to herbal tea and comes up with very slanderous names for it."

"Some of that stuff does smell like dirty gym socks," Rocky said. "Peter and I have a do-not-brew list at the office for Trudy."

Everyone laughed as they settled around the picnic table or in lawn chairs to dig in. Rocky waited nervously for feedback from his chili and hoped it wouldn't come in the form of retching.

The first compliment came from the last person Rocky expected when Dandridge hovered over Eddie's bowl and inhaled deeply. "Damn, that chili smells like heaven."

Eddie pivoted a half turn on the bench to keep Dandridge away from his food. He raised a spoonful to his mouth and straightened. Rocky held his breath while waiting for a reaction. Eddie let out a little moan as he finished chewing. Then he turned back around to face Dandridge. "I'd planned to say you're not missing out on anything, but damn, you really are." He looked around the table. "Who made this? I will marry you right now."

Several hands went up at once, including Rocky's.

"I'd never planned on marrying one man, let alone five." Eddie shrugged. "Fuck it. This is damn good chili."

One by one, the guys lowered their hands, leaving Rocky as the sole survivor.

"I'm already taken," he said with a casual shrug.

Eddie chuckled. "So I can see."

Rocky turned his head and caught Asher glaring menacingly at Eddie. He kissed Asher's firm lips. "Very taken," he added, hoping to soften the frown lines marring his handsome face.

"Permanently taken," Asher amended.

After Eddie's high praise, the others tried the chili too. Some of them added it as toppers on their hot dogs and burgers, others ate it as a soup as God had intended it, and Dandridge moped.

"I'll figure out a good vegan recipe," Rocky promised him.

The debates over food continued through the meal, then segued into bets on who played cornhole the best, and so the tournament began.

"Hold my hat, baby," Marla said to Amos. "Mama is going to whip some ass." And she did.

Afterward, Amos showed everyone who was boss at horseshoes. Watching his and Asher's two worlds merging so beautifully filled Rocky with happiness he'd never experienced before because of Duggins's hostility right out of the gate. Rocky understood the source of it and even sympathized at first. He'd hate to watch Asher fall in love with someone else too. The mere thought caused him to tighten his hold on his man. Asher dropped a kiss on top of his head when he pulled free to take his turn.

Asher silenced a few more calls as the barbecue progressed. Were they all from Duggins? A sense of foreboding grew in Rocky's gut. There was no way in hell Asher's former partner would accept being ignored for long. In fact, when Rocky's cell phone rang twenty minutes later, he expected to see Duggins's name appear on the screen.

"Something wrong?" Asher asked.

"I don't know," Rocky replied. "It's somebody local." He accepted the call and said, "Rocky Jacobs."

"Hi, Mr. Jacobs, this is Grant Duncan. Do you have a minute to talk?"

Rocky stiffened, then turned to find Felix and Jonah in the crowd. "Yes, I do. Give me just a second to step away from a party."

"Oh, I don't want to disrupt your evening."

"It's no problem," Rocky assured Grant, waving to get his friends' attention. Felix and Jonah stood up and headed toward him, and Rocky nodded his head toward the house so they'd follow. He turned and held up his index finger to Asher, who looked more curious than annoyed.

The guys followed Rocky to his office, which was way too small for the three of them. "Okay," he said, "I'm going to put you on speakerphone so my podcast partners can hear you too."

"Oh, great. Hi, guys." Felix and Jonah both said hello in return. "Listen," Grant said, "against my better judgment, my mom has agreed to meet with you."

Rocky forgot their close quarters and nearly punched Felix in the face when he did his celebration fist pump. Felix playfully pushed Rocky's shoulders while Jonah scowled at both of them.

"That came out sounding wrong," Grant said. "I didn't mean to imply I think you're bad people."

"We get it," Felix assured him. "Your mom has been through a lot, and you're just looking to protect her. I respect that."

"We all do," Jonah said, reaching out to rub the tip of Felix's nose.

Rocky squelched a laugh because Felix was such a brownnoser when it suited him.

Unaware of their immature antics, Grant continued, "I can't promise she will participate in the podcast, but she'd like to meet with you to discuss it."

"Fair enough," Rocky said, liking their odds. "When would be a good time for your mom?"

"She and her friend will be leaving on a much-deserved cruise on Friday. She has a lot to do before then, so her only free evening is Wednesday. Will that work for you?"

Rocky had a therapy appointment, but he could easily reschedule it. "I'm free," he said. "What about you guys?"

"I need to juggle a few things, but I'll make it happen," Felix said.

Jonah checked his phone. "I'm free. What time?"

"Would six thirty work?" Grant asked.

They all agreed.

"Thanks, Grant," Rocky said.

"Don't thank me yet, fellas. My mother is a handful." He got quiet for a second. "And don't make me regret this." Grant hung up before they could assure him of their good intentions.

"Well, Major," Felix said. "It looks like you're going to get your crack at solving the mysteries of Tess Hamilton."

"No way she'll resist your charm," Jonah said.

"Just try not to scare her with your intimidating stare, big guy," Felix said as he reached for the door. "I gotta get out of this tiny space. One of you added too many onions to your chili."

They followed Felix out into the hallway.

"I'll try not to scare her if you try not to shove your nose too far up her ass," Jonah told Felix.

"It'd be the most excitement she's had in a long time," Felix countered. He pointed at Rocky. "Don't lay your charm on too thick, or you might suffocate the poor woman."

The three of them jerked to a stop when they reached the archway between the kitchen and the living room. Dandridge stood at the stove, eating chili directly from the pot.

"Come on," Felix said. "Surely your mama taught you better manners."

Dandridge snapped his head up. The guilt and shame etched on his face might've been comical if the man weren't truly devastated. "This is so wrong."

Jonah patted his shoulder. "Buddy, we caught you eating chili, not sucking some other dude's dick."

Dandridge dropped the spoon into the chili pot, then wiped the back of his hand over his mouth. Rocky was grossed out by both reactions. "My boyfriend would rather I suck someone else's dick than eat meat or dairy."

"Fiancé," Felix corrected.

Rocky kicked Felix to shut him up. There was clearly a big problem with the relationship if Dandridge kept forgetting they were engaged, not to mention the shame eating they'd witnessed.

"Yeah," Dandridge said. "I can't go home with meat on my breath."

Jesus. Rocky was suddenly glad Dandridge hadn't brought his guy to dinner. "I have a spare toothbrush in the bathroom."

"Yeah, okay," Dandridge said, looking longingly at the chili before walking away. The trio of trouble stepped aside so he could head toward the bathroom.

"The second drawer on the left," Rocky told him.

Dandridge held up a hand to acknowledge him but didn't say anything.

"Poor guy," Felix said. "He should be glad Marla didn't witness this, or she'd be at his house first thing in the morning trying to fix his life too."

"And a damn fine job I did with you ungrateful lot," she said from the open sliding glass door. "Did I hear that some little lamb chop is in trouble?"

"Dandridge," Felix said quickly, then looked at Rocky. "What? If I can throw your ass to the wolf, I surely wouldn't hesitate to feed Gingersnap to her."

"Wolf," Marla said. "I like it. You boys clear out of here and leave that fine man to me."

"Yes, ma'am," they all replied.

"Not so fast," Marla said, wrapping her wrist around Rocky's bicep to stop him.

Felix and Jonah practically ran to evade capture. Rocky shook his head as he met her warm brown gaze. "Hi, Mama."

"Hello, Pretty Boy. You look so much better. Are you okay?"

"Getting there."

Marla studied him for a second and must've liked what she saw because she nodded. "Give me a kiss and get out."

Rocky kissed her cheek before hustling out the back door. Asher met him at the bottom of the steps, and Rocky walked into his embrace.

"Everything okay?" he asked.

"Yeah. We finally got a break on a new case." Rocky kissed his lips. "Sorry it took me away from the party." He wanted to point out that he'd noticed Asher silencing Duggins's calls but didn't want to get into it right now. It would ruin their perfect day.

"Don't worry," he said, nuzzling his nose against Rocky's neck. "It's starting to break up anyway. Soon I'll get you all to myself."

"You have to share me with the Roses," Rocky reminded him. "We need to start season four, and it's my favorite."

Marla came out a few minutes later without Dandridge. "Sweet Kurt had to head home. He asked me to tell everyone goodbye for him."

"Is he okay?" Asher asked.

"Time will tell," Marla said.

Ugh. There was that damn phrase again.

As Asher said, their guests started heading home after their offer to help clean up was rebuffed. Rocky had loved their company, but like Asher, he was ready to hang with his man. And the Roses.

"Bring the ice cream," Asher said as he started down the hallway.

"How do you have room for it?" Rocky countered.

"Fine," Asher said. "We'll share a pint instead of eating our own."

Rocky shook his head but grabbed a pint from the freezer before following Asher to their bedroom. His husband had already stripped down and was lying between the sheets when Rocky walked in. He handed the carton to Asher, then divested himself of his clothes before crawling into bed beside him. Asher returned the ice cream to Rocky while he turned the television on and found the next *Schitt's Creek* episode in the queue.

Asher raised his arm, and Rocky tucked himself beneath it. Maybe Rocky would get fully aroused, and they'd make love; perhaps he wouldn't. He'd started to see a significant improvement after consecutive nights of good sleep and markedly fewer anxiety attacks. He wasn't cured; he was a long way from it. The important takeaway was that Rocky finally understood the difference between intimacy and sex. Yes, he wanted his sex life to return to what it was before the shooting, but he was grateful for the lessons in intimacy and discovering the beauty in connecting on a deeper level.

"What flavor ice cream did you pick out?" Asher asked when the opening scene started on TV.

"Why don't you try to guess?"

"Okay."

Instead of spooning the ice cream into Asher's mouth, Rocky took a bite. "Mmmm," he said as he tasted the peanut butter ice cream mixed with chunks of salty pretzels and fudgy brownies. He took a second bite before he kissed Asher.

His husband slid his tongue between Rocky's lips, flicking the tip against his. Asher moaned when he got a hint of the flavor, then cupped the back of Rocky's head and deepened the kiss until he devoured all traces of the ice cream.

Asher pulled back and studied Rocky's face. "We've never had this flavor before. I tasted peanut butter and chocolate, though."

Rocky fed him his own spoonful, smiling when Asher immediately opened for a second bite. He fed Asher again before taking a spoonful for himself. "It's called Netflix and Chill'd."

"I have a new favorite." Asher opened for another bite.

They took turns feeding one another and exchanged sticky kisses. Eventually, they forgot about both the ice cream and the show on TV. Rocky straddled Asher's lap, loving the feel of his husband's big hands all over his body. Before, Asher's urgent erection would've induced panic. Now, Rocky closed his eyes and gave his pleasure over to Asher. He focused on how his husband made him feel, not what he was supposed to make Asher feel.

Asher brought him to a full erection with his patient touches, tender kisses, and encouraging whispers. Rather than rolling Rocky to his back, Asher held him on his lap.

"Ride me. Just like this," Asher said.

Rocky drizzled lube on Asher's cock while his husband teased and stretched his opening. Asher kissed him deeply, possessing every part of Rocky that he could reach. When Rocky couldn't take it any longer, he lowered himself onto Asher's cock. He fisted his hands in Asher's hair when he started to move, eating at his mouth as the pleasure built inside him. Asher kept his hands on Rocky's hips, anchoring them together as they moved in unison. The invisible hold Asher had on his heart tightened too, causing him to lose his breath in the best ways.

Rocky came sooner than he'd wanted, but it was hard to get upset when he felt so fucking phenomenal. Seeing Asher's pleasure wash over his face and ripple through his body meant more than experiencing his own climax.

Sticky and replete, they clung to one another for a long time afterward.

"We missed the show," Asher said in between kisses to Rocky's neck.

Rocky aimed the remote at the television. "Now that we've chilled, we can Netflix again."

Asher chuckled. "Do we have more of that ice cream?"

"We have half a pint left plus another one in the freezer."

"You go start the shower, and I'll grab the other pint of ice cream."

Asher's phone rang inside his jeans pocket. Rocky moved to get off his lap, but his husband tightened his grip. "I like you here."

"Two seconds ago, you wanted me to go start the shower." Rocky tipped his head toward Asher's jeans. "We're going to need to talk about this."

"I'm a slob. I know."

Rocky smirked. "Not about your slovenly ways, although it is true. We need to discuss why you're not taking Duggins's calls."

"Saw that, did ya?"

"I am a private detective. I also have a very overactive brain, so letting me draw my own conclusions can get dangerous."

Asher winced. "Duggins and I haven't… We didn't…"

"Hey," Rocky said. "You told me you haven't been with anyone else. I believe you. Not all my conclusions involve you getting naked with another man."

"They better never include that scenario. You're the only one I want." He heaved a deep sigh. "Things with Duggins have gotten really complicated. I'll tell you everything but not tonight, okay?"

Rocky held his stare for a few seconds. The sense of foreboding from earlier returned. Whatever the problem was between the former partners, it wouldn't go away just by ignoring it. Rocky also knew he couldn't force Asher to address it until he was ready, so he nodded and gave him a quick kiss before easing off his softening cock.

"Meet you in the shower," Rocky said.

CHAPTER 18

"Thanks for juggling my appointment around," Rocky said as he sat on Karen's couch.

He'd called her office first thing Monday morning to reschedule his appointment and was surprised when her receptionist offered him a same-day slot that had just become available. Usually, he wanted a full day to psych himself up for the sessions, but erecting shields was part of the reason he'd sought therapy in the first place. So, Rocky accepted the offer with only a slight hesitation. He'd been too busy at work to work himself into a tizzy over talking about his problems.

Could he be any more cliché? He'd laugh if it weren't so sad. If women figured out how to procreate without men, Rocky knew his species would soon go the way of the dinosaurs.

"Of course," she replied. "You look more rested than last week. Are you sleeping better?"

Instead of lying back and staring at the ceiling, Rocky remained in an upright position and maintained eye contact. It was a big step for him, one that Karen's shrewd gaze hadn't missed.

"I am."

"That's great news." She picked up her pen and began making notes. Rocky noticed she still wore the same navy blue nail polish. "What techniques are working for you?"

Images of the past few nights flooded Rocky's brain, all of them starring Asher. They'd unpacked his boxes when they arrived and merged his belongings with Rocky's. Sunday morning had been breakfast and crosswords in bed. Then they'd done domestic tasks like cleaning, reorganizing the closets, and grocery shopping—mundane things other couples took for granted. Rocky had never been so excited to fondle produce or pick out beef and chicken. They'd swung by the retirement village to see Queen Bea, and she'd talked them into staying for dinner and playing cards. They returned home sixty dollars poorer but happy. Rocky had fallen asleep with Asher's arms wrapped around him and his dick nestled in Rocky's ass.

He wasn't sure that was the kind of detail Karen was looking for, so he said, "My husband and I started working through our differences."

"Husband?" Karen asked as she rifled through previous notes. When she met his gaze again, Rocky saw curiosity instead of accusation. "You included a lot of information on your intake forms, but there's no mention of a husband."

"It hurt too much to even write it down," Rocky said. "I fucked up so badly, Karen."

"One person can't destroy a relationship on their own."

"Conventional wisdom says so, but I gave it the old college try anyway."

"Do you want to talk about it now?" Karen asked.

Rocky ran his hand through his hair. Did he? Weren't these things he should say to Asher? They kept dancing around the "big talk" because neither of them wanted to ruin the joy they'd rediscovered. Rocky worried it would blow up in their faces if they kept putting it off. Why not talk to an objective person about his doubts and fears? Isn't that why he'd started going to therapy?

"Yes, I do."

Rocky had only meant to give her an overview of their problems, but everything came gushing out once he opened the floodgates. He told her about his impotence and how he'd masked it by drinking heavily. "I hated the fucking taste of whiskey, so sometimes I only pretended to be drunk."

He hung his head in shame. "I'd drink a shot or two before Asher got home so he'd smell it on my breath, then pour the rest down the drain." Rocky met Karen's gaze once more. "I think I was a meaner fake drunk than when I was actually drunk."

"Rocky, you were acting as any wounded animal would in survival mode. I hope we can reach a point in therapy where you recognize it."

"I'll try." And he meant it. Rocky continued talking about how their marriage had deteriorated over the next few months. "When Asher got passed over for a promotion due to my embarrassing media coverage, I realized what I had to do."

"Hang on a second," Karen said. "How do you know he missed out on a promotion? Did he tell you that?"

"Of course not," Rocky said. "He'd never hurt me that way, no matter how much I deserved it."

"If he didn't tell you, who did?"

"His partner."

Karen tapped her pen against her lip, then said, "Tell me more."

Rocky told her about Duggins's behavior and how he'd suspected Asher's partner was in love with his husband. "The last confrontation about the promotion was the worst. I'd been researching why men experience erectile dysfunction and the various treatments for it. I must've left my laptop open."

"Or maybe not," Karen said. "This guy sounds like he doesn't adhere to personal boundaries."

"Yeah, I guess not," Rocky replied. "That came on the heels of Duggins telling me about the lost promotion opportunity. I can't recall a time where I felt more heartbroken and humiliated, and I believed Duggins had Asher's best interest at heart."

"You think differently now?"

"I *know* otherwise now." Rocky took a deep breath. "But, boy, was I dumb and gullible back then." He felt his face heating as he recalled just how easy he'd made Duggins's job for him.

"You were neither dumb nor gullible," Karen said. She pointed her pen at Rocky. "What's the first rule here?"

"We do not talk about fight club."

Karen snorted. "That's the second rule."

"Oh, yeah," Rocky said. "I'm not allowed to insult myself."

Karen nodded. "Now tell me what happened next, but do it in a kinder, more constructive way."

"About this time, my nana had decided to move into a retirement home. She was really struggling with the decision and scared about her future. Nana worried she'd feel trapped and regret selling her house. She'd been an independent woman long before it was cool."

"Sounds like my kind of gal."

"She's the best, our Queen Bea," Rocky said. "Anyway, it broke my heart to hear her so sad and confused. Asher was out of town on an assignment, and the media attention had turned our apartment into a prison. I think Asher volunteered for extra work just to get away from me, and I couldn't blame him. Bunkering down by myself was the absolute worst thing for me, so I decided to fly home to help her transition. I needed to be needed."

"We all do," Karen said.

Rocky nodded. "When I arrived back home in Savannah, I felt like I could breathe again. Considering the humidity, that says a lot." Remembering the time made his lungs feel heavy, so he rubbed the spot over his sternum. "Reconnecting with my family was exactly what I'd needed. My first full-blown panic attack hit me when I stepped inside the airport to fly back to Vegas."

"Had you decided to fight for your marriage?" Karen asked.

Rocky shook his head. "No, but ending our relationship in person felt important. I missed the first flight, then a second and a third. So, I took the easy way out and told Asher I was leaving him over the phone."

"How'd your husband respond?"

"By getting on a plane," Rocky said. "We argued for days, but I wouldn't budge. He went back to Vegas by himself, and I filed for a divorce a few months later."

"Yet, you're still married?"

Rocky nodded. "Asher contested the divorce and applied for a transfer. He had big plans to win me back. His first request was granted right away, but the latter didn't come through until recently." He smiled. "But it came with the promotion he'd been denied in Vegas."

They continued talking about the recent changes in Rocky's life. And even though it was embarrassing, he spoke of his erectile dysfunction and the various things that seemed to improve his condition. "Sleep helps the most." Heat flushed Rocky's neck and face. "And, um, Asher employs other techniques to distract my over-busy brain."

"Erectile dysfunction is a prevalent side effect for people suffering from PTSD," Karen said. "There's absolutely nothing to feel ashamed about, and I applaud all methods as long as they are safe and consensual."

"Absolutely." And, oh, so very sexy.

"Look, I don't want to come off sounding like a rep for a pharmaceutical company, but there are reliable and safe prescriptions. Not only for ED but for sleeping."

"I know," Rocky said. "I don't want to come off like some nut job who doesn't believe in science or medicine either. I know how valuable and important medications are. I just have issues with giving up control. I also don't want something that makes me groggy. I have to stay sharp in my line of work."

"I fully understand," Karen said. "You said Asher travels a lot as a marshal, right?"

"He does."

"What happens when he's not home? Will you return to sleeping poorly?"

Rocky hadn't given it much thought, but she had a valid point. "It's possible."

"During your recovery, you're at a higher risk for falling into codependent relationships. While it seems less addictive and dangerous than medications, I assure you it's not." She held up her hand when Rocky started to object. "I'm not saying your marriage falls into that category. I'm just asking you to be aware. I would've had this conversation with you sooner if I'd known you were in a relationship."

"Point taken."

"What else has been going on with you this week?"

Rocky told her about the changes at the office that resulted in him taking on more responsibility. He even showed her the picture Trudy had taken of him holding Skylar Rose when they met. Rocky wouldn't divulge details about the new clients he signed but expressed excitement to work with them. He talked; Karen listened. She only interrupted if she wanted to clarify something or delve deeper into his feelings.

As they neared the end of his session, Rocky still hadn't broached the shooting in Vegas. Maybe he'd work up his courage at their next session.

"See you next week, Karen."

"Looking forward to it, Rocky."

When he got to his car, Rocky checked his phone for messages and saw he had one from Asher. The text was short with only two words, but they happened to be two of Rocky's favorites. *Irish stew.*

On my way, he replied, then aimed his car toward home.

When he turned on to his street, Rocky expected to see Lady Luck parked in his driveway but instead found a shiny, gold Mazda Miata convertible in her place. Rocky laughed so hard he nearly sideswiped the car when he pulled up beside it. He was still laughing when he let himself into the house.

"Wow, someone is having a really good time at your expense," Rocky said after kissing Asher hello. "That car is hideous, and it's not big enough for your dick to fit in it, let alone the rest of your body."

Asher shrugged, then continued stirring the pot. "To each their own."

Rocky sniffed the air appreciatively. "Damn, dinner smells good."

"Thanks. The bread will be done in a few minutes, then we can eat."

"So, who owned that glittery gold Miata before the marshals confiscated it?" Rocky asked.

Asher chuckled. "The mistress of an investment capitalist who started a Ponzi scheme. Boy, was she pissed when we arrived to take it away. She tried to claw Dandridge's eyes out. Poor fella."

"I hope it wasn't my cousin."

Asher released the spoon and turned his full attention on Rocky. "I forget about your ties to some of Atlanta's wealthiest people through your mom."

"I think most of them would like to forget about it too."

His maternal grandparents had been less than thrilled when their only daughter ran off with the contractor they'd hired to remodel their home. Their resentment only grew stronger when she died a few years later after giving birth to Rocky. His relationship with the Duttons was tumultuous at best, and he only tugged on those familial strings when he needed a favor, such as gaining entrance into an exclusive nightclub to spy on a mob boss with his best friend.

"How was therapy?" Asher asked.

"Good," Rocky said, stepping into his husband's embrace.

Being in Asher's arms and having his scent all around him brought Rocky so much happiness and peace. It also reminded him of Karen's cautionary remark about the dangers and allure of codependency. Rocky understood at that moment what she meant. He didn't need or want Asher to be his crutch or his cure. It could breed resentment, a poison that would erode their relationship. Asher's embrace would start to feel suffocating instead of comforting.

"Ford," Asher said, rubbing his hands up and down Rocky's back. "You stiffened suddenly. Is it okay if I ask?"

Asher dropped his hands and tried to take a step away, but Rocky tightened his arms around his husband's waist. *Just another second.* Asher chuckled, then resumed rubbing Rocky's back.

"Of course you can ask," Rocky said. "There's no need to tiptoe around it. That's kind of how we got into this mess in the first place."

Asher was the one who stiffened this time, and Rocky was the one who regretted his remark. No. They had to stop dancing around this. The timer on the stove went off, so Asher dropped a kiss on top of Rocky's head before lowering his arms and pulling away.

"Um, do you think dinner could wait for a bit?" Rocky almost changed his mind when Asher pulled out the loaf of soda bread. Nothing was better than freshly baked carbs. He didn't want to ruin Asher's lovely dinner, but if they didn't air this out now, they'd just bury their troubles under another layer of sand and silt. This felt like a now-or-never moment.

Asher set the bread on top of the stove, dropped the mitts on the countertop, then turned off the oven. Worry lines furrowed Asher's brow when he faced Rocky again.

"It's going to be okay," he said, smoothing his fingers over his husband's forehead. It fucking had to be. Rocky led Asher over to the small table tucked into the corner of the room. Their knees bumped together when they sat down, but Rocky liked the connection. Taking Asher's hands in his, he said, "Did you get passed over for a promotion in Vegas because of me?"

The confusion on Asher's face should've been comical, cartoonish even, but it was the equivalent of setting a match to a fuse in Rocky's soul. Duggins had played him like a fucking violin, and Rocky had let it happen.

"No. I turned down a promotion because it came with a transfer to DC. Why would you think—" Asher pulled his hands free and crossed his arms over his chest. Rocky couldn't be sure if he was bracing himself for combat or trying to shield his heart. "Did Duggins feed you that line of bullshit?"

Rocky took a steady breath to calm his nerves and control his temper. Asher wasn't his enemy; he was an innocent victim in all of this. *So were you, goddamn it.* "Yes."

"And you believed his lies?" Asher's voice shook with rage.

Rocky's pulse sped up in response, but he focused on the rhythm of his breathing. Nice and steady. "I did. Even though Duggins hated my guts, I thought he had your best interest at heart."

"Clearly, he didn't." Asher looked so betrayed; it broke Rocky's heart.

"Are you sure there's no truth to it? Could Duggins have overheard something? Would Bradshaw have confided in him?"

"No fucking way," Asher growled. "How could I have been so fucking stupid?"

"Hey," Rocky said, "neither one of us is stupid. We got played by a liar and a manipulator who took advantage of a bad situation. Duggins had one thing on his mind, well, maybe two. He wanted to get rid of me to have a chance at you."

A guilty expression washed over Asher's face, and he turned his head to break eye contact.

Breathing suddenly got harder as if a boa constrictor had wrapped itself around Rocky's chest. He inhaled deeply to prove to his brain that he wasn't suffocating, then released it slowly. He repeated it a few more times until the tightness eased up.

"But you knew this already," Rocky prodded. "When I left Vegas, you were still oblivious to Duggins's feelings for you. When did that change?"

Asher met his gaze again. "He came on to me during my going-away party. Duggins leaned in to kiss me, and I jerked my head away. He'd tried to blame it on the alcohol, but I'd seen him drunk enough to recognize the difference." Asher rubbed his eyes for a second before reaching for Rocky's hands. "I swear to you, I never knew Duggins was into me like that. He was out at work but never flirted or indicated he was attracted to me."

"Would it have made a difference?" Rocky asked. "Would Duggins have been your first male lover instead of me?"

Asher shook his head. "No. Even if he hadn't been my partner, I only felt friendship for Duggins." He took a deep breath. "Things have been strained between us ever since I rejected him."

"It didn't sound like it when you talked to him on your first night here," Rocky said. He'd tried to keep the bitterness from his voice but failed miserably. "Sorry."

"Don't be. I'm the one who's sorry." Asher blew out a deep breath. "Is Karen's couch big enough for both of us?"

Rocky chuckled. "Probably."

"With thousands of miles separating Duggins and me, I attempted to get our friendship back on track. Chances are good that I'll have to work with him again someday. I didn't bring up the botched kiss and kept our conversation to neutral topics." Asher shook his head. "Things seemed better between us, and I started to think maybe Duggins had been drunk when he tried to kiss me."

"But then," Rocky prodded.

"Duggins started probing into our relationship. Subtle things at first," Asher added. "I figured evading his questions would only spark more interest, so I kept my answers vague."

"I'm guessing your method didn't work because now you're avoiding his calls altogether."

Asher cringed. "He went too far."

"Do I even want to know?" Rocky asked.

"Duggins somehow got ahold of Dandridge's number and called him in the guise of a friend looking out for another. He wanted to be sure my new partner had my back and knew the score."

Rocky stiffened. The fuse he thought he'd extinguished burned closer and closer to the dynamite. "You mean Duggins bared my personal business." Rocky stood up suddenly and fisted his hands in his hair. "Fuck."

"Ford, I'm sorry," Asher said as he stood up. "I know this might not help, but Dandridge was furious on your behalf. He told Duggins to lose his number."

Rocky jerked away from Asher's touch. "Which part did Dandridge pity most? That I'd watched a woman gun down her husband and sister-in-law after I unwittingly led her to them? Or that—" His voice broke, and tears streamed down his face. Rocky couldn't voice his worst fear. Had Duggins told Dandridge Rocky couldn't pleasure Asher because his brain was so fucked up?

Asher snagged his wrists and tugged Rocky back into his arms. "Don't pull away from me, baby," Asher said. "Scream, rage, and throw things if you need to, but please don't shut me out again."

"I used to pity Duggins because I couldn't imagine what it would be like to watch you fall in love with someone else," Rocky said, fisting his hands in Asher's shirt. "I fucking hate him now."

"I'm so sorry, Ford. I'll make this right somehow."

How could Asher fix this? "Savannah was my safe place."

Asher kissed his forehead. "It still is. Don't let Duggins undo the progress you've made. We're going to have the life we always talked about. Right here in your safe place." He pointed out the window and said, "Our kids will play under that magnolia tree with Fifi by their side." Asher's words created a striking piece of art to rival his mother's watercolor paintings. "I'll deal with Duggins."

"By ignoring his calls and hoping he gives up?"

Asher puffed out his cheeks on a deep exhale. "I know it was a mistake, and I probably made the situation worse. I'm sorry."

Rocky shook his head. "You don't even know half the things he's done to us."

Asher slid a hand inside Rocky's hair and massaged his scalp. "So tell me. I'll listen."

Therapy had already zapped a lot of his energy, and an emotional conversation would drain the rest of his battery. Rocky had initiated this confrontation, so he wouldn't give up now.

They sat back down at the table, and Rocky told him everything that had happened with Duggins, both the little digs and the massive betrayals. Asher's face turned pale when he found out his so-called best friend had invaded Rocky's privacy and used his trauma to humiliate him.

"I'm going to kill him," Asher said.

Rocky chuckled a little. "That's one solution, but I think we can come up with something that will keep you out of prison. We've got to beat him at his own game."

"I'm all ears."

"Feed me first," Rocky said. "I can't thwart evil on an empty stomach."

Asher stood up, then leaned over to kiss him hard on the mouth. "My seanmháthair always said Irish stew can fix anything that ails us. Have a broken heart? Eat stew. Need to conquer a villain? Eat stew. Want to win a man's heart? Make stew."

Rocky snagged his hand to prevent Asher from walking away. Craning his neck to look up at his husband hurt, so he rose to his feet. "You made it for me a lot after that night. I never thanked you for the many ways you took good care of me. I appreciated it so much."

Asher cupped his face and rested his forehead against Rocky's. "I... Christ." He swallowed hard and held Rocky tighter. "I'll never forget the sound of those gunshots or the way your voice shook when you told me goodbye. I have never felt so fucking helpless in my life. And you hung up before I could say it back."

Rocky had told Asher he loved him, but he'd meant it as a goodbye.

"It felt like an eternity before I reached someone in the Vegas PD who could tell me what the hell happened," Asher continued. "Do you have any idea how relieved I was to find out you'd been taken to a hospital instead of the morgue?" His voice cracked, and tears filled his eyes. "You were practically catatonic when I was finally able to see you. You were alive, but I feared I'd lost you anyway. The only thing I could think of was to take you home and make the fucking stew."

"The best fucking stew," Rocky corrected.

Asher grinned. "It didn't work. The harder I tried, the more you pulled away. I didn't know what to do or how to make things better."

Rocky shook his head. "You were everything I needed then, and you're everything I need now."

"You'll always have me," Asher said tenderly.

"Now, how about that fucking stew?"

Two bowls and half a loaf of soda bread later, Rocky and Asher had mapped out a plan to take down Duggy Bear.

CHAPTER 19

"**R**emember, don't glare at the woman," Felix said to Jonah as they approached Tess's house.

The ranch-style home was slightly bigger than Rocky's bungalow. The yellow exterior was tidy and cheerful with perfectly groomed flower beds. A blue jay was frolicking in one of the ornate birdbaths but flew away when the men got too close. Glancing around, Rocky noted several feeders hanging from trees on the property. Queen Bea would approve of both the color scheme and attention given to both the floral and feathered fauna.

"Jonah won't scare the lady if you promise not to stick your nose up her ass," Rocky said.

Felix snickered. "Keep your charm in check, Major. She might be on the prowl."

They dropped their shenanigans as they reached the porch steps. Grant opened the front door before they had a chance to ring the doorbell. Rocky made quick introductions, then Grant stepped aside for them to enter.

Rocky was the last one through the door, and Grant stepped in front of him. Nothing about his demeanor or expression was menacing, though. Rocky only saw concern. "Is this a terrible mistake?"

Rocky shook his head. "You said your mother is innocent of any wrongdoing."

"That didn't stop them from charging her with fraud," Grant pointed out. "Luckily, they just couldn't make it stick."

"Everything okay here?" Felix asked as he joined them.

"We're fine," Rocky replied, meeting his curious gaze. "Grant is just looking out for his mother." Rocky smiled at Grant, hoping to reassure him. "You don't have anything to worry about if there are no skeletons to dig up."

"We all have skeletons," Grant said.

Rocky nodded. "I know this all too well. All I can promise is that we approach each investigation with utmost respect and care. You might not always like what we have to say, but you can rest assured our words will be spoken without malicious intent."

Grant studied him long enough for it to become awkward. He finally relented with a nod and stepped aside. "It's best not to keep my mother waiting."

He led the trio of trouble past an unoccupied formal living space that looked like something from *Southern Living* magazine. Rocky never understood the concept of a space created for looking and not living, but it was common among Tess's generation or high-society homes. Why even call it a formal living room, then? Why not a formal looking room?

The kitchen and dining areas were in the middle of the home, bisected by a walkway leading to the family room in the rear. Rocky could see through the wall of windows that Tess's lush gardens continued to the back of the property as well. She had a Southern magnolia tree similar in size to Rocky's. A well-used rope swing hung from one of its lower branches.

"Magnificent, isn't it?" a soft, genteel voice asked.

Rocky turned his head and met Tess's gaze. "It is."

"My grandchildren argue over it when they visit," she said, extending her hand. "Tess Hamilton." She wore a pale pink blouse, ivory slacks, and pink ballet flats. The woman couldn't be much over five feet tall, but her direct gaze and confident movement gave her a larger presence.

"Rocky Jacobs." Her hand felt dainty in Rocky's, but her grip was firm. "These are my partners, Felix Franklin and Jonah St. John."

Felix and Jonah both shook Tess's hand, then she led them over to a cozy seating area. The space was as beautifully decorated as the formal living room, but it had a lived-in vibe. Bookshelves lined an entire wall, and they were packed full of books, movies, and family photographs. In the opposite corner sat a velvet club chair and a matching ottoman, where a paperback lay facedown beside a pair of discarded house slippers. Steam rose from a dainty teacup on the antique side table.

Rocky had a strong urge to examine the book Tess had set aside to meet with them, as well as the ones lining her shelves. You could tell a lot about a person by their choice of entertainment. He glanced over at the bookcase once more, this time focusing on the photographs. His eyes homed in on a particular image that snagged his attention. It was a much younger Tess Hamilton with her arm wrapped around a woman with vibrant red hair and memorable blue eyes. Helen Girard's hair might be white as snow now, but there was no mistaking her identity.

Rocky's attempts to find out why Helen no longer worked at Whispering Willows were wholly unsuccessful. The HR rep had been friendly but stated he'd have to submit a written request before they'd respond. He'd tracked down Bethany Fields, but she wasn't willing to speak, not even off the record. Those two things only made him more curious about the woman who seemed so devoted to Tess Hamilton.

"That's my dear friend, Helen," Tess said. "You might've seen her pictures from the trial." Not a longtime friend. Not a best friend. Tess called Helen her dear friend. Was there a deeper meaning, or was he grasping at straws?

He hadn't meant to be so damn obvious about his interest and latched on to the excuse Tess had given him. Smiling, Rocky said, "That's why she looks familiar." The photo looked like it had been taken on the set of $M*A*S*H$. Tess and Helen wore green fatigues and appeared to be in their early twenties. The ladies stood next to a group of wounded soldiers. "Army?" he asked.

"Yes," she said. "We met in 1968 during Vietnam. It's also where I met my first husband. Bob was a chopper pilot who transported the wounded soldiers for treatment."

Rocky already knew these things, but they established a baseline for what Tess was eager to discuss. He scanned the rest of the framed photographs, noticing that not even one included a husband—only Tess with her kids, grandkids, and Helen.

"Why don't we have a seat," Tess said. "Can I get you gentlemen something to drink?" The men declined, but a true Southerner never stopped there. "Are you sure? I have hot and cold beverages."

Jonah finally caved and accepted a Coke, and Felix asked for water.

"I'll get it," Grant said to his mother. "I think I'll make myself a cup of coffee. Any other takers?" he asked, looking around the room.

A cup of coffee suddenly sounded great to Rocky, but he'd be up all night if he drank caffeine this late. "You don't happen to have decaf, do you?" he asked when Grant's gaze landed on his.

"Decaf?" Felix and Jonah asked at the same time.

"Since when?" Felix wanted to know.

"Since I like sleeping at night," Rocky countered.

"Fake meat and fake coffee," Jonah grumbled. "What's next?"

Grant chuckled. "Mom, do you have *decaf* coffee?" He, too, made the word sound like a loathsome thing.

"Of course," she said. "In the freezer."

"How do you take it?" Grant asked.

"A splash of creamer or milk and a little sugar. Don't go to any trouble on my account," Rocky said. "I can drink water."

"Nonsense," Tess said as she returned to her club chair. She propped her feet up on her ottoman, put her book on the end table, and picked up her cup of tea. "I like the three of you already."

"Should we place bets on how long that lasts?" Felix quipped.

Tess laughed and saluted him with her cup before taking a sip. She set it back down and folded her hands in her lap. Nothing about her demeanor signaled Tess was anxious about the meeting. She was calm, relaxed, and refined, reminding him of his maternal grandmother, Matilda Dutton. Still waters ran deep, and one couldn't assume a quiet façade meant nothing sinister lurked beneath the surface.

They made small talk while Grant got their drinks. Tess asked a little about their careers and the podcast.

"I'd never even heard of such a thing. I associate the word pod with alien movies." She shivered dramatically. "Have they been around a long time?"

Felix was most familiar with the history of podcasting since he'd hosted a few over the years, so Rocky and Jonah were happy to let him field her questions.

"Are there podcasts about other things besides crime?" she wanted to know.

"There are podcasts about everything," Grant said when he entered the room. "If you'd like, I can help you find ones about gardening for your trip."

"Really?" she asked. "I already downloaded an audiobook for the flight, but I think I'd like the podcast better. Now that everyone is settled with a beverage," she said, making eye contact around the room, "do you think I killed any or all of my husbands?"

Direct hit. Rocky respected Tess for it. Felix and Jonah both deferred to him since he was the one who pursued the investigation. He could lie and tell her that all three of them thought she was innocent, or he could be brutally honest. One option would probably have a much higher success rate than the other, but which one? Tess tilted her head slightly as she awaited a response.

"The truth is we don't know," Rocky said. "We're approaching this investigation from three different angles."

"Christ," Grant snarled, slamming his cup on the table hard enough to make the coffee slosh over the side. "I told you not to make me regret this meeting."

Rocky met his hostile gaze. "You'd rather I lie to your mother and blindside her later?"

"I'd prefer you weren't here at all."

"Grant," Tess said softly. "He's being honest, which is more than we can say for most people." She shifted her attention back to Rocky. She held up a finger. "I'm innocent." A second finger joined the first. "Or I'm guilty. What's the third angle?"

"Mercy killing," Rocky replied.

From his periphery, Rocky saw Grant leap to his feet. "The fuck you say. I want the three of you out of here right now."

Rocky kept his gaze locked on Tess, and she didn't so much as flinch. She wasn't just a cool cucumber; she might be the coolest to ever live. "Mrs. Hamilton?" he asked. If she wanted them to leave, they would go. No questions asked.

"I want to know more." She broke her eye contact long enough to look at her son. "Really, Grant? They haven't said a single word I haven't already heard or read a hundred times."

Rocky felt the man's eyes burning holes into him, so he turned his head and met Grant's gaze. Tess's son wasn't just hot under the collar; he was burning with rage. If this were a cartoon, steam would be coming out of Grant's ears. "What did I tell you a few minutes ago?" Rocky asked.

Grant took a deep breath and sat back down. "You said I wouldn't always like what you had to say, but your words wouldn't be spoken with malicious intent."

"I meant it then, and I mean it now." He turned his attention back to Tess, who kept her eyes on her son for a few seconds before meeting Rocky's gaze once more.

"Isn't a mercy killing still murder?" she asked.

"Legally?" Jonah asked. "In most states, yes. The perception is vastly different, though. One is committed through cold and calculating means, and some consider the other to be an act of compassion."

"Mom," Grant said. "Come on. You can't be serious about participating in this podcast."

Tess ignored him and focused on Rocky. "Are you going to continue this investigation if I don't cooperate?"

"Yes."

She nodded. "Then I'd rather have my say."

"Mom," Grant said once more. "What could they possibly do to clear your name?"

Tess looked at her son, but Rocky's gaze was riveted on her. She was either completely innocent or more talented than any Hollywood actress. "They can help sort out the facts from the fiction, Grant. I've already been acquitted of fraud, so they can't charge me again."

"Mom, double jeopardy doesn't extend to new charges. Nothing is preventing a power-hungry DA from filing murder charges against you."

"Based on what?" Tess asked.

Rocky turned and looked at Grant. Tess had an excellent point. What the hell did he think Rocky might find if he dug too deep? The man seemed lost in thought as he stared at the coffee table.

"Do you think I killed your father or your stepfathers?" she asked when her son remained quiet.

Grant snapped his head up and looked at Tess. "Of course I don't. That doesn't mean these guys won't paint you as a cold-blooded killer."

Tess made a frustrated sound, pulling Rocky's attention back to her. He saw the first ripple in the water as she continued to stare at her son. "I loved Arnie with all my heart, and I miss him every day," Tess said. "I hate that the world lost a good man, but more than anything, I loathe how cynical this situation has made you. Will you please get the boxes out of the spare bedroom and bring them in here?"

"Mom," Grant said softly. He let out a little growl, then ran his hands through his hair. "This is a big mistake."

"Maybe," she said. "But it's mine to make, and I'm still your mother. Will you do as I've asked, or shall I hoist those heavy boxes all by myself?"

Grant chuckled dryly and shook his head. "I'll do it." He stood up and pointed at Rocky. "And you can help."

Jonah and Felix didn't look comfortable, but Rocky thought it would be an excellent opportunity to soothe some ruffled feathers. So, he rose to his feet and said, "Sure."

Grant stood up and walked out of the room without another word or even a backward glance to make sure Rocky followed. As soon as they reached a hallway leading back to the bedrooms, Grant stopped and turned so fast Rocky nearly plowed into his chest.

"You're not taking these boxes out of here, so don't even ask," he told Rocky.

"What's in them?" Rocky countered. He couldn't agree to something if he didn't have all the facts.

"Everything you could possibly need to know about my mother's husbands."

"I don't need to know their shoe size," Rocky said.

Grant narrowed his eyes. "You're a real smartass, aren't you?"

"Yes, but you knew this already."

"Would having access to medical records make you happy?" Grant asked.

Rocky tried hard not to let on just how happy it made him, but he wasn't as cool as Tess. "I'm not opposed to viewing them."

Grant snorted. "You can scan them with your phone or take pictures, but you're not taking a single document out of this house. Also, you need to obtain written permission from my mother before posting any of these documents on your website or social media accounts for the podcast."

"Deal," Rocky said.

Grant studied him for a few more moments before he pivoted and led Rocky to a spare bedroom in the back of the house. The area wasn't much larger than his home office, and the stacks of boxes and storage containers made it seem even smaller. In the center of the room sat three boxes, each labeled with a husband's name. Grant stacked Donald Trout's box on top of his father's and lifted them, leaving Rocky to carry Arnold Hamilton's back to the family room.

"What's in here? Bowling balls?" Rocky asked.

"My mom is a bit of a packrat," Grant replied. "I'm carrying two, so quit your bitching."

"Okay."

Grant shook his head and kept walking.

The mood in the family room seemed relaxed when they walked in. Tess searched Grant's face for a few seconds, then smiled.

"Jonah was telling me about supercomputers," she said to Grant. "Have you ever heard of those?"

"Yeah," he said. "It exceeds my technical skill level, but I've heard they can accomplish pretty cool things." Grant looked at Jonah. "You're the GBI agent, right?"

"I am," he said. "But I'm not here in an official capacity. This isn't some kind of gotcha game."

Tess gestured to the three boxes. "These are important documents for all three of my husbands. I have everything from their birth records to their death certificates and everything in between."

On the one hand, it made sense that these boxes were heavy. On the other, how sad was it to think their lives could be whittled down to fit in a single cardboard box? Rocky couldn't help but think of his mother's possessions that he kept tucked away or her paintings and photographs hanging on his walls. Legacies weren't defined by keepsakes but by the emotions they evoked. Bloodlines died out, but the stories lived on.

Grant went over the ground rules with Felix and Jonah, and they agreed as readily as Rocky had. They each picked a box and sat on the floor to examine the contents. It felt kind of weird with Tess and Grant supervising, but Rocky set his discomfort aside and scanned and photographed any important-looking documents.

"What would your computer tell you if you scanned all the information from these three boxes?" Tess asked Jonah.

He looked up from his work and smiled. "It would assimilate the information and highlight similarities in their lifestyles, medical histories, and even their deaths."

"Fascinating," Tess said. "Is this method of investigation respected?"

"Not fully," Jonah said. "People don't like change and are suspicious of technology. I think law enforcement officers dislike those things even more."

"Do you plan to enter this data into your computer to see what it comes up with?" Tess asked him.

"Yes."

"Good," Tess said with a nod.

"Mom, a machine can't paint a full picture," Grant said cautiously. "It can only analyze the facts it's given. There's room for error and manipulation."

"Which is why we plan to interview a lot of people who can speak on your mom's behalf," Felix told Grant.

"Your son has a valid point," Jonah said. "Stella isn't a detective, but she's an extremely intuitive tool to help officers in the field."

"I'm going to start making phone calls this evening," Tess said. "I'll continue working my contact list until I have to leave for my cruise with my dear friend, but Grant can do the rest."

"Great," her son said dryly. "I know how long your average phone call lasts. You might scratch two people off the list before I take you to the airport."

Tess just shrugged. She continued chatting with them as they worked, answering any questions they had about documents they found in the boxes. Tess permitted them to record her answers so they could refer back to them when necessary. They couldn't have asked for better cooperation from her.

"Why won't you let me feed you?" Tess asked them at one point. "I have plenty of leftovers, or I can order takeout or pizza."

"They're afraid you'll poison them, Mom," Grant said.

She rolled her eyes. "We'll make Grant test all the food first."

They all laughed but still declined since they'd already met for dinner before they came over. Then she mentioned homemade blueberry cobbler and the guys suddenly found room in their stomachs.

After they finished, the guys stacked everything neatly in the boxes once more.

"Where to?" Jonah asked, hoisting two of them.

"Follow me," Tess said.

Felix grabbed the third box and aimed a grin at Rocky. "You two play nice. If Major weren't already married, I'd recommend you go on a date."

"You're married?" Grant asked when they were alone.

"I am."

"I never would've guessed," Grant replied.

"Because I don't wear a ring?"

"No," he said. "Because you flirted with me the day we met."

"It's in my DNA, man."

"Okay, Blanche."

Rocky grinned. "Maybe we could be friends."

Grant chuckled. "Perhaps."

Rocky, Jonah, and Felix thanked Tess when she walked them outside, then wished her a safe and fun vacation.

"How quickly can you upload the scans and photos?" Rocky asked Felix and Jonah when they were out of earshot. "I want to put together a strategy and hit it hard this weekend before Tess changes her mind or Grant changes it for her."

"I'll get on it as soon as I get home," Felix said.

"Me too," Jonah added.

Rocky rubbed his hands together. "Perfect."

Things were finally clicking into place for this investigation.

"What about you?" Felix asked. "Deputy Delicious won't be home?"

Rocky chuckled. "He's been in Atlanta since yesterday working on a joint task force with the DEA and FBI. He should be back sometime this weekend."

The busy work would keep Rocky's mind occupied with something productive instead of worrying about Asher's safety or fretting about why Duggins had suddenly stopped calling. His husband thought his former friend and partner finally got the message, but Rocky knew better. Duggins was just biding his time before springing his attack. Rocky wanted to think they'd be ready and spent too much of his free time preparing for every conceivable possibility. It was exhausting.

Karen had been right about Rocky falling back on bad habits when Asher was away. He'd slept horribly the night before, and even though his husband was expected back soon, he decided to fill the prescription for the sleep aid. Karen had written it out during their first visit, but Rocky had been reluctant to take it. The key to recovery was sleep, so he would start making it a top priority.

Tess's investigation wasn't the only thing moving in the right direction. Rocky was proud of himself in ways he hadn't been for a long time.

CHAPTER 20

"**Y**our car or mine?" Asher asked.

Rocky halted and looked at his husband. "You've got to be kidding me."

Asher looked at the shiny Miata, then back at Rocky. "What's wrong with Goldie?"

"Besides the name?" Before Asher could answer, Rocky pointed at the large picnic basket his husband carried. "That won't fit in the trunk."

"Would so," Asher argued. "It's a summer day and she's a convertible."

The ornery grin on Asher's face made Rocky want to drag his husband back inside the house. A picnic in bed was starting to sound like an excellent idea. Asher had arrived home during the wee hours of the night, much later than Rocky expected. His husband had to be exhausted, even though Rocky let him sleep until almost noon. Rocky had kept himself busy making the last few phone calls to Tess's friends and family leftover on the list. The trio of trouble had reached all but three people during their marathon of interviews the day before.

"Huh-uh. August in the South means the humidity will be a thousand percent," Rocky countered. "We will need the air-conditioning blowing on full blast."

"Fine," Asher said with a shrug as he walked toward Rocky's car. "Where did we get this basket, anyway?"

"I borrowed it from Marla. I guess she used it for a drag performance of *The Wizard of Oz*. Miss Betty got to play Toto."

"I hope that's on video someplace," Asher said.

Asher stowed the picnic basket in the trunk, then pulled Rocky into his arms.

"Hi," Asher whispered before dropping a kiss on his lips.

"Hi back," Rocky said when they parted. "I missed you."

"I missed you too."

"We could stay here and explore this further," Rocky suggested again.

Asher narrowed his eyes. "Are you ashamed of me? Is that why you want to hide me in the house?"

Rocky laughed and stepped from his embrace. "Don't be ridiculous. Get in the car."

"How'd you sleep while I was gone?" Asher asked as Rocky backed down the driveway.

His first instinct was to sugarcoat it for his husband, but he decided to go with honesty. "Rough at first, but then I put on my big boy pants and took the sleep aid."

Asher placed his hand on the back of Rocky's neck and massaged the muscles. "Don't do that."

"What?" Rocky asked. "Take the sleep aid?"

"No, demean yourself."

Rocky forced himself to relax. "It's become a habit. A survival mechanism, I think."

"You don't need to put up shields or try to impress me. In case you haven't figured it out, I'm already crazy about you."

Rocky glanced over and smiled. "I'm crazy about you too."

"The prescription helped, then?"

Rocky chuckled. "The first night was hard because my brain tried to fight the effects of the drug, so it triggered a panic attack. I huffed and puffed and breathed my way through it and slept really well once I calmed myself down."

"That happened to me the one and only time I tried pot in college,"

Asher said. "Everyone else is mellow as fuck on the shit. Not me. My friends told me to sleep it off, but I couldn't. I was convinced my lungs would forget to work if I didn't stay awake. It was an awful feeling."

Rocky rested his hand on Asher's thigh. "The medication wasn't a heavy sedative, so it didn't turn me into a zombie the morning after. The second night went smoother."

"I can attest that you weren't knocked out cold."

Rocky had woken up when Asher slid between the sheets, and they'd given each other a proper hello. Rocky still had the bite marks on his inner thigh to remind him it hadn't been a dream. Maybe he wasn't firing on all cylinders yet, but four out of six wasn't bad.

"Better get your mind out of the gutter before you drive into a parked car," Asher said. "That would derail our afternoon plans for sure."

"My mind isn't in the gutter."

Asher chuckled. "Your hand on my dick says otherwise."

Rocky stopped at a light, then looked over. Sure enough, his hand was full-on groping Asher's crotch. He smiled sheepishly and returned the rogue appendage to the steering wheel. "Should I apologize?"

"Hell no," Asher replied. "How'd the phone calls go? Did you get in touch with everyone?"

"I did."

"Why don't you sound happy?"

Rocky took a deep breath. "All together, Felix, Jonah, and I interviewed almost three dozen people. Each of us recorded our phone conversations and uploaded them into our shared drive. I haven't listened to Felix's or Jonah's interviews yet, but all the people we talked to virtually said the same things about Tess and her husbands."

"Could their accounts be similar because they're the truth?"

"I thought about that," Rocky replied. "Even if they're being a hundred percent honest, wouldn't there be some variance in their recollections of the same events?"

"Give me an example."

Rocky had so many thoughts it was like searching for the proverbial needle in the haystack to find one that would capture what was bothering him. He grabbed ahold of the first shiny thing his overactive brain landed on. "Okay. Here's one. Everyone in Augusta mentioned a New Year's Eve party at Bob and Tess's house. I guess their parties were legendary among their friends, but this one was particularly memorable because Tess had gone into labor with Grant."

The more Rocky talked, the clearer his concerns became.

"Everyone's account of the night leading up to Tess's water breaking is virtually the same. I know these people are in their seventies, and memories can be tricky things at any age, but why would they all see and hear exactly the same thing? Hadn't they used the bathroom at any point or stepped into the kitchen for a refill?"

"I see your point," Asher said. "You feel like their responses were rehearsed or even fabricated."

"Yeah, I do. I can't think of another reason why everyone I talked to chose that night to define the Duncans' relationship."

"Hmmm," Asher said. "You didn't accidentally steer them toward talking about it?"

"No. Obviously, I was interested the first time I heard about Tess going into labor. Bob, who was allegedly calm and cool under fire, had acted out of character. He was comically anxious and worried, according to their friends. Tess, the one going into labor, had been the calm one. She also had to drive herself to the hospital because everyone else had been drinking. They talked about how Bob paced the floor after she left."

"Why not call an ambulance?" Asher asked.

"Here's the only place where their accounts varied," Rocky said. "A few said a bad storm had recently passed through, taking out the phone lines. Another said Tess was stubborn like that, and the others couldn't remember why. Oh, and one said they didn't even know anything about it until after she'd left."

"That doesn't explain why no one went with her, especially Bob."

"She was a trauma nurse," Rocky explained. "I imagine she was pretty tough under pressure."

"Why didn't someone stay sober just in case?"

"Tess's due date wasn't for another month," Rocky explained. "Bob probably thought it would be okay. Maybe Tess's first three kids were born on time or late, but she was forty when she got pregnant with Grant and not twentysomething like when she'd carried her older children. Maybe her uterus was like 'enough, bitch' and kicked his ass out early."

"If the story was rehearsed, who were they protecting, or what were they trying to cover up?" Asher asked.

"Exactly."

Asher hummed again. It reminded him of the noises his husband made when Rocky found an especially sensitive spot on his body. It wasn't too late to turn the car around.

"I'm curious if the same thing happened with Felix and Jonah," Asher said.

"We each called a different group of friends," Rocky replied. "I called the folks in Augusta to interview them about Bob and Tess's relationship. Felix called the folks in Albany to chat about Donald and Tess. We let Jonah call Arnold Hamilton's family because it was a bit more of a delicate dance since there was a trial and an acquittal."

"Even Arnold Hamilton's family had nothing bad to say about Tess?" Asher asked.

"Nope. Mr. Hamilton's kids said that Tess had made their father very happy and she'd taken good care of him."

"What about the life insurance fraud? They wouldn't be singing the same tune if she'd gotten the inheritance."

Rocky shrugged. "I have to listen to the recordings, but Jonah said they'd forgiven her. They said her actions were derived from fear, not malice. In fact, they're the ones paying for her cruise."

"Oh my God. The Hamiltons probably hired someone to push Tess overboard."

"What?" Rocky asked, jerking his head in Asher's direction.

"Watch out," Asher said, leaning across the car and jerking the steering wheel to the right. "You swerved into the other lane."

"You just implied the Hamiltons hired a hit on Tess."

"I was joking," Asher said. "But seriously, she tried to take all their money, and they send her on a cruise?"

"Who said Tess tried to steal all the money?" Rocky asked.

"No one said it, but it's been implied in the media coverage. So, Tess allegedly just tried to steal some of the money?"

Rocky nodded. "She was set to inherit a hundred thousand dollars, and the rest went to his children. To be honest, that's barely a dent in the man's assets."

"Huh."

"What?" Rocky asked.

"I think forging a document for only a portion of the money was genius," Asher said. "It shouldn't have raised any flags. Most husbands would make sure their wives were cared for after their passing, especially if they knew their death was imminent. Are you sure the document is even a forgery?"

"No," Rocky admitted honestly. "Jennifer Blossom had been ready to pay out the proceeds until an anonymous phone call tipped them off."

"It could've been nothing more than a disgruntled kid," Asher scoffed. "It's really easy for them to imply they don't hold a grudge against Tess because they've robbed her of the money. They send her on a cruise to cover their guilt and tell you guys how amazing she is. What was the DA's basis for bringing charges against Tess?"

"The handwriting expert said Arnold Hamilton's signature was forged."

"Bullshit science," Asher said. "What else?"

"The witness to the signature is a fake person, as far as I can tell. No one by the name lives at that address, and the phone number wasn't valid."

"Maybe they're dyslexic," Asher suggested. "A transposed number gets you a completely different address and phone number."

"I thought of that," Rocky said. "I've searched high and low for this person, but Rona Danielson doesn't exist."

"Is Rona a nickname?" Asher asked.

"I thought so at first, but I've called every Danielson in a two-hundred-mile radius. No Rona. I've accepted the forgery is real. I'm just not convinced Tess was behind it."

"Okay," Asher said. "If Tess didn't do it, who did?"

"Someone looking out for her best interest, perhaps." Rocky thought of Grant's fierce protectiveness toward his mother. While he understood it, Rocky had to wonder if Grant wasn't protecting something else. Hadn't he said that they all had skeletons in their closets? What were Grant's? And what about Helen? Rocky had reviewed Hamilton's medical records at length and was confident the man had died as a direct cause of his illness. No one helped Arnold Hamilton to an early grave. Had Helen seen the writing on the wall and taken steps to ensure Tess was cared for?

"What's the son say about all this?"

"I haven't asked him yet. I'm saving his interview for second to last," Rocky said as he turned into Joseph Tribble Park.

"Who's last?"

"Tess's friend, Helen Girard. She's on the cruise with Tess, so I'll chat with her next weekend. I want to assimilate the information from these interviews before I chat with Grant, even though I don't anticipate he'll be much help since he disapproved of his mother's participation." Rocky parked the car. "Enough chat about the investigation. I want to show you my favorite park."

They got out of the car and walked around to the trunk. Asher hoisted the heavy picnic basket and Rocky grabbed the blanket while lusting after his husband's bunched biceps.

"What's in this thing?" Asher asked. "It weighs a ton."

"I've never gone on a romantic picnic before and might've gone overboard."

"What did you make? Feels like a Thanksgiving feast."

Rocky laughed. "I didn't make anything, but I did buy lots of yummy stuff from the deli."

Asher leaned over and kissed his temple. "I'll love it all." He looked around at the lush space and commented on the many ways people were entertaining themselves. You could expect to find everything from bicycles to roller skates on the trails. More adventurous people enjoyed kayaks, canoes, pedal boats, and paddleboards on the lake. "Ever tried to kayak?"

"Once," Rocky said. "It didn't go well. You?"

"I'm afraid of getting stuck and drowning when it capsizes. I'm all in for canoeing, though."

"We'll look into buying one." Rocky gestured to a replica of an old-fashioned schoolhouse on a post near one of the pavilions. "I want to show you something."

Asher followed him over. "It's a tiny library," he said.

"My dad built and installed them all over the city. Queen Bea was a school librarian, and he wanted to honor her when she retired."

"Roger is good people."

"He is," Rocky agreed. He opened the picnic basket, removed a stack of books, and set them inside the little schoolhouse. "Adult books on the top shelf and children's books on the bottom." Rocky had contributed some to each row. Then he selected a book someone else had donated to the library. Gesturing to the heaving bosom of the woman bent over a roguish pirate's arm, Rocky said, "Marla will love this."

He tucked it under his arm and watched Asher rifle through the picnic basket contents.

Asher looked up. "Is this chicken salad on croissants?"

"Yep."

Asher linked his fingers through Rocky's and headed toward one of the empty picnic tables. Rocky squeezed Asher's fingers to halt his forward progress. "No?" Asher asked.

Rocky shook his head. "Not secluded enough."

Asher leaned in. "Just what are you planning to do to me in this very public park?"

Rocky rolled his eyes. "Dream on, big guy. This way," he said, tugging on Asher's hand. "I have an extraordinary spot in mind."

"How much farther?" Asher asked after a few minutes. "I'm starving."

"Just over there." Rocky pointed to a huge shade tree that provided a fantastic view of the water.

Rocky spread out the blanket once they reached the tree. Asher set the basket in the middle, then sat down beside it. Rather than dig in immediately, his husband stared across the little lake for several moments before looking at Rocky.

"This spot feels so familiar to me, but I've never been here."

"Yes, you have," Rocky said. "This exact view was captured in watercolor and hangs over the couch."

"Oh, wow," Asher said. "Your mom was so talented. The trees are taller and fuller, but otherwise little has changed. Thank you for sharing it with me." He leaned over and captured Rocky's lips for a sweet kiss.

"I will hopefully have another surprise for you later this afternoon."

"What is it?" Asher asked.

"It wouldn't be a surprise if I told you. Besides, I don't want to get your hopes up in case it falls through."

Happiness hummed through Rocky as Asher continued to prod him for clues while they unpacked the basket. His husband was easy to distract when Rocky started feeding him various bites of food.

"You people are really loose with your definitions of a salad," Asher said after sampling potato salad, broccoli salad, and even fruit salad. Maybe Rocky had gone a little overboard with his selection.

"If it has mayo or marshmallow fluff, it's a salad. Here's a nonsalad picnic staple," Rocky said, feeding Asher a kettle chip dusted in Carolina barbecue seasoning.

"I'm not complaining," Asher said, then took a massive bite of his chicken salad croissant.

Once they finished eating, Asher sat against the tree and Rocky lay on the blanket, using Asher's thigh as a pillow. His husband lazily stroked his fingers through Rocky's hair while reading the smutty romance out loud.

"Oh, yeah, Marla will love this," Rocky said as his eyes grew heavier.

He'd just about drifted to sleep when his phone vibrated in his pocket. Rocky thought about ignoring it but remembered he was waiting to hear back about Asher's surprise. He sat up and scooted over to the far corner of the blanket so his husband couldn't see the message.

"Better not be dick pics."

"Shut up," Rocky said as he checked the message. His pulse picked up when he received the answer he'd hoped for. Jerking his head up, he said, "I found our girl."

"Um, what?"

"Fifi," Rocky said. "Well, ironically, her name is Fiona, but we can work with it, right?"

Asher grinned. "Are you kidding?"

Rocky shook his head. "I've been thinking about the dog a lot since you brought it up."

"Because it's a freaking great idea," Asher said. He practically vibrated with excitement.

"Karen agrees. I called her while you were gone, and she told me the right kind of dog will help me with my recovery. She referred me to several different sites where they train dogs for emotional support and personal protection. Fiona is a two-year-old German shepherd trained to do both." Rocky thought of the videos he'd seen of Fiona on their site and started laughing. "Most of these dogs failed out of K9 school for various reasons. Fiona was a little bit wackadoodle as a pup, so we might see remnants of it on some days."

Asher laughed. "How wackadoodle?"

Rocky scooted over to sit beside his husband, then pulled up the website and clicked on the video. "See for yourself. Keep in mind she was just a baby in the beginning."

Asher started chuckling as soon as the video played. They'd put Fiona through several different tests, and her hyper ass had failed every single one. Instead of attacking the guy dressed in pads, she peed on his foot. Instead of calmly aiding the trainer who was using a walker, Fiona jerked it out of the woman's hands and attacked the tennis balls on the bottom of the legs. Luckily, it was just a training exercise and the lady wasn't dependent on the walker, or she would've fallen over and gotten hurt.

"Come on," Asher said, pointing to the screen. "She saw those tennis balls and couldn't resist. Who could blame her?"

The video continued, showing Fiona progressing from a rowdy pup to a regal lady who proudly wore her service vest. In a mock attack, the dog thwarted the aggressor and saved the day. The final demonstration showed Fiona reacting to a trainer mimicking an emotional crisis. The beauty of her intuition brought tears to Rocky's eyes. He'd filled out the adoption paperwork two days ago and felt like he'd been holding his breath while waiting for a response. Tess's investigation had been a very welcome distraction.

"Our application has been approved," Rocky said. "We can go meet her to see if we're a good fit."

Asher scoffed. "Let's go get our dog."

"She's smiling," Asher said when the three of them walked into the pet store two hours later. They'd fallen madly in love with Fiona, and the beautiful girl seemed quite smitten with them too. "Smugly, I might add."

"Because she knows she's the prettiest girl in all the land," Rocky said, looking down at the dog walking by his side. "Smartest too. Look how she's trained you to ride in the back seat already."

"She wants to be near you," Asher said, wrapping his arm around Rocky's waist. "I can't blame her."

They went through the store and bought anything and everything they thought she might need. They'd debated on getting a crate for Fiona, then decided to wait and see how she did without one first. Rocky had every intention of taking her to work with him, and she could sleep on a plush dog bed in their room at night.

"You know she's not really going to sleep on that, right?" Asher said when Rocky put the bed in the cart.

"Where is she going to sleep?"

"With you," Asher said. "I'll probably be the one relegated to the dog bed." He gave it a good squeeze and added, "It's memory foam, so it might work out okay."

Rocky laughed and kissed his cheek. "Never. Fifi and I will make room for you."

"You better," Asher said, then growled playfully. Fiona froze and studied him; her head cocked to the side. Asher let go of Rocky and held up his hands in peace.

Rocky's phone rang as they were checking out. He looked at the caller ID and saw it was Queen Bea calling.

"I don't owe you money, do I?"

"Rockford, is that any way to answer a telephone?" Queen Bea asked.

"No, ma'am."

She huffed. "Kids these days."

"We can start over if you'd like."

"Who has time for that?" she grumbled. "I could die before we get to the reason for my call."

Alarm raced through Rocky's nervous system. "Are you ill?" Fiona sat down in front of him, bumping his free hand with her nose. Rocky stroked the top of her head and willed himself to calm down. Asher nudged him aside and slid his card into the machine to pay for their purchases. "Have you called the nurse?"

"Don't be so dramatic, Rockford. I was teasing you. I'm not dying. I just don't want to waste precious moments restarting phone conversations."

Like this detour wasn't a complete waste of time, breath, and anxiety. Rather than point it out and cause further delay, Rocky shook his head and said, "To what do I owe this great pleasure?"

"Smartass," his nana mumbled. "You can solve the case regarding Nurse Ratchet so she'll keep her greedy mitts off my man."

"Your man?"

"Remember Harvey?" she asked. "It's a good thing you didn't take the bet. You'd be owing me a hundred and twenty dollars by now."

Rocky laughed. "The bet was going to be forty dollars."

"Per visit."

"Eww," he said. Eager to change the subject, Rocky said, "What's this about Nurse Ratchet? You told me she quit."

Queen Bea heaved a heavy sigh. "Rockford, the name isn't owned by one nurse. We assign the moniker to whomever loses favor with the residents."

"Who's on your shit list now?"

"You know who," she replied. "The one you're investigating."

"Helen Girard?" he asked. "What did she do?"

"Put the moves on my man."

Rocky's brow furrowed. "How? She's on a cruise ship in the middle of the ocean."

"The hell she is," Queen Bea said. "Harvey hurt his hip while—"

"I get the idea, Nana. Are you telling me you've seen Helen Girard this weekend? The nurse with the pretty white hair and pale blue eyes."

"I saw her five minutes ago when she collected Harvey for his next rehab session. I'm pretty sure the asshole is milking this for the extra attention."

"I'm on my way, Nana."

"That's my boy." She hung up, leaving Rocky to stare at his phone.

Asher placed his hand at the small of Rocky's back and urged him forward. "Is everything okay?" he asked as he steered the cart around a group of people looking at the rows of puppies and kittens available for adoption.

"I'm not sure," Rocky said, then repeated the conversation he'd had with his nana.

"I thought you said Helen was on a trip with Tess."

"Tess said she was going with her dear friend. I thought she meant Helen. I mean, there are photographs of the woman mixed in with Tess's children and grandchildren."

Asher quirked a brow. "Dear friends can sometimes imply a deeper connection than friendship, especially among the older generations. They don't say boyfriend and girlfriend. They refer to their love interests as dear or special friends."

"Who did Tess go on the cruise with?" Rocky asked.

"I'm sure her friend Helen can tell you."

"Yes, but will she?"

CHAPTER 21

Rocky left Asher and Fiona with Queen Bea, then followed his nana's directions to locate the onsite rehabilitation facility. He was initially suspicious when Nana said Harvey was getting physical therapy on a Sunday, but Queen Bea had reminded him how easily senior citizens got injured.

"Someone is always falling around here," she'd said.

"Is that what happened to your friend, Harvey?" Asher had asked.

Rocky had shaken his head. "You don't want to go there."

Queen Bea had still been cackling when Rocky walked away after coaxing a promise from his nana that she'd be on her best behavior.

Rocky found the rehabilitation center quickly enough. No one was in the waiting room, and the glass walls separating it from the facility were frosted. He tried the doors, but they were locked. Rocky could tell the lights were on, but he couldn't confirm if Helen and Harvey were inside. The only options were to take a seat and wait to see if they came out, bang on the doors, or track down another nurse who might be able to unlock the doors for him.

He decided to wait a bit since plan B would make him look like an idiot and plan C involved a lot of questions. His patience paid off because Helen and Harvey came through the double doors a few minutes later. Helen halted so fast that Harvey tipped forward in the wheelchair.

"Easy, doll," Harvey said. "I'm not wearing a seat belt."

"Sorry, Mr. Marks," Helen said without looking away from Rocky. He saw recognition in her eyes but not fear or guilt.

"I know you," Harvey said, pointing a bony finger at Rocky. "You're Beatrice's boy."

"And I know you," Rocky replied. "I also know why you need physical therapy."

The older man's cheeks turned pink, and Helen chuckled.

"I bet he's here to find out what your intentions are toward his grandmother," Helen teased Harvey.

The older man's cheeks continued to flush, and Rocky worried about his health. Queen Bea would kill him if he gave Harvey a stroke.

"Nah," Rocky said. "I'm here to speak to Ms. Girard."

Helen nodded, then picked up the phone from the reception desk and dialed an extension. She spoke softly, but Rocky heard her request assistance getting Harvey back to his room. She hung up and knelt down next to Harvey's chair. "Deidre is coming to take you back to your room."

"I'd rather go to Beatrice's."

"Might want to slow it down there a bit, Mr. Marks," Helen said.

The older man chuckled. "She's a hell of a woman, your nana."

"This I know," Rocky said. "I'm expecting you to treat her right."

"Deal," Harvey agreed, extending a hand toward Rocky.

The two men shook, then lulled into an awkward silence while waiting for Deidre. Luckily, she didn't take long. The nurse studied Rocky for a second before looking at Helen. He saw a silent communication between them. Helen nodded, and Deidre wheeled Harvey away.

"Care to step into my office?" she asked, gesturing to one of the frosted doors she and Harvey had passed through.

"Sure."

Helen punched a code into the keypad and pushed open the door when it unlocked. The rehabilitation room was exactly what he'd expect to find in any physical therapy facility, but the equipment was modified for seniors with impaired balance and other disadvantages. It smelled like Clorox and Bengay.

Helen passed through the room and led Rocky to a small office at the rear of the facility. The space was neat and tidy with very few personal items on any of the surfaces. One of them was the same photograph Tess had on her bookshelf.

Rocky picked it up off Helen's desk and studied it closely. "You love her," he said.

"I do."

Rocky looked up. "You're in love with her."

Helen said, "I always have been and always will be."

Rocky returned the photo to its place of honor, then sat down.

Helen folded her hands on the desk and leveled a direct gaze at Rocky. "I told Tess I didn't want to participate in this investigation, but she asked me to do it anyway. She believes in you. Do you really think Tess is innocent?"

"My gut tells me she is. Help me clear her name."

Helen took a deep breath. "What do you want to know?"

There were so many things. Like earlier, Rocky's thoughts swirled around in his head like a cerebral cyclone. "Who'd Tess go on a cruise with?"

Helen looked down. "Richard Beauford."

"Her attorney?" Rocky asked, hoping he kept the judgment from his voice.

Helen chuckled dryly. "Tess isn't the kind of person to live by herself for long."

"Weren't there a dozen years or so between Bob Duncan's death and her marriage to Donald Trout?"

"Fifteen," Helen said. "Tess and I traveled a lot. We settled in Albany because her oldest daughter lived there. We took jobs and shared a home."

"You were a couple?"

Helen pinched her lips together and sat quietly for a second before answering. "No. We've never had a sexual relationship." He noticed she hadn't said intimate. Thanks to Asher, Rocky understood that a couple could be intimate without sex. But was Helen's remark wordplay or deliberate? "Do you believe in soulmates, Mr. Jacobs?"

He thought about the love he felt for Asher. "I do."

Helen nodded. "Tess and I are soulmates, even though we're not romantically involved." She cleared her throat. "To be clear, yes, I'd happily enter a romantic relationship, but Tess doesn't love me like that." How lonely was her life?

"Don't you want to find someone who will?"

"No," she said without hesitation. "Tess isn't happy without a man in her life for long. She dated a lot between Bob's death and meeting Donald Trout." Helen shook her head. "Bless her heart, she has horrible taste in men, but she's still looking for the epic romance she reads about in her books. Bob Duncan was an awful man, and she met a string of losers afterward."

Rocky sat up straighter in his chair. This was the first time someone expressed a negative opinion about Bob. He knew he had to take her thoughts with a grain of salt, but it felt important to him. Rather than interrupt her to ask questions, Rocky let her talk.

"So, I decided to take action by steering her toward men who were worthy of her. I met Don through some charity work I did for the hospital. I knew he was right for Tess the moment we met, so I introduced them. They were happy for a few years, but his health spiraled toward the end. Don hadn't made any financial arrangements to care for Tess, so she moved back in with me after his passing. She grew despondent after a while, and Grant suggested we come to Savannah. He wanted to keep a closer eye on her."

"And you introduced her to Arnold Hamilton?"

Helen nodded. "I met him while working at a facility similar to this one." She arched a brow. "I'm sure you know the name of my previous employer. Your grandmother isn't as discreet as she thinks she is."

Rocky shook his head. "I'm sorry. I didn't ask her to look into your background. I recognized you from the trial photos and asked your name."

"She's a hoot."

Rocky chuckled. "She's something."

"Anyway," Helen said, "like before, I introduced Tess to Arnie. She never knew I was setting her up, and I liked it that way. Tess wanted to get caught up in the romance of her relationships. I didn't want anything to ruin it for her."

"And Arnie was a good guy too?"

"Yeah," Helen said softly. "I thought he'd do better than Don and make sure Tess was taken care of. The only good thing Bob Duncan ever did for Tess was taking out that life insurance policy. Arnie and Don, the kind gentlemen who'd treated her with respect, hadn't shown her the same courtesy."

"You think Arnie's beneficiary change form was forged?"

"It's the only conclusion I can draw since we couldn't find the witness who supposedly signed the form." She widened her eyes suddenly. "You're a PI. Finding people is what you do."

"I've tried, believe me." He recapped the steps he'd taken to find Rona Danielson.

"Tess didn't forge the document, and she sure as hell didn't kill any of her husbands."

"Did you?" Rocky asked.

"What? Kill her husbands or forge the document?"

"Either."

Helen's pale eyes looked like twin blue fires. Hadn't Rocky read somewhere that those were the hottest-burning flames? "I would never have hurt Don or Arnie. They loved and deserved Tess."

"And Bob? I spent twelve hours yesterday hearing how wonderful he was."

"He was a fucking son of a bitch if ever one lived," Helen hissed. Her eyes seemed to lose focus as she stared off into space. Rocky didn't dare say or do anything to interrupt her. "I wanted to kill him. I begged Tess to let me do it. It would've been so easy. The man was taking a fairly high dosage of digitalis, which is a derivative of foxglove. The right amount saves your life, and the wrong one takes it. Just an extra pill or two, and she would've been rid of him." Helen continued staring off into space long after her words trailed off.

"Tess didn't agree?"

Helen flinched like she'd forgotten his presence, then met his gaze once more. "She loved the asshole, no matter how many times he hit her or sexually assaulted her."

Rocky tried to hide his shock, but his mouth went slack anyway.

"You don't believe me?"

"I do," Rocky said. And he did. "I'm just trying to figure out why no one, not friends, family, or former coworkers mentioned anything about it. Did they love him so much they'd lie to protect him all these years later?"

Helen scoffed. "They're not protecting him, Mr. Jacobs. Hell, they might've even convinced themselves that they believe the lies. Every single one of them knew he was physically abusing her."

"Even the kids?"

Helen shook her head. "Tess moved heaven and earth to protect them. She'd sense a dark spell coming and make sure they weren't home. Bob was smart enough not to hit her where people could see it."

"If they were masters at hiding the violence from their children who'd lived in the same house, is it fair to blame the friend who hadn't?"

Helen's nostrils flared, and she clenched her jaw. She took a deep breath and released it slowly. Rocky sensed she was trying to get ahold of her emotions. "They knew."

"How? You should've heard these people yammer on about their famous parties. I heard a dozen accounts of the New Year's Eve party where Tess went into labor. They all talked about Bob's—"

Helen slammed her fist down on the desk, startling him. "Do you know why she went into labor four weeks early?" Rocky started to speak, but she cut him off. "Bob knocked her down the stairs during an altercation, even though their house was filled with their friends."

"Christ," Rocky said with a wince.

"Bob had followed her up to their bedroom and confronted her about flirting with his friend, Dave. Tess tried to get away and return to the party, but Bob followed, and the argument became physical. Her water broke during the fall." Helen paused to pull herself together. "He told everyone she'd tripped down the steps, but they had to have overheard their argument. It's a miracle Grant wasn't seriously hurt. Then again, she wouldn't have been pregnant in the first place if he hadn't forced himself on her after losing badly at poker. I hated that fucker. Still do."

"My God."

"Tess didn't trust any of them to help her, so she drove herself to the hospital, which was forty minutes away. Once she got there, she called me collect. It took me four hours to reach her side, and I've never left since." Helen took a deep breath. "I told him he better never lay another motherfucking finger on her again. I warned Bob that I'd kill him. I meant it too."

"Your threat worked?"

Helen nodded. "Or so I believed. He switched to verbal abuse, which was just as damaging. He had one affair after the other to demoralize her spirit. I didn't find out about these things until his health took a hard turn. You can believe that he spent every remaining minute of his life wondering when I was going to strike."

"But you didn't."

"No. Tess and I argued about it a lot toward the end of his life. I asked how she could defend a man who'd beaten and raped her. I begged her. Just a few extra pills. He wouldn't suffer."

"Sounds easier than he deserved."

Helen snorted. "Probably."

"Did Tess love him that much?" Rocky asked.

"She wasn't trying to save Bob," Helen said softly.

Then he understood. "She didn't want his death on your conscience."

"Yes. Tess can't love me the way I want her to, and it's not her fault. She still loves me more than anyone else has. I'd do anything for her, but I didn't kill Bob, and I didn't forge the life insurance documents." She tipped her head. "I wish I'd thought of it because I probably would've done a better job."

"So, why'd you part ways with Whispering Willows, and why the secrecy?"

"Arnie's shitty kids lodged a complaint after he died," Helen replied.

"The facility told you that?"

"No, but they didn't have to. The kids claimed I used my position to introduce Tess to wealthy men."

"Didn't you?" Rocky asked.

"Yes, but not due to a nefarious plan. I wasn't choosing the one most likely to die quickest so Tess could make bank."

Rocky chuckled. "Fair enough."

"Whispering Willows wasn't willing to listen to my side, so they offered me a severance package and made me sign an NDA. It's a good thing I did too because Tess needed the money to pay for a good attorney."

The man Tess took on a cruise instead of Helen. Tess was starting to slip in Rocky's estimation, although he tried his best not to judge. Besides, Helen wouldn't want to hear his thoughts on Tess's shoddy treatment of her. "About this cruise," he said. "Are you aware Mr. Hamilton's children paid for the trip?"

Helen sniffed. "It's the least the little ungrateful assholes could do for her. Where the hell were they when their father needed care around the clock toward the end? Tess and I took care of Arnie. They just wanted to collect the money after he died."

"If they're so awful, why would they pay for the cruise?"

Helen shrugged. "Guilt."

"Because their father didn't leave her any money?"

"Or were they grateful she didn't get more? There's a far cry between a seven-thousand-dollar cruise and a hundred-thousand-dollar beneficiary payout."

"What if they worried Tess would contest the will?" Rocky asked. Then a thought occurred to him. "Or they had reason to believe the insurance forms weren't falsified. Maybe they wanted to stop Tess from looking into it further."

"Arnie's kids are jerks but sending Tess to jail just so she doesn't get that money?" Helen shook her head. "I don't think so."

"People have done a lot less for a hundred grand."

"True," Helen agreed. "But that's like a hundred bucks to them."

Rocky tilted his head to the side. "Do you know what rich people like?"

"I honestly wouldn't know."

"Getting richer," Rocky told her. "Arnie's children might not have wanted to share a dime with a woman their father had only known for four or five years. If they believed the allegations they made against you, they probably even felt justified in keeping the money from Tess."

Helen sat back and considered what he said. For the first time since he'd arrived, Rocky realized how exhausted the woman looked. "The cruise might've been an attempt to distract her." Helen's shoulders slumped for a second before she stiffened her spine. "How are you going to find the truth?"

"That's the million-dollar question."

Helen nodded and wrote down her phone number on a piece of paper. "Call me anytime."

Rocky pocketed the number, thanked her for her time, and then retrieved his man and beast.

CHAPTER 22

"**W**elcome back to the show, guys," Mad Dog Mulroney said. "I see you've brought your mascot with you." He gestured to the sleeping dog at Rocky's feet. "What's her name?"

"Fiona," Rocky said. The dog jerked her head up and looked at him. He reached down and scratched her ears. "She's the best girl ever." Adopting her was the second-best decision he'd ever made. Marrying Asher was the first.

"She's beautiful," Mad Dog said.

"Thank you."

"So, we have a huge treat for fans of the show. We set up a live question and answer session, and my producer told me the lines are jammed with callers. Are you ready?"

"Go easy. It's our first time," Jonah quipped.

While Felix had been over the moon with the live caller aspect, Rocky and Jonah were more hesitant. It wasn't like they'd avoided the nut jobs on social media. There'd been all kinds of false information shared about them on various sites like Reddit, and some gung-ho keyboard jockeys had even infiltrated their fan group on Facebook. Those things were easy to ignore or resolve, but a live caller during a popular radio show was different. Mad Dog made it clear they weren't screening the questions first, which meant they could face anything from furious accusations to marriage proposals and everything in between.

"Our first caller is Jane. Are you still with us?" Mad Dog asked.

"Yes, I'm here," she said. "Hi, guys. I absolutely love your podcast."

"Hi, Jane. Thanks so much for listening," Felix said.

Rocky and Jonah also said hello and thanked her for tuning in. Then Mad Dog spurred Jane onto her question.

"How do you separate fact from rumors when interviewing people for your investigation?" Jane asked.

"That's a great question," Felix said. "You have to take what people say with a grain of salt until you can find the hard evidence to back it up. There are many things that can influence a person's memory, and it's irresponsible for us to report supposition and rumor as facts."

"Sometimes that means we walk away from a case without getting answers," Jonah said. "Not all investigations will lead to a resolution, and we don't manufacture things just to get good ratings. It's another reason why we don't discuss cases until we've thoroughly investigated them."

"I think that's what sets your podcast apart from some of the others that are only looking to share salacious gossip," Mad Dog said. "Jane, thank you so much for your question. Our next caller is Miles. What question would you like to pose to the fellas?"

"Are any of you single?" he asked.

The guys laughed and said, "No," at the same time. They softened their responses by thanking him for supporting the show.

"Sorry, Miles," Mad Dog said. "Who's next? Ah, yes, Sarah. Hello, love. You've got the trio of trouble's full attention. What would you like to know?"

"Hi, guys. Love your show." She paused so they could return her greeting and thank her for listening. "Have you considered doing live shows?"

"That's a great question," Jonah replied. "I've heard it's a popular trend among podcasters, but we haven't discussed it yet."

"Sounds really fun," Felix said.

"We'd need a super cool location," Rocky added. "Something historical or true-crime related."

"What about attending Crime Con?" Sarah asked.

"Don't get greedy with your questions," Mad Dog admonished mildly.

"Sorry," she said. "Please consider both things to give your fans a chance to meet you."

With each new question, Rocky relaxed more. No one accused them of anything or tried to trip them up. Midway through, the show's producer appeared at the window and gestured wildly at her phone. It distracted the hell out of Rocky, but Mad Dog just rolled with it. He introduced the next caller while pulling his phone from his pocket.

Rocky was too busy studying the DJ's face to hear the question or the answer Felix started to give before Mad Dog looked up with wide eyes and cut him off.

"Forgive my rudeness, Felix," the DJ said, "but there's some breaking news out of Governor Stanton's office that the guys will want to hear."

Rocky's pulse kicked into high gear. He looked over at Felix and Jonah who looked as anxious as he felt.

"Don't edge us, Mad Dog," Felix said.

Rocky snorted. "I don't think you can say that on the radio, Fee."

Felix cringed. "Sorry."

Mad Dog laughed and shook his head. "The fine will be worth it because I get to tell you that Stanton has just signed Bo Cahill's posthumous pardon. Congratulations."

It felt like a giant vacuum had sucked the air out of the room. Then the three of them were on their feet hugging one another. Tears welled in their eyes, and Rocky knew his friends were thinking about sweet Agnes and all the pain she and her children had endured over the years.

"How does it feel?" Mad Dog asked after a few moments.

"Euphoric," Rocky replied, feeling breathless. "We couldn't have done this without the help of so many."

"Especially the fans," Felix said. "They made the Cahills' fight their own and kept pushing until we got the job done."

"God, this is incredible," Jonah added. "I can't wait to talk to the Cahills."

"I'm honored to share this moment with the three of you," Mad Dog said, sounding a little choked up. He cleared his throat. "Looks like we lost our caller. I'm so pumped up about the news that I can't remember what the guy had asked. Can you?" he asked Felix.

"It completely slipped my mind too."

When Rocky and Jonah couldn't remember either, Mad Dog decided to move on to the next caller. "We have Tim on the line. Go ahead with your question."

"Hey, guys," the caller said. Rocky's heart sank. He'd know that voice anywhere. Motherfucking Tim Duggins. He'd known damn well this asshole wasn't going to just go away without a fight. Oh fuck, this wasn't going to be pretty. "I'd like to know how you expect anyone to take you seriously when your resident private investigator is too stupid to avoid the classic setup and led a woman straight to her husband's fuck pad. She gunned down her cheating husband and his mistress, who turned out to be her sister-in-law. Then she shot herself right in front of this moron. Google his name plus pretty poison or Vegas and see what you find. He escaped criminal charges, but he should've been sued in civil court. It's not too late. I hope the victims hear this and take my advice."

Rocky tensed, and his breath caught in his throat. He wanted to signal to Mad Dog to cut the caller off, but he couldn't move, speak, or even think. Fiona stood up and softly whined as she nudged his hand with her nose. Rocky slid his fingers into her fur, reminding himself to breathe. He felt Jonah's and Felix's attention yet couldn't do anything but close his eyes and picture something serene while he fought off the rising panic.

He heard voices, some of them loud, but he couldn't comprehend a single thing. Felix threw his arm around Rocky's shoulders and pulled him into an embrace. He kissed the top of Rocky's head while rubbing his hand up and down Rocky's back. Black dots danced in his vision as Rocky's chest felt tighter and tighter.

"Breathe, Major," Felix whispered. "Come on."

Rocky inhaled a deep, shaky breath, which cleared the dots and brought the room back into focus. Fiona whimpered again and pushed harder against him, nudging his other hand with her nose. Rocky buried the second hand in her fur, focusing on the slide of silky strands between his fingers. He leaned forward to hug her as his breathing regulated, and Fiona licked his face. In his pocket, Rocky's cell phone started buzzing. As soon as the call went to voice mail, it immediately started vibrating again. He continued ignoring it to focus on pulling himself together.

"I cut off the caller and sent the show to a commercial break," Mad Dog said. "I'm really sorry."

Rocky shook his head. "It's not your fault. Honestly, I'm surprised it's taken this long for someone to match my name to the incident in Vegas."

"Do you guys want to take the final questions or call it a day?" the DJ asked.

"We'll finish," Rocky said. "Can't let people like Tim win."

"You sure?" Jonah asked.

Rocky met his gaze and nodded. "Yeah. Sorry for my minimeltdown."

"Shut up," Jonah replied.

Rocky's mouth twitched. "You shut up."

"And he's back," Felix said.

"We have another minute before we're back on the air," Mad Dog told them. "How do you guys want to play this off?"

"We could just pretend it didn't happen," Jonah said.

"That will only make people more suspicious," Rocky replied. "I'll have to address it."

"Are you sure?" Mad Dog said. "I'm really sorry this happened. It wasn't what I had in mind when I set it up."

"I know," Rocky said. "It was inevitable, though. Someone was bound to get upset over our mission and start looking for ways to humiliate us."

As soon as the words left his mouth, Rocky realized how true they were. He'd dreaded every appearance or interview because he knew this could happen. While it was a wholly unpleasant experience, it wasn't as awful as his subconscious had imagined. Oddly, it helped that the assault was instigated by the one person who hated him most rather than a random stranger.

"Attaboy, Major," Felix said.

"Today, I'm their huckleberry. Tomorrow, it could be one of you. We'll have to pick and choose the way we combat the attacks. One method won't fit all. And we can't let it alter our course. We have hell to raise and wrongs to right."

Jonah looked at him and said, "This kind of feels like a *Braveheart* moment."

Felix snorted. "I'm not painting my face blue."

Laughing, Rocky said, "And I'm not mooning anyone."

"Back in five," Mad Dog told them, then silently counted down before they were back on the air. "And we're back with the *Sinister in Savannah* podcasters, also known as the trio of trouble. Rather than pretend the last call didn't happen, I'm allowing Rocky to address the accusations Tim made against him."

"I appreciate it," Rocky said before launching into an overview of the night Julia Warner killed her husband and sister-in-law before taking her own life. He stuck to public facts and didn't dredge up his personal thoughts or feelings, except when it came to the aftermath. "Julia's family has been harassed enough as it is. I'm begging everyone to please leave them alone. Let them heal and move on with their lives as best they can. There are plenty of unresolved cases and instances of injustice to explore. Don't do it as a favor to me. Do it because you're good people who care about the damage you'd cause to her children. The media has exploited her death and turned their lives into a living hell once already."

"And yours too," Felix said softly. "You deserve to heal too." He turned to face Rocky. "It's a miracle we're friends after what the press put you through."

Rocky laughed, which helped ease the tension in his shoulders. "Yeah, I wasn't really keen on you at first. But then I started to pay attention to the kind of reporter you are and stopped lumping you in with the ones who live to sensationalize everyone's personal tragedy." Rocky smiled at his two best friends. "Meeting the two of you was the best thing to happen to me in a long time. Your friendship helped patch my broken heart, and the podcast gave me a purpose. Because of you, I found the courage to seek treatment for PTSD and reconnected with the love of my life. Thanks for believing in me."

"We love you, Major," Felix said. "Right, Jonah?"

The big guy wiped a tear and cleared his throat. "Very much."

"I love you guys too."

Mad Dog sniffled and said, "Oh, man. That's beautiful. We just took one small step into bromance history and one giant leap toward ending toxic masculinity."

"New podcast idea?" Rocky teased.

"Maybe if this gig doesn't pan out," Felix replied.

"We should all be lucky to have friends like the three of you. And on that note, this is Mad Dog Mulroney wishing you all a rockin' day." He gave them a thumbs-up. "We're off the air. This is the time where I normally ask popular guests to come back, but I'm not sure the three of you would be willing."

Felix and Jonah deferred to Rocky, who said, "We'd love to. Have your people contact our people."

They should've stuck around to exchange pleasantries, but Rocky's phone kept going off in his pocket, and he needed fresh air. They shook hands with the DJ and headed toward the bank of elevators.

"Do you think this Tim guy was someone acting on the governor's behalf?" Felix asked. "This was the kind of blowback you worried about, Major."

"Christ," Jonah said.

"Relax," Rocky said as he led Fiona into the elevator. "I know exactly who Tim is, and it has nothing to do with the hit piece you wrote on the governor."

"Who is he?" Felix asked.

Rocky gave them the equivalent of an elevator pitch because he didn't want to waste more breath and energy than Tim Duggins deserved.

"Some best friend he is," Jonah said when they got off the elevator on the ground floor.

Rocky heard his name called from across the lobby. Jonah stiffened, and Felix tried to place himself between Rocky and an unknown threat, but Rocky wasn't worried. He'd recognize that voice anywhere. Stepping around Felix, Rocky walked into Asher's embrace.

"I've been calling you," Asher said.

"I was still on the air," he replied. "I'm sorry I worried you."

"I changed my mind. I'm going to kill Duggins," Asher said, holding Rocky tighter.

"I can't overhear this," Jonah said, sticking his fingers in his ears.

"You can still hear them, big guy," Felix pointed out.

"Nope," Jonah said.

Fiona whined, pulling everyone's attention to her. Asher released Rocky and dropped to one knee in front of the dog. "Were you a good girl for Daddy?"

"The best," Rocky said, running a hand over her head.

"Is it safe for me to remove my fingers now?" Jonah asked.

Felix snorted. "Define safe? They're using daddy talk."

Jonah hooked his arm around Felix's neck and rubbed his knuckles over the reporter's head. Felix squirmed and tried to get away, so Jonah increased his hold and the friction.

"My hair. My hair," Felix said.

Jonah let go so Felix could repair the damage.

Rocky and Asher laughed at their antics, then Rocky hugged his friends goodbye and followed his husband outside. The humidity felt good on his cold, clammy skin for once, but he immediately stepped into the shade to avoid getting incinerated beneath the hot sun.

"What are we going to do about Duggins?" Asher asked. "I can't let this go."

"Of course not. We don't strike back yet. We let the asshole keep digging a bigger hole for himself," Rocky replied.

Asher blew out a long breath. "I can't just sit by and watch it all happen. Dandridge votes that we fly to Vegas and beat his ass. I think it's a good idea."

"Oh God," Rocky moaned. "Dandridge heard."

Asher cringed but nodded.

"Who else? All the goons?"

"They were excited for you, baby," Asher said.

"Now they know you're married to a los—"

Asher cut him off with a fierce but short kiss. "Shut the hell up and listen to me."

"We're not in bed," Rocky reminded him.

"Listen good," Asher growled. "None of the goons hold you responsible for any of this. I won't be able to make you see this, though. They'll prove it to you if you give them a chance. I know it's hard to trust, but will you try?"

Rocky nodded. "I'll do my best."

Asher kissed him briefly and said, "Now, what are we going to do about Duggins?"

"We let him dig himself a bigger hole," Rocky replied.

His husband blew out a long breath. "I don't think I can."

"Focus on one of your other talents."

Smiling, Asher asked, "Such as?"

"Making the fucking stew that fixes everything."

"Be patient and make stew," Asher said. "Got it. *Anything* else?"

Rocky winked. "We'll discuss the options at home tonight."

"Are you going into the office now?"

"Hell yes," Rocky said. "I'm not running anymore."

Asher caressed his cheek and said, "I'm proud of you."

"I'm proud of me too."

Asher walked him to his car. He turned on the engine and got the air-conditioning going for Fifi before facing his sexy husband. The goodbye kiss they shared was hotter than a Carolina Reaper and sweeter than his nana's tea.

"I probably don't have to go directly to the office," Rocky said once they pulled apart.

Asher checked the time and frowned. "I wish. I need to get back and deliver a briefing on this afternoon's raids."

"Be safe."

"Always." Asher gave Rocky one last kiss before walking away.

Rocky took a few minutes to appreciate the cool air in the car before driving to work.

Trudy jumped out of her seat and launched herself into his arms when he and Fiona walked in. "I heard what happened. I'm so sorry."

"It's okay. The world is filled with assholes."

"And all of them stink," Trudy said. She pulled back and studied his expression. She must've liked what she saw because she nodded. "Okay, then."

"Any messages or new issues I need to address right away?"

Trudy shook her head. "No, but the day is young."

Rocky made himself a cup of coffee and put fresh water in Fiona's bowl in his office. He'd brought her plush dog bed here since Asher had been right about their sleeping arrangements. Fiona had barely glanced at the bed covered in pretty pink corduroy before she'd leaped onto their mattress on her first night at home. Rocky unhooked the leash from her harness and showered her with affection before sitting at his desk.

Fiona had developed a routine. She noshed on food, got a drink, and chose a toy from her basket before flopping down onto her bed. Rocky wondered how he'd ever worked without her occasional toy squeaks and soft snores.

Around noon, Peter, Shelly, and baby Skylar Rose paid them a visit. Fiona had gone on high alert when his door opened unexpectedly, but she calmed at Rocky's command.

"Is this our newest staff member I've heard so much about?" Peter asked. He started to extend his hand to Fiona, then checked himself. "May I?"

Fiona's harness identified her as a service animal followed by the words "do not pet" in multiple places. To best utilize her training, Rocky needed to uphold the boundaries her trainers taught her, but there were exceptions for friends and family.

"Of course," he told his partner.

Peter extended his hand to Fiona, who wagged her tail and soaked up the attention.

"She's beautiful," Shelly said. Skylar was strapped to her chest, so she sat down so Fiona could investigate the sleeping baby. "What a good girl you are," Shelly said as she stroked Fiona's soft fur.

"We heard about the radio interview," Peter said once introductions were over.

Rocky cringed. "I should've called you right away."

"No," Peter said, taking a seat next to Shelly. "That insult shouldn't have happened."

"I don't want my personal trauma to reflect badly on the agency. You're building something special here."

"*We're* building something special here," Peter corrected. "Stop downplaying your value to the business."

"I appreciate your support, Peter, but I'll step away if we start to lose clients. I won't hold any grudges."

"I will," Shelly said, looking at Peter. "We don't turn our backs on family."

Peter nodded. "She's right. We just came by to make sure you're okay."

"Do you need Peter to come back to the office?" Shelly hadn't bothered to dim her eagerness.

Peter snorted and shook his head. "You just want to hog the baby."

Rocky laughed. "Is he hovering?"

"Just a little." Then Shelly mouthed, "A whole lot."

"I think I have everything under control here, but you could always work from home if you need to feel productive," Rocky suggested.

"There's an idea," Shelly said. "Now, let's close the office and all go to lunch."

Rocky looked down at Fiona. He didn't want to leave her here, but restaurants didn't welcome furry beasts, even though he knew Fifi was cleaner than many human patrons they let in. "Maybe someplace with an outdoor café," he suggested.

"Great idea," Shelly said. "I know just the place." She stood up slowly so she didn't jar Skylar Rose. "I'll go tell Trudy."

Once they were alone, Peter studied him quietly.

"I'm okay, Peter. I promise." It felt good to mean it.

CHAPTER 23

Rocky's mettle was put to the test over the next week. Duggins's hits kept coming in the form of petty attacks on social media via fake accounts. Rocky wasn't just guessing where to lay the blame because Avery tracked each of the posts to an IP address in Vegas registered to Timothy Reginald Duggins III. He was either too stupid or lazy to hide his petty acts or wanted Rocky to know it was him. Either way, the podcasters documented and deleted the smears when they could and ignored the rest. Rocky hoped it pushed Duggins toward a confrontation, even though waiting was brutal.

The radio interview and the subsequent media hit job had both a positive and negative effect. Sinister and Savannah saw a record week of downloads on the various sites where their podcast was available, but it coaxed all the conspiracy theorists and whack jobs out of the woodwork.

The agency received an influx of calls also, which Trudy deftly screened. Rocky had a few weird encounters outside the office, which Fiona quickly thwarted. Some clients expressed concerns about continuing their association with the agency, but only one of them actually pulled their account. It had upset Rocky, but Peter remained nonplussed.

"Fuck them. We're family," Peter had said.

Rocky worked through the highs and lows in the healthiest ways possible. He'd finally delved into the traumatic event with Karen during his most recent therapy session. He couldn't say he felt miraculously healed, but her unbiased thoughts on the night and the fallout helped him put things in perspective. He was starting to view himself as a victim and that was a big step. His anxiety attacks didn't entirely disappear, but they were less frequent and not as severe. Karen emphasized avoiding triggers and being kind to himself when he had a setback, both lessons that would come in handy.

Asher was home more than he was away during this stretch, which was the ultimate balm to Rocky's soul as he worked through his frustrations and fears. Karen had recommended re-evaluating his diet and exercise regimen but cautioned him about making too many changes at once. He and Asher enjoyed cooking healthier meals together and taking their nightly walks with Fiona. He wasn't quite ready to say goodbye to caffeine and sugar altogether, but he noticed a significant improvement after cutting back on just those two things.

During lunchtime, Rocky took Fiona to the park to stretch her legs and get exercise. It cleared his head so he could analyze better and stay sharper. Unfortunately, it didn't give him a solution to Tess Hamilton's investigation. He'd started to think the case was a dead end until an unexpected clue landed on his desk one day after one of his outings with Fiona.

Lillian Travers was waiting in reception when he returned to the office. He was pleasantly surprised to see her. Rocky had expected to receive her list of candidates for the board position the previous week. When it didn't arrive, he assumed Lillian's account was a casualty of Duggins's smear campaign.

"I probably should've called before stopping by," she said after he greeted her. "Do you have a few minutes to meet with me?"

"Of course." He gestured for Lillian to follow him to his office.

Once there, she spent a long time fussing over Fiona's beauty before pulling several files from her briefcase. Lillian made no attempt to reach for his dog, and Rocky didn't encourage it. "I had intended to provide these to you last week, but life got in the way."

"It's what life does best," Rocky said. He accepted the stack and met her shrewd gaze. "I thought maybe you'd changed your mind about working with our agency."

"Why? Because of the idiot who called the radio station and made baseless accusations? Surely you think I'm a better judge of character." When put like that, Rocky felt kind of silly for doubting her. Before he could apologize, Lillian continued, "I have a better understanding of the pain I saw in your eyes during our first meeting. If anything, my respect for you has grown, not diminished."

"Thank you."

"I started listening to your podcast, and it's riveting," Lillian said. "Not just the stories, but the chemistry between you and your friends."

Rocky smiled. "I'd hate to think where I'd be without their friendship."

"And I pray you never have to find out." Lillian tilted her head slightly. "You know, your show has opened my eyes a lot. Our system is more flawed than I realized. We have bad people being set free too soon and innocent people going to prison. You can be pissed about both those things at the same time. It doesn't have to be one or the other."

"Very true."

"I'd like to ask a question, but please don't feel obligated to say yes. And saying no won't jeopardize my commitment to working with your agency," Lillian added.

"Okay. You've got my attention."

"Would you consider featuring my Halianna on your show? It would bring much-needed attention to my causes and help raise awareness among young women."

"I think it sounds like a wonderful idea." As their personal lives got busier, the guys would have less time for chasing down leads and investigating unsolved cases. Halianna's tragedy and Lillian's triumph was the kind of story they could feature in between those lengthier investigations. "I'll absolutely bring it up to my partners to see how they feel."

"Thank you so much," she said. After checking her watch, Lillian rose to her feet. "I have another meeting in thirty minutes. I'd like to choose my board by the end of the month. Is that enough time?"

"Plenty," Rocky assured her. "Thanks for sticking with me."

"No thanks necessary," she said as Rocky walked her back to reception. "Take care of yourself. Let me know what your friends think."

"I'll be in touch soon."

Fiona was waiting for him in the doorway when he returned. Rocky scratched her ears and told her she was the best girl for at least the twentieth time that day. He sent a group message to Jonah and Felix and pitched Lillian's idea to them. Their replies were enthusiastic and eager, so he sent an email to Lillian. The logistics could come later, but he didn't want to keep her waiting for an answer.

Afterward, he immediately began looking through Lillian's candidates and was surprised to see a file with Grant Duncan's name on it. Rocky knew very little about the guy except he was protective of his mother, worked in management at Arnold Hamilton's trucking company, and owned a spooky house. He'd called Grant a few times to interview him, but he'd always had an excuse for why they couldn't meet. Rocky hadn't expected a different reaction, so it hadn't bothered him.

What skill set or quality would make him attractive to Lillian's charity? There was only one way to find out, so Rocky opened the file and began looking through his dossier. Like a work resume, the profile separated the candidate's information into categories: education, work history, and philanthropy experience. Rocky started at the top and read all the way through, then went back to the beginning and reviewed it again.

Everything about Grant aligned perfectly with Lillian's mission. His education was in social work and philanthropy. He had professional and personal experience utilizing both skill sets that would help her succeed. His first job out of college was counseling abused children. During that time, he'd volunteered for several nonprofit organizations. Eventually, his career shifted away from social work and more toward his philanthropic endeavors. Grant's current position was listed as Director of Gift Planning and Donor Services for Hamilton's trucking company.

Still? If the Hamilton kids were so horrible, wouldn't they have fired Grant? Or were they not involved in the daily operations of the corporation?

The trucking company was well known for the staggering amount of money they gifted to charities. Rocky pulled up their website and read through the annual donations list for the previous year and the one before that. A pattern began to emerge, and the hint of an epiphany tickled Rocky's brain. Fiona raised her head and looked at him. She must've sensed his excitement.

"It's all good, sweet girl."

Fiona laid her head back down but watched him through curious eyes.

Rocky switched his attention back to Grant's dossier, reading it from top to bottom again. Everything Grant Duncan did after high school, both professionally and personally, revolved around helping abused children and women. He'd volunteered at shelters, counseled kids, raised money for these causes, then later accepted a position which allowed him to funnel millions of corporate dollars to them too.

Were these the acts of someone who'd experienced abuse firsthand or just a selfless man? What was it Grant had said to him? *We all have skeletons.* Perhaps his philanthropy came from a place of guilt.

Rocky pulled up Helen's interview and played it back. He fast-forwarded to the parts where she discussed her fights with Tess over Bob and her desire to kill him. What were the odds Grant hadn't overheard those arguments? Had he learned that he only existed because his father had forced himself on his mother? Had Grant learned about his father pushing Tess down the stairs and causing her to go into early labor? More importantly, had Grant Duncan learned at age fifteen how easy it would be to kill the man who'd done those awful things to his mother?

Could Grant's hostility toward the investigation stem from a fear of getting caught? Proving the man killed his father would be impossible. Rocky had no actionable proof to give to the authorities. What about the insurance policy? If Tess hadn't forged the form, then it was someone who was looking out for her. Helen claimed she didn't do it, and Rocky believed her. Grant had motive, and as a director for Hamilton's company, he'd have access to the man's signature.

Would he have let his mother go to prison? It was the only part that didn't make sense. Was his faith in the justice system that strong? After years of working with abused kids, he had to know better. What would he have done if the jury had convicted her? Or would he have never allowed it to go that far? Rocky couldn't imagine a scenario where Grant allowed his mother to go to prison, even if she had been the guilty one.

Rocky rested his elbows on his desk and funneled his fingers through his hair. He had so many questions but suddenly no longer wanted the answers. He set Tess's investigation on the back burner and focused on doing deep-dive background checks on the candidates for Lillian's board of directors.

As his dossier claimed, Grant's background was spotless, which didn't change the opinion solidifying in Rocky's mind. He just didn't know what, if anything, he was willing to do about it. Rocky had made a big dent in the stack of candidates when Trudy ran him out of the office.

He hadn't planned to go to Grant's house on his way home; he'd just headed there on autopilot. Instead of driving past the spooky house, Rocky parked in front of it when he spotted the silver SUV in the driveway.

Rocky hooked the leash into Fiona's harness, and the two of them made their way to the front of the house. Grant answered on the second ring, but this time he was fully dressed. He held a paintbrush in his hand and had a smear of burgundy paint across his handsome face.

"I've caught you at a bad time again, I see."

"At least I'm dressed. Who's this?" Grant asked. He didn't reach for her and just waited for her to react. Fiona surprised Rocky by stepping forward and sniffing his hand. She wagged her tail and nuzzled her nose against him. Fiona made a soft whining noise like when she sensed a storm brewing inside Rocky.

"This is Fiona," he said, then formally introduced them.

"She's beautiful."

Rocky smiled. "Thanks. We think so."

"I forgot you're married."

"And I forgot to ask how your date went that night," Rocky countered.

Grant shook his head. "I've given up on men," he said dramatically. "I've decided to spend my energy on fixing up this old house." He looked at Fiona. "Maybe I should get a dog, yeah?" She just wagged her tail. Grant stepped aside and said, "Come on in. You can ask your questions while I paint, but no making fun of my awful skills."

"Actually," Rocky said when Grant started to turn away. "I didn't come here to interview you."

"Cookies?"

Rocky laughed. "No."

"Bibles?"

Rocky shook his head.

"No vacuums either?"

"Fiona wants to hoover up food, but no," Rocky said. "I've come to tell you that we're no longer pursuing your mom's investigation." He hadn't talked it over with the guys, but he knew they'd support his decision.

Grant cocked his head and studied Rocky. "Why? You were so persistent."

This was the hard part. If Rocky told Grant precisely what he thought, he'd force the man to admit or deny his role in either his father's death or the attempt at insurance fraud. Anything he said could incriminate him, and Rocky wasn't looking for that. This wasn't his cross to bear. He didn't have to right every wrong, just the ones within his power.

Rocky wasn't sorry Bob was dead. If given a chance, he'd dig up the man's ashes and piss on them. As far as he could tell, Rona Danielson wasn't a real person. Maybe her name was a combination of a romance book heroine and the nickname Mr. Miyagi gave Daniel in *Karate Kid*. Did it matter? Not really. If Tess, or anyone associated with her, had forged the life insurance form, they hadn't gotten away with it. That was enough for Rocky. He thought his fictional hero, Sam Spade, would agree with him.

But he did hope Grant found some peace. If Rocky was right, this had been weighing heavily on the man's conscience for twenty years.

He took a deep breath for fortitude and said, "You know why."

Grant's mouth went slack, and his eyes took on a blank expression as if his mind had left the building.

"Grant?"

The man blinked and refocused on Rocky. "I—"

"You know why," Rocky repeated. "No good will come out of me digging deeper. In this case, it's wisest to let the dead rest."

"What am I supposed to tell my mother?" Grant asked.

"The truth."

He flinched as if Rocky had hit him.

"Take care of yourself, Grant." He whistled softly, and Fiona followed him down the steps.

"Wait," Grant called out.

Rocky stopped and faced him. The expression on the man's face was as haunted as the home he'd purchased. He didn't look vacuous as Julia had, so Rocky felt hope for the man. He believed Grant could excise his ghosts if he found the right help.

"How'd you know?" he asked.

Rocky recalled the words Lillian said to him. "I know trauma when I see it."

He hadn't detected it right away. If not for Lillian, Rocky might never have made the connection. Sometimes you just have to accept that things happen for a reason. The universe gives and the universe takes. Rocky wished Grant well and hoped he found peace because dwelling in perpetual purgatory wasn't living at all.

His phone rang when he was a few blocks from home, and Jude's name popped up on the screen. Rocky accepted the call and sang, "'Hey, Jude.'"

"Very funny," he said dryly. "And so original."

"An oldie but a goodie," Rocky argued. "What's up?"

"Well, I have good news, and I have great news. Which do you want to hear first?"

"Surprise me," Rocky replied.

"I found a news reporter in Vegas who was willing to tell me who leaked the Julia Warner information to him."

"Is that the good news or the great news?"

"It's kind of lukewarm, really," Jude replied. "It gets better. Much better."

"Quit being a tease and get on with it," Rocky said sternly.

Jude laughed. "Tim Duggins was definitely the leak. Duggins has buddies on the police force who were all too willing to tell him the sordid details of that woman's last days."

"Is that the great news?" Rocky asked. Because it made him feel terrible inside.

"It's the good. I'm about to unleash the great."

"Do I need to pull over?" Rocky asked.

Jude snorted. "I recorded the conversation for you. I'd prefer you don't go public with it and destroy the man's career. He seemed genuinely remorseful for his part in keeping the scandal alive."

"I'm not out to ruin the reporter's career. I'm just looking for leverage. Besides, it's the reporter's word against Duggins's. I just know that Bradshaw is a by-the-book guy and won't take these allegations lightly. Thanks for the ammunition, Jude."

"But wait, there's more," Jude said.

"I get a second box for free? I just need to pay a separate shipping and handling charge, right?"

Jude chuckled. "Why do I like you?"

"Because Felix loves me."

"Yeah, there's that. The reporter backed up his claim with recorded phone calls and copies of his emails. Duggins was stupid enough to send a copy of the goodbye Julia wrote to her family from his USMS email address."

"Holy shit."

"Yeah, this guy is no criminal mastermind."

"Will you send those things to me?"

"Already did it." Rocky thanked Jude, then disconnected.

Asher was in the backyard chatting with Cal over the fence when they arrived home. Fiona leaped and bounded across the yard to get to him, and he crouched down to greet her.

"She sure is a pretty thing," the neighbor said.

"Thanks, Cal."

Asher must've heard something off in Rocky's tone because he snapped his head up and met his gaze. He stood up and gently clapped the neighbor's shoulder. "It was good catching up with you, Cal. I'm going to head inside so we can start dinner."

"See you guys later," the older man said. "Bye, Fiona."

Once inside the kitchen, Asher placed his hands on Rocky's hips. "What's wrong?"

Rocky repeated his conversation with Jude before pulling up the documentation he'd emailed.

"Jesus," Asher said. "He's going to lose his job for this."

"Someone like him doesn't deserve to wear a badge and carry a gun," Rocky replied. "Do you want to talk to Director Bradshaw, or do you want me to do it?"

"I'll call him."

"When?"

Asher took a deep breath. "Now. Mind if I borrow your office?"

"Of course not." Rocky kissed Asher, then turned to the refrigerator. "I'll get dinner started."

Rocky could hear the timbre of Asher's voice but not the individual words. He could tell the conversation was solemn and mostly one-sided, with Asher doing most of the heavy lifting. By the time his husband returned to the kitchen, Rocky had diced the onions and peppers and was sautéing them in olive oil.

"Are you okay?" Rocky asked.

Asher wrapped his arms around his waist and rested his chin on Rocky's shoulder. "Not really. Bradshaw is pissed. It was the right thing to do, but it doesn't feel good."

"I'm sorry."

Asher tightened his hold. "Don't be. I'd love to think this is the end, but we both know better."

"We do. We'll handle it when the time comes."

Hours? Days? Weeks? The wait wouldn't be fun, but Rocky had

plenty of ideas about how they could distract themselves. He was just about to demonstrate one of those ways a few hours later when his cell phone rang. He checked the caller ID and said, "Showtime."

Asher sat up straighter. He held out his phone, but Rocky shook his head.

"This is my battle to fight." Then he opened his recorder app and hit the red button before answering the call on speakerphone. He briefly pressed his finger to his lips urging Asher to let him handle this. "Duggins," Rocky said calmly.

"You think you won, don't you?"

"You sound a little drunk, Duggy."

"Only my friends can call me that."

"Nah," Rocky said. "They all call you dumbass and douchebag. What do you want?"

"Fuck you," Duggins slurred.

"Nah. There's no room at the inn."

"Look who's become a smug little bastard. To be honest, I didn't think you had it in you, Jacobs." Duggins chuckled. "You let that crazy bitch turn you into a limped-dick, sniveling crybaby. That's why I kept feeding those tidbits to the journalist to keep that story alive. I'd hoped you'd eat a bullet, but I settled for you leaving Vegas. I hadn't anticipated Asher turning into a mopey, pathetic man once you did. He got sloppy and ended up with a knife in his back. I thought it would be the wake-up call he needed, but he chose you again."

Thinking of how close he'd come to losing Asher made Rocky seethe with anger. When black dots swam in front of his eyes, he knew he was close to losing control. Rocky pushed the thoughts out of his mind and took a steadying breath. "What you did to Julia Warner's mother and children was inexcusable. It's one thing to fuck up my life, but those kids…"

"Boo-fucking-hoo," Duggins jeered. "They're better off without her as far as I'm concerned. This isn't over between us, Jacobs. First you took Asher away from me, and now my job. I'm going to destroy you."

Rocky took a deep breath. "No," he said calmly. "And here's why.

You're not smart enough, Duggy. You're sloppy and leave a mile-wide trail of evidence in your wake. Someone stupid enough to use their USMS email addy to leak information to the press is not a worthy opponent. And if you're going to keep making harassing posts on social media, don't use a computer or device attached to your own IP address. I've got the receipts for those too, asshole. You make those mustache-twirling cartoon villains look smart. We're going to hang up this phone, and we're never going to speak again. You're never going to call Asher either."

"You can't do shit to me."

"That's where you're wrong. I've recorded this conversation, and I won't hesitate to use it."

"You recorded it without my permission, so you can't use it against me."

Rocky chuckled. "Georgia is a single-party consent state, asshole. Fuck with me or Asher again, and I will take you down. I could use my podcast to expose your behavior, or I could sue you for defamation of character. Maybe I won't win, but your reputation will be ruined, and you won't even be able to land a job as a mall cop. For fuck's sake, man, seek professional help."

"You arrogant little shit. I oughta—"

"Warmest regards, Duggins," Rocky said before disconnecting. He stopped the recording and looked at his husband. "Damn, that felt good."

Asher's grin was big and contagious.

"What?"

"Warmest regards?"

Rocky shrugged. "It just felt right."

"I'm so fucking sorry, Rocky. I knew there was tension between the two of you, but I was oblivious to the source and the depth of his betrayal. I promise I won't ever let you down like that again."

"I should've spoken up and been honest with you about everything. I should've had enough faith in us to know you would've chosen me."

"I'll always choose you, baby," Asher said. "Do you think he'll leave us alone?"

"Maybe. Maybe not. I meant what I told him, though. My brain has been my real nemesis, and I'll beat its mustache-twirling ass too. You promised me forever, and I'm not settling for anything less."

Asher moved closer to kiss Rocky, but Fiona got between them. "How's Daddy's little cockblocker?" he asked in a sweet voice.

Rocky gasped and covered her ears. "You know what time it is."

Asher laughed and lifted the leash off the coffee table. "Is this what you want?"

Fiona barked and spun around in circles. Asher stood up and held out his hand to Rocky. "We'll resume this when we return." He tugged Rocky into his arms for a short, hard kiss.

"Because you always keep your promises."

"I do."

CHAPTER 24

"**I** feel underdressed," Asher said.

Rocky looked over at his husband who was dressed in a sexy-as-fuck black suit and a crisp white shirt opened at the throat. "Why? I'm not wearing a tie."

"No, but you have those fancy black-diamond cuff links." Asher strode across the room and lifted Rocky's hand. "You wore those on our wedding day too."

"My grandpa Dutton gave them to me when I graduated from college. They belonged to his grandfather or great-grandfather. They're supposed to bring me good luck, so I wear them on important days."

Marla's life celebration ranked up there at the top. He wanted everything to be perfect for her special day. Rocky took a shaky breath as he checked his reflection in the mirror. He met Asher's gaze.

"Will I pass muster?"

"You set the bar, baby," Asher said huskily.

"Oh no. Don't you look at me like that. We'll be late, and Marla will rip our balls off and laugh while doing it. Have you seen her long nails?"

Asher grimaced. "They're more like talons."

"Exactly. No one wants to be on the business end of those claws." Rocky turned around and kissed Asher. "Did you take Fiona to Cal and

Elaine's already?" They would've taken her with them, but they worried the rambunctious celebration would be too much for their girl.

"Do you see her at your feet?"

Rocky quirked a brow and said, "I don't see you at my feet either." Heat and hunger burned in Asher's eyes, and he looked ready to make a liar out of Rocky, so he wagged his finger. "Talons, babe."

"We better get going, then," Asher said.

Once outside, they got in Asher's car that had arrived from Vegas the day before. The sleek black Dodge Challenger suited his husband perfectly.

"I kind of miss Goldie," Rocky said as he fastened his seat belt.

"Really? She's still on the lot."

"Imagine that. I can't believe no one wants to buy a shiny gold Miata."

"I bet I could get a good deal for you," Asher insisted.

"I'll pass," Rocky said. "I do have something else gold on my mind, though."

Asher glanced over at him and smiled. "A tooth?"

"Damn, you know me so well," Rocky said dryly. "I was thinking about rings."

"Ear or belly button?" Asher waggled his brows. "Or cock?"

"Wedding," Rocky said.

Asher stopped at a red light and looked at him. "I'm listening."

"I know we kind of dismissed them when we got married the first time around."

"First time?"

Rocky chuckled. "I'm blowing this."

"No, I wanted to blow you, but you said we couldn't be late."

"Green light."

"Oh, now you're giving me the go-ahead?" Asher asked.

"The light is green."

"Oh," Asher said. He turned his attention back to the road and accelerated his hot rod through the intersection. The growling engine was almost as sexy as the man behind the wheel.

"What I was trying to say," Rocky said, "is that I want to renew our vows. Here in Savannah where we're making our fresh start. I'm picturing a small event with just our families and closest friends." He looked at Asher. "I want to wear your ring."

"I really want to wear yours too."

"And?"

"Yes, I will marry you again," Asher said. "And again. And Again. For however many times it takes."

"One more time will do the trick."

"I'm going to sing my vows."

Rocky groaned. "No. I've heard you sing. It's not pretty."

Ignoring him, Asher rattled off various songs from any and all genres he could choose from to represent the epic love he had for Rocky. The lyrics ranged from the sweet to the ridiculous. Rocky nixed them all.

"Can we do one of those cool first dances?"

Rocky snorted. "You're smooth in the sack, but you can't dance for shit."

"Can't sing. Can't dance. I'm not exactly sure why you'd want to marry me all over again."

"For the fucking stew, of course."

"Of course," Asher agreed.

The Dive Bar parking lot was packed to the brim when they arrived, even though they were twenty minutes early. Asher found a spot in the lot for an adjacent business that was closed for the day.

"It looks like all of Savannah showed up tonight," Rocky said as he took Asher's hand.

"Marla will soak it up like a sponge."

"As she should," Rocky said. His cell phone rang before they reached the door to the bar and he pulled it from his pocket to see who was calling.

"Something important?" Asher asked.

"Not sure. I don't recognize the number," Rocky replied before answering. "Rocky Jacobs."

"Mr. Jacobs, it's Tess Hamilton."

He pulled up short and Asher stopped too. Tess was the last person

Rocky expected to be on the other end. He mouthed her name and Asher nodded. "Hello, Mrs. Hamilton. How was your vacation?"

"It was lovely, dear. Please call me Tess."

"What can I do for you, Tess?"

"When Grant picked me up from the airport, he informed me that you won't be continuing your investigation. I just wanted a chance to say thank you." ·

"For what? I wasn't very helpful." Rocky still struggled with his decision on occasion, but his conscience was clear.

"I think we both know that's not true, Mr. Jacobs."

"Rocky," he told her.

"Okay, Rocky. You believed in me when not many others did. That's not all, but we'll let the other things remain unspoken."

"You're welcome, Tess. I wish your family the best."

"Likewise, my dear. Take care."

"What was that all about?" Asher asked after Rocky pocketed the phone.

"She just wanted to thank me for believing in her," Rocky replied as he reclaimed Asher's hand.

"We all need a Rocky Jacobs in our corner," Asher said, kissing him on the cheek.

"Well, look at you two," Daisy said when they stepped inside the bar. "I don't think I've seen a more beautiful couple."

Her burly husband, Edgar, guffawed and straightened his leather dinner jacket. "I think we can still show these youngsters a thing or two, baby," he told her.

Daisy kissed her husband's cheek, then asked him to show them to their seats. They followed Edgar to a large table located at the front and center of the stage. Jonah, Avery, Jude, and Felix were already seated with Amos and Marla's parents, Thomas and Jessa Rae. They hugged Marla's mom and shook her father's hand.

"This event is so Marla," Jessa Rae said, looking around at the glitz and glam. "Catered dinner and themed cocktails. No one shines brighter than my baby."

"I'm grateful for this opportunity to see her perform live," Thomas said. "We missed so much time with her."

Amos patted the older man's back. "You know the rules, Thom."

"No mourning her while she's still alive," everyone at the table said, making her parents chuckle.

The guest of honor appeared a few minutes later, wearing a strapless teal ball gown. Rocky wasn't sure what the dress was made of, but it was satiny and poofy and fit for royalty. Marla loved the attention, waving and blowing kisses at her adoring friends as she wove her way through the tables until she reached theirs.

She went around the table, greeting them with a hug and a kiss. "You look so happy, Pretty Boy," she said.

"And you are the most divine creature ever made."

Marla batted her eyelashes. "You think?"

"I know."

Her lips trembled as she looked around the room. "This celebration has rendered me speechless."

"Since when?" Amos asked.

Marla spun around and slapped him playfully on the arm. "Oh, you."

Amos took her hand and brought it to his lips. "You are my greatest treasure, and you deserve this wonderful night."

"You are a big softie," Marla said, then leaned down to kiss him. "I love you." She stood up and fanned her face. "Don't none of you assholes make me cry and ruin my makeup before my performance."

Once Marla sat down, the caterers began serving the elegant dinner. At first, the conversation was stilted because no one had ever attended a life celebration for a person who was still alive.

"They better serve mashed potatoes this good in heaven," Marla said, breaking the silence.

Jessa Rae made a strangled noise, then cleared her throat. "They will if your grandmother has a say."

"She did make the best, didn't she?" Marla said before forking another bite into her mouth.

The caterers moved fluidly between tables, replenishing drinks and whisking away empty plates. The lights dimmed as soon as the guests had their dessert plates and coffee.

"Oh, it's showtime," Marla said.

Queen after amazing queen took to the stage to pay tribute to the woman who'd touched their lives. Each of them shared a story or gave a speech before they performed a song. Marla's parents had contributed dozens of photos and the video montage to music was heart wrenching and beautiful. The evening was the most moving display of love Rocky had ever witnessed. A ceremony that had felt a little odd in the beginning now felt like the bar they should all aim for.

Marla wiped away an occasional stray tear, but mostly she sang along and danced in her chair. She was living every minute to the fullest and setting an example for the rest of them to follow. Marla stood up when it was almost time for her to take center stage.

"I hope you enjoy my performance, Mama and Daddy," she said.

"We will, angel," Thom said.

"Is someone recording this?" Jessa Rae asked. "I want to be able to watch it over and over."

"Absolutely," Jonah said.

"I'll record it on my cell phone, too, just in case," Avery added.

You could've heard a pin drop when Marla walked onto the stage. Then the room erupted into clapping and cheering, which went on until she gestured for everyone to settle down.

"I had a hard time deciding what song to perform for you tonight. What lyrics could encompass my journey? The ups and the downs and everything in between. What one song could sum up my story? You're the loves of my life. Each and every one of you in this room. You've given me more love and shown me more kindness in one lifetime than most people would experience in ten," Marla said. "I decided I wanted this performance to be about you and how lucky and loved you make me feel. You're simply the best."

She gestured for the DJ to play the music. Tears filled Rocky's eyes as soon as Tina Turner's "Simply the Best" began to play, but he joined everyone else who rose to their feet and sang along with her. There wasn't a dry eye in the room by the time she finished. She might be able to whip a few of their asses, but she couldn't take them all.

Rocky hugged Marla tight when she returned to the table. "I love you."

"I love you too, Pretty Boy." She pulled back and cupped his face. "The first thing I'm going to do when I get to heaven is find your mama and tell her how wonderful you are. Then, I'll go find Bea, Rue, and Estelle."

"I'm not ready to say goodbye," Rocky said.

"Then we won't," she said. "Listen, now. I'll never be too far away. When you get to missing me, you just need to look up at the sky. I'll be the star burning the brightest."

Of that, he had no doubt. Jessa Rae was right. No one shined brighter than her girl.

EPILOGUE

They gathered on a freakishly warm day in September. It was still too hot to wear suits, but the occasion called for them anyway, and Southerners were big on tradition. They'd strung lanterns and fairy lights throughout the backyard, bathing the space in a soft, romantic glow. The ole magnolia tree had never looked as majestic as when Rocky and Asher joined hands beneath it.

The backyard was packed with friends and family as they exchanged vows and golden rings at dusk. They'd gone with a simple menu and cupcakes over something elegant and fussy. It might not have been the perfect venue, but it was right for them, and everyone genuinely seemed happy.

The oppressive heat and tiny house meant people didn't linger a long time after the ceremony, but that didn't bother Rocky. He was ready to have his husband all to himself, but the Southern goodbye tour was lasting a ridiculously long time.

"I've never seen anything quite like it," Asher said, hooking his arm around Rocky's waist. "I'm pretty sure I've seen Marla tell your nana goodbye three times and my mother twice."

"They lose track during the rounds. No one stands still, so who can blame them?"

"Maybe they should line up in two rows like athletes and high-five," Asher suggested.

"Is that what you Yanks do?"

"No," Asher scoffed. "But we don't make five trips around the room or yard either."

"What do you do?"

"We stand by the door and say goodnight to everyone at once."

"Expedient," Rocky said. "And a little rude." He looked up at his husband. "You won't get away with that down here. You're a proper Southern gentleman now."

Asher nuzzled his nose against Rocky's neck. "I'm not feeling gentle or proper right now."

"Oh," Rocky said. "Let's see if we can't steer these well-meaning people off our lawn before they start round six."

"Good idea. How?" Asher asked.

"Start singing."

"Smartass." Asher pulled Rocky into his arms and kissed him soundly on the mouth. "I love you."

"I love you too."

"Looks like it's time for us to leave, people," Marla yelled. "These husbands want to be doing husbandly things. Let's move out."

Rocky mouthed, "Thank you."

She used her index fingers to draw a heart in the air, then blew him a kiss.

Rocky spread a blanket beneath the tree after the last guest left, and they lay on their backs staring up at the sky while holding hands. With low cloud cover, they had a fantastic view of the starlit sky. Soon, the simple touch wasn't enough, so they rolled onto their sides, facing one another. Rocky ghosted his fingers over Asher's brow and cheek and chiseled jaw. When he reached his husband's chin dimple, Rocky slid his finger upward to trace Asher's lips.

"They're not going to kiss themselves," Asher said.

"No, they won't," Rocky said, leaning forward and pressing his mouth to Asher's. The kiss started out as teasing and light but quickly progressed to a deeper foray that included roaming hands.

A shadow crept over them, and a heavy panting sound intruded on their moment.

Rocky pulled back and looked at Asher. "Was that you doing the heavy breathing?"

"I hadn't worked up to it yet," he replied.

They turned their heads simultaneously and found Fiona standing over them with her leash hanging from her mouth.

"It's our wedding night, Fifi," Asher said. "You have this nice yard to do your business in."

"Her walks wait for no one." Rocky stood up and held out his hand to Asher. "If you think this dog is a cockblocker, just wait until we have kids."

Asher wrapped Rocky in his arms. "I can't wait."

Fiona let out a series of short barks.

Rocky laughed. "This dog won't walk herself."

"Okay, Fi," Asher said to her as he attached the leash to her harness. "One quick walk around the block."

Fiona barked again.

Asher smiled at Rocky. "She said okay." Asher leaned closer and said, "Then I promise alone time with Daddy."

"You've made a lifetime of promises today."

Asher kissed Rocky's smiling lips. "I'll keep every damn one."

The End!

Though *Pretty Poison* is officially the last book in the Sinister in Savannah series, there are more stories yet to be told. I'm currently writing a book for Jimmy, who I introduced as the young reporter in Mr. Perfect. Kurt Dandridge is also demanding a story, and I cannot forget sweet Kendall from Sinister in Savannah. Jimmy's story is supposed to be a light and funny contemporary romance to give me a little break between heavier plotlines. My objective is to write these three books as standalones. We also haven't heard the last from Royce and Sawyer. We'll be hanging around Savannah for quite some time. I hope that makes you as happy as I am right now.

Want to be the first to know about my book releases and have access to extra content? You can sign up for my newsletter here: http://eepurl.com/dlhPYj

My favorite place to hang out and chat with my readers is my Facebook group. Would you like to be a member of Aimee's Dye Hards? We'd love to have you! Go here: www.facebook.com/groups/AimeesDyeHards

OTHER BOOKS BY
AIMEE NICOLE WALKER

Only You

The Fated Hearts Series
Chasing Mr. Wright, Book 1
Rhythm of Us, Book 2
Surrender Your Heart, Book 3
Perfect Fit, Book 4
Return to Me, Book 5
Always You, Book 6
Any Means Necessary, Book 7

Curl Up and Dye Mysteries
Dyeing to be Loved
Something to Dye For
Dyed and Gone to Heaven
I Do, or Dye Trying
A Dye Hard Holiday
Ride or Dye

Road to Blissville Series
Unscripted Love
Someone to Call My Own
Nobody's Prince Charming
This Time Around
Smoke in the Mirror
Inside Out
Prescription for Love

ACKNOWLEDGMENTS

First, I need to thank my husband and children for their constant support and encouragement. It's not easy living with a writer who often disappears into a fictional world for long periods of time. They do so many things to help me so that I can realize my dream. I love you guys more than words can ever express.

To my creative dream team, thanks seem hardly enough for all that you do. Miranda Turner of V8 Editing and Proofreading, thank you for your tireless work, feedback, and many laughs while editing. Jay Aheer of Simply Defined art is an incredible artist, and I love how she brings my words to life. Stacey Blake of Champagne Formats is also an amazing artist who does incredible interior formatting, illustrating, and designing for e-books and paperbacks. It truly takes a village to whip me into shape. Judy Zweifel of Judy's' Proofreading and Susie Selva did a great job of proofreading and polishing to make my manuscript shine.

To my lovely PA, Michelle Slagan. I'm not sure how I ever did this without you. I love you to the moon and back!

I want to thank Brittany for being a wonderful critique partner and Jill Wexler for giving me invaluable feedback during her deep-dive beta read. I'm grateful to Racheal and Melinda for being amazing alpha readers. And to my betas, Kim, Michael, Dana, and Laurel, I appreciate your honest feedback. I love working with you all.

ABOUT
AIMEE NICOLE WALKER

Ever since she was a little girl, Aimee Nicole Walker entertained herself with stories that popped into her head. Now she gets paid to tell those stories to other people. She wears many titles—wife, mom, and animal lover are just a few of them. Her absolute favorite title is champion of the happily ever after. Love inspires everything she does, music keeps her sane, and coffee is the magic elixir that fuels her day.

I'd love to hear from you.

Want to connect with me? All my links are in one nifty location.
Click here:
linktr.ee/AimeeNicoleWalker